MARIN'S PROMISE

Borderland Ladies, Book 1

MADELINE MARTIN

Cover Design by Teresa Spreckelmeyer @ The Midnight Muse Designs.

To Lori and Eliza

We are there to celebrate our victories together, comfort our losses, make each other laugh endlessly, share a bottle of good wine and keep us all from going crazy. Thank you for your incredible friendship - it means more than I could ever possibly say.

July 1333
Brampton, England

L ady Marin Barrington was used to attacks from the reivers. As the eldest daughter to the third Earl of Werrick, the English West March Warden, she was even used to acting as his unofficial constable in his absence.

Threat of an impending battle in Berwick had resulted in the earl bringing a majority of his forces with him to go to King Edward's side. The remaining soldiers looked to her for guidance, to ensure the people within the castle remained properly defended and safe.

The castle had not been breached, not in the last eleven years when the last raid forced them to erect fortified curtain walls so great no marauders could penetrate them to reach the castle within. Not until this moment.

Marin kept her arrow nocked and pointed toward the dark-haired man below. The blonde girl in his arms did not move. It was that last fact which made Marin's heart chill.

"Open yer gates," he shouted.

The army around him was larger than the one remaining to defend the castle. Well over one hundred men. If the gates were opened, her forces would be easily overwhelmed.

"Open yer gates, or I will kill yer sister." The man leapt from his stocky reiver's horse and dragged Catriona with him, her hair streaming in the summer wind like a banner of gold.

As soon as his feet hit the ground, Catriona jumped to life, launching her elbow at his face. He jerked hard to the side from the impact but kept his hold on her.

Marin lowered her bow and edged to the castle wall.

"Don't give in to him, Marin—" Cat opened her mouth to say more, but the reiver snagged her around the waist and pulled her toward him. A knife flashed at his side and pressed to her neck.

He sniffed hard, the way one often did when a blow to their face resulted in a bloody nose. "Open the gate or I will kill her."

Marin's heart plunged into her stomach.

It was in moments like this that she wished Father was not in Berwick. As Warden to the West March on the English side, he would typically have been home. Yet as one of the king's wealthiest earls, he was with their king. When she needed him most.

She was glad Geordie was with him. It would cut the lad to the quick to see Cat in such a predicament.

Sunlight glared down on her and did nothing to quell the bite in the air while she wrestled with her decision, with the life of her sister as well as the lives of all her people.

"Marin, please." Marin did not have to turn to see her sister's face. She could read the horror and fear in Anice's voice.

"If we let them in, every man, woman and child will be at their mercy," Marin said numbly.

Anice and Cat were the only sisters Marin had permitted thus far on the battlements. Now though, Marin regretted having

Anice to join her. And she especially regretted allowing Cat to go out and pick flowers that afternoon.

Cat, who always saw the best in people, who always knew how to lighten any dark situation, whose bright smile was for everyone no matter how awful a person might be. A girl of only sixteen whose life had not yet had a chance to blossom. If it were Marin below instead, Cat would have nocked an arrow and killed the reiver in one shot.

Marin did not possess such a skill. But she would cut out her own heart if it would save her sister.

Only it was not her heart the reiver wanted.

"My lady?" Sir Richard regarded her. As the knight with the most experience and Werrick's Captain of the Guard, she often looked to him for advice. His kind brown eyes were bright with concern.

Marin shook her head, unsure what to do, unsure what to say. Her soul was on fire with indecision. How could she choose between sacrificing her people, or seeing her sister murdered?

"We can fight," he said levelly.

"Aye," Anice agreed quickly. "Let us fight. I'll get our swords. We can tell Ella to get her axe, and Leila to get her daggers. Please, Marin."

The reiver jerked Cat harder against him and pushed the blade closer. Cat did not make a sound, but Marin cried out as if she had been struck.

God help her and her people, for she was not strong enough to endure this.

"There are too many of them to fight," she said weakly. "Let us keep this as peaceful as possible. Open the gates."

"Open the gates," Sir Richard bellowed with such readiness, Marin knew he had been hoping to hear those very words.

She didn't wait to see the reivers amass below on their anxious mounts. Nay, she ran down the stone stairs to the gatehouse with Anice close at her heels. If they came in with weapons raised, she could at least head them off, give the women and children an opportunity to flee.

"My lady, please." Sir Richard followed Marin down the stairs. "I do not trust them."

"This was my choice," she replied, her decision made. "I will be the first to face the consequences. Take Anice back into the castle."

"My lady, your mother—" he broke off before digging deeper into a wound that had not healed in any of them these past eleven years.

Anice's mouth opened as if to protest.

"I am not my mother," Marin replied. "Take Anice into the castle." She lifted her head and turned from him. Her steps were confident as she strode to the gatehouse. No doubt the reivers could smell fear. She would not give them the satisfaction.

The heavy metal portcullis gave great groaning squeals and protests as it rose and revealed to her the force of an army. Still it was not enough to cover Anice's pleas to remain.

But Marin was not focusing on Anice. Not when Cat was locked against the man with a blade set to her neck, defeated, her face ruddy from silent tears. "Marin, please don't do this," she said miserably.

But it was already done.

"Ye dinna have enough men to fight us, so dinna bother trying." The reiver removed the blade from Cat's throat and shoved her forward on stumbling legs. Marin caught her second youngest sister before the girl could fall. Cat clung to her, her slender body trembling.

"Do you mean to attack us?" Marin pushed Cat behind her and regarded the reiver who had craftily forced his way past their fortifications.

He was tall with deep set eyes of the most intense, dark brown she'd ever seen. His black hair fell in messy waves to his shoulders from beneath his steel helm and an unruly beard covered his entire jaw. A trail of blood showed beneath his sharp nose from where Cat had struck him.

"Who are ye?" He sniffed hard again and wiped at the injury. Marin's lip curled in disgust. The man was a beast. And so was the younger man, barely more than a lad, standing stoically next to him.

"I am Lady Marin, eldest daughter of the Earl of Werrick." Marin spoke with strength and authority. This man would not intimidate her. "We are mostly women and children here. We do not want to fight."

"Ye mean ye dinna want to die." The dark eyes scanned up her body and came to rest on her face, assessing.

She wasn't wearing her chainmail and hated her own vulnerability. Her simple blue kirtle was of fine Italian brocade with bits of silver thread embroidered at the ends of her sleeves. It was a poor substitute for chainmail and a solid sword in her palm. She straightened as tall as she could and stared directly back at him.

She could assess as well, and he had been found wanting.

"Are ye the mistress of the castle?" he asked.

"Aye," Marin replied.

"Cede the castle to me, or we attack." He folded his arms over his chest while the whole of his army pressed at his back.

Cede the castle? Marin nearly blanched. And yet...there were too many of them. Even if she gave the order for the portcullis to be closed, it wouldn't be done in time to block out the storming reivers. Her own men would be not strong enough to defend Werrick Castle. It could not be like last time the castle had been taken, not like with the Grahams.

"Nay, Marin," Cat whimpered behind her. "Please."

Marin gritted her teeth. Better to give her castle without a fight than allow all of them to be killed. She squared her shoulders with determination. "I will cede my castle only on the condition that my people remain unharmed."

The reiver lifted his brows. "Ye're negotiating with me?"

"Aye." Marin was in no position to do so, and they both knew it, but she refused to back down. "If you do not agree, we will be forced to attack."

He smirked. "Ye would lose."

"And many of your men would die." Marin crossed her arms over her chest as well, mirroring his easy confidence.

He gave a mirthless chuckle. "Verra well, my lady." He bowed mockingly. "Cede yer castle and I give ye my word yer people willna be hurt."

The word of a reiver held as much honesty as a basket held water, but she had no choice.

"Then I cede Werrick Castle to you." She infused her capitulation with all the force of her bitterness.

The cur grinned at her, a flash of brilliant white teeth beneath his dark beard.

Cat sobbed, a gut-wrenching cry.

Marin spun about to her younger sister. "Are you injured?"

"You should have let them kill me," Cat cried.

Was there blood? An injury Marin could not see?

She cupped her hands around her sister's face, turning her this way and that. Aside from wide eyed terror and the moisture of shed tears, Cat appeared otherwise unharmed. Even the blade to her slender throat had not left so much as a mark. Thanks be to God for such a gift.

"I could never let anyone kill you, Catriona. I love you too much." Marin's voice caught.

Out of the corner of her eye, Marin noted the dark-haired reiver's approach.

She released Cat and shifted to put herself between Cat and the fiend. In no way would Marin allow her sister to become this man's victim once more.

"I'll have supper for my men." He gestured behind him. "And lodging for our horses."

"You wish me to treat you as though you are guests?" she

asked incredulously. It was nearly an hour until supper. How could there possibly be time to accommodate so many men?

"This is my castle." He cocked his head arrogantly. "And yer people are unharmed."

Marin balled her hand into a fist within her skirt. "I will see to it." She drew a deep breath to still her frantic pulse. "I wish to speak with you alone later, as well."

The reiver's gaze dipped to her body. "Aye?"

Her cheeks flared with heat. "To discuss your intentions."

He made an agreeable humming sound and strode forward, toward the keep. A black cat trotted from the stables and wound his way around the man's feet. Fitting. Bixby always did have an affinity for rats.

Marin did not wish the little feline to be kicked by a man so brutal, and quickly stepped forward to shoo Bixby away. Before she could reach him, the reiver lifted the animal into his arms and scratched at the place Bixby liked best, right between his ears.

Very well. She would leave the rat-lover to the rat.

Marin put an arm around her sister's shoulders to gently indicate they should follow. A splash of red on the skirt of Cat's pink cotehardie caught Marin's eye.

"Is that blood?" Marin pulled at Cat's gown, fanning it out to reveal the spot. "Are you hurt?"

The reiver stopped and looked back at them.

"It's Eversham's blood." Cat's lower lip trembled, but she bit it and held back the tears swimming in her large blue eyes. "He came out with me to ensure I stayed safe." She stared down at the blood on her skirt. "He's...he's..." She sucked in a hard breath and her body began to shake.

Marin brushed Cat's hair from her pretty face. As often as she'd wished Cat's incessant chatter would cease, she realized now that was far preferable to seeing her younger sister rendered mute by fear and sorrow.

"Marin, it was my fault," Cat whimpered.

"Aye, it was," the reiver said.

Marin shot him a dark look. "Don't listen to him."

"Nay, it was my fault." Cat shook her head miserably. "It was so lovely outside and I wanted to see if there were more of those yellow flowers Ella loves on the other side of the hill." Cat turned her luminous gaze on Marin. "You said it was fine so long as I brought a soldier."

"Then it was *yer* fault." The reiver looked to Marin. "Marin." He said her name as though he were testing it out, and Marin didn't like it anymore than she liked the implication of wrong-doing on her part.

"*Lady* Marin." In truth, she did not remember allowing Catriona to go outside. She recalled dealing with the ledger of the accounts she'd gone over with the steward; then there had been the inventory of the larder.

Ah, yes. There it was in her memory—Catriona spinning about the room with a little song and asking if she might pick flowers for Ella. Marin had half-heard the silly request and flippantly agreed so long as she took a soldier to attend her.

In truth, she merely wanted Cat out of the room so she might finish the growing pile of work in peace, before one of their other three sisters came to ask for something.

And now Eversham was dead and their impenetrable home breached.

The reiver continued toward the castle, nonplussed, with Bixby contentedly curled in his arms.

Marin gently rubbed Catriona's slender back. "There now, you needn't blame yourself. It is not your fault."

And it wasn't at all her fault. Nay, the danger hovering over them all, threatening violence and fear and death—it was entirely Marin's fault.

Bran Davidson strode into the keep like he owned it. And he did, at least for now. He lowered the black cat to the ground where it continued to follow him, trotting at his feet.

"Drake, see to the men," he said to his most trusted reiver at his right. The young man had joined Bran three years back when he was barely a lad and had been invaluable ever since. He never questioned his tasks and was always willing to do anything to earn his keep, as he had a mother and several sisters back home that he supported.

For the first time since Bran had known Drake, the young man paused. He regarded the figures of the sisters behind them, the older one with her arm around the younger, and a muscle clenched in his jaw. Drake didn't like this any more than Bran did. But he knew what he'd agreed to. The same as Bran. And he too knew what was at stake.

Finally, Drake gave an obliging nod and disappeared to follow orders.

Bran gave his own final glance back at the ladies. Catriona who had bowed into her sister's embrace, and the bonny Marin. And damn, but she was so bonny. Only a blind man would not have noticed her angelic beauty with her pale blonde hair and wide blue eyes. Even with the barely suppressed rage she afforded him, she was lovely.

Guilt stabbed at him for having used the younger girl to gain entrance into the castle. But with the walls so damn high and well built, it had been his only option. He'd taken considerable care to ensure the girl wasn't hurt.

In truth, he wouldn't have killed her, but Marin need not know. God, how he hated this whole damn thing. Kerr had better uphold his end of the bargain after this was done. One never knew with that crooked warden.

Bran entered the keep and stopped short. He'd heard rumors of Werrick's wealth from the Grahams, but he hadn't believed it. After all, who could really afford tapestries sewn in silk to cover the walls, and thick carpet lining the cold stone floors, as well as so much furniture? Even the hallways were furnished and decorated.

Apparently Werrick could. No doubt money scraped from those who barely had enough to give, extorted from those who were too poor to be anything but vulnerable.

The scent of savory meat and herbs hung in the air. Bran's mouth watered with hunger. How long since he'd last eaten a solid meal? Aye, a bit of cheese and bread here and there as he could afford, but a real meal–hot and running with juices that hadn't congealed or gone rancid?

Too bloody long.

Maybe this task wouldn't be as bad as he'd thought. After all, he'd been able to take the keep with only having caused one death.

Only a few days observation of the castle had revealed no additional troops were returning to guard the high walls. It was left as theirs for the taking. No doubt Kerr had suspected as much when he'd sent Bran.

A peasant woman leapt in surprise at his presence, and ran, slamming a door behind her. Another stab of guilt thrust into him. The people within the keep would be scared for only a short while, until they knew Bran meant no harm. At least until Kerr and his men arrived.

Bran made his way deeper into the castle, each hall and room seeming more opulent and ostentatious than the last. A waste, the lot of it. The coin used could have fed an army for a lifetime. With some to spare.

For the whole of his life, he had survived. Not lived, survived. Every damn day brought a new struggle to find food or shelter or both. It ground away at him until he could scarcely take another day of hunger or danger. Suddenly taking the castle held a note of vindication.

He climbed the stairs to the second floor and wandered into a room luxuriously decorated with tapestries of unicorns and lions. The rich furniture was polished to a high shine and shelves filled with books. Paintings of animals and flowers and whorls covered the great wooden beams along the ceiling in a colorful array of blue and red and green and yellow.

Sunlight poured in from a leaded window, each pane of glass carefully constructed in a circle, like the bottom of a bottle, and cast in iron. The light cast pure warmth against his hand where it touched him. He'd seen glass in a chapel once, several years back, but he had never seen it up close. He hadn't realized castles now had glass windows.

He stepped closer and was startled to discover a woman sitting on the cushioned bench under the glass window. She'd been so still, and he'd been so awed by the room, he hadn't noticed.

Her legs were curled toward her with a book resting on her knees. She had her fingers daintily propped on either side of the leather-bound cover and her blonde head leaned over the pages.

The mother? Another sister?

He cleared his throat. She held up a finger and did not bother to raise her head.

"A moment," she murmured.

He waited. She turned the page and sighed to herself, a whimsical little hum of a sound. She slid a ribbon to the center of the book before closing it and lifted her brows with mild impatience. "Aye?"

She was young, but not as young as the girl he'd held hostage only moments ago. Another sister, then.

"I'm in charge of this castle now." He stood with his feet planted wide.

She tilted her head pensively. "I heard no battle."

"There was no battle."

"Then you must be quite clever or quite bold." Her eyes narrowed slightly in obvious assessment. "I think bold."

The saucy chit. He opened his mouth to protest but was interrupted before he had the chance.

"You should come to supper."

Bran turned toward the feminine voice and found yet another golden-haired sister. She was older than the one he currently spoke to, a woman more his age, and stunningly beautiful. Her hair was lighter and hung in glossy waves, her eyes larger, her lips fuller, her curves more apparent.

She waved him toward her, the movement graceful and beguiling. There was not the steely exterior about her that Marin had possessed. This one might be a good lass for bed sport, if she was willing. It'd been longer than he liked since he'd had a woman in his bedroll.

He drew off his helm and grinned at her. He knew his smile to be one of his finer attributes, not just for enlisting new reivers to his side, but also winning over ladies. His teeth were white and strong, and he still had them all.

The new sister did not return his gesture. "You threatened to kill Catriona." A hardness touched her almond-shaped eyes and she appeared more likely to run him through with a sword than allow him in her bed. A massive dog came from behind her, a beast so tall, its haunches came higher than her waist. It regarded him with glittering black eyes from a face of drooping brown fur.

"He did what?" The other sister exclaimed from behind him.

"I dinna hurt her." He held up his hands. If he wanted her in his bed that night and didn't want to end up that beast of a dog's supper, he'd need to approach the topic with diplomacy.

In truth, if Lady Marin hadn't opened the portcullis when she did, the situation would have been a difficult one to navigate. He didn't hurt women or children. Ever.

His men had all been warned off ever hurting them as well, upon punishment of death. And it was one he would readily mete out. He didn't care if he took the life of a man, especially one who preyed upon the weak.

"You could have hurt her," the younger sister said. She moved to his side. The curious interest in her eyes had frosted over with icy disdain.

"Come now if you want food, or don't and starve." The older one departed with her dog, leaving only her swirling hem trailing behind her.

Bran strode quickly to follow and found the younger sister at his side. "What are you called?" he asked.

"A scholar." She lifted her chin. "And you?"

"A reiver." If she wouldn't answer him with naught but a quip, he could do likewise.

Ahead of him, the older sister and her giant beast led at a ridiculous pace, her leather shoes far quieter than the wooden patens of his. She did not slow, not until they reached the great hall where his men had settled in. Conversations buzzed around him, heavy with the baritone of his reivers. The inhabitants of the castle were easily detected by their soundlessness. As if those who had dared to attend supper might remain safe by remaining quiet.

The ceiling of the great hall had similar paintings across the great wooden beams stretching out overhead. Unicorns and lions and flowers and graceful arcing whorls throughout. Had the sisters done them, or had they come at an exorbitant price as with everything in the castle?

Servants laid out trenchers filled with steaming food on the tables. So much food. Root vegetables roasted and steaming, thick slabs of meat drenched in gravy, and loaves of crusty bread as big as his forearm.

Never had he seen so much food in one place.

The younger sister disappeared from his side and the dog trotted off toward a servant who waved the beast over. The one who had led him there swept past him, intending to leave as well. He caught her hand. It was soft, her fingers slender and dainty.

She stopped and her lashes lowered as she regarded their joined hands. Her palm was warm, and she had a delicate floral scent about her. It was pleasant and he liked the thought of smelling her on his skin the next morning.

"What is yer name?" He brushed her wrist with his thumb, a suggestive caress to imply so, so much more, and released his hold on her.

Her eyes narrowed in a way that said Bran wouldn't get her name, let alone her favors.

Rejection.

He'd expected nothing less. The wealthy always thought themselves so above everyone else.

"May I show you to your table?" Marin stepped from the doorway and wedged herself in front of her sister.

By comparison between the women, Marin held an authoritative demeanor and unquestioned confidence. A challenge. He decided then and there he liked her the best. Bran nodded for her to lead him to the table, and she did, skirting the edge of the great hall to the front. To the dais.

He wouldn't sit at the head of the great hall, like some over-privileged noble. "Nay. This is fine here." He indicated the bench as she turned to face him.

There was a strength about her, a fortitude which drew him. Everything about her indicated she would be supple and sweet, and yet her influence, her tone, all suggested she was nothing fragile.

"Will ye join me?" he asked.

Marin's lips curled into a slow smile of obvious interest. "I was hoping we might dine together."

She stood nearly a head taller than any of her sisters, her stance proud. Candlelight sparkled off her glossy hair and something enticing glittered in her blue eyes.

His gaze slipped to her full, kissable lips. No doubt they'd be supple beneath his mouth, sweet.

"I know what men like you want." Her own stare dipped in assessment of his body.

He was sure of what she thought she knew. Mayhap of what she'd even seen living on the border. He frowned. "I dinna take women by force."

She stepped closer, bringing with her the clean scent of lavender. "What if she comes to you by choice?"

Her face was flawless, lovely, most likely soaked each night in milk that could feed families instead. He should hate her for it, and yet he found all he wanted to do was stroke her to see if she would be as smooth as she looked, caressing such creamy skin, having her flush with passion...

"Depends." He cocked his head to the side. "Is that woman ye?"

Marin's tongue darted between her pink lips, leaving them glistening. "Aye."

"I was hoping ye'd say that." He winked and her cheeks went pink. Aye, he would have the bonny lass tonight, after a meal fit for a king, in a castle he'd taken with only one death.

This was the best damn day of his life.

❧ 2 ❧

Bran gazed down at Marin in eager anticipation. His blood roared with the victory of seizing this impossible castle, and at the prospect of possessing this beauty.

He craned his head closer, near enough to touch her and yet he did not, mindful of maintaining respect for the lady of the castle. His lips whispered over her hair as he spoke just over her ear. "Tonight, come to my chambers." He let his gaze dip to the swell of her breasts. "I eagerly await our mutual pleasure."

His cock stirred at the thought of taking her, thrusting between milky white thighs, slick with her passion.

He backed away and observed her flushed cheeks and bright eyes, clearly as keen on their pairing. He'd heard of castle ladies and their boring lives, desperate for a real man. And he truly was a real man. No doubt more so than anyone she'd had before.

Perhaps her husband was away at war. Or dead. Widows made the best lovers, as they were experienced and starved for pleasure.

He sat on the hard bench and gestured for her to join him. Her gaze flicked to where the other sisters were locked in conversation, their heads bent together.

"Invite yer sisters to sup with us," he said. After all, it would do well for harmony in the castle if he got to know the earl's daughters. Who knew how long Kerr would take to arrive?

He only hoped for Ena's sake it was sooner than later.

She hesitated, her expression suddenly guarded. Aye, the protective older sister.

"I willna hurt any of them." He gently brushed her slender hand with his own. Her skin was flawless and silky. The hands of a true lady.

She flicked him a coy glance that coiled low in his belly. "Mayhap it would be better with only us."

"Nay, I should like to meet them. If we are all to live here peacefully, should we not get to know one another?" He waved the sisters over.

Marin's pleasant countenance slipped slightly. "I confess, I am curious as to why you are here, and what it is you want?"

"What are yer names?" he asked as the two sisters approached. The air around them was heavy with wariness and distrust.

The beast of a dog was back at the side of the prettiest sister. The cold one who had rejected him. "Lady Anice." She carefully threaded a loose curl back behind her ear and pointedly looked at her nails before passing him a nod of acknowledgement. "And this is Piquette."

The dog glowered at him and gave a low rumble of disapproval.

She was the kind of woman who could build a man up, or knowingly tear him down. He was glad for a woman more like Marin, one who wouldn't play coquettish games.

"And Lady Ella." Marin nodded toward the scholar, whose far-off expression pulled back from where it had been and settled on Bran as if she didn't know what to make of him.

Marin indicated a black-haired girl making her way across the crowded room toward them. "And here is Lady Leila."

The lass was a wee thing, most likely not even on her tenth year, and aside from the sea-blue eyes, appeared nothing at all like her sisters. Not just for the darkness of her hair, but in the rounder shape of her face and her small, set mouth. She watched him solemnly with eyes too large for her face.

He expected another chastisement from this sister for his manner of getting into the castle using...Catriona, was it?

"Are you the one they call the lion?" Leila's voice was so fragile, almost unheard beneath the raucous din of hungry men.

Her question was unusual. He'd been called many things in his life before, but never the lion. He shook his head. "Nay."

Her slender shoulders relaxed, and she took the seat to his left, the only one willing to do so of her own volition.

"I think you can understand why our other sister will not be joining us," Marin said in a gentle voice. "Lady Catriona has had a trying day."

"It hasn't been my best," a female voice spoke up. "But do you really think I'd let that keep me from supper?"

Bran found the final sister standing by the doorway nearest their table, her small chest puffed bravely out. She had changed from her blood-stained dress and wore an orange kirtle with her hair bound into a neat braid coiled around her head.

"I couldn't possibly stay up in my room smelling such delicious fare, could I?" She approached the table.

"Cat, you don't have to do this." Marin said it lovingly, but the admonishment in her tone and the concern furrowing her brow suggested she was not happy with her sister's decision.

Catriona took a seat on Marin's right, with a smile plastered to her face. It did not reach the flatness of her blue eyes. "It is a pity the troubadour who comes sometimes is not about. He is quite witty and tells the most wonderful tales." She chattered on, her words too quick, her laughs too breathy, as if doing so might force everything to rights.

Looking at the lass compared to her older sisters, she was a wee bit of a thing. Only a little larger than Leila. Guilt stabbed at Bran's chest, deeper than last time, its effects radiating farther.

Ena would be disappointed in him if she knew. But then, he hadn't had much choice in the matter.

After all, Catriona being outside the castle walls had afforded him the opportunity to capture the castle without loss of life on either side, save the single soldier valiantly guarding the girl. His death could not have been avoided.

"Besides, you did not change any part of your life after you were taken, Marin," Catriona said brightly. "I will not either."

Marin looked sharply at the girl and Catriona stopped talking long enough to leave one wondering what had happened. Bran frowned. He knew well what happened to most women abducted in these parts. "Taken by who?" he asked.

Each of the sisters' attention turned toward him.

Anger sizzled through him at the knowledge of what men oftentimes did to women they took. A noble's brat Marin might be, but it made him want to kill anyone who dared lay a harmful hand to her. Especially after witnessing how caring and protective she was of those around her. "Did they hurt ye?" he demanded.

Anice scoffed. "You're one to ask such a question."

"Anice," Marin said in a firm tone. Anice lowered her gaze at the chastisement.

Marin regarded him, her expression revealing nothing. "It was nothing. Truly." Her gaze lingered on him, bright with interest.

His fears quelled, the tension in his shoulders eased.

"Besides, Father always says we should be proper ladies and welcome our guests." Catriona spoke as though reciting the words from memory. "I cannot imagine they will stay long. After all, there are only so many beds to be had here, and so much food to eat. We cannot support so many in the castle for long. Therefore, they must be guests and treated thus." She turned her face toward him, her brows lifted in hope. "Isn't that correct, sir...lord...uh..."

"Bran," he replied.

A servant set a platter of venison at the table's center. Steam rose from it and the herbaceous scent of roasted meat drew every bit of his attention. His mouth watered. It had been two days since he'd eaten a hot meal. And yet he would be foolish to blindly consume food placed in front of him in a castle he'd just usurped.

He sliced off a generous hunk and set it on the trencher in front of Anice. The meat broke apart, more succulent than anything he'd ever eaten before. Rich man's food. His stomach gave a vicious snarl of hunger.

"Eat it." He motioned to the meat.

"You think it's poisoned." Ella smirked up at him. "Perhaps you've read more than I presumed. Or mayhap you've heard too many troubadour tales."

Anice pushed the plate away with disinterest. "I have no appetite."

Marin shot her sister a hard look before turning once more to Bran. "The food is not poisoned."

"I'll no' take my chances." He nodded to Anice. "Eat."

She glowered at him. Marin gave a little laugh, as though this was all some silly thing and pulled the trencher toward her. She sliced off a piece with a knife from her belt, plucked it free with her fingers and slid it between her lips.

Bran swallowed. He was so bloody hungry that he would probably eat the food even if it was poisoned. Hell, he wanted to lick her fingers clean.

Marin chewed the small bite, then slid the trencher before him. She lifted his goblet and put it to her sensual mouth. He did not once take his eyes from her, watching as her slender throat squeezed in a swallow. His own throat burned, desperate for the flow of rich wine.

"Not poison." She set the goblet in front of him. Her fingers slowly released the cup, the movement almost a caress. His blood went hot. A fine meal and a finer lass. All his baser needs would be sated tonight.

He let his gaze slide down her in appreciation, making the

effort to keep from looking as desperately hungry as he truly was. And dear God, he was ravenous. "Thank ye."

Her mouth lifted at the corner, coy and welcoming. His stomach gave a savage growl. He only hoped the din of the room was such that she hadn't heard. Leila, however, grinned impishly up at him.

He raised his brows at her and waggled them. The grin widened.

Bran sliced a hunk of venison with his blade. Thick gravy dripped from the meat and his hand began to quiver with near desperation when he pulled it off his eating dagger.

These women had doubtless never gone a day without eating. Despite the bitter thought, he forced his movements to slow as he ate the first bite.

The morsel was tender, and his teeth sank through it without having to even chew. The herbs hit his tongue with more flavor than he'd ever tasted in his life, something pleasantly savory with a hint of earthiness. Exquisite.

He took a second bite and third, then noticed the sisters pointedly watching him. He popped a fourth into his mouth and regarded them as he chewed. Ire rankled him. He'd tried to follow all the rules of the table for the ladies and still his eating had somehow caused offense.

He hadn't wiped his mouth on his sleeve; he'd pulled the meat from his eating dagger rather than biting it directly off the blade. He hadn't even used the blade to pick his teeth. A bowl of water sat beside him. *Shite*. Rich men always washed their hands before eating. Damn their ostentatious and foolish ways, and damn him for trying to appeal to the lot of them.

His eyes narrowed.

"My sisters were wondering at the cause of your arrival and questioned the length of your stay," Marin said sweetly. "They also would like to know what has happened to our soldiers. I was uncertain how to answer."

In truth, he didn't know how long he'd be there. At least until Warden Kerr could get enough troops over to take the castle. All of it would be based on how events played out at Berwick. A war was brewing between England and Scotland, and this land was a crucial piece in the chess game of wealthy men.

Like all those without a title, Bran was simply a pawn.

"The soldiers are alive." He put another bite into his mouth. It was exactly as good as the first few. He could happily become a fat man on food such as this. "They're in the dungeon, but we dinna intend to harm them."

"Why are you doing this?" Anice asked. "Why would you threaten to hurt Cat, and bring your men in here? What do you want from us?" She glared at him openly now, no longer fearing Marin's wrath.

Marin, for her part, did not tell her sister to stop this time.

"I took this castle intentionally without harming more than the one unfortunate soldier and I've no intention to hurt any of ye or yer guards." He took another bite and waited until he swallowed before speaking again. "That's all ye need to know."

It was ridiculous to put on such airs for the benefit of these ladies. But then again, to do so, to win their affection, would make the people of Werrick Castle more compliant. He'd heard too many tales of the people rising up against usurpers. And who knew how long Kerr would take to come for Werrick Castle?

His gaze skimmed over Marin's face, noting the lusciousness of her lips, the fairness of her skin. He could only imagine her flushed with pleasure, her mouth and cheeks red, her blue eyes heavy lidded.

Aye, having the lovely noblewoman would be the perfect bit of sweetness after so filling a meal. He cut another piece of venison for himself and noticed none of the sisters had taken any for themselves. Now he was grateful he'd made them test it for poison.

"But surely you will not harm our soldiers." Catriona offered a tentative smile, even as hurt flashed in her eyes, despite the optimism of her words. She looked away, no doubt recalling the man Bran had cut down .

He ate another slice of venison and drank deeply from the goblet of wine at his side. He didn't have the opportunity to drink wine often. Even when he had, it was usually sour with age and of poor quality, certainly nothing so fine as the rich spiced wine in his cup. He drained it in one gulp and found his starved stomach already overly full.

"We will discuss yer soldiers when I speak privately with Lady Marin." He rose from the table and winked at the eldest sister. "I'm ready to retire."

Her face went red. Aye, like that. He wanted all of her flushed exactly like that, under him and moaning in passion. His cock began to swell with longing.

"What does he mean?" Ella asked. "Are you going to have a private discussion without us?"

Marin put up a hand to cease her sisters' complaints and got to her feet. She turned from her sisters and lightly bit her lip. "I'd like a moment to prepare first." Her voice was low, sultry; it teased over every nerve in his body and left prickles of gooseflesh, raising the hair on his arms.

Most likely she wanted to wipe her body off and apply more of her clean-smelling lavender water to her intimate places, the very places he intended to explore.

But, if Lady Marin of Werrick Castle needed a few minutes, he'd give her the time she needed. For soon, she would in his bed. And in the meantime, he had a missive to pen for Kerr. Bran's end of the bargain had been fulfilled.

MARIN WAS GOING TO KILL BRAN.

Her decision had seemed so easy earlier in the evening when

she'd seen him with Anice, when he had reached out and caught her hand. Marin had wanted to kill him then, but when his men outnumbered her own two to one, it was wise to be prudent.

Nay, it would be best to do it alone, when there would be no surrounding army. And there was no better way to get a man alone than to seduce him.

Marin's hands shook so badly, she could scarcely fasten the jeweled belt around her waist.

Anice pushed Marin's hands aside and deftly fastened the clasp before readjusting it into place. "Is there nothing else we can do? Entertain him, get him drunk. You saw how fast he drained his wine. It would be easily done." Her gaze was desperate when she looked up at Marin, desperate and scared. An uncommon look for the sister who was always so effortlessly composed. "Please, Marin."

"I must do this." And Marin would. She had to. In order to protect her sisters, her home. This was her mistake to make right, and she would do so without putting anyone else at risk.

"At least take Piquette," Anice said. The large dog lying next to the hearth lifted his head at the sound of his name. "He'll keep you safe."

Marin shook her head. "I cannot attempt this with Piquette in the room."

The dog watched the exchange with dark eyes, his floppy ears perking at the second mention of his name.

"This is foolish." Even as Anice spoke, her fingers were at work plucking at Marin's fabric and fiddling with her jewelry to make it all just so. "You cannot let the reiver have you. No man will marry you after that."

"Have her?" Catriona flopped down on a cushion on the ground near them. "Why wouldn't a man marry you?"

At only sixteen, Catriona had remained blissfully ignorant of what transpired between a man and a woman. That all the sisters had been able to remain innocent in such dangerous times was a testament to their father's diligence to their care and the strong-hold that was Werrick Castle. But the older three had heard stories of what happened to captured women and had tried their best to keep the younger two sheltered.

Bran had said he would not take a woman by force, but what of his men?

"You know I have no intention to marry." Marin ran her fingers through her long hair to ensure no tangles remained. "It's why you've been able to become betrothed to your Timothy before any engagement was announced for me. Besides..." Marin lowered her voice. "It will not come to any of that."

"Any of what?" Catriona grinned impishly.

Piquette, who apparently realized he was no longer part of the sisters' conversation, rested his large head back on the floor.

Ella gave an excited gasp. "What if we can find poison to apply onto your dagger? Leila, can it be done?"

Leila, who had watched everything with her small lips tucked against themselves, shook her dark head. "I'm unaware of a poison that can coat a dagger. At least one to kill a man." Her mouth screwed to the side. "And I chance it to say, it might not be good to have him dead."

The sisters all went still and stared at her.

"Because he's a good person in his heart?" Cat guessed. "And this will truly become the greatest love story of all time?" She put her hands dramatically over her chest and pretended to swoon. "Ella, you must write all this down."

Marin laughed, her nerves making the sound high-pitched. In truth, she knew exactly what she was getting into. Not through experience, but through knowledge gleaned. It had been she, after all, who had caught their Master of the Horse with the maid in the stables.

It had piqued her curiosity. And while she did not anticipate getting to the point of...of...copulation, the anticipation of a kiss held great appeal.

Because she *would* have to kiss him and touch him. A trill of excitement shivered through her, no matter how much she tried to tamp it down. He was handsome in a wild way, those dark eyes intense as they devoured her.

She shivered and the tips of her nipples tingled. But she could not think such things. Nay, she would need to focus on him as the opponent he was. He was clever; he'd proven that by how he'd gotten into the castle. And he was strong, at least in her summation based on how his visible forearms and neck were corded with muscle.

What would it be like to touch such a strong body? What would he feel like under her fingertips?

Death. She reminded herself with the word in steely resolve. For she would need to kill him.

"I do not wish you to hurt him," Leila said with finality.

Of everything said in Marin's preparation, this was the one that gave her pause. Leila saw things others didn't, felt things in ways others could not.

Anice carefully slipped the dagger into the front of Marin's belt where the length of gold metalwork fell in the fashionable "Y." It perfectly concealed the dagger, which was why she'd borrowed the belt from Anice. Likewise, the dress she'd borrowed had been one of the latest styles with a lower-cut neckline, hopefully a better distraction than her own more modestly cut gowns.

She only wished it was as easy for Anice to lend her effortless charisma and confidence.

"If not his dagger, then we could poison his wine," Ella offered, ignoring Leila. "I read in a text once where a bit of belladonna could be added to his cup. Anice was right; he drank quickly at supper. He would never know until it was too late."

"And if he makes me drink it again?" Marin said. "Nay, I must kill him if we want them all gone. His reivers are not loyal men. No reiver is. His men will be easily dispatched when they no longer have their leader to guide them."

"What if he's a good man?" Catriona asked. "Did you see something, Leila?"

Leila simply shrugged, either unable or unwilling to share what she might know. Oftentimes she did not see everything fully. It was a skill Marin did not encourage either, not when it was so dangerous.

Anice scoffed and set to work brushing Marin's hair over her shoulder and pinching her cheeks to give them color. Marin waved off her sister's preening. "He's taken over our castle, Cat. He's not a good man."

"Yet he did so without killing any soldiers other than Eversham and that was because Eversham—" Cat's voice caught. "Eversham wouldn't have let anyone take me." She pursed her lips and gently shook her head. "But Bran didn't once hit me, even when I hit him. Nor did he leave a mark from his dagger on my throat. He was careful. Intentionally so. I could tell."

It was true. Cat had emerged without even a scratch on her. Marin had noticed as much. Most men would have struck Cat back when she hit him, but the reiver had not.

Marin swept her hands over the length of her borrowed gown. "I'm ready." At least as ready as she might ever be.

Anice set her slender hand on Marin's forearm. "Please don't do this, Marin. What if you are caught?"

Marin met her sister's eyes. "I won't be."

Ella rushed forward and hugged Marin with all the strength in her seventeen-year-old body. "I do wish you'd try the belladonna."

Cat came next and threw her slender arms around Marin in a hug. "Please give him a chance."

Marin knelt in front of Leila, who had watched and listened with her customary pensive silence. "You needn't worry, Leila." She smoothed the girl's dark hair from her face.

The youngest sister nodded with sage wisdom. "I know." Her smile was shy and secretive. She did not protest Marin's departure again, making Marin wonder at what little Leila might be foreshadowing with her sight.

Regardless, her assuredness helped quell some of the anxiety rattling through Marin. With a final kiss on each sisters' head, the way their father always did before battle, Marin departed.

Her nerves returned as she traversed the darkened passageways and tried not to hear the echo of strange men's voices around her. The candle in her hand trembled and cast a wavering light over her path as she headed toward the chamber Bran had claimed—her father's chambers.

She had never even kissed a man, and yet she was intent on seducing one. What sort of a fool was she to assume she could?

He was an attractive man; she would give him that. The thought of his lips on hers made her pulse race a little faster with anticipation. Would his dark beard prickle against her mouth? Would it be bristling, or downy? Would he touch her body?

The thought left her breathless.

These musings made her question her decision to have her father refrain from contracting any betrothals for her. Clearly, she had interest in a husband. Or at least copulation.

And mayhap Catriona was right. He might be kind.

Marin paused in front of the door and her heart slammed against her ribs. This man would touch his mouth to hers, put his hands to her body, at least until he was cajoled into a sense of complete unawareness and then she would attack.

She had killed men in battle on many occasions. This would be no different. Bran's strength would outmatch hers, aye, but she had the benefit of proper training. His skills would be rough and hers refined.

Suddenly, she found herself hoping he would not be kind after all. For if he touched her affectionately and gave her consideration, how could she watch the light fade from his eyes as he died?

Her breath came out in a shaky exhale. If she had so many

advantages in her favor, why then was she so nervous? If he had taken the castle, how could he truly be a good man?

Yet if he was, could she bring herself to kill him?

"Are ye going to stand outside my door all night?" The masculine voice came from the other side of the door. "Or are ye going to come in?"

Marin started. This was it. She would need him to put down his guard with her, to lull him into a sense of comfort. She had to be a seductress.

She pressed the latch on the door. It creaked open, the sound low and ominous as it scraped over her nerves. Light from the hearth glowed orange gold in the room, transporting the familiar room into a place of sin and temptation. He stood just before the flames, his dark hair combed sleek and his stance wide with authority. The man she intended to kill.

3

Bran forced himself to remain by the fire as Marin entered. The woman looked like an angel with her blonde hair swept becomingly over one shoulder. She'd put on a new gown, this one cut lower over her chest, revealing the rounded tops of her breasts. His heart pounded in a hard, steady rhythm of lust.

"Close the door and approach," he ordered.

The lass did as he bid, gently closing the door behind her and sauntering toward him. Her hips swayed back and forth enticingly. He wanted to skim his hands over them and up her narrow waist. His cock was already beginning to thicken at the very thought. She stopped in front of him and looked up, taking him in.

He'd bathed. For her. The bath had arrived without his orders, the suggested request apparent. He'd resented it, knowing he wasn't clean enough for the likes of her, that he wasn't good enough. But he'd done it, and now it was time for his prize.

His dark hair still dripped at the ends and soaked through his shirt. The heat of the fire had dried his skin and kept the chill of the night at bay. Of course, with this beauty in his bed, he would not feel any bit of the cold.

He touched her cheek. God's bones, her skin was impossibly smooth. He swept his thumb over her full bottom lip. Her breath whispered over the back of his hand. Every part of his body seemed to be on a level of heightened awareness and soaring sensitivity. He regretted having not rubbed away his longing earlier, to ensure he did not lose himself too quickly with her.

He lowered his face and brushed his mouth against hers. Aye, she was sweet. He gently swept his tongue inside the heat of her mouth. A little moan sounded in the back of her throat.

Aye, she'd never been kissed like this before.

He stroked his tongue against hers and reveled in the chords of pleasure humming through him, building the fire rising within him. She was bold with the spice of wine on her lips and the kisses she offered him in return, more curious than confident. He slid his hand from her waist, up higher to cup the swell of her breast, and she stiffened.

He paused. Perhaps she was not as experienced as she had implied.

He hesitated, but she leaned toward him, her mouth seeking his with the kind of carnal appetite he enjoyed. His hands found her waist and he ran his palms over the curve of her hips down to the pleasant firmness of her bottom. She arched against his touch like a cat being pet.

He pulled her against him and fit their pelvises against one another where his powerful erection raged at full force. She gave a jolt of surprise.

He pulled away. The open-mouthed expression on her face was not one of uncertain delight, it was one of shock and inexperience. Damn it.

He adjusted the rock-solid shaft of his cock, so it fit more comfortably within his trews. "Where's yer husband?"

"I don't have a husband," she said resolutely.

"Are ye betrothed?"

"Does it matter?"

He smirked. In truth, it didn't.

"Are ye a maiden?" he asked.

"Nay." She shifted her gaze to the left and pressed her tongue between her full lips. Honeyed lips he'd been kissing only a moment ago.

Encouraged, he stepped closer once more, and traced a finger over her delicate earlobe, down the length of her slender neck. He pulled his fingers back from her momentarily. "Have ye been ill-treated, Marin?" he asked.

She shook her head, but the tension in her body did not dissipate. There was something she was not telling him.

"Do ye want to be here, lass?"

She caught his hand and brought his fingertips to her low neckline. Using his hand for him, she drew his touch over the tops of her breasts. Her nipples hardened merely an inch under his fingers, the tight buds apparent beneath the fabric of her dress.

She pulled in a breath. "I want to be here." Her eyes met his with starlight dancing in them. "With you."

He circled the pad of his thumb lower, to graze over one taut nipple. She gave a shaky inhale, and her lashes swept briefly closed.

"I'll be different than what ye've had before, I vow," he said in a low, sensual tone. "I want to take my time with ye, love ye all through the night. I want to ensure ye're fully ready for me. Do ye know what that means?"

Her breath quickened and her cheeks were a lovely shade of pink.

He circled her nipple as he spoke and watched the pleasure play over Marin's bonny face. "It means ye go slick between yer legs." His fingernail drew over the bud and her eyelashes fluttered. "Are ye wet for me, Marin?" he whispered.

Her cheeks went deep red.

"If ye're no', we'll have to change that, aye?" He caught her face gently in his hand and those large blue eyes turned up to gaze at him, burning with desire.

Many of these noble lasses had been married off to the worst of men, aging bastards who used them like mares to sire children and nothing more. Or they'd been seduced by some courtier who used them to slake their own desire. None of the noblemen he'd ever heard of knew how to handle a lady. At least not like Bran.

There would be no stiff coupling where she lay beneath him with her eyes tightly closed. Nay, he would have her crying out, her hips meeting his with matched urgency, her hands on his body.

He pressed his lips to hers. This time when he brushed his tongue against her mouth, she opened for him immediately, like a flower parting its petals to the sun. He drank her in, teasing and tasting her sweetness. She gave a moan and her tongue flicked against his with tentative curiosity.

Aye, there. That was what he wanted.

His body was on fire, his cock throbbing with want of her. He wanted to tear the kirtle off her and spread her legs to reveal her pink, damp center. In his mind he could see it perfectly, him positioning the head of his manhood at her entrance and sheathing himself in her tight, wet heat until they both cried out.

He gave a little growl of desire and deepened the kiss, so his tongue tangled with hers. His hands moved down her back to the round shape of her bottom. He drew her to him again, so her legs spread over his thigh and his cock nestled against her.

She curled her hips toward him in an instinctive motion of coupling. The pressure of her body against the raging lust of his erection tightened pleasantly through him. He grunted and pushed against her.

He had taken off his quilted gambeson earlier and now drew back to pull his leine over his head. It fell to the floor, leaving him in only his trews with his cock straining at the leather.

He'd never wanted a woman so badly in all his life as he

wanted this fine noblewoman. To show her what loving truly was, to bring her more pleasure than she'd ever had in the whole of her life.

❧

MARIN COULDN'T DRAG HER STARE FROM BRAN'S NAKED TORSO, his powerful muscles rippling in the firelight. Dark hairs dusted over his chest and various scars left his skin puckered. The body of a warrior. He was a man who had seen much war in his life. And doubtless many lovers.

Everything within her spun with the most thrilling, dizzying sensation and her heartbeat pounded between her legs with a wetness she was too shy to admit.

"Take off yer kirtle." His voice was silky and so sensual, it made prickles of desire shiver down her skin.

He wanted to have her, which had been her intention. He was sufficiently lulled into a sense of trust. Though she had not expected it so quickly, nor so enjoyably. A deep part of her wanted to comply with his request, to slip off her kirtle and let her curiosity be sated. But the blade was in her belt, and she would need the dagger to kill him.

"I am not ready yet," she said in a strong voice.

He stepped back and put his hands up in an innocent gesture. "I willna force ye. In fact, ye may leave any time ye like." His dark eyes glittered. "If ye stay, I'll kiss ye and touch ye until ye beg me to take ye. I want ye aching with longing. But I'll no' have ye with yer dress on. Ye're far too lovely to no' see all of ye."

Suddenly it was almost impossible to breathe.

"Will ye leave?" he queried. "Or stay?"

He closed the scant distance between them, and the light spice of the oil he'd used while bathing swirled around them both.

"Stay." She swallowed. "I want to stay." And oh, how she

wanted to stay. She wished she was in a different time, a different place, a different woman. She *wanted* this.

His gaze drifted down her body and her nipples tingled as though he'd caressed her again. "I wager if I swept my fingers against yer center, they'd come away wet."

Fire flashed in her cheeks and she licked her lips. She wanted to squirm from the words he spoke, as if he knew the sinful sensation between her legs.

His dark stare fixed on her mouth. "It drives me mad when ye do that, Marin."

She shouldn't like the way he said her name. And yet she did, his Scottish brogue making her name sound like a sensual purr. "When I do what?"

"When ye lick yer lips." He cradled her jaw in one large, powerful hand, his touch light. "It leaves them glistening and makes me want to kiss ye."

Her pulse raced faster at the thought of his kisses and the heat of his tongue against hers. "Oh."

"And it makes me want to feed ye my cock to suck."

Even as surprise took her, the lust between her thighs pulsed harder, burned hotter.

"It isna only women who pleasure men with their mouths." He stroked his thumb against her mouth, the blunt edge of the digit against the seam of her lips. "Men can also pleasure women in such a fashion."

His thumb probed between her lips and, heaven help her, she could not help but let it pass into her mouth. He groaned, a low, desperate sound that elicited a wild, thrilling power within her. Emboldened, she sucked at the digit. His brows flinched.

"Aye," he gritted through clenched teeth. "Like that." He eased more of his thumb into her mouth. "And I would part yer legs and lap at ye with my tongue."

Such a wicked thing should have shocked her, and yet it did not. Nay, it made her hot with curiosity. She ran her tongue over the length of his thumb, the sensitivity of her mouth letting her discern every whorl of his fingerprint and the roughness of a callus.

His eyes were half-lidded and dark as he watched his finger in her mouth. "I want to lick ye, Marin. I want to taste ye until ye cry out."

A greater part of her wanted that too, a wanton, hungry side. But the stronger part of her knew what she needed to do. It stuck in her mind like a thorn, through each tempting kiss and all the wonderful, lurid descriptions.

He drew his thumb from her mouth and kissed her again, his mouth hot and tasting of the spiced wine he'd drunk earlier. It would be too easy to give in to the seductive words.

Rather than allow herself lustful thoughts, Marin pushed to the forefront the things she ought to recall.

Eversham's sacrifice in his attempt to save Cat. The way her sister had so valiantly hit Bran, a man twice her size, and how the younger girl had pleaded with Marin to let her die to save the castle. Her soldiers locked in the dungeon below the castle. The anticipation of Father's reaction when he discovered Marin had lost Werrick Castle.

She touched Bran's naked chest. His skin was warm and soft, the soap clean scent heady. The coarseness of his hair was masculine and appealing. He pushed closer to her, so her hands pressed to him more firmly. She let her fingers work down the bands of his flat stomach to where their hips touched. To where she hid her dagger.

The metal had heated from where it sat between the heat of their bodies. Marin had to skim its surface several times before finding the hilt. In her efforts, her fingers brushed the hard column of manhood beneath Bran's leather trews. He groaned and ground his hips harder against her.

Pleasure tingled through Marin and made her want to elicit more of his groans, more of his enjoyment. She steeled herself, closed her hand around the hilt and drew out the blade. It slid from its sheath with a telltale metallic hiss. Before surprise could reflect in Bran's eyes, Marin pushed it to his throat.

She meant to keep shoving it until her hands were wet with the life gushing from his body. She meant to kill him and remove his head from his body to show to his men and strike fear into their hearts.

Except he stared at her with as much hurt as he did surprise. It should not have stayed her hand, but it did. And *that* was her greatest mistake.

It took only that one fractured moment of doubt, of care, for him to grip her hand and twist it so all the strength drained from her fingers and the dagger clattered to the floor. Marin was familiar with the move; she'd used it many times herself. She knew better.

The dagger glinted from the floor.

"Marin," Bran said, his voice light with chastisement.

That was when she slammed her forehead into his, for no daughter of Werrick went down without a fight.

✥ 4 ✥

Marin pulled free from Bran's grip, out of danger. He clutched his face with his hands where she'd injured him.

He loosed a string of curses, but she was not done with him yet. She swooped down to reclaim the dagger, then swept her leg toward his, knocking his feet out from underneath him. He crashed to the ground with an "Oof!".

Marin would not hesitate this time. The man had to die. It was the only way to keep everyone else safe.

She fell on top of him, her legs spread over his hips to keep him pinned in place. His body was solid beneath her, and his panting breath made every sinewy muscle in his torso show against his skin.

His manhood still rose hard with lust between her legs where she straddled him. Even in such a dire circumstance, lust teased the back of her mind, begging her to rub the length of her body against his. She shoved aside all the innate yearnings. She drew the dagger up and thrust it down with all the strength she possessed.

Bran brought his arm across his body and pushed her blow off course. A thin line of blood arched over his chest. Merely a scratch. Marin tried to jerk her arm up once more, but Bran had his fingers locked around her wrist in a powerful grip.

"Drop the blade, Marin." He spoke in a low voice, not unlike the one he used when they were so intimate only minutes ago.

She didn't need a dagger to kill him. She did as she was asked and twisted her arm free from his grip. Using all of her body weight, she shoved her elbow toward his throat. Again, he shoved her assault aside, his movement far defter than a man of his size would usually possess.

He locked her elbow in his vise-like hold and rolled them both over. His weight atop her was considerable, certainly enough to keep her in place. He had his hands atop hers, so she couldn't defend herself, his legs spread over hers in an effort to still her kicking. She was completely pinned into place with his hips resting between her legs, the column of his arousal quite obvious.

This time the connection between them sent a jolt of fear through her. She had lost her power. Women in such situations could be easily raped.

Exactly like what had happened to her mother. Marin dragged in a harsh breath, but it did not quell the rise of panic.

"Don't," she gasped. "Please."

Bran's grip on her loosened immediately, though not enough for her to break away from his hold. "Marin." He said her name gently and she realized he had been calling to her several times. "I willna hurt ye, lass, but I canna allow ye to try to kill me either."

"What will you do with me?" She writhed under him, still desperate to be free. "What will you do to my people? My sisters?"

"I dinna intend anyone harm. I told ye that. But I will have to put ye in the dungeon." He gritted his teeth. "Damn it, woman. Be still."

"Afraid I will escape your hold and kill you?" she asked, trying to appear as though she'd recovered more than she had.

His expression relaxed with lust. "Ye're driving me to distraction as ye continue to grind yer heat against me."

Mayhap it was his reassurance he would not hurt her, or the draw pulling her to him, but prickles of desire warmed through her center. He was not like the man who had taken her mother, she knew that. She was also old enough now to realize many men gave pleasure to their women, as this one obviously intended to do for her.

Still, she should not enjoy this so much. Rather than give in, she glared up at Bran. "If you put me in the dungeon, I will escape, and I will kill you. I do not know what you want with my home, but I cannot allow you to take it."

He held her for a moment longer and Marin's skin tingled with incredible awareness. It wasn't the same as when she battled, but it was as primal. Lust.

A new sensation for certain, yet one she would not soon forget.

"If I let ye up, will ye fight me?" he asked.

She narrowed her eyes. "Aye."

He nodded. "As I thought." He sighed and appeared regretful. "Ye're going to the dungeon whether I have to take ye, or my men have to drag ye, there. I'll give ye the option."

"How kind."

"Considering your intent to murder me, I think ye should appreciate my generosity." He spoke slowly, as if he had limitless patience.

"You killed my soldier, held a child hostage, forced your way into my keep and declared it yours. You expect me to be gracious?"

"I expect yer love for them would extend to ye having a wee more care for yer person. Yer cooperation is better for the whole of yer household and ye know it."

He was right, and it only served to make her seethe more. Bran slowly got to his feet. She remained where she lay, refraining from leaping to attack him. He extended his hand down to her, as cordial as any courtier. "My lady."

She slapped her hand into his and curled her fingers around him with the force she'd use on a blade hilt. He drew her to her feet, ignoring her powerful grip.

Once he had her standing, he locked her arms behind her back. "I dinna want to do this."

The room spun. "And yet you are." She twisted and pain laced up her arm. She tried to keep from crying out, the sound squelched into something of a grunt.

"This will only hurt if ye move," he cautioned. "If ye thrash, ye could break yer arm."

His hold on her was strong and the heat of lust she'd experienced only moments before chilled into something cold and ugly. "You have no soul."

"If I had no soul, ye'd be dead, as would yer sister the moment the portcullis opened." Bran nudged Marin forward, forcing her to walk.

Frantic fear scrabbled through her. "Will you hurt them now?"

"I told ye I wouldna." He detained her with only one hand, his grip still strong, and unlatched the door and pulled it open.

"And I'm to trust you? A reiver." She glared at him over her shoulder.

He returned his second hand to restraining her and steered her forward. "It would appear ye dinna have a choice."

Tears of helplessness blurred in her eyes. Some of Bran's men appeared in the halls as she was led through, their gazes bright with malicious curiosity. She hated the low-cut kirtle she wore now, and the way it left her vulnerable to the molestation of their leering stares.

She blinked rapidly to keep the tears from spilling over. And then she saw them, the solemn faces of her sisters, bearing witness to her great failure. She had put them all at risk.

Of all her stricken sisters, it was little Leila who strode

forward and stood in Bran's path. "Where are you taking her?" Piquette left Anice's side to accompany Leila, his front paws squared so the bulk of his chest stood out menacingly.

"To the dungeon." Bran steered Marin around her sister and Piquette. "And if ye try to stop me, little lass, ye'll join her."

"Leila, no," Marin cried. "Please. Leave it be."

Leila's large eyes went luminous with unshed tears. "But I love you."

The reivers watching elbowed each other and shared a chuckle over the display of emotion.

"Enough," a reiver said. The dark-haired serious one who had first walked in with Bran. He cast a hard glare at the men who immediately went silent.

"Please, Leila." Marin nodded to her sister, willing her to wait with the other girls. "Stay with your sisters and remain safe."

Anice approached their youngest sister and whispered something in her ear. Leila's face turned solemn and she nodded, finally moving from Bran's path and shuffling back to her sisters. The dog did not move.

"Piquette," Anice called gently. Finally, he ambled from their path, but not without a long look of regret first.

Marin's blood roared with rage, with a need to exact vengeance on the man holding her. He had exploited her love to seize the castle and would soon see the effects of her wrath. Or she would die trying.

⚜

BRAN DID NOT PLAN TO KEEP MARIN LOCKED IN THE CELL forever. In fact, he had made it a point to instruct his men to see that the imprisoned soldiers were properly fed and cared for.

After a poor night of sleep in a rich man's bed, he found his mind returning to the spitfire, and how her potent energy had been beautiful when it had been used not for anger, but for passion.

In the great hall, crusty rolls were waiting for him, so fresh that steam curled from them when broken open. There was a pot of honey waiting to be drizzled, a pat of butter for smearing, the salt bowl filled once more, and even oats thickened with fresh milk and perfectly hot.

He'd enjoyed breaking his fast so much that the kitchen was his first stop that morning in his assessment of the castle. The stables appeared to be in good order; he'd seen that when he left his horse there the day before. The Master of the Horse seemed competent, albeit evidently displeased with the castle's loss.

Bran had already written the letter to Kerr informing him of having taken Werrick Castle. He'd secured a runner for its delivery and the lad was already on his way. Once the Scottish Warden sent reinforcements, he could put this whole mess behind him and Ena would be free.

Ena. The name charged a feeling of powerful protection through him. She had been so foolish, and yet his being here proved he would do anything for her. He only hoped Kerr kept his side of the bargain.

Bran entered the kitchen and found a large round rump thrust up in front of a fire pit.

"Are ye the cook?" He asked the massive, flour-dusted bottom.

A woman spun around, her face flushed rosy from heat and hard work, her hair wiry with strands of brassy gray jutting out in all directions from under her simple cap.

She propped a meaty fist on her hip and regarded him with an assessing gaze. "Are you the marauder who threatened to kill our wee Catriona?" Before she could answer, she clicked her tongue and turned away from him. "For shame."

"I want an inventory of yer food stores," he said.

"You're not the mistress of the keep."

"Nay, but I am its head currently."

She hissed an exasperated sigh and hefted a great pot onto the metal hook over the fire. "You won't get an answer from me." She turned and wiped her hands on the white apron she wore over her brown kirtle.

"Ye may verra well be the only one in the castle no' afraid of me." Bran narrowed his eyes, intentionally offering her one of his fiercest looks, one known to make men cower in battle.

The cook, however, gave a hoot of laughter. "Aren't you a cocky one?" She scoffed. "No man would bother taking this body by force and if you kill me, you'll save me from a life of my back hurting like the very devil every day." She waved her hands to get him to leave. "You want information, bring Lady Marin with you."

A black cat leapt onto the table beside him and stroked itself against his hand. The same one he'd seen the prior day. It appeared the little beast remembered him.

The cook smirked. "'Tis fitting Bixby likes you so."

"Why is that?" Bran stroked a hand over the cat's head.

"He always knows where to find the rats." With that, she turned and lifted a second kettle to the fire with a hearty grunt.

Bran strode from the kitchens with a muttered curse. Bixby trotted behind him, following as he made his rounds to the various servants. The Master of the Horse who had been compliant enough the prior day would give Bran no information on the horses, their supply of food, or even the names of the stable lads. The chatelaine would not speak with him regarding any of the household upkeep. And the steward offered a stuttered refusal over reviewing any of the earl's accounts with Bran.

They all declined to offer their assistance without Lady Marin present.

Frustrated and greatly begrudging his decision to keep the castle peaceful until reinforcement arrived, Bran made his way to the solar. Sunlight flowed in through the wide display of clear glass and filled the room with a comfortable golden heat. It was soundless within, away from the noise and bustle of the greater part of the castle. Motes of dust floated lazily in the still air. It was unlike anywhere he'd ever been; it was peaceful.

So, this was how the rich lived. With their painted walls and the safety behind their fortified stone, with good food served to them every day and bits of heaven shining down upon them. He wanted to turn away in disgust from the gross display of wealth, evident in the shelves of books and fine furnishings.

And yet the draw was too much, even for him.

Indulging, he sank into the chair behind the desk and savored the stillness.

Bixby hopped soundlessly onto the desk and blinked wide green eyes at him. The cat nudged closer. Bran stretched a hand out and stroked the glossy black fur until Bixby's eyes began to slowly drift closed and Bran's fingertips vibrated with a rhythmic purring.

Exhaustion pulled at Bran as well. A quick bit of slumber promised him more rest than the previous night had allotted.

The earl's bed had been a luxury. The feather-stuffed mattress, thick and downy, had cradled his body like a cloud, and the sheets had been of the best linen, cool and welcoming. None of it had mattered. Regardless of where he slept or how fine the bed, he would always be followed by his ghosts.

He scrubbed a hand over his beard and stretched back to rouse himself to wakefulness. Combing over the accounts would take extensive concentration without the aid of the bloody steward but was necessary to uncover anything that might be of import before Bran vacated the castle upon the reinforcements' arrival. That, and letting the castle fall apart would not bode well for the inhabitants. The last thing he needed was Werrick's people rallying against him.

He pulled open a drawer and encountered several lengths of parchment. Bixby's ears flicked with irritation. Bran moved the contents about carefully so as not to make too much noise. He shook his head at his own efforts, all for the sake of a cat.

Ridiculous.

From what Bran could gather, the parchment was little more than a reply to a friend with nothing of note. He drew a book from beneath and flipped through the fragile pages. Numbers filled either side with words that made no sense. He set it on the desk splayed open, and pushed the drawer closed. This might be a fruitless task. Bran hesitated before opening the second drawer.

There was great unease in going through another man's belongings. It seemed strange that in taking the earl's castle, eating his food, drinking his wine, kissing his daughter and sleeping in his bed had not struck Bran with any level of invasion until the moment he opened personal correspondence to read.

"I do not believe Marin would like you being in here." Ella entered the solar without asking permission. A length of green silk had been sewn to the bottom of her pink cotehardie, an alternative to purchasing a new gown when the old had become too short or its hem too worn.

Bran could only imagine the expense of clothing five daughters. How was it the earl hadn't married any of them off?

"In fact, I know she would not like it." Ella approached the desk and rubbed a hand over Bixby's back. "I've never seen him take to a man. He usually favors rats."

"So I've been told," Bran muttered.

Ella glanced to where his hand hovered over the knob of the drawer.

"I think you're a good man despite what you've done." Catriona appeared from behind her sister and watched him carefully with her large blue eyes, as if expecting him to contradict her.

"You didn't hurt me," she went on. "I think you only killed Eversham because he would never..." She swallowed hard. "He would have never allowed you to take me. It didn't appear you hurt Marin either. Mayhap..." she pursed her lips. "Mayhap you might let her go?"

"Can I get either of ye to help me with the cook, or the steward? Hell, even the chatelaine?" Bran asked, ignoring the request. "No one will speak with me."

"Marin would be the only one they will speak with." Catriona offered a tentative smile. "If you let her free—"

"Catriona! Ella!" A voice hissed from the hallways, and Anice swept into the room. Piquette was at her side, of course, and both cast Bran a cold look.

"This man is not worth our time." Anice stared at him with the impact of all the scorn a beautiful woman could muster. "Especially considering how he has handled Marin."

Ella turned contemptuously to him. "He is indeed a vile cur."

Bran lifted a brow. Vile cur seemed a bit strong. "The lass did try to kill me." His bland defense fell on deaf ears, however, for at that exact moment, Lady Ella gave a gasp of outrage and snatched up the book from the desk.

"You do not leave them open like this." She fondly caressed the leather spine where a deep crease showed. "Do you not know how to handle books?"

Apparently, he did not. "I dinna realize there was a certain way."

She stroked her book while Anice approached, her gaze going from him to the top of the desk where the cat snoozed in front of Bran. "How fitting Bixby should find you."

"Aye, because he likes rats." Bran rubbed a hand over the aching muscles of his neck and prayed for patience. God knew he was failing with these daughters of Werrick. "I'd ask ye if ye knew how I might get the servants to speak with me but assume ye'll tell me to speak with Marin."

"Mayhap you ought to free Marin from imprisonment." Anice put an arm around each sister and led them to the doorway. "Come, Piquette."

The dog followed, but Ella glanced over her shoulder before

being guided out. "Marin is the heart of Werrick Castle, in more ways than one."

The heart of Werrick Castle. Bran bit back the bitter laugh. The situation was quickly becoming absurd. Not a damn thing could be done in the castle without Marin's blessing.

He pushed back from his seat. Bixby startled at the sound. If he needed to see Marin for the castle to function, then he would see Marin, but he'd be damned if he released her simply at the nagging of meddlesome women and obdurate servants.

He stalked through the castle, left with no choice but to talk with Marin.

The soft lilt of singing greeted Bran as he descended the stairs. Singing? In a dungeon? He quickened his pace, hastened by the need to chastise his men for not putting a stop to such foolishness.

His men didn't notice his arrival for they stared into the dungeon, their faces serene with concentration. Closer now, Bran could better hear the woman's voice, and the beauty behind it.

The song was in a language he didn't know, but the sweet melody seemed to imply a story both calm and light, a song one might sing to a child. It was no wonder his men did not order the musician to cease when they so obviously found her talent enjoyable.

Bran pushed aside his men to enter the dank dungeon. A candle glowed on the floor next to Marin's cell beside a bundle of furs and a glossy dark head resting against the iron bars.

Marin's arms extended from her prison where she lay flush with the barrier of her cell to cradle her youngest sister. Her delicate hands stroked the girl's shiny black hair. It was Marin who sung so beautifully.

Every man stood enthralled. Not only Bran's men, but her

father's soldiers held prisoner not far from her. Her singing filled the ugly darkness and made it somehow light—a transition so remarkable, it might be considered magic.

Her voice quelled and the singing drew to an end. Marin opened her eyes and looked at Leila with love shining in her eyes. For her part, Leila appeared to be asleep, her fingers curled loosely around one of the thick iron bars of Marin's captivity.

Marin is the heart of Werrick Castle, in more ways than one.

Bran was beginning to understand as much now. The room remained silent enough that the delicate flicker of the decorated candle's flame could be heard. Small flowers had been pressed into the white wax and whorls of paint showed along its sides.

One of Bran's men sighed and turned away from the sisters.

Bran approached the cell, foolishly trying to still the sound of his wooden soled shoes clattering over the hard ground. Marin's head snapped up and she put her finger to her lips.

He glanced down at Leila. Her hair fell over her cheek and her face was tranquil with the relaxation of slumber. Initially he'd thought her to be ten. Now he questioned whether she was even that old.

"Why is she here?" He whispered.

Marin carefully pulled her arms from her sister and secured the furs more snugly about her shoulders before standing to face Bran.

"She's scared." Marin paused and regarded him for a long considering moment. "Mayhap you can bring another candle if you wish for us to see."

He glanced at the one at his feet where the fine wax candle still shone with brilliance. "What's wrong with this one?"

Marin gently swept her fingers along the top of the glossy dark head of little Leila. "It's her Candlemas candle. She's been saving it all year. I'd like her to still keep it in case she needs her own prayers for reassurance later."

Irritation tightened along the back of Bran's shoulders. "I said I wouldna harm ye."

"Yet you've imprisoned the guards and you've imprisoned me." Shadows stained the fair skin under Marin's eyes. She'd clearly had little sleep as well. "Leila is a sensitive child. She feels things differently than most." Marin glanced down at her sleeping sister, a look akin to maternal worry and affection crossing her features. "Locking me in the dungeon only heightened her concern."

"Ye did try to kill me." He turned to his men behind him. "Ye, bring me another candle. And ye," he nodded at a burly man with a large barrel chest, the strongest among those guarding the dungeon. "Go to the kitchens to aid the cook with lifting heavy items. If her back goes, we'll no' be eating well."

Both men nodded and went about their orders.

"You saw Nan?" Marin lifted her neat brows in amusement. "And I see Bixby found you." A smile teased at her full lips.

Bran cast a frown down at the cat. Bixby licked at his paw with supreme disinterest. "I know about Bixby, before ye attempt the jest."

The ghost of a smile pulled higher on her mouth and she gave a simple hum of acknowledgement.

"If ye mean the cook, then aye, I went to see Nan. I also saw yer Master of the Horse, steward and even the chatelaine." Bran shifted. "It appears no one will provide me any information. Nothing in the castle can happen without ye."

The lighthearted expression on Marin's face tightened. "What did you do to them?"

"No' a damn thing, which I now regret." Bran shot her a dark look. "I dinna come here to harm ye or yer people."

One of the reivers came forward and handed him a candle which he passed to Marin. She nodded her thanks, then knelt to light it with the Candlemas candle before blowing Leila's out to preserve the girl's blessings.

Marin rose amid a thread of smoke. "I assumed the role of

mistress of the keep when my mother died years ago, and I assume something of a Castellan when my father is summoned to the king's side. I handle every account of the castle and am responsible for every person here."

"In that case, I need yer help. I dinna want the order of things to fall apart. Nor do ye, I am certain." In truth, he needed her support with more than simply the accounts. He needed her to stop bloody fighting him, lest the people eventually rose up against him. Then he would need to flex his force, as fleeing was not an option. Not with so much at stake.

Marin tilted her head toward him. "It's difficult to perform such a task from my current location."

Bran grunted.

Marin crossed her arms.

"I'll let ye out today to help me," Bran offered. "But if ye cross me, there will be consequences."

"And I want a bath drawn for me in my room."

Her airy disregard for his threat rankled. In fact, everything about this woman left him in a state of agitation. And yet, he found himself tempted to offer the bath only if he could join her. "Ye have to promise to try not to kill me," he said instead.

"Try not to, or don't actually, kill you?" She gave him a feral grin. "If I try again, I *will* be successful."

His cock twitched. Damn but this woman stoked desire deep within him. "Dinna kill me, or even attempt to, and I'll let ye have yer bath."

"In my own room. Alone."

The thought of her naked in a tub of water filled his mind. The mirrored surface reflecting her image back to her, the curve of her creamy shoulders, her breasts round and high on her chest. Her skin slick and glossy in the firelight.

"Verra well. Ye'll have an hour." He pulled the dungeon's only key from his pocket and unlocked her cell door. She carefully eased it open, came around to the other side of her prison and bent to lift her sister.

Bran opened his arms to accept the girl's weight, but Marin shook her head, choosing to carry her sister instead. It was familiar, the undying loyalty holding them together. The same as what he shared with Ena.

A twinge pulled at his heart and he jerked away from the two sisters. He was tempted to tell Marin of Ena's plight, and yet feared her knowing his sister's name. With the Earl of Werrick being a warden, he could bring down punishment upon Ena, and Bran would be right back where he started. Another pawn in the rich man's quest for power.

He strode from the dungeon to see about coordinating Marin's bath. Being here, surrounded by wealth when he had so little, reminded of sisterly love as his own sibling clung to the edge of life, it was more than he could bear. Surely Kerr would have received the missive by now, or at least would get it soon, and would arrive to claim this coveted castle.

It was only a matter of time.

MARIN HAD WANTED TO LINGER FOREVER AMID THE PERFUMED steam of her bath. After a night in the dungeon, among the darkness and the things moving within, she had craved such luxuries as her daily bath.

While down there, she had noticed the captured guards were not her entire force. Sir Richard had been able to discreetly convey some were in hiding. Not all was lost, then. For a plan could be devised with those in hiding.

Anice helped Marin into a simple gray kirtle with a side-less surcoat of deep sapphire blue, while Piquette snored on the floor.

"I wish you'd killed Bran," Anice said. Her fingers flew deftly over the lacings. "Ella said she found him pawing through Papa's journal today. No doubt to read through our accounts."

Marin put her fingertips to her temples and applied pressure to the thrumming pain there. She wanted a trencher of hot food and the embrace of her comfortable bed.

"He has refrained from harming our people," Marin said.

"And what of you?" Anice whispered, despite them being alone in the room together. "What did he do to you before he dragged you through the castle and threw you in the dungeon?"

Marin's cheeks went hot with the searing memory of his mouth on hers, the power of his naked torso. How he'd put his thumb to her lips, and she'd sucked the blunt tip. The eager heat of lust pulsed to life between her legs at the memory. She swallowed. "He kissed me."

"Are you still a maiden?" Anice hissed.

"Aye."

Anice's expression relaxed as she affixed a gauzy veil over Marin's hair and secured it with a gold circlet. Perhaps it was foolish to wear such a modest headdress indoors when she considered the intimacy she'd shared with Bran the prior evening.

Anice's gaze skimmed over her in a final survey. "You look beautiful, my dear sister." She settled her hands on Marin's shoulders and met her eyes levelly. "Be careful with him."

"I thought I was supposed to be the mother to us all," Marin said in jest.

Anice smirked and nudged Marin toward the door. Marin paused to rub the top of Piquette's velvety head before departing the room.

Bran stood in the hall, awaiting her, his arms crossed over the red doublet he wore. His sleeves had been rolled up to his elbows, exposing his forearms that were powerful with muscle, a reminder to the way his body had been when he'd taken off his leine. He was terribly strong. Such knowledge left the baser part of her swelling with feminine appreciation.

"You didn't trust me?" She put her hand to her hip.

"Ye did try to kill me."

It was a fair argument. Not that she would admit as much. "Where shall we go? To see Nan?"

Her stomach clenched even as she spoke. She was about to lay bare their lives, their possessions, to this thief. Aye, it kept her people safe, but it did not mean she had to like the abysmal task.

If he noticed the bitterness in her tone, he ignored it and simply nodded. "Aye, we can start in the kitchen."

Together they made their way down the hall. "Leila seems verra fond of ye," he said.

Marin slid him a side glance. Was he truly attempting to be conversational?

"Our mother died as a result of a reiver's attack." She did not bother to keep the disgust from her voice this time. "She died soon after Leila's birth."

"Ye became her mother."

"Of sorts. I knew Leila wouldn't have the years of our mother's affection like the rest of us had. My mother was..." Marin couldn't finish her sentence. She couldn't share the goodness——the kindness and love——everything wonderful her mother had embodied. Not with this man who exploited love as a means to an end.

"My mother was extraordinary," she said finally.

"Was that when ye were taken? When she was attacked by the reivers?" he pressed.

Marin pursed her lips. She didn't want to talk about the incident, not now or ever. And certainly not with this marauder.

They arrived in the sunny kitchen before he could insist on an answer and found Nan pointing to a corner as she directed an unfamiliar man.

"Put it there," Nan said in her authoritative tone. "Then you need to get the pheasant from the ovens."

The man had dark hair and a stocky torso blanketed with a

reiver's gambeson. He followed Nan's orders with ready obedience.

"I'd like information on the stores," Bran said.

"I told you, not until you come with Lady Marin." Nan swiveled toward him. The look of consternation on her face stretched into a pleasant smile. "Ah, I see you did. And was it her idea you put one of your brutes to work in the kitchens to help save my old back?"

Marin remembered suddenly the order Bran had issued in the dungeon. It explained why he'd sent one of his men to the kitchen. The consideration was surprising. No doubt Cat would be pleased at such a discovery, but then she always tried to see the best in people. Even those who did not deserve it. Marin, however, held tight to her suspicions.

Bran shrugged as if the act were of little consequence. "Ye make fine food, which means ye should remain happy."

Nan wiped her hands on her white apron. "Ach, the way to a man's appreciation is always through his stomach. My Hewie had an appreciation for my cooking, he did. 'Course he showed me all I know." She nodded with pride. "And he said I was the loveliest lass in all of England and Scotland." Her eyes glittered with the joy of memories, the way they always did when she spoke of her late husband.

"He taught ye well. Yer oat cakes were some of the best I've ever had." Bran gave her a charming grin and it lightened the fierceness of his face.

"You should try my meat pies." Nan waggled her hands excitedly in the air. "I'll make them for supper this eve. It was the one thing I always done better than my Hewie, God rest his soul."

"I will anticipate it," Bran said with such earnestness, Marin knew he truly did.

This man speaking to the cook, who had gone out of his way to see to Nan's comfort, was not the same man who had put Marin in the dungeon. Nor was he the same man who had used his tongue to kiss her, tease her, seduce her. She shivered at the memory of who that man had been.

"May I show him the stores, my lady?" Nan asked.

Marin nodded and quickly averted her face so Nan wouldn't see how much it truly did bother her for the inner workings and intricacies of the castle to be laid open before this usurper. He followed Nan to the larder. At some point, Bixby had emerged from the shadows and trotted at Bran's heels.

"Are these peaches?" Bran pulled the jar from its shelf and pulled the stopper free. The cinnamon and sharp vinegar scent of the sweet peaches filled the room. He pulled one free before Marin could protest and plucked a succulent peach from the juice. He held it out to Marin.

Any appetite she might have had evaporated. She shook her head.

He stepped closer. "I want it tasted to ensure it hasna been poisoned." He held the peach before her mouth and his gaze darkened. Like when he'd put his thumb to her lips, and she'd sucked it into her mouth.

Heavens, what *had* she been thinking?

Her cheeks scorched with the memory. "I am without appetite." She backed away.

"I love peaches and will gladly taste for you." Nan stepped between them and opened her mouth wide enough so the hairs along her chin prickled.

Bran dropped the peach into her mouth. It was all Marin could do to keep from laughing when Nan snapped her mouth shut and noisily chewed the pickled fruit. She winked at Marin and nodded definitively to Bran. "'Tis not poisoned."

He nodded his appreciation and placed the stopper back in the jar. "It appears I'm no' hungry either." He handed her the remainder of the peaches. "For ye."

Nan tucked the jar on a shelf and returned to the larder with Bran.

"What's in there?" he asked.

Marin didn't bother to come closer to see where he indicated.

At least, not until Nan hesitated a long while before answering, "Those are preserved eels."

"I love eel," Bran declared. "Cook them for supper tonight."

"Nay." Marin entered the larder. "We're to have meat pies if you recall."

"Aye." He clapped his hands together. "On the morrow then."

"Nay."

He gave her an exasperated frown. "Why?"

"They're my father's favorite," Marin said by way of explanation.

"He's no' here."

"But he will be," she insisted. "We always have his favorite meal prepared the night he returns home."

Her heart lightened to think of it, her father at the head of the table once more, regal and full of perfect authority. He would set everything to rights.

Her stomach dropped. *Could* it be set to rights?

Bran grunted at her refusal to allow him to eat the eels, but he did not press the issue. "The stores appear sufficient." His tone was airy, as though he meant to sound important in his declaration.

"Aye, for now." Nan returned to a table with several bowls covered with linen. She lifted a ball of dough from one and began to knead it. "I think we will be needing more on account of so many men to feed."

Bran's brow furrowed.

"I'll see to it, Nan," Marin offered. She'd be damned if she allowed Bran to disturb the order of things in her carefully constructed world.

Nan graciously inclined her head. "Aye, my lady."

"Matters here are now settled." Bran indicated the door. "Next I've a mind to see the solar and examine the accounts."

Marin's chest tightened. "The accounts for the kitchen?"

"For the castle."

Her stomach knotted at the prospect. If seeing him go through the larder was terrible, how would she handle him reading through her father's accounts? Suddenly she found herself regretting her promise not to kill him.

❧ 6 ❧

Bran knew Marin didn't want him to look through the accounts. It was evident in the snap of her hem at her ankles as she strode onward in an angry march. As much as he knew he had to see the accounts to ensure the castle continued to run without issue, going through the earl's personal effects left him discomfited.

She pushed through the door and led him to the desk. Ella lay curled on the window seat, her head bent over yet another book. This one had a blue cover with gold paint scrolling up along its spine. She didn't bother to look up as they entered.

Marin swept a bit of hair from Ella's eye, the way a mother might do to a child. "Is the light sufficient?"

"Mmm..." Ella murmured. Then her head snapped up and her blue eyes went wide. "Marin." She leapt to her feet with her finger carefully pinched in the book's pages and threw her arms around her sister. "You've been freed?"

"Depends," Bran said.

They both turned toward him, smiles fading.

He braced his hand over the polished top of the desk. "I need compliance."

Marin touched her sister's shoulder. "Please leave us, Ella."

"Mayhap I—"

Marin nudged her toward the door and Ella cast a regretful look back at him before leaving the room. The door clicked closed.

"I know ye dinna want to do this," he said.

Marin shot him a sharp glare. "Do you?"

He hardened his resolve against her ire. "The accounts."

"It's there." She pointed to the second drawer. The one where he'd found the book Ella had deemed he'd mistreated and taken from the solar.

"Ella has it," he countered. "She took it the other day."

Marin frowned. "That's ridiculous. It never leaves this drawer." She pulled the drawer and bent over it, her fingers graceful as they gently sifted through the parchments and vellum within. Her delicate lavender scent rose around him, teasing and alluring.

She wore a modest veil over her fair hair. While it looked lovely on her, he much preferred her hair uncovered, the unbound strands flowing and free for him to stroke. Though their time alone had been brief, he remembered too well the softness of her skin, the silky coolness of her hair. He could all too easily see himself laying abed with her, playing his fingers over those golden locks in a moment of post-coital reverence.

Oblivious to his thoughts, she rose and looked at the desk's barren surface. "You're correct. It appears to be missing." She put a hand to her hip. "Why would Ella have taken it?"

He wanted to pull the veil off her head and let the little circlet fall to the ground. He needed her in his arms, making those lusty moans she had the night before, her slender body arching in help-less abandon against him. "She said I wasna treating a book properly."

Marin smiled secretly to herself. "Aye, that sounds like Ella."

Bran found his gaze drifting to Marin's pink mouth and he imagined his thumb between her lips, the shy, curious way she'd suckled the digit. "We can reclaim it and speak to the steward," he suggested.

Though it was not truly what he'd wanted to suggest. He didn't like this hard Marin, the one who treated him with contempt and ire. Nay, he wanted the woman last night, the seductress who was surprised at her own enjoyment of their light play.

Her sweet mouth thinned with agitation. "Why is it you wish to speak to the steward, to discover everything you've gained in your capture of Werrick Castle?"

"That isna it."

"What is it then?" She lifted her head defiantly and the gold circlet around her head winked in the light shining in through the leaded glass window.

If he told her he was securing the castle for the Kerr warden, she would no doubt fight him even more than she did now. Nay, this lass did not have cause to know the true plan. He merely required her assistance, which she already had promised.

His gut twisted with unease. He hated this using of women, forcing them into compliance. More than anything, he hated being at the beck and call of a privileged noble. His life, and that of Ena's, was expendable and exploitable.

"I need yer support," he answered finally.

The skin around Marin's eyes tightened, giving her a shrewd appearance. Even shrewd, she was still bonny.

"More than simply speaking to Nan and the other servants," she surmised.

He nodded. "It will keep everyone safe. Yer people and mine."

"And give you exactly what you want without the risk of having us revolt." She gave a knowing smirk. "Aye, I know that is why you seek my permission. You know your men are fickle in their loyalty, and you know eventually my people might rise up if your numbers lessen."

Damn but the woman was too clever for her own good. "People will die on both sides."

"And you may lose all you have purloined."

He stared at Marin, who was as stubborn as she was lovely. "It will keep us all from loss."

She folded her arms over her chest.

"Will ye help me?"

"Nay." Her brows drew together, and her face went pink. "I will not let you stand there and gloat about how in one day you have managed to acquire what one man took a lifetime to garner."

Her words plucked at a nerve Bran had not realized he had. If her people did revolt, if they took back Werrick, Ena would die. A band of tension worked its way around his chest. "Ye will help me," he said in a low, threatening tone.

"Or what?" Her chin angled toward him with defiance. "Will you hit me? After all your reassurances we would be left unharmed. Will you be a liar as well as a thief?" She tensed. "And I warn you, I will hit back."

Anger lashed through Bran. He fell prey to her goading and it only served to increase the ferocity of his rage.

"I dinna hit women."

She scoffed. "Due to your noble character, I presume."

He stared down at her. His blood boiled to scalding in his veins, and his breath came hard and fast. "Ye're the most stubborn and maddening woman I've ever met," he growled.

A wicked grin curled her sensual mouth. "Such knowledge brings me great delight."

The emotions snapping through him were too overwhelming; her face too alight with the passion of their argument for him to ignore. He wouldn't hit Marin, but he certainly could kiss her.

Marin had won their little battle. It was as evident in Bran's glare as it was in the pounding of her heart. His eyes were bright with something unsaid and his stare was so intense, it reminded her of when she'd gone to him. His kiss, his touch, both played out in her mind more often than they ought to, and they were doing so again now.

"Will you hit me?" she asked. Her voice came out with a throaty quality, a note of sensuality she had not intended.

"Nay." He slid his hands to her face. "No' when I'd rather kiss ye."

His mouth came down on hers and Marin's world blossomed to life in a wave of undeniable anticipation. His lips were softer than she remembered, the rasp of his beard over her sensitive skin rougher. His hands, the delight at his touch far more thrilling. She ran her hands over his shirt where his chest was firm with muscle beneath.

It was all too easy to recall the lines of his body, the strength shadowed by the light from the hearth. She opened her mouth to him, and his ready tongue swept against hers. A whimper slipped from her throat.

He growled at the sound she made, and it sent lovely shivers running through her. His hands slid from her face, delicately brushing down the naked skin of her neck and collarbones before skimming down the length of her body to her waist. He pulled her to him, against the wonderful solid wall of his body. And she melted.

She leaned into his strength with a sigh shared between their kisses, her hands moving over his powerful back. The desire humming through her drew her hips toward him in a slow, eager rhythm he all too easily matched. She ought to push him away, she knew, to be firm in her defiance. But these kisses were heaven, and they awakened in her something she had thought never to experience: desire.

His palm swept up to brush the side of her breast and gently cup it. Marin arched her chest toward him before she knew what she was doing, her entire being transformed by the power of need. He sucked at her bottom lip while his thumb played over the swollen bud of her nipple. She cried out with pleasure, but he muted the sound with a hungry sweep of his tongue.

He kissed her mouth, her chin, her neck, his mouth suckling, his teeth ever so gently nipping. Tingles of bliss danced up and down her spine. Her breath came in panting gasps.

Bran cupped her bottom with his free hand and drew her hips flush with his, where the hardness that had been there the night before now strained between them again.

Marin was not so ignorant of the ways between a man and a woman that she did not know what the column was. A trill of power shot through her. She had caused that. His want of her. His yearning.

His leg nudged against hers and she found herself parting her knees for him. His thigh pressed into the wild thrum of lust at her cleft. He straightened to kiss her once more, gliding his hand up her lower back to catch the back of her head in his large palm. Somewhere in the distance came the ring of thin metal hitting the ground. She paid it little mind, her mouth impatiently tasting his with greedy abandon.

"I want ye," he moaned into her mouth.

It would be so easy to give in to this lust, to let it ignite her body and soul. The voice in the back of her mind ticked off reasons she ought to cease, with one glaring reason that was louder than curiosity and excitement combined–responsibility.

She could not do this with the man who had taken her father's castle and taken them all hostage. She could not do this at all with a man to whom she was not wed. If her father ever needed her for an advantageous match, she could not tell him she had given away her maidenhead. She could not let him down.

"Stop," she murmured.

Bran's mouth lifted from her and his hands fell away.

"Marin." He stared down at her; his voice ragged. "I dinna want to fight with ye."

She stepped back on wobbly legs and tried to regain her composure. "You cannot take such liberties with me."

His hair had become tousled at some point and his mouth was red beneath his beard. Desire blazed in his eyes and set a new tempo to the pulse pounding through her. "I want ye."

"I'm not for the wanting," she whispered. "Or the having." She bent and lifted her veil from where it had floated to the ground.

"Ye want me." He met her gaze.

She did not deny it. Indeed, heat seared through her anew. But she could not give in, not when she was without the freedom to give into her pleasures. She had been trained as a man in battle, aye, but she knew the many restrictions she still held as a woman. And there was the consideration that he meant to intentionally seduce her to secure her compliance.

He picked up her delicate circlet between large, gentle fingers, the delicate clink she'd heard.

"What is between us doesna need to be difficult." He handed her the circlet. "It could be so verra good."

Marin nodded her thanks and put the veil atop her hair before affixing the circlet back in place. Her cheeks went hot thinking of what they'd done, at what this marauder had somehow awoken within her. "Everything you want goes against everything I protect." She shook her head. "I can't give you my body any more than I can give you my obedience."

He closed his eyes and rested his brow against hers. It would be so easy to tip her chin upward and catch his lips with hers.

"I want there to be harmony between us," he said.

She turned her head from his. "You seek to destroy everything I hold dear."

"Ye willna give me yer support then," he surmised.

Marin pulled away. "Nay."

"Please, Marin."

"Nay." She said it more firmly this time and met his gaze so he might see her resolve. "I am an earl's daughter."

Something dangerous flashed in his eyes. "And too good for the likes of me."

The words jabbed into her. She pressed her lips together to keep from apologizing. He had forced his way into Werrick. She would not show him sympathy.

He ran a hand through his thick, dark hair. A tuft jutted up at his right temple. It gave him a pleasant boyishness she hated, for it was far too endearing.

"I said I willna harm ye, and I mean it," he said. "But I canna have yer disobedience either."

Marin said nothing, watching him and awaiting his next move. It was a complicated chess game, and both wanted to be the victor.

He braced his hands on the desk as though he had the weight of the world sitting on his shoulders. "If ye dinna help me, eventually yer people will attempt to revolt."

Marin laid her hand on the cool surface of the table and leaned toward him. "They might succeed."

"And if they do not, they will all be killed."

"What do you want us for?" She clenched her hands at her sides. "Why are you doing this?"

He did not answer. Instead he stared at her for a long space of time, as though possibly considering telling her. "I willna get yer support."

The statement was without question.

"I will need to send you back to the dungeon to reconsider." A corner of his mouth tucked downward in what appeared to be disappointment. "Mayhap tomorrow we can meet with the steward and the Master of the Horse."

She lifted her head even as her insides shuddered at the

thought of being locked in the dark once more.

"Will ye be compliant?" he asked.

Marin said nothing. Not when tears burned in her eyes and she feared her voice would tremble if she spoke.

"As I thought." Bran lowered his head and motioned for her to follow.

She did, lest she be paraded through her own home like a prize again and begrudged her passivity. It made her feel as though she were a willing participant, which she vehemently was not.

Except she had been when they had kissed. How she regretted those kisses with this awful man and hated the passion he awoke within her. He was not her lover. He was her enemy.

The shadowed hallway of the dungeon came into view and a damp coldness pressed at her skirts upon their approach. Panic welled up within her chest, spreading into icy fear the closer they drew. She did not want this. And yet, she did not fear it enough to offer her compliance to Bran.

He led her to the cell door as though he were leading her to a dance, his touch gentle on her lower back. "I dinna want to do this." The flex of his jaw and the pull at his brows indicated the truth behind his words.

"You can't keep us locked down here forever." Marin put her hand to the cold iron and curled her fingers around the bar.

"Until I get what I need, aye, I can leave ye here as long as it takes." With that, he twisted the key in the lock.

Hopelessness washed over her in desolate waves, tightening her muscles and weighing at her heart. She could not fail her family in this manner, to leave her sisters unattended upstairs, to leave her father's wealth potentially exposed.

"I will escape from here," she said through gritted teeth. "And I will kill you."

He held up something that glinted in the low light. "I have the only key."

She watched him leave with an angry fire flaring to life in her chest. Aye, he did have the only key, but there had to be some way to break out, something she could do to free herself and get her sisters to safety. And part of that safety would be seeing Bran dead.

7

True to his word, Bran summoned Marin from the dungeon again the following day. He had a bath and a hot meal waiting in her room in the hopes he might draw more compliance from her with kindly actions.

He waited outside her chamber while Anice tended to her. Thus far the other girls had been compliant, simply watching him and his soldiers with wide eyes. They did not cause problems and, based on the reports he'd received from Drake, they spent a majority of their time reading or working needlepoint. Women's tasks.

The door opened and he straightened to attention. Marin wore another veil, this time with a silver circlet which made the gilded stitching on her deep blue kirtle sparkle like stars.

"Lady Marin." He inclined his head respectfully.

She said nothing, but her gaze discreetly settled on him. Though her regard was cool, he knew her to be more interested in him than she bothered to show. No woman without interest kissed with such heat, such passion. It made him want to pull her back into his arms.

"Shall we see the steward today?" he inquired.

Her head lifted in a look that was almost arrogant. "Aye, but first I should like to see to my sisters and meet with Nan to confirm the meals are properly planned."

The haughty attitude did not become her, though her request was unsurprising. He had expected her to want to ensure the safety of her sisters.

"Ye will find them all in good health." Bran indicated she precede him.

True to his word, on their way to see to her sisters, her vassals appeared to be relaxed in their safety and at ease. All the sisters but Anice were in the solar, with Ella reading, Cat plaiting several flowers into Ella's hair, and Leila sitting beside the glow of the fire. The three looked up at the sound of the door opening and ran to Marin.

He waited patiently as Marin addressed each girl affectionately, asking after their care and getting the reassurance she'd requested. Leila clung to Marin's waist and refused to let go for a time before Cat lured her away with the promise of teaching her to loop the flowers together into a necklace.

As Marin cast one final glance back at her sisters, her heart clearly heavy, Bran leaned close to her ear. "If ye can promise me the support I need, I can see to ye being free of the dungeon for good."

In response, Marin merely frowned.

In the kitchen, Marin made certain the meal for the day was sufficiently planned and Bran once more attracted the attention of Bixby. Fie on what they'd all said about the little beast. The cat was good company.

He lifted the furred weight of the creature into his arms and caught a slight twitch to Marin's lips.

"I know what ye're thinking." He rubbed at Bixby's ears and the cat pushed into the caress, the air practically vibrating with his ready purr. "Mayhap I think this wee creature has good taste."

Nan scoffed at this, but Marin did not bother to comment as

71

she left the kitchen. Bran settled Bixby on the ground and went after Marin.

"Bixby certainly is drawn to you." Marin said when Bran caught up. "Though I confess I find his affections questionable."

No one else was in the hall with them. He leaned closer to her. "Do ye?" He spoke into her ear with a low voice.

Marin pulled in a deep breath. "Aye, I do." Small bumps of gooseflesh showed on her skin and a flush spread over her cheeks. She stared up at him, her attention fixed on his mouth as she gently bit her bottom lip.

Oh, aye—she was interested.

He chuckled at her obvious pleasure in his closeness and shifted closer still. Marin lifted her hand and rapped at the door they stood before.

She quirked a brow at him, as though in silent rebuke. A voice on the other side bid them enter. Bran opened the door for Marin and found a middle-aged man with sandy hair and a blunt nose waiting for them amid several open ledgers. He rose from his place behind the desk as they entered. Resplendent tapestries depicting biblical scenes adorned the whitewashed walls. Aside from those splashes of color, the room was otherwise bland and orderly to the point of being sparse.

"Lady Marin." The steward smiled broadly, revealing a wide gap between his two front teeth. His gaze fixed on Bran and the ready greeting wilted.

"This is Bran Davidson," Marin said. "It would appear he has needs to see the accounts to ensure all is in order. Bran, this is William, my father's steward."

Introductions made, she folded herself gracefully into one of the two seats before the desk.

William hesitated to sit and remained poised above his own chair. "Are you sure, my lady?"

"I do not believe we have a choice," Marin said bitterly.

William indicated the other chair to Bran and sat himself. "What exactly is it you wish to know?"

"I'd like to ensure the castle will continue to be maintained properly." In truth, Bran was unsure what he ought to ask. He was no landowner, no warden, no rich man with more wealth than any one person ought to possess. Regardless, he was certain it was important to stay privy to all activities within the castle.

Marin gave an irritated huff. "William is perfectly capable of handling Werrick without your guidance."

The steward dipped his head graciously toward his mistress. "I can assure you that the entire household will be maintained accordingly."

Bran fought the urge to clear his throat at the discomfort congealing in the room. Apparently, his words had been offensive. "I'd like to be informed of everything pertaining to the castle's care."

William's gaze slid to Marin, as though to confirm Bran's request. Marin's fingers on the arms of her chair tensed. Her knuckles went white, but she gave a stiff nod.

Though Bran had taken the castle, Marin was still very much in charge. This would need to change.

"Of course," William said with congenial kindness. "Will that be all?"

"Nay." Bran gazed about the room where ledgers were stacked neatly on the shelves amid the colorful tapestries. The room was tidy and plain with a roaring fire crackling in the hearth.

It was all too easy to recall the humble cottage Bran had acquired for himself and Ena. The meager fire in the center of the home was never sufficient to heat the space completely, the task to keep it going nearly endless. This man had no idea what it was like to cut his own wood, haul it through snow and ice and wait for it to dry to finally be warm.

Marin didn't either. None of them did, the spoiled lot of them.

"I want to see the coffers," Bran said.

"Nay." The confident sneer Marin curled in his direction told him everything he needed to know. She thought herself untouchable, infallible, in control.

So like the bloody rich.

Attempting to quell the residents' fears with the assurance he would not bring anyone harm had been a poor decision. Bran had made himself appear weak and malleable—a misconception that would end now.

He surged to his feet. "Ye will give me what I've asked for and ye will stop fighting me every step of the way."

She met his threat with bored disinterest.

Aye, he'd made a foolish mistake in his attempt to placate. He reached across the desk and grabbed William's tunic before the man could sense danger. "Get me the coffers posthaste."

"Leave, m-m-my l-l-l-lady," William stuttered and squeezed his eyes into a hard blink. "I c-c-can handle h-h-him."

Marin leapt out of her chair, outrage apparent on her face. "You said you would not hurt my people."

"Ye said ye would cooperate." Bran pulled his knife from his belt. "It would appear we've both lied."

A flush crept up Marin's slender neck and stained her cheeks. "I do not lie."

"It would appear otherwise." He turned his head toward the door and bellowed Drake's name.

"Let him go," Marin said in a low, calm voice. "William, get the coffer."

Bran released his hold on William.

The steward looked between Marin and Bran. "Only i-i-if you p-p-promise n-n-not t-t-to h-h-h-h-h-h-" He stopped and drew in a long breath before letting it exhale. "Only if you p-promise not to hurt Lady Marin," he said with careful concentration.

Bran nodded. But though he put forth an uncaring demeanor, his gut twisted with self-revulsion. He'd known a lad in his youth who had been plagued by a stammer, an affliction other children had teased and tormented him about with pointed cruelty. Though it had earned Bran their scorn as well, he had shielded the boy and found in him a trustworthy and loyal companion. Duncan had been his name. He'd died in the attack that had killed Bran's mother and older brother, but Bran had never forgotten him.

Attacking Werrick's steward now made Bran as low as the boys who had teased poor Duncan, and it cut deeply into his soul.

The steward bent toward the floor with his eyes still locked on Bran to ensure he kept his promise. A jangle of keys sounded, followed by the click of an unlatching lock. William hefted a box of obvious weight onto the table. The dark, polished wood trunk was the size of a man's head and had a heavy iron lock at its front. William turned a key in that one as well and Bran drew the cover back.

Blue velvet lined the inside and cradled a wealth of more coins than Bran had seen collectively in the entirety of his life. Coin enough to feed him and his troops for a considerable amount of time, or to see to Drake's sisters and widowed mother for years to come, or enough that his own mother might not have had to work so hard to give them a life that was barely above starvation.

If he'd had coin like this in his youth, his world would have been so, so drastically different. And no doubt, so too would he. To have had food enough, safety enough. His mother and brother would still be alive, and Ena would never have been used in a manner that would have caused him to turn against his own morals.

This wealth represented everything he never had, and how he had suffered for it.

MARIN GRITTED HER TEETH AT THE RAPACIOUS GLEAM IN Bran's eyes. Her stomach churned with disgust.

"It would appear you have what it is you came for," she bit out.

"Ye have no idea what it is I've come for." His gleaming gaze did not stray from the pile of her father's wealth.

"Aye, you will not tell me." She slammed closed the lid, unable to take for even a moment longer the avarice practically glowing around him. "Though I'm certain this is close to what it is you wanted. A life gleaned off the earnings of other men."

Bran snapped his stare to her. "'Tis a fine thing to say from a woman who hasna ever known hardship."

Her eyes glinted. "I've known hardship." She'd borne her own woes like an anchor in her soul, keeping her leashed to this place and its people.

"Ye know what it is to go to bed at night with yer gut gnawing with hunger, then?" he demanded. "Or to no' even know where it is ye'll rest yer head, or if ye'll have the benefit of a roof over yer head."

"Not all suffering is caused by a lack of funds, Bran." Her cheeks went hot with rage. "In fact, some has been caused by people who were set on taking that which does not belong to them." She lowered her voice to a dangerous whisper, the way her father did when he was truly enraged. "Do not think you know me, or my life, based on your own assumptions."

Bran's eyes narrowed. "Mind yerself, lass, or ye'll be in the dungeon once more."

William slowly rose from his own chair, a dagger trembling in his grip, aimed in Bran's direction. "L-l-leave her a-a-alone."

It was all Marin could do to keep from putting herself between Bran and her would-be protector. William had suffered his own terrible fate when his wife had died in childbirth with their stillborn son. Yet when the Grahams had attacked, he had gone to the great hall to defend the women and children gathered there. It had nearly cost him his life when he was struck down, yet his efforts had saved countless lives. The man's body was not that of a warrior, though he had the heart of one to be sure.

Bran's eyes closed with what appeared to be measured patience, or mayhap regret. "William," he said in a tired voice. "Please, dinna do this."

"I c-c-can't l-l-let—"

The door flew open and a large man filled the doorway, thick with muscle, black eyes devoid of any emotion. He marched across the open space like a predator. He was on poor William in an instant, twisting the older man's wrist so that the blade dropped with a clank to the floor. The marauder shifted his gaze to Bran, as if awaiting further instruction.

"Take his blade and let him go." Bran sighed heavily.

The tension in Marin's shoulders drained away. William had always been kind. He was a good man. If he'd been killed on her behalf, she never would have forgiven herself.

Drake released William and retrieved the blade in a stealthy move. The steward rubbed at his freed wrist; his jaw locked with dejection.

Marin knew well the feeling of impotence caused by defeat. Its impact had stung since the day she'd been forced to allow Bran into Werrick's fortified gates.

"Drake, have a look at this." Bran shoved open the chest once more.

Her father's wealth glinted within. Not all of it, of course. There was far more than that. It was their good fortune the marauders were too obtuse to guess as much.

Drake glanced within, his eyes glittering in the firelight. Marin's insides twisted. More greed. It was unbearable, truly.

Bran reached a hand in and drew out a fistful. "Get yer Ma a new roof, lad, and see those sisters of yers get a decent meal, aye?"

He held the bounty toward Drake, who did not move from his militaristic stance. His jaw worked and he dragged his gaze from the pile of coin. "I canna accept that." His words were crisp like that of an Englishman with a lilt of Scottish burr.

"Ye will accept." Bran pushed a fisted handful of coins into a bag at Drake's waist. Not once, but thrice.

Drake shook his head. "It's too much. It isna ours."

At least one of them had a conscience. Marin would spare his life later.

"Take it," Bran said with finality. "That's an order. For yer family."

Drake's jaw set and he slid his gaze from where Marin sat, observing her father's wealth being passed from thief to thief, however unintending the latter may be.

"Ye do this for yer ma and sisters." Bran clapped him on the back. "Remember that."

Drake turned to Marin then and nodded, as if she had given him the coin of her own volition. "This will get my family through the winter, my lady. Thank ye."

It was impertinent. But it was also respectful and thoughtful.

Marin slid a glance to William and found him watching the exchange between the two with a private smile, one he dropped immediately once he noticed Marin's attention on him.

"Now I need ye to do something," Bran said to the young warrior.

Marin smirked. Here it was, a terrible request. After all, nothing good came without a cost.

Drake snapped to attention, a ready soldier. "Of course."

Bran turned to regard Marin, his face cold despite the generous act he'd just done for his fellow reiver. "I need ye to take Lady Marin to the dungeon."

8

B ran had made several mistakes when he'd decided to take
Werrick Castle. The first of which, obviously, had been
assuring everyone they would not be hurt. The second had been
underestimating Werrick's five daughters, especially Marin.

In truth, he did not like leaving her in the dungeon, especially
when he would much rather have her in his bed. But the dungeon
served as a lesson for her attempts to murder him, and for being
so obstinate.

It was a pity, though. He hadn't had a woman raise that kind
of passion in him in some time. Perhaps ever. She was wild, unpre-
dictable and exhilarating, like trying to contain lightning in his
hand.

The lass was stubborn though, and strong, and sensual and
powerful. And so damn beautiful. His cock echoed his words with
a steady pulse of approval. Aye, he wanted her in a fierce way, to
claim as his.

If only she were not so fixated on seeing him dead.

The rest of the day passed in relative calm with his men
contented enough to maintain peace with the inhabitants of
Werrick. He knew keeping the reivers from getting bored would

be a difficult task, especially with the thrill of the capture complete. Their security had been established, food was plentiful, and every man had a clean, dry place to sleep. Their needs were met, and the excitement had passed.

The reivers were not bound to him by blood and were mercurial by nature, with little loyalty. How long could he maintain peace at Werrick?

The sun had set long before he finally made his way to his room. Attempting to see to affairs of the castle was an arduous task, one made doubly difficult without Marin's assistance. The door to his room stood unguarded, the two reivers stationed there having abandoned their post.

Bran groaned. Their comfort had already begun to steer them from duty, and toward drink and revelry. He couldn't blame them. His own body raged for release in a way his fist couldn't allay. Not after having kissed Marin, not after feeling her body and tasting her passion.

The door to his room stood ajar, but he was unconcerned. With the bulk of the coin currently in the chest locked within the floor beneath William's great desk, even if someone had entered his room, they'd find naught but the earl's belongings.

He pushed the door the rest of the way open, strode in and froze. There in the semi-dark stood exactly the woman he'd been thinking of only moments before.

Marin.

He didn't think of how she had gotten there, or why she was there, or even if this might be some nefarious ploy. Nay, his mind went blank and his prick went hard. *Need.* He *needed* her.

Marin was in his room and by God, he would have her.

Firelight shone behind her, putting her face in shadows, a face he knew so damn well. She'd removed her kirtle and wore only a chemise, which had gone translucent against the backdrop of the flames and left her curvy body outlined in tantalizing detail. Only a scant layer of fine linen would lay between his hands and her warm, naked skin.

"Bran." Her voice came out as a coquettish purr, in a way she'd never spoken to him before.

His feet continued forward, bringing him to her. Her fingers played lightly over the hollow of her collarbone. She peered up at him and he stopped short.

This woman was not Marin.

"You took a long time to come upstairs." Anice gave a pretty pout. She drew a graceful hand down the length of her hair.

"I've been lonely." Anice bit her lip and thrust her breasts forward. Her nipples were hard beneath the thin white fabric.

The memory of Marin's pert little nubs straining the glossy silk of her dress rose in his mind.

Anice stepped toward him and boldly placed her hands on his hips. "Marin didn't satisfy you, did she?" Her hands slipped over his chest and then ran down his back as she pressed her body to him. "I could."

She was ready and willing. The kind of woman Bran enjoyed. And yet, Marin had implied Anice was a maiden, as readily as she had indicated she herself was not. Bran had no mind for maidens.

And damn him, he could not clear Marin from his thoughts. The way she fought him left his blood boiling in a mix of frustration and rage and sexual need so that they all blended together in an indecipherable mix of searing passion.

"Get to bed," Bran said.

Anice slipped her hands away from his body and turned toward his bed.

"Yer own," he amended.

She regarded him with incredulity. "You don't want me?"

"I've had it with the lot of ye meddlesome daughters of the warden." He folded his arms over his chest. "Ye rich lasses think ye own the world and every man in it."

Anice remained where she stood. "Release my sister."

Ah, and there it was. Bran scoffed. "Would ye have tried to kill me too?"

The coquettish expression transformed into one of smugness. "I'd have done whatever necessary to see my sister safe."

How flattering.

These women would be the death of him, either through a successfully plotted murder or by driving him utterly mad with their scheming.

He pointed his finger toward the door. "Get out now if ye ever want to see yer sister alive again."

Anice lifted her mantle from where she'd draped it over a chair and pulled it to her shoulders as she spun away in a wave of blonde hair. Without another word, she stomped from his room.

He waited for the slap of her bare feet to dissipate before he locked the door and wearily approached the bed. Hopefully snakes hadn't been put beneath the furs, or poison poured atop his pillow, or any other horrors the daughters of Werrick might have concocted.

But at this point, he was just too tired to bother with any of it. He climbed over the feather mattress. The blanket beneath the furs was decadently thick. He slid under the finest linen sheets, cool and welcoming.

The plush mattress cradled his weight in wealth and luxury. The delicate scent of lavender and meadowsweet rose around him. His eyes fell closed.

Catriona's face rose in his mind. Her eyes were wide with fear, her cry to Marin to let her die. Another face swam up from his memory, another voice pleading for death to save the ones they loved.

His mother, with her long dark hair tangled in the fist of the reivers. The beast of a man with his blade to her throat. Ena's voice ringing out to kill her instead, and Gregor charging.

He opened his eyes rather than let his mind play out the rest of the memory.

He would not go through such loss again. No matter how difficult, he would succeed with Werrick. He would not let Ena die.

👁️✨👁️

MARIN PACED HER CELL LIKE A CAGED BEAST. EVERY MOMENT
that dragged on brought thoughts of her sisters, of their compromised safety. And her anger grew.

She had failed them. Her hesitation to kill Bran could cost
them all their lives. He had sworn he would not hurt them and
then he had put a knife to William's throat. William, of all people.
The kindest, most generous man who aided the poor in the
village with his earnings and had been so terribly brave in trying
to protect her.

She had failed.

The words echoed in the beating of her heart and hammered
through her soul.

She had done them all a horrible wrong. Mistake after
mistake, all ones her father would never have made.

"Your father would be proud of everything you've done, my
lady."

The familiar voice startled Marin from the downward pull of
her self-castigation. She stopped pacing and shook her head. Her
jaw ached from clenching it.

"He would be," Sir Richard continued. "You kept Lady
Catriona safe and you nearly sacrificed yourself for your people.
He will also be glad you didn't succeed in getting yourself killed."

Marin frowned. Her efforts had only put the entire castle in
danger. There was no way out of this predicament. She'd combed
over the cell, testing every stone for anything loose, kicking at the
ground to possibly uncover the beginnings of a hole she
might dig.

As with everything in Werrick Castle, the dungeon was
soundly built.

A giggle sounded in the hall outside the dungeon followed by the murmurings of a feminine voice.

"Of course," the woman's flirtatious voice echoed. "If you were here, I'd make sure you had bread and cheese too."

Anice appeared then, a flickering candle clutched in one hand and a platter of food in the other. The coy smile still teased the corners of her mouth. Piquette lumbered along at her side.

"Oh, Marin." Anice rushed to the cell and the white of her chemise flashed between the partings of a hastily-donned mantle.

Marin's blood went cold at Anice's state of partial undress. "Did they hurt you?" Marin reached for her sister with a desperate hand, hating the iron keeping her restrained. "Has something happened?"

Piquette settled on the ground near Marin's cage and slid a glance toward the tray.

Anice took Marin's hand in the cradle of hers. "You're so cold, Sister." She looked at the cell and grimaced. "And it's so filthy."

"Did they hurt you?" Marin repeated, her voice stern.

Anice's attention returned to her and she shook her head. She took a heel of bread and a slab of cheese from the tray where Piquette had begun to sniff and offered them to Marin.

Marin ignored the food and gestured to her sister's chemise. "What is this? What's happened?"

"It's nothing—it's not as it appears." Anice flipped her hair over her shoulder. "But I got this."

She pressed something cool and hard into Marin's palm. Some kind of metal. Marin looked down and found a key within her hand.

"For the dungeon." Anice gave a proud smile.

Marin's joy was short-lived when she remembered who had the key. The only key. Bran. "How did you get this?"

Anice shrugged with a little grin.

Fear jabbed through Marin for Anice's maidenhead, for the

welfare of her younger sister. Would her betrothed still take her if she were compromised? "What happened?"

Anice rolled her eyes. "Nothing. I tried to seduce him, to free you. It didn't work." She lifted one shoulder. "I ran my hands over his hips in an attempt to persuade him and slipped the key out."

Marin eyed her sister warily. "That is all? He didn't...touch you?"

"Nay. That was all." Anice leaned closer, her eyes sparkling in the candlelight. "Though he is strong, and quite fine looking."

Marin didn't reply. How could she protest such bold statements when she herself agreed with Anice's assessment of the man?

She'd been listening to her guards, waiting for one of them to mention the bounty waiting within William's work room. Yet not one had mentioned the coin.

They didn't know. The man Bran had called Drake had kept his newfound wealth a secret. Mayhap he was loyal, and mayhap he did need the coin for his family.

Marin shook her head. "You are safe, then?" she asked her sister.

Anice nodded distractedly and pushed the food toward Marin a second time. "Within the hour, there will be a guard change." Her tone had changed from the lightness of a girlish joy to the seriousness of a plan in action. "We can supplement their guards with our own, the ones who have remained hidden."

Marin straightened and tightened her grip on the key. "You've spoken with them?" She glanced toward the cells across from hers, where most of her army stood.

"Aye. They will take the place of these guards. We will have the opportunity to slip from the dungeon without detection, and easily out of the castle through the secret passage."

Their father had commissioned the hidden tunnel after the first attack on Werrick, accessed through the larder beneath the wine stores. From there, it ran under the castle and came out in the woods through an iron grate.

Marin always wore the key to that hidden entry on her person, in a locket on her belt. Even if someone could find the metal gate and somehow wrest it open, the tunnel broke off in different directions beneath the castle. If the intruder didn't identify the correct tunnel, they could wander about forever without finding their way into the keep. The entrance had been masked by a trap door at the top, stained to appear as part of the earthen ceiling. If one didn't know where to look, it would never be found.

Aye, the passage would be the perfect escape.

"I know exactly what to do," Marin said resolutely.

"I knew you would." Anice smiled. "Enjoy your food, dear sister," she said with more volume to her voice. "I do hope they release you soon. It's so dank and awful in here." Her lip curled with sincerity.

"Thank you for thinking of me," Marin replied with equal volume. This was a second chance. Another opportunity to save them all.

Anice's hand squeezed Marin's, and with that, she and Piquette were gone, taking with them the glowing light of the candle. Marin's world plunged into a sea of black once more.

"Did you hear everything?" Marin asked into the darkness.

"Aye," Sir Richard answered.

"We ought to go to Mabrick Castle and seek the aid of Baron Carlyle there. We will need a good portion of the soldiers and can formulate a plan there."

"A good plan, my lady," Sir Richard said. "They've always been loyal supporters of the English crown and are strong allies."

Marin nodded to herself. A surge of confidence roared through her for the first time since Bran entered Werrick Castle. "Then it's time to begin, for we'll be freed soon."

The servants would need to remain behind for the time being, though she was loath to do so. But to move them all would be too obvious. Marin, however, would not be going to Mabrick.

She would slip away before her sisters would notice. They would be safe, but she still wanted to protect the remaining people. She wanted her castle back, and the safety it had afforded them all once before. The only way to obtain that would be to follow her original plan and kill Bran.

❧ 9 ❧

Marin was at the head of the procession, leading her men. After all, this was her folly to repair.

The task of getting the soldiers from their cells had been quick and easy, and the guards who had been in hiding replaced the reivers without incident. As Marin had anticipated, the reivers were not familiar enough with one another to question the men who replaced them.

Now the group of liberated soldiers moved as silently through the castle as was possible. Many of the men were without their chainmail, as only a few were able to procure a full suit for their escape. The minimal armor helped make them somewhat quieter. Weapons had been snuck out of the armory earlier by brave servants, so at least nearly all were armed.

Bran's men had imbibed heavily on the Highland whisky they'd found in the castle's stores. The men had been all too eager to partake and now most lay splayed on the ground in a spirit-induced slumber.

Marin's wooden patens had been left off, so her leather clad feet padded soundlessly over the stone.

A shadow caught her attention at the end of the hall. A guard?

Aye, it was, one lone man who did not appear to have drunk as much as the others.

Her heart slid to her stomach. She hadn't wanted to kill these men. Yet she'd been given no choice. Her people's freedom for a life. She readied her dagger and reminded herself this man and the other reivers had stolen her home, eaten her food. They posed a dangerous threat.

The guard lifted a cup to his mouth, drank and casually strolled in the opposite direction. His pace was slow, his relaxed shoulders indicating he had not seen them.

Marin waited with her breath locked in her chest for several moments after he was out of sight.

Sir Richard nodded to her and waved them all across, taking the lead with Anice, Ella, Catriona and Leila in the middle of the small band of Werrick's remaining troops. Fortunately, there were no more reivers on their way to the larder where the trap door lay beneath heavy casks of fine wine.

"You took a fine bit of time getting here, my lady," Nan admonished. A fine sheen of sweat glistened on the cook's brow.

Marin leveled her own gaze at the old cook. "We didn't want to start a battle on our way out."

Nan nodded. "'Tis a smart thing to do."

"You're so brave to help us, Nan." Cat wrapped her skinny arms around the cook. "Will you not come with us?"

An affectionate smile spread over Nan's face and she wrapped an arm around Cat. "Nay, lass. I'll see your tracks covered."

"Will you be safe?" Ella asked as Sir Richard and several of the men tugged the casks of wine off the trap door.

"Men love their food." Nan chuckled and pulled Leila toward her in an embrace similar to the one she held Cat in. "Old Nan will be fine. I want to ensure my girls are safe."

"You could always poison them," Ella offered.

"I'll keep that in mind." Nan winked.

Once the casks were cleared and the rushes brushed aside, Sir

Richard tugged at the door's latch. It opened with a creaking groan as the musty odor of disuse and wet earth emerged from the gaping black pit.

"I'll go first," Sir Richard offered. He took a torch from the wall and held it over the pit. The darkness within seemed to swallow the light so only blackness showed beyond the feeble flames.

Regardless, brave Sir Richard leapt without fear into the entrance to the tunnel. He landed with a solid thud of feet on dirt. The light cast around him showing walls of tightly packed soil around him.

Marin's heart pounded with what she knew she'd have to do. For though she would make a show of going with her sisters, she would not be escaping with them. Not yet. She had her own battle to wage.

The rest of the Werrick soldiers made their way into the awaiting tunnel.

"We shall be back soon, dear Nan." Marin embraced the plump cook and whispered into her ear. "Leave the wine casks off the door once it's closed."

Nan asked no questions, but simply nodded slowly to the request.

Marin lowered herself into the pit among Werrick's soldiers. The walls pressed a chill into her bones. All around her was the scent of wet earth and stale air. Their footsteps ground against the gritty floor, the sound absorbed into the thickness of the walls.

Once Marin's sisters had either leapt or been lowered into the entrance, along with Anice's dog, Piquette, the lot of them set off through the maze of tunnels. Marin's heart thundered in her chest, the sound filling her ears. She had to do it now, while she still had the fortitude to do so. For if she did not, the castle and its people would be lost to her forever.

Aye, Baron Carlyle would undoubtedly help them, but she

knew how impenetrable the keep's walls were. Bran had demonstrated he was not without a streak of violence with his threat against poor William. What would he do to the servants if he was under attack?

She had to turn back now. To cut the head off the snake so that the rest of the body might also die.

She took the key to the gate from the small locket at her belt and passed it to Anice. Her sister looked at the key in her hand and frowned.

"Is something wrong?" Leila looked up between them, her eyes luminous beneath the glint of her small helm.

"Nay, lamb," Anice said. "'Tis nothing to concern yourself over."

Ella took Leila's hand and drew her away, but not before casting a suspicious glance at her elder sisters first.

"I must do this," Marin whispered. "Otherwise we will lose Werrick Castle."

Anice nodded slowly, and Marin knew her sister understood. Piquette gave a whimper and nudged Marin's palm with his large wet nose.

"Go with God, Sister." Anice clasped Marin's shoulder with her free one.

Marin lowered her head in reverence and remained thus as the soldiers marched past her. Sir Richard, who led at the front, did not notice her absence, and for that she was grateful. He would never condone the risk she was about to take.

The light of the torches bled away as Marin let the last of the soldiers pass by with their curious glances. But they did not question their lady. They moved on at the sweep of her hand until she was alone in the dark with only the sound of her breathing echoing around her. So deep was the darkness, she could not see her hand passing before her face.

She waited for the jumble of footsteps to shuffle out of range before she fished out the stub of a candle from her pocket and struck at her flint to light it. Now able to see, she turned and quickly made her way down the tunnel, retracing her steps to the trap door. This would be her one opportunity to truly save them all.

৵৵৵

BRAN'S FITFUL SLEEP CAME ABRUPTLY TO AN END WITH AN insistent pounding on the door. He bolted awake, sitting up and nearly sinking in the downy mattress beneath him. "What is it?"

"Bran." Drake's voice on the other side of the door came with urgency.

Bran climbed out of the ridiculously large bed. "Aye, come in."

The door opened and Drake entered, his mouth set in a thin line. "The prisoners are no' in their cells."

A chill of apprehension trickled down Bran's back. "Where are they?"

"I dinna know, but all the cells are empty." Drake paced the room. "We searched the castle before I came to ye. No' much to be found save for the servants left behind and our reivers."

"How did they not know an entire dungeon full of prisoners escaped?" Bran demanded.

Drake folded his arms over his chest. "I believe they were too far into the whisky."

He was most likely correct. When Bran went to bed, most were too drunk to know their head from their arse.

A panicked thought pounded through Bran's skull. "What of the warden's daughters?"

Drake shook his head. "Gone as well."

Bran ran to the windows and pushed open the shutters. A harsh wind blew in and spattered him with rain water. He ignored the discomfort and stared into the downpour, half expecting to see a trail of soldiers trekking over the moonlit land before him. No such luck.

He pulled the shutters closed. "Round up the men sober enough to be of use. I want those lasses found. Having the warden's daughters on hand is part of the deal."

"I willna let ye down." Drake gave a stiff nod and quickly departed.

Without Marin or any of the other sisters present, the servants were more likely to revolt. Aye, they were only servants, but the mass of them could still take on the reivers if they were sufficiently enraged. He'd seen it happen enough times to not underestimate their force.

A crack of thunder sounded from outside and the patter of rain against the shutters intensified.

Bran snatched up his trews and pulled them on. He caught sight of the gambeson he'd flopped over the back of a wooden chair after Anice had left. He lifted it and checked the pocket where he'd tucked the key to the dungeon. His fingertips grazed over fabric without catching the coolness of metal. Irritation and rage seared into the muscles along the back of his neck. Anice had not been there to seduce him. The chit had stolen the key.

Damn the daughters of Werrick.

The shutters banged open and made him jump. Evidently, he had not latched them properly. They rattled and smacked the stone walls with the frenzy of the storm. Bran cursed and stalked across the room. He slammed the shutters closed and snapped down the narrow clasp to lock them.

The hair along the back of his neck prickled in warning. All at once, the scent of lavender teased at his senses and his body immediately hardened.

"I told you I would kill you." The voice purred in his ear and an arm curled around his torso.

Marin.

She tensed behind him and he could imagine her in his mind's eye, pulling back her dagger to deliver the death blow. But he would not go down so easily. Not when he'd come so far.

He ducked down low and jerked backward. Her concentration had been centered on the blow she'd intended to deliver, and not on her hold on him, which made it easy to evade her. This time.

She had her hair braided back, exposing more of her beautiful face, and she wore men's hose along with a surcoat. She lunged forward with a grunt and arced her blade at him.

He deflected her strike and backed up once more. "Where did ye send yer sisters and all the soldiers?"

She dove at him, hitting him with her full body weight. They both slammed to the floor. She kicked at him, landing a solid blow on his shin. He flinched from the injury and just managed to catch her intent to drive her elbow toward his face. He spun to the side as her arm came down on the hard-stone floor.

She cried out and cradled her elbow. Bran scrambled to his feet, grabbed his sword and held it to her throat.

"Why did ye stay?" he asked. "To kill me?"

She edged away from the blade and slowly lowered her hand from her injured elbow. "Your men are unorganized. Your leadership of them is tenuously established at best. If you were dead, they would disperse, and my sisters could safely return home. And your men are well-behaved for now, but for how long? I will not stand by while my servants are raped and killed."

He gritted his teeth. He hated that his precarious leadership was so apparent. Damn the reivers for making so pathetic an army and damn the Middle March Warden for sending him on this fool's errand in the first place. "Where are yer sisters? Where are the soldiers?"

"It doesn't matter what you do to me. They'll stay safe." She gave him a smug grin. "They're gathering reinforcements, allies strong enough to withstand your forces no matter how underhanded your schemes."

"Reinforcements?" he asked. If they went for reinforcements, then surely, they would seek a castle nearby.

"They left well over an hour ago." She stood slowly, keeping her blue gaze fixed on the blade pointed at her. "I went with them but snuck back here for you." Her hand slowly moved at her sleeve.

"Toss the dagger to the ground or I'll see it lodged in your throat." He threw her an exasperated look.

She jerked the blade from her sleeve, but she did not toss it to the ground. Instead, she let it fly toward him, determined in her decision to see him dead.

M arin would not fail again. Bran had ducked to avoid the hurtling dagger. She took advantage of his new position and launched a solid kick into his chest, pushing him backward. His sword clattered to the ground, too far for him to quickly grab. He coughed out an exhale and widened his stance in preparation for a fight.

A swift glance at the floor did not reveal the dagger or sword within her reach. Damn.

She threw a fist at him, but he batted it aside with his forearm. The strike of his solid arm jarred her. She swung again, and again he deflected. Each blocked hit resulted in a jab of pain shooting through Marin's hand.

Her gauntlets were in her chambers with the rest of her armor. Though she regretted their absence now, slipping quietly into Bran's room had been more important than protection. At least it had been before she realized she'd be engaging in hand-to-hand combat with a man twice her size.

Bran grabbed her wrists in his large hands and restrained her with impossible strength. She wrestled against him, twisting and turning, her legs kicking at him seemingly without effect. No matter what she did, he did not lighten his grip. She arched back in preparation to smash his forehead with her own.

"Nay, lass. No' this time." He knocked her feet out from under her.

She fell back, unable to stop herself, and landed atop something downy. The bed.

Bran's weight fell on top of her and set her heart beating wildly.

"Stop attacking me." His gaze searched hers. "Stop trying to kill me. I dinna want it to be this way."

"What way did you want it to be?" She didn't bother to stifle her incredulity. "Did you expect us to allow you to come into the castle and welcome you?"

His brow furrowed. "Mabrick Castle," he muttered.

Marin stiffened. The soldiers and her sisters were on their way there now. Why would he mention it?

"What of it?" she demanded.

Had he known? Damn her for taunting him. And still, even if he left now, he would not be able to catch up with her sisters. Nay, they would be within the walls of the stronghold by then, safe.

"Ye dinna send them to Mabrick Castle, did ye?" There was a hesitation to his tone that made her skin prickle with a wave of apprehension.

"Why?" she whispered.

"The castle was taken by the Grahams two days past."

Her veins ran cold with horror. The Grahams. The fiercest and most brutal of all the reivers to strike the borders. They attacked without discretion, killed without mercy—men, women, children. And what they did to the women...

It had been a Graham who had attacked her mother a decade before. He'd raped her in the attack and left her for dead, leaving before he could be struck down. Aye, the Grahams were the cruelest, and Marin had sent her sisters and the remaining brave soldiers directly in their path.

Marin shook her head. "Nay." Tears blurred her vision. "Nay, you lie."

The earnestness on his face, the gravity in those dark eyes spoke for him. He was not lying.

"My sisters..." her throat choked off the remaining words, unable to even form the thought.

"May already be dead," he finished for her.

"Nay." Marin thrashed against him. "Let me be. Let me go to them. Let me—"

"Marin." He spoke gently in her ear, his voice soothing.

She jerked and stared up at him. "You. You can help. You and your men. You must save them, Bran." Her words came fast and frantic, for she was mad with hope.

He smirked. "I have what I came for, as well as the eldest daughter of the Earl of Werrick. The Grahams have no qualms with me as yet, nor I with them."

She shook her head. All she could see in her mind was her sisters marching out with the meager army of soldiers, the brave group moving steadily over the rugged terrain of the borderlands toward what they thought was safety. Only it wouldn't be safety— it would be a slaughter.

Desperation rose with her panicked heartbeat. She blinked away her tears and gazed imploringly at him. "Please, Bran. Please."

His jaw tightened. "They made their choice. It's all a rich man's game. No doubt that's why the Grahams attacked Mabrick. Men like me, we're simply pawns."

"I'll do anything." Marin lay back in supplication and pushed up her breasts toward him. "Take me, do what you will with me, just please, please save my sisters."

She couldn't stop the hot tears from leaking from the corners of her eyes. The force of agony radiating from her chest was more than she could bear. How could she be so helpless? How could there be nothing she could do?

She could not lose her sisters. They could *not* die.

"I will be cooperative in any way you require. I will ensure the servants accept you." She clenched her fists. "I will do *anything*."

He smirked. "Attacking the Grahams would cause a war I will spend a lifetime fighting. I canna risk my men. I canna risk losing this castle. No' when I've worked so hard to secure it." He shook his head. "Yer sisters left my protection. They made their own decisions. I canna be responsible for their fates."

But her sisters hadn't made their own decision. Marin had made it for them. She had sent them to be cut down like beasts on the hunt.

An idea struck her so suddenly, it wrought a cry from her lips. "I will marry you."

Shock lit his gaze.

She gazed up at him. "Please. If you help my sisters, I will marry you."

BRAN EASED HIS GRIP FROM MARIN, BUT SHE DID NOT LAUNCH at him in an attack. Her eyes were red rimmed from her tears, her cheeks and nose pink.

"Marrying me will give you an earl's eldest daughter for a wife," she explained. "You will have the acquiescence of the entire castle. You will have the security of my wealth. And if you were so generous as to save the earl's four other daughters from being massacred, I assure you my father would bestow upon you a great reward in gratitude. You will no longer be a pawn in a game of rich men. You will be a player."

Bran studied the lovely, miserable woman beneath him. She was clever. Clever and shrewd and made as weak by her love for her sisters as he was by his love for Ena.

Her suggestion was an ideal opportunity, and an appealing one at that.

Marriage to Marin would give him the protection of a March Warden, a lifetime of safety for Ena as long as she didn't do anything foolish.

He stared down at Marin, taking in her beauty. He would be lying if he said he had no interest in her carnally. God's teeth, he wanted her with every bit of his being. And it was true her people would accept him if she voluntarily wed him. It might complicate matters when Kerr arrived, but then Bran would not be in such a position of weakness.

"If I release ye, will ye stop fighting me?" he asked.

Marin nodded with her watery blue gaze fixed piteously on him. He knew the helpless desperation she felt, as well as the chest-splitting pain of loss.

Bran released Marin and straightened. Every moment he considered her proposal was one that could cost one of her sisters their lives. And yet it was not a decision made easily.

"Ye're no' wed?" he asked. After all, it could be a trick.

She sat up. "Nay, I am not wed. I never have been."

Yet she claimed to not be a virgin. An interesting situation.

"Betrothed then?" he pressed. He wouldn't want some fool-hardy intended coming after him over this.

She shook her head.

"And yet ye are no' a maiden." He frowned. "Were ye compromised when ye were held captive before?"

Her cheeks went red. "I am a maiden." Marin folded her arms stiffly over her chest. "I only said I wasn't in an attempt to seduce you and kill you." She paused before saying with vehemence, "I'll do anything to save my sisters."

He scoffed. "Including seducing me and marrying me, aye?"

She lowered her eyes. "The advantage of a marriage to me would be beneficial to you."

All the strength she possessed before now wilted beneath the crippling effects of her helplessness. She pressed her hands over her heart and her shoulders curled forward, as if the pain were too great to bear. For truly, it no doubt was. She lifted her eyes to him, and another tear rolled down her cheek. "Please save my sisters."

He could not bring himself to let anyone hurt as he had, especially not a woman.

"Aye," he said at long last. "I'll help ye in exchange for marriage to ye."

Marin leapt to her feet. "Thank you." She clutched his hand. "We must make haste." She paused and looked around the room for a frantic moment. "I must get my armor."

Her armor? Surely, she did not expect to fight with men on the battlefield. "Ye willna be joining us."

"I'm trained in battle. All of us have been. I can fight."

"Ach, aye, I know ye can fight." He grinned at her. "But ye willna be joining us in battle."

Her mouth fell open. "I have to come."

"Ye are to be my wife, Marin." He touched a hand to her shoulder. "As yer husband, I will protect ye no matter what. Whether with my life, or by demand that ye stay put."

"You will not keep me here while I might be the extra soldier to tip the scales in battle." She stood stubbornly in front of him. "This needs to be included in our negotiations."

Bran grunted with disapproval, but now was not the time to argue with his intended. Not when every moment wasted could mean death.

"I'll accompany ye to get yer armor, but we must make haste." Bran led her from the room. "The forces were already assembling to come after ye. They should be ready to depart."

As quickly as was possible, she donned her armor and they were mounted on their steeds outside in the pouring rain. Marin's full mouth was set in a grim line under her helm.

Bran called out for his men to move. And move they did, pouring from the gates of the castle in a wave, riding as though the devil himself were chasing them.

"We will catch them," Bran shouted to her. "I dinna see their horses missing from the stables. They are on foot. Even with over an hour advantage, we will be able to gain on them. Especially with our hobblers."

She looked at his horse, then down at her own.

"They dinna look like much." He patted his steed's strong neck. "But they can navigate this terrain like a selkie does the sea."

"We must arrive in time." Marin's emphatic words were not meant for him.

"Aye," he said with all the conviction he could muster. "We will."

And he hoped to God he was right.

Mabrick Castle was not much further when they came
upon a body. Marin spotted him first, her heart and mind
having trained a lifetime to recognize the Werrick hawk on the
familiar green background with the yellow stripe. Even in the
moonlight, she could make out her family crest.

She stopped her horse, but before she could leap from its
back, Bran was already on the ground. He pulled the man over
and her stomach clenched.

"Dinna look, Marin," Bran said.

But she had to look. She was responsible for the man being
there.

He was young and blond, an archer, one not trained to
perform in close combat. As a result, he'd been one of the men
without chainmail, left unprotected. The gaping wounds glistening in the moonlight and the horror of his death etched upon
his face bore witness to his terrible end.

There were many men in her father's forces who said they had
seen death so often in battle, it no longer affected them, or so
they said. But Marin did not think she would ever be able to make
such a claim.

Especially not when several feet away lay another body. And then another. The rain had stopped, but the trail of death continued, their blood an eerie purple in the silvery light.

She covered her face with her hands and tried to still the growing tension welling in her throat. The wind shifted, no longer sweeping from behind them. It billowed toward their faces, carrying with it the odor of blood and the frenzied cries of war.

Marin leapt back onto her horse, but Bran stopped the horse by grabbing the reins.

"Stay back," he said to Marin. He mounted his stubby-legged horse and shot forward.

Marin ignored his request and followed close behind him.

He bared his teeth at her, his expression dark and ferocious. "Damn it, woman. If ye ever listen to me, listen now. Dinna sacrifice their lives and yers by riding out there without assessing the battle."

Stunned, she slowed her horse while his men rode onward toward the clash of metal and the piteous wailing of the dying. He was right, she knew. Charging into battle would only cause her sisters to be distracted. Such distractions quickly led to death. The thought made her shudder.

The warrior in her knew this, but the blood the five of them shared, the blood running through her veins, raced with helplessness. Time seemed to drag on for the agony of a lifetime. Her sisters needed her, and she was having to wait.

The horse shifted under her weight, as if he detected her anxiety. She tightened her grip on the hilt of her sword. Every muscle in her body was tensed with the need to charge into action.

Wait.

Her throat burned to scream her frustration, yet she swallowed it down and remained in place.

Finally, finally, finally a bellow came from the tree line, followed by the cries of attacking men. Marin punched her sword in the air and her voice joined their lusty shouts. Her horse flew over the bloodied ground where bodies lay, unmoving in death. It was hard not to see them as she raced past the men who had not been prepared for war.

Marin gritted her teeth as if doing so might tamp down the horror ripping through her. She had ordered her men to charge into a slaughter.

The clashing of blades and grunts of fighting became louder, a sound welcome to her ears.

There were still survivors. Her sisters would hopefully be among them.

And at least in battle, Marin would not be a helpless observer, left to see what the fates had cast her way. Nay, she would be fighting, with control over where her blade fell and how her body moved. She would be with her sisters. Three more dead men lay on the ground. Only one was not a man from Werrick Castle. The slain reiver lay face up, his eyes staring at nothing, an arrow jutting from his chest with a white sprigged fletching.

Catriona's arrows.

A harsh breath tore from Marin's chest. There was still hope. She raced up the hill toward the battle. As she crested the top, she could make out the swarm of men below, Graham reivers and Bran's reivers blended together in a chaos of bodies. Marin searched frantically, her gaze moving to the center of the fray.

She caught sight of her soldiers and her heart gave a wild skip.

Only about half of them remained alive by her count, and they had formed a protective circle around Marin's sisters, fighting valiantly even as the Grahams pressed in on them. Catriona's hands flew at her bow, nocking arrows and launching them into the onslaught.

Bran's men hit the outskirts of the Graham reivers and fought with the same degree of merciless ferocity. While the Grahams were a large force, it appeared only a few dozen were outside the castle. Bran's reivers easily outnumbered them.

The odds would be in Bran's favor. Hopefully, time would be as well.

Marin continued to race down the hill toward the maelstrom, unable to tear her gaze from the cluster of Werrick soldiers. Her soldiers fought bravely, regardless of some being without proper armor. These were men she had grown up caring for and respecting, men who were sacrificing themselves so that her sisters would live.

Marin met the first Graham reiver with the swing of her blade. It tore through his neck in a fatal blow. She didn't stop, not until the bulk of her steed crashed into the solid wall of soldiers. Only then did she lose sight of her sisters as she fought her way toward them. She pushed her horse forward, her sword hacking and slashing as she made her way through the outskirts of battle until her horse refused to continue.

The small stout-legged pony was ideal for the difficult border terrain, but it was not prepared for battle. Marin followed Bran's men and leapt from her horse. Her feet landed on the spongy marshland and sank slightly with each step. The small horse abandoned her, leaving her moving more slowly.

Too slowly.

Panic rattled in the back of her mind, threatening to let a wave of fear consume her. But she'd trained for too long at her father's side to give in to such weakness.

She drew a steady breath, even as she lashed out at her enemy. Worry cleared from her and all her thoughts shifted to the moves of her blade. In. Out. Block. Feint. Left, jab.

Sweat trickled down her face and her feet slid and stumbled over the bodies lying beneath her. Still, she did not allow herself to break her concentration.

A reiver beside her fell, and Marin whipped right with her blade drawn back. Bran glowered back at her from under his helm.

She hesitated, finding him at her side thus.

She could kill him. Then she wouldn't have to marry him. His men wouldn't notice his fall until after the battle when her sisters were safe. They would no doubt disband, and she could return to Werrick Castle with her sisters. They could all be safe.

And yet she could not bring herself to thrust her sword into him as he was occupied in battle, set on saving her sisters. Instead, it was he who lifted his weapon and charged in her direction.

BRAN SWUNG HIS AXE WITH ALL HIS MIGHT, SO IT CONNECTED with a satisfying thunk into the head of the Graham bastard lunging at Marin. Her blue eyes went wide beneath her helm and she jerked her attention to the man who was dead before Bran could even pull his axe free.

She nodded her thanks, and her expression blinked from surprise to the narrowed ferocity of determination. He returned her gesture and together they fought, blade and axe, side by side.

She wielded the sword as though it weighed nothing, using its heft to propel the weapon rather than fighting against it, and she moved with an ability wrought by years of repeated practice. Her skills were admirable for any warrior, but especially so for a woman. It did not escape his notice that she managed to cut down as many Graham reivers as did he. At least until the scream.

It rent from the heart of the melee. High-pitched and feminine.

"Nay," Marin cried. Her blade whipped faster, her face set with concentration. But such power could not be maintained. One wild jab went awry and only nicked the arm of the man she fought. The man took advantage and sliced at her. She was knocked back a step and Bran took the place in front of her.

He roared his rage and brought the axe down hard on the man.

"I didn't need you to do that." Marin appeared at his side, her blade moving with less speed.

He grunted and kept his focus on the man before him, one with a dirk and a frenzied glint in his eye.

"My chainmail protected me," she offered.

He grunted again and ducked to miss the man's attack. His opponent lifted his head up to the sky and screamed out like a banshee, which gave Bran the perfect opportunity to cut him down.

A clang of metal echoed in Bran's right ear, where Marin stood. He glanced to his side and found her stopping a man who had intended to strike his killing blow as Bran delivered his own. The corner of her lip curled up. The favor was repaid already, and she was damn proud of herself for it.

"Marin!" The high-pitched voice rose from the center of the battle and Marin's cocky smile disappeared.

Her gaze shot to where the heads of Werrick's soldiers showed through the battle between the Grahams and Bran's men. So close. So far.

Bran sliced through a Graham, splitting the man's gambeson as well as his chest, then swung his axe again, catching a man who intended to attack Marin. "We'll save them."

The shiny helms of Werrick's soldiers came into view over the heads of several Graham reivers. They were getting nearer. They truly might get there in time.

Marin's blade flashed at Bran's side, blocking a man who sought to attack him. Apparently, the passion they shared was not their only compatibility. They fought together without effort, keeping each other safe as easily as they charged their enemy.

The muscles along Bran's back and arms ached with the effort of his swings. The axe continued to grow heavier in his grip. But he had been more tired in his life, more beaten down. He dug deep in the well of his reserved strength and swung with vigor.

They were close enough now to make out the Werrick soldiers

better. Several were bloodied, one could scarcely lift his weapon, doing so with one arm while the other hung limply at his side. They were exhausted, injured and fighting for survival.

A soldier fell, a man with no chainmail or helm. Then another followed, and the line of defense around the women broke.

All of Bran's senses became sharper in battle. He discerned the hiss of a blade over the cries of the dying and the clanging of weapons, the odor of an impending attacker over the horrors of death and dying redolent around him. His awareness worked to keep his body strong and his focus intact.

When a slight blonde woman wearing chain mail and wielding a mace stepped forward into the gap where the soldiers had fallen, however, his focus shattered. She was too little for battle, barely a woman at all.

His body moved with memorized action, blocking and killing as needed, but his gaze remained fixed on where young Ella whirled the spiked metal ball of her mace. Her lip curled back in a vicious snarl as she let the heavy head of her weapon slam into a man's face, its impact wet and hollow. Blood exploded where the Graham's face had been.

Ella kept her attention fixed on another reiver and tugged her weapon free with a jerk. Anice appeared at her side with her arm outstretched, as if the action might keep the two younger sisters behind them safe. In front of her, Piquette stood like a sentry, his mouth colored with blood and his snout peeled back from his bared teeth.

Like Marin, Anice wielded a blade, arcing and slicing with a skill only slightly less than that of her older sister.

Another man in the distance gave a wild shriek into the air, followed by another and another until the wild cries rose above even the chaos of war. Then it stopped, as suddenly as it'd begun.

The women paid it no mind and continued to fight with their exceptional skill. While Bran didn't know much about the Earl of Werrick, he was well aware the man had trained his daughters to fight like men. And in doing so, the earl had undoubtedly saved their lives.

A bellowed order came from the parapet of Mabrick Castle, one single word that struck fear into Bran's heart: archers.

The only way the leader of an army of men might readily sacrifice his own men in a volley of arrows was if he anticipated killing more of the enemy. Meaning there were more of Bran's men than there were surviving Graham reivers. And most likely the Grahams knew this when they gave the call.

A neat line of men appeared on the parapet, staggered against the crenellations, their bows jutting up from them like staffs. They drew back in unison, aimed their arrows and let them fly.

Bran braced for the impact of several arrows. They soared through the air in a unified hiss and landed in errant thunks on the battlefield. For the briefest of moments, the battle seemed to pause in wait for the impact, for the powerful hit upon the band of battling men and women. Some sank harmlessly into the ground or against shields, but others buried into flesh. Men cried out in surprise and agony, and opponents took advantage of their weakened state.

Two of Werrick's guards were struck by arrows and fell. They were immediately replaced by Leila, who put her small body in the space once occupied by two men. Catriona stood in the shelter of men and her sisters, pulling arrow after arrow to feed into her bow. Graham after Graham fell around them as a result.

Bran swept his axe at a reiver who lunged in his direction. The weapon caught the man on the side of the head and sent him to his knees, before crashing to the blood and dirt below. The circle of English soldiers and the sisters was in view. Finally.

If the older sisters' skills were exceptional, young Leila's were truly extraordinary. Her small hands lashed out with daggers at such speed, he could scarcely make out her movements. A call sounded from the parapets above once more, and the archers readied another volley of arrows.

Marin rushed forward to her sisters with a desperate speed Bran could not match. A man headed her off, too far for Bran to stop him, and whipped a blade at her head. She arched backward, but it still came so close, Bran heard a ping as the edge of the weapon glanced off the bottom of her helm as it was pulled free from her head. She spun around, dazed and blinking.

Anice cried out and ran forward, her sword drawn to cut down the man who had struck out at Marin.

The sky hummed with the impending rain of arrows and every man and woman tensed for its impact. Everyone save Anice, whose determination propelled her forward. And Leila, who stopped fighting as suddenly as she started, and darted protectively toward Anice.

Leila braced herself, small and brave, at Anice's back, and stared up at the arrows with steely determination as they continued to suck down toward the earth. Bran's voice rasped out with his cry. He tried to run toward her, through the layer of bodies at his feet and the blood-slick ground.

The harder he tried to get to Leila, the further away she seemed. The arrows thrust down upon them. One glanced off his shoulder, but he barely registered it as he saw two arrows punch through Leila's body—one in the arm and one in her narrow chest.

Something heavy and massive struck Bran in the back of his head. Stars winked in and out of his vision. But Leila needed him.

He swung his weapon blindly until it connected with a body, and the grunt of death sounded. The ringing in Bran's head left his mind thick, as though it'd been stuffed with wool. The sharpness of his hearing went muffled and distorted, as if underwater.

He shook his head and turned back to Leila in time to see her body curl around her injuries as she began to pitch toward the ground. Bran reached out to her, nearly falling himself, and snagged her in the safety of his arms. Blood dotted her cheeks and narrow chin. She'd lost her helm and her dark hair spilled free. Pain shone in her large blue eyes.

Nay, this was not Leila. This young girl was Ena. His sister.

Panic locked around his heart and gripped its erratic pounding in a vice. Suddenly, he was a scared boy again, tucked up beneath the cabinets with his hand pressed over his ears to block out the screams. Ena was crying for him. He had to go to Ena. To save her. Because he had not been able to save anyone else.

"Ena, I—"

"Behind you," she said in a weak voice.

He had to save her. He *must*.

Gingerly, he set her down. He exploded upward while swinging his axe with all the power of his roiling emotions–the blaze of rage and the enormity of his fear. The man fell amid a spray of blood.

Bran stood over the dark-haired girl, his breath coming in great huffs, while his blood pounded molten through his veins. Men continued to come, and he continued to fight.

The rain had started once more in a heavy downpour that stung at his eyes and made him blink hard to clear his vision. Still, on he fought, until a cry sounded from the castle and the Graham men eased back, defeated.

They had won.

And yet it was a sad victory when faced with so much loss.

The fight dropped out of Bran and he crashed to his knees at Ena's side. His body was heavy with exhaustion. He pushed aside the pain. It was not uncommon to receive flesh wounds in battle. Nor was it rare to be so tired.

Nay, mayhap not this tired. His eyes began to close. He wanted to lay his head in the dirt and sleep.

But he could not.

Ena.

He said her name aloud and her eyes fluttered open. Blue. Not brown. Confusion prickled through him. Not Ena's eyes.

He scooped her into his arms, trying as hard as he could to be mindful of her wounds. The arrows lay on the ground, glistening with her blood. Who had taken them out? His thoughts were too slow in his mind, muddy as they swirled in a fog of confusion.

"We must get her to safety." A blonde woman reached for Ena.

Bran stared at the woman, this stranger who sought to take his sister. His body turned to protectively block Ena from the woman, to ensure his sister could not be taken from his arms. "I'll kill ye if ye touch her."

She looked behind her, where the Graham soldiers had run. How long had passed since they had been there? Damn it, he could not keep his thoughts in one place.

"We may not have enough time." Worry creased her brow, but she was still beautiful. Familiar?

Damn but he couldn't think.

"We must go now, and you can hardly stand." She gestured to him and her eyes flashed.

Of course, he could stand. He hugged Ena more tightly to him. The blonde woman cursed and grabbed the padding of his gambeson and dragged him forward. His legs were weighted and awkward. He stumbled and caught himself, only to stumble once more.

"Anice, take Leila. Bran, come with me." She spoke with authority, a leader.

Another woman who looked much like the one who gave the order snatched Ena out of his arms with a warning look in her eye. The air vibrated with danger and the stench of congealing blood hovered around him. It clogged his throat and nose and left his head spinning. The authoritative woman pushed at him to walk.

"If we don't get to the horses, we're dead." She pulled at him, but his steps were clumsy and too slow to move.

His feet met the uneven surface of the dead, their stares vacant, their faces like cold marble chiseled into masks of horror. The odor of blood was so thick, it seemed to coat the back of his tongue with its coppery tang. His mouth filled with water and his stomach wrenched into his throat. The woman didn't stop tugging at him.

Marin.

The name slid into the swirling mess of his thoughts. "Marin."

"Aye," the woman confirmed. "And you're Bran, and that is Leila, not Ena."

His gaze moved to the three blonde young women running ahead, one with a black-haired girl in her arms.

Ena.

His heart lurched and he quickened his pace. He had to get to her. He had to save her.

"Bran." Marin's voice was gentle with something he didn't recognize, something he didn't like. Pity? "Bran, what ails you?"

"Where is Ena?" His words slurred together, his tongue too thick and uncooperative in his mouth.

Marin merely looked at him but did not answer.

His heart pounded faster. Where was Ena? Was she dead?

"Where is she?" He pulled his hand from Marin's.

By God, he could not lose Ena. She was all he had left.

Marin glanced behind him and the muscles at her neck tensed. "She's just ahead. Don't you see her?"

Bran followed her gaze to where the dark-haired girl was being handed to a woman on horseback. Ena's name choked in the back of his throat.

He ran forward then, as fast as his stubborn legs could take him, running with the urgency he'd suppressed before. His aware-ness waned and threatened to wink out, but still he ran. He continued on until his body had nothing left to give, and the ground rushed up to meet him.

Ena.

MARIN STARED DOWN AT BRAN'S UNMOVING FORM. THE Graham reinforcements who charged from the castle were gaining on them. If she did not get everyone out soon, they would all be massacred.

She could leave him, of course. He might already be dead after the knock he'd taken to his skull. And yet every one of her sisters and a handful of her men had survived because of him. He'd fought like a beast, tearing through scores of Graham reivers, hovering over Leila protectively and keeping her from the worst of the melee that might have otherwise killed her in her weakened state.

Marin fixed her stare on Sir Richard, who limped several paces behind her. "Have our two strongest, uninjured men get him to a horse, and quickly."

If her captain of the guard questioned her orders, it did not show on his face. Sir Richard nodded, and pulled two men forward. Drake had been assisting Marin's sisters, but stopped and took the place of one of the men.

Marin stood by Bran's side with her blade in her hand as he was carted to the nearest horse. Drake nodded in gratitude as he passed, his mouth set in a grim line as he helped Bran to safety. All around them, Bran's reivers were claiming the horses and abandoning the area. Some did not ride in the direction of Werrick Castle.

Perhaps they thought Bran was dead. Even if they did, the number who abandoned him was not enough to allow Marin the opportunity to seize control of her home once more. Not with the number of men she had lost. And certainly not with her promise to marry Bran.

She suspected many had grown weary of their time at Werrick Castle. A full belly only went so far when one's pockets were not being padded with coin.

Sir Richard waited by her side until Bran was put onto a horse with Drake. An arrow shot from somewhere unseen and sank into the earth between them.

The Grahams were too close. It was time to go whether they were ready or not. Drake nodded and took off with Bran secured on the horse with him. Sir Richard and Marin urged their horses onward but remained at the rear of the band of her father's soldiers and Bran's reivers. They rode as hard from battle as they'd ridden into it, both man and beast sweating with the effort to avoid the storm of Graham fighters thundering at their heels.

There were so few soldiers ahead of them. Leila slumped limp against Anice, with Piquette running to keep up with the horses. Marin's heart clenched. Ella and Cat's horses remained close to Anice; their concern echoed by their proximity to their fallen sister. She'd come so close to losing them all. And so many men had been slain.

They had yet to assess those killed today, but she knew the number would be significant to her small force. She gritted her teeth against the icy wind pelting her face with shards of rain and wished she could equally stand up to tearing pain within.

"They've gone, my lady," Sir Richard shouted over the wind.

She whipped her head to peer behind her. The Grahams were in the distance, their horses turned back in the direction of Mabrick. Apparently, they had decided the chase was not worth it with their stolen castle now secure.

Tears burned in her eyes and leaked hot at the corners. She angrily wiped them away before Sir Richard could see and sniffed hard. Her face was chaffed from the wind, as raw outside as she was on the inside.

She slowed their horses to a canter, as did the soldiers and reivers in front of them. All but Anice and Drake, who continued to sprint onward to get Leila and Bran to the healer with haste.

Marin gasped for breath, her heart still going too fast. Beneath her legs, her horse's sides swelled in and out as he attempted to catch his breath as well. It had been close for all of them.

"Richard, I..." Marin's words choked off as tears threatened to overwhelm her. Instead, she took a moment and looked down at her hands. She'd lost her gloves in the fray and her fingers had gone pink with bitter cold beneath the stains of fresh blood. "I'm sorry I sent you to Mabrick. All of you. I didn't know." Her words broke again, and she shook her head in an attempt to clear the ache from her throat.

The lines of Sir Richard's brow deepened. "You couldn't possibly have known, my lady."

Marin offered a distracted nod, unconvinced. Her father always seemed to know what was safe, and what was treacherous. It was a skill she had not yet had the opportunity to master. Her limited experience had incurred a steep cost.

How she missed him, and longed for him to be home, to have made all these decisions instead of her.

"Do you think enough of Bran's men have abandoned him?" Sir Richard nodded to Drake's horse in the distance ahead of them.

Her sigh billowed white in front of her face for a split second before being torn away by the wind. "Even if they did, retaking the castle isn't possible." Marin's heart slid lower in her chest by the tug of regret. "I made an agreement."

"To save them." Sir Richard regarded her sisters.

She nodded.

"Your father will be proud of you, my lady."

The captain of the guard always had encouraged her at her lower moments, except this time she couldn't tolerate Sir Richard's praise. Not with everything she was giving up. For what would her father do when he returned from war and found his castle belonging to a marauder? And that Marin had married him?

She merely nodded, unable to speak, unable to quell the gnawing unease in her stomach. Bran had been limp where he lay against Drake before they rode ahead. In truth, Bran might not live through the remainder of the journey back to the castle.

And she would have nothing to uphold if he was dead.

❧ 13 ❧

Marin ran through the halls of the castle to where Leila shared chambers with the other three sisters. Bran's men did not stop her. In fact, many of his men had left the castle after seeing him in such an injured state.

Bran was alive from what she'd heard, but his head wound had left him confused and disoriented. Marin had ordered him sent to the healer and would check on him later. But first she had to see to Leila, to know she was safe.

Marin entered the room and found Anice standing over where Leila's small form lay in bed with Piquette on the floor by the foot of the bed. Anice looked up, tears bright in her eyes.

"How is she?" Marin asked, even as she made her own assessment of their youngest sister's pale face.

"Fortunate." Anice spun the delicate ruby ring on her finger. Their mother had given it to her for her namesake day before the castle had been taken. It served to remind those who could remember of better times.

"The arrow stuck fast into a rib, and the other in her arm, and will cause some discomfort." Anice's voice choked off. She swallowed and continued. "Isla says Leila will need several days of rest but will otherwise be fine."

Marin's throat went tight with the threat of tears. She settled her hand on Leila's small cheek. The littlest of her sisters did not register the caress, but the warmth of her skin against Marin's palm was sufficient reassurance.

"Isla gave her a tea to help her sleep," Anice said.

Marin nodded, unable to break her gaze from Leila's precious face. Their healer had extraordinary skills, and never was Marin more grateful for those skills than now.

Leila's long dark lashes fanned down over pale cheeks. She had the pert nose of their mother and her deep blue eyes, but that was where the similarities ended. Marin's mind flinched away from any further thoughts of Leila's appearance, the way all the sisters did in avoidance of such thoughts.

"She saw my death." Anice's whisper was threaded with anguish. "She said she knew if she did not block those arrows, I would have died." Piquette issued forth a whine and shifted on the floor, as if understanding his mistress' words.

Marin glanced up at Anice in time to see the tears run down her cheeks.

"She thought to sacrifice herself to save me." Anice's voice broke on a sob. Piquette leapt to his feet and was immediately at her side, his great muzzle bumping into her palm.

Marin opened her arms and Anice ran to her with the large dog in tow, the way she had done so often after their mother died. Anice tucked her face into Marin's shoulder and her back jerked with the force of her sobs.

Marin offered soothing shushes and rubbed small circles over her sister's back until the worst of her weeping had ceased. All the while, Piquette wriggled his tail nervously and pressed his massive body against the two of them, almost knocking them over in his clumsy attempt to comfort.

In truth, it was hardest to console in times such as these,

when Marin's own heart was breaking. Little Leila's near-sacrifice had been so altruistic, one of incredible generosity and love. And yet they had almost lost her. For a child of only ten, she was selfless when it came to those she loved—mayhap to a fault.

"Leila will be fine," Marin said resolutely, as much for herself as for Anice. "And you are alive, my beautiful sister."

Anice pulled away from Marin and wiped at her red-rimmed eyes. Even after having cried, Anice was still lovely.

"Marin, I was so scared." She shook her head. "If Bran and his reivers had not arrived, I do not think..." She sucked in a pained breath and did not finish the sentence they both knew the answer to. "Why did Bran come? Are his hostages worth so much? And where had you gone?"

Marin's heart sank low into her belly. "I'd gone to kill him. I intended to secure our castle into our possession without risking anyone else. When I found out the Grahams had Mabrick, I asked him for help." She tried to keep her head lifted, to stand by her decision made in a moment of desperation. For soon she would be honoring her vow.

"And he did?" Anice ran her fingers through Piquette's hair. "Why?"

"I promised to marry him."

Anice's eyes went wide. "You did what?" She spoke too sharply, and Leila stirred on the bed. "Marin, say it isn't so," she said in a whisper.

"He needs the cooperation of the castle to hold it. I promised to marry him, and to convince the people to allow him to stay in peace without trying to kill him. He feels he has always been at the mercy of rich men." She hesitated. "I also had to vow to cease my attempts to kill him."

"What of Papa?" Anice put her hand over her mouth. "Will he be barred from entering his own home?"

Marin's eyes prickled with wet heat and she knew tears would soon be upon her once more. It was true. After all her father had taught her, after everything he'd entrusted her with, she had completely, ultimately and horrendously failed.

"If Bran and his men hadn't come, you would all be dead." Marin drew in a shaking breath. "I could not lose all of you."

"Oh, Marin." Anice gazed at her with such sadness, it cut into the quick of Marin's heart. "You gave up everything."

Though they hadn't been meant to be cruel, Anice's words hit Marin like a slap.

The angry emotion thickened into a knot in Marin's throat. At her helplessness, at her choice, at her perceived loss carved so evidently on Anice's face. But Marin refused to allow her sister to know how much the statement hurt.

Marin had to appear strong, the way she always did, especially when they had already experienced so much sorrow and strife.

Piquette nudged his cold nose against Marin's palm, a mute offering of comfort that nearly undid her control.

"I will be back to check on Leila later." Marin made her way to the door to keep Anice from seeing any of her hurt.

"I will remain by her side." Anice's vow of loyalty plunged the dagger of agony deeper into Marin's soul. After all, it was Marin's fault Leila had been wounded. It ought to be Marin who remained in vigil.

She closed her eyes and a hot tear rolled down her cheek. There was nothing she wanted to do more than stay in this room she had shared with her sisters in the years after their mother's death, with its walls painted with red and gold whorls, and various dressing tables. She wanted to curl against Leila on the bed as she'd done when they were children, to watch the rise and fall of her breathing, to be perpetually reassured Leila would live.

But as mistress and master of the castle, Marin had too many obligations to handle. She had soldiers to see to, lives lost to pray over, and a man to tend to—a man who would soon become her husband if he lived.

Nay, she could not linger. She had to endure the emotional torment of her decisions, even when she was so close to breaking.

⚜

BRAN WRAPPED HIS ARMS AROUND HIS LEGS, DRAWING THEM MORE tightly to his stomach. The men shouted and threw a chair across the room, where it clattered against the wall of their simple home. The men were angry; even Bran could see that through the cracked door in the cabinet. Their faces were red and snarling beneath the limp chainmail coifs drawn over their heads.

One of them stalked over to the table.

Bran's heart nearly beat out from his chest.

Ena was under that table.

She put her hands over her head and shrunk down, as if she might be able to make herself blend into the floor below. Bran scrunched lower in his own hiding place.

They couldn't find her. They couldn't—

The man threw the table on its side and Ena screamed. A long, high pitched note that pierced Bran's soul.

She ran, but the man caught her by the hair and jerked her back. Mum came out from where she was hiding behind a small trunk, her hair wild and her eyes wide with fear, with Gregor leaping in front of her.

Gregor, the brave elder brother with their father's sword in his hand, though it was nearly as tall as he.

"No' my child," Mum cried. "Take me but leave my child."

The man gave a snarling grin in reply and drew back his blade.

The sharp, wet scent of brewing herbs pulled at Bran. Jars clinked together and the subtle pop and hiss of a fire sounded in the background. Beneath him was the downy thickness of a feather bed, and smooth fine linens. Despite the luxuries of heat and bedding, his body was in hell.

His head thundered with agony. He shifted slightly and the room dipped into a dizzying spin.

"That's enough out of ye." An older woman's voice spoke over him. "Drink this. It'll ease the need to purge yerself again."

Again? Had he been ill?

"How is he?" the voice was a new one, feminine and familiar. *Marin.*

"He isna doing well, my lady," the healer replied.

"I'll give that to him." Marin's voice was closer now.

He opened his eyes and the brilliance of the firelight seared into his skull. He winced back.

"You need to drink this," Marin said. The bed shifted slightly on his right and he knew she settled herself beside him. The clean scent of lavender drifted toward him like a cooling balm. He breathed it in and some of the tension drained from his stiff muscles.

The whoosh of a breath exhaling sounded several times. He cracked an eye open and looked up to find Marin next to him, gently blowing onto a steaming mug of tea.

"Come now." She eased a hand behind him and helped him sit forward.

His side pinched at the simple action and dizziness caught him in a swirling grip. He grunted, unable to even warn her he might retch.

Marin's hand was firm behind him. "Lean against me, Bran. I am stronger than I look."

"I know," he ground out.

"At least you haven't fully lost your senses." There was a smile in her voice, and it was as beautiful as she.

A cup pressed to his mouth.

"Drink," she said. "It should not be too hot."

Obediently, he opened his lips and the liquid poured into his mouth. As promised, the temperature was comfortable. Warm and appeasing on his dry throat. It quelled a ragged thirst he did not know he possessed, and he drank it until there was naught left.

Marin settled him back against the bed, and her fingers swept over his brow. A pleasant, heated glow followed the graze of her skin over his. He wanted to turn into her touch, to encourage more.

The bed shifted again, and the welcome presence of her body left his side. He wanted her back beside him. He craved her gentle voice as much as he did more of her delicate caresses.

The pull of sleep grew stronger. It wrapped around him in a cradled embrace and dragged him toward the temptation of oblivion. And yet the vestiges of his nightmare hovered at the edge of consciousness, ragged and raw. Ena.

Ena.

"Ena." He spoke without meaning to.

Marin was at his side once more, her delicate hand set atop his. "She is well. The arrow missed her heart. She is resting now."

"My lady, do ye speak of Leila?" The healer's voice sounded distant.

He'd begun to relax at Marin's words, but the healer jarred him in his confusion.

There was a pause, then Marin continued. "Ena is well, Bran. She is abed resting but will heal." Something cool stroked over his face, and her perfume of lavender water washed over him as surely as did the need to sleep.

"Rest," she breathed in a whisper.

The tension drained from his body as if by magic and he floated toward the deep darkness of sleep with the knowledge Ena was safe.

"Will he live?" Marin spoke low in a volume meant to not be heard by others.

Bran roused back to awareness once more, his ears straining around the thickness of his jumbled thoughts.

"Aye, he'll live." The healer's voice was just as quiet. "He's got a few cuts. I wager he's had worse by the look of him. But it's the knock to the head that's got him addled. He'll be well upon the morrow when he's had a fine bit of sleep."

There was a click of something glass set atop a hard surface, followed by silence.

He'd almost thought the conversation was done when the healer spoke again, so discreetly he wouldn't have heard her had he not been straining. "He doesna have to recover, my lady." The simple words were heavy with a suffocating implication.

Marin did not respond. Her lack of a reply pressed upon him, crushing at his rapidly beating heart.

"I could poison him," the healer whispered. "A mix of herbs and no one would be the wiser."

"You mean to say," Marin said slowly. "You would kill him?"

"Aye."

Marin's answer did not come readily, and with that great hesitation, Bran was sure he knew her choice.

❧ 14 ❧

Poisoning Bran would be such an easy solution. A lightness filled Marin at how many problems his death would alleviate. Her father would not need to fight for his home upon returning from battle, peace would be restored through the castle and Marin could remain unwed and free. She gazed at the man lying abed, his face peaceful with sleep.

Her mind still echoed with the pained way he'd called out for Ena. Whoever the girl was, or had been, it was obvious she meant a great deal to him. Somehow, she imagined that affection was part of the reason he'd agreed to help her rescue her sisters.

He had risked his own life and the lives and loyalty of his men. Even after she had betrayed him, even after she had returned with the intent to kill him. He had protected her in battle, and he'd saved Leila from certain death.

She could not bring herself to give the order to have him poisoned, not when he had spared her from so much loss.

"Nay," Marin answered Isla finally. She pulled in a breath for fortitude. If she were to keep him alive, she needed to uphold their agreement—not only marry him, but to put forth a credible performance that their union was one she wanted.

"He will live," Marin said. "And once he has fully recovered, we will marry."

"Marry?" Isla chuckled with incredulity, flashing her impossibly white teeth. It was whispered that they had been taken from the mouths of the dead. A distasteful rumor, but then there were many surrounding the aged healer.

"Aye." Marin glanced once more to Bran's sleeping form. He lay on his back with his hands folded peacefully over his flat stomach.

She needed to convince her people that their union was what she truly wanted. Otherwise the effort would be for naught.

The healer squinted with skepticism and she gave a little grunt. "Him?"

"Of course." Marin was not doing well with this. "He is a much better man than he seems." She almost winced at how bad her attempt sounded. "That is to say, he is…"

This was far more difficult than she had anticipated, but she must be more genuine. If she couldn't fool one old woman, how could she convince an entire castle?

She pulled her lower lip into her mouth and remembered his kiss, how his mouth had set her aflame.

What other good attributes had he that she could elaborate on?

"He is brave," she said sincerely. "He saved my sisters and our soldiers. None of them would have returned had he not agreed to help. And he is a fierce warrior. I…care for him." She stumbled over the last part, unable to say she loved him. Surely caring was sufficient.

Isla regarded Bran with consideration. "He's a fine-looking man, I'll give ye that. Wrought with hard muscle and easy on the eyes. Other bits of him are nay so bad either." She winked. "Ye could do far worse than the likes of him for certes."

Marin's cheeks heated and she breathed a discreet sigh of relief.

The older woman patted Marin gently on the face. Her withered fingers were dry and held the clean scents of sage and meadowsweet. "Dinna ye fash, lass. I'll have yer man well enough to give ye a worthy wedding night, aye?" She issued forth a cackling laugh and shooed Marin from the room.

Marin said nothing as she was pushed out the door, grateful to be free of the awkward conversation. Isla had been fooled, but Marin would need to improve on her earnest declarations of affection if she was going to sway the castle into believing she truly wished to marry Bran. Part of that lie would involve visiting him daily while he recovered, sitting by him with care and affected fondness.

And so it was that Marin found herself going often between Leila's bedside and Bran's. Leila had healed quickly with the resiliency of youth and was sitting up within days of receiving her injuries, smiling and nodding as Cat chattered on about all Leila had missed.

And so it was that Marin remained at Bran's sleeping form for hours on end in an effort to play the part of the doting betrothed.

The days were mind-numbingly dull. She found herself speaking to him as she stitched silk embroidery over a fine new gown she was making for Leila, or reading to him from one of the ornately decorated books from the solar. She even took to going over accounts and replying to correspondence while in the confines of his room. None of the missives received had been from her father as yet, though it was common for him to be unable to reply on his missions with the king.

Never had she been more grateful for his lack of communication.

Oftentimes, Bixby kept them both company from where he curled up along Bran's sleeping body and watched Marin as she read.

Her time was not all spent attending Bran as he slept, though it was the larger part of it. She also helped feed him the drinking broth Nan sent up from the kitchens when he was awake, fortified with cattle bones and goose fat. She saw to his medicine to ensure he took what was needed without fail, and she swept a cool cloth over his face before and after his meager meals.

Isla was there to do most of the other things he needed, things she insisted Marin not have to deal with, like bathing his body and seeing his clothing changed. Though in truth, Marin harbored a suspicion the older woman found much enjoyment in those tasks.

Regardless, it was in those respites where Marin found herself seeing to the wounded soldiers, all of whom were recovering well. They had lost twenty-eight men in the attack. More than half of their remaining force. In truth, having Bran as Marin's husband would be beneficial in affording her more troops to stand guard. As long as the reivers could remain loyal.

His man, Drake, came to visit Bran daily, despite his newfound wealth. A man without loyalty would have taken the treasure and never returned. Yet the man came every day with concern bright in his dark eyes.

Marin took care to visit with Bran's men as well, to make certain they received proper treatment for their wounds and were fed well enough. She even went so far as to speak with Drake regularly to confirm the men had all they needed.

It was not until the fourth day that Marin found Bran sitting up in his bed, his gaze fixed on the fire in the hearth. She stopped short when she entered and held her book close to her chest. She had intended to read it aloud, not necessarily for his benefit, but to fill the gaps of empty silence.

His stare shifted mutely from the hearth to her and her heart gave an unexpected little squeeze. Bran was awake. Which meant soon she would have to make good on her vow and marry him.

BRAN'S GAZE LINGERED OVER MARIN. SHE CLUTCHED A BLUE bejeweled book in her arms, the encrusted volume nearly large enough to cover her whole chest. Her purple gown had been trimmed in black fur and called to attention the dark smudges under her eyes.

"You're awake." The sweet sound of her voice pulled at his memories, of the ebb and flow of her speaking to him as he lay in recovery.

There had been pieces of stories and the whisper of parchment pages turning. Other times there had been mention of tales from her youth with her sisters and her father and even some of her mother, all fractured through moments of sleep. And yet all had been told in her beautiful, soothing tone.

"Aye, I woke this morning." Bran's voice came out craggy from disuse.

She nodded and swept into the room as though she hadn't stalled in the entryway at all. "And are you feeling well?" She set aside her book and handed him a glass of ale, which he drank gratefully.

The cool liquid glided down his throat and eased the rasping dryness. His body was in good enough repair, with the wounds not giving him much trouble. Apparently, the arrow he'd thought had glanced off him had actually grazed the skin, and a slash at his side had left a wee bit of a mark. Both were nothing more than pink scars now. Even his head had finally stopped aching, which had brought about the clarity of his mind, and the memory of his family's fate on that fateful night.

For during those blurry days of his recovery, when he had been worried after his family, they had been alive. At least, to him. Now, awake, he knew they were merely distorted memories. Ena lived, but she was not safe, while Mum and Gregor...

The realization plunged into his heart as sure as any dagger. He had lost them. Again.

"I'm well enough," he answered simply. "I was told ye'd be by today. That ye've been by me every day."

She approached his bed and turned abruptly to examine a neat row of bottles set along the back of his bedside table. "I wanted to be certain you were well." Her fingers plucked at various bottles, unstopping them and plugging them up once more after a brief sniff.

No longer without his wits, he was well aware of what her options had been with him ill. He knew also how much easier her life would be with him conveniently absent. There had even been a dream somewhere in the fog of his memory of her being asked if she would like him dead.

"Why would ye check on me?" he asked.

She gave a surreptitious glance around the room, then leaned forward over the bed. Her unbound hair fell around her shoulders like a gilded cape and draped over the bed sheets, a mere inch from his hand. He wanted to lift his forefinger and stroke the silkiness of the cool golden strands.

"It's part of the facade," she said levelly. "To safeguard the acceptance of our marriage."

The delicate scent of her enveloped him like an embrace, reminding him of her soothing touches and tenderly spoken words.

"Ye're standing by yer word then?" He eyed her, half-expecting her to change her mind.

"As you held by yours." She inclined her head graciously.

A knock sounded at the door and Marin pulled away. Bran feared it might be the healer, come to take Marin's place to see to his bathing and the changing of his clothing and the sheets. He waited in bed, unable to see the visitor from around the door, helpless.

Agitation rippled through his restless limbs. He'd been abed too long, treated as an invalid. He was trapped, cared for, like some silly bird in a cage, and it rankled him.

Marin returned with a tray in her hands and the door shut behind her. "I've asked the kitchen to bring you some bread to go with your broth." She said it as though she thought he might be glad for the bowl of clear liquid.

"I could do with a hunk of venison and some ale," he offered irritably.

She ignored him and sat on the chair beside the bed. He'd noticed it earlier and had wondered if that was where she'd bided her time with him. She held the bowl in her palms and gently blew at the steaming broth. The steady rise of steam broke in quivers that resumed between her breaths.

"I dinna need ye to care for me like a child." He held out his hand for the soup. "Ye'll do anything for yer sisters, it would appear. Even feed me."

"You certainly were easier to care for when you were sleeping." She set the bowl into his waiting hand.

Bran put his lips to the bowl and drank the broth. It splashed over his tongue like molten lava. He swallowed fast and got the sting of it at the back of his throat for his efforts. His entire mouth was prickly and thick with the effects of the burn.

"Who is Ena?" she asked. "And Gregor?"

His heart caught and he lowered the bowl from his mouth. The broth churned in his stomach and soured. "Gregor is dead." He stared down at the murky brown broth.

"And your mother?"

"Dead.

"Ena?"

"Alive. For now." He lifted the bowl and drained the rest in one burning swallow before handing it back to Marin.

Marin took it from him. "Loss is by far the most painful of all wounds."

Words spoken by one who understood. His renewed grief cut him to the quick. As sharp and poignant as it had been twenty years ago.

She set the bowl on the tray with a clink. "What happened?" she asked. Her voice was kind, the way it'd been when he was ill, when she'd cared for him.

She leaned on her knees. So wonderfully near. She focused her full attention on him. "Tell me what happened."

Mayhap it was the comfort of her voice, or his addled state, or even the pressing guilt for having taken the castle in the first place, but he found himself ready to tell his story for the first time in his life.

❧ 15 ❧

Regardless of what had triggered his need to speak, Bran found the memories rising inside him and bared them before Marin for her mercy.

He welcomed the angry, frustrated rage firing through him. It was an easier emotion to handle than the ugliness of his hurt. He couldn't fall prey to such pain. Not again.

"I know Leila is not Ena," he said.

Marin nodded.

"Ena was the same age, with the same long dark hair..." Brown eyes surfaced in his mind, doe-like and dark, fringed with long lashes. "She doesna have blue eyes like Leila. The hit to my head knocked my wits about." He put his hand to the back of his skull in demonstration and found his scalp still sensitive.

Marin leaned forward to rest both elbows on her knees, as if she needed to be as close as he yearned for her to be. "Who is Ena?"

"My sister." His voice was gravelly with disuse, from the ragged pain of his loss.

"And Gregor?"

The pain of that name tore a fresh rawness in Bran's heart. "My brother."

"Will you tell me what happened?" Marin's request was equally as kind and calm as her expression—an invitation, but not in any way a demand.

"I was still a lad, the youngest of the three of us." He drew in a deep breath, but it did not ease the band of tension squeezing at his chest. "We lived on the border as ye do now, but we didna have yer wealth. We didna have yer stone castle and yer guards. We were villagers, with homes that barely kept out the wind, let alone reivers, and with walls thin enough for us to hear them coming."

A scream rang out in the dusk and immediately cut off. Mum edged toward the door and brought down the latch over the frame, a meager means of protection. "Hide."

Another scream rent the air, this one longer, tinged with anguish. And far closer. Bran didn't move. He stared, watching the door, uncertain where to go. What to do.

"Now," Mum hissed.

Gregor, the eldest of the three of them, grabbed the sword their da had used before he died. "I'll protect us, Mum."

"Nay." She reached for the sword. "They'll kill ye."

Bran looked to Ena, the way he always did in times of crisis. She always knew what to do. Her arms closed around Bran, enveloping him in safety.

She gave him a reassuring smile and pulled at him. "The cupboards are safest."

She tucked him into the darkness within, but he reached out to her.

"There's only room for one, sweet Bran." She stroked his hair and kissed his brow. "All will be well."

A thump sounded at the door and her eyes went wide.

Mum hid on the opposite side of the cupboard, buried in the shadows. Near him. He knew she'd done that for him, to make him feel safe. Gregor was at her side, sword in hand. Brave Gregor, who was ready to defend them all.

Ena ran to the center of the room and stood for one panicked moment. Time crawled to stillness then, in the hissing pop of the fire and the distant cries of loss and pain. Ena dove under the table just as the door flew open in an explosion of splintered wood.

"Ena hid me, then went under the table," he said around the rawness—of his throat, of his memories, of his heart. "My mum and older brother had hidden near me to ensure I'd be safe." Bran balled his fists. The action echoed in a light sting on his shoulder where the arrow had nicked him days before. He reveled in the physical pain, even wished it was more, anything to distract from the blaze in his chest. "Four of them came in, broke through the door as though it were nothing. They threw the furniture about in their search for food, coin, whatever they could take. Then they flipped the table and saw Ena."

Marin pulled in a hard breath.

Bran dragged his gaze from her, unable to bear her sympathy. "Ena tried to run, but they grabbed her by her hair and yanked her back. They pulled out their swords, ready to run her through. My mum came from her hiding place, screaming, and Gregor was there too, running toward them with that damn sword."

His mother's voice cut through his mind, filled with terror.

No' my bairn.

No' my bairn.

He shuddered. "Gregor stabbed one in the neck and the man fell. Two reivers caught him and held him down while the third ran him through. He'd only seen eight summers, still a lad." He hesitated, trying to ward off the memory and falling prey to its clutches regardless. "My mum was next, and then Ena."

The blade shoved through Gregor's skinny chest and he dropped like a sack. Mum's screams were like an animal, feral and wild with grief before they too cut off with a choked cry.

Bran's hair stood on end and he buried his face in his knees to keep from seeing anymore. He wished he could close his ears too, to keep out the sounds of Ena's cries, of how she struggled.

Bran stared at the coverlet of the bed, where a wrinkle in the fabric shaded the other side. "I waited a long time before I came out and that's when I found them all. Ena was still alive, only barely. And so, I did what I could to care for her."

The shame of it all pressed hard on him, the way it always did when he thought of that day. Deep, burning shame for having been the cause of their deaths. If he hadn't frozen, Ena would have hidden better. If his mother hadn't thought he needed protection, she and Gregor would have as well. They would have both been alive.

"Ena lived." He swallowed. "But it took several days before she was strong enough to leave."

"You stayed with their bodies?" she asked softly.

Their bodies. Those of his mother and brother. He nodded. "Aye. I didn't want to leave them, but I couldn't bury them. I was too small." *Too weak.* "Leaving them was hard. It made their deaths so real."

"I understand." She eased from the chair and settled on the bed beside him, the way she'd done when she was nursing him through his wounds. "I struggled with the finality of it all when my mother died."

He wanted to curl against her and breathe in her sweet, soothing scent, to sweep away these awful memories. Hell, he didn't know why he was telling her now. For a cathartic cleansing of his soul?

"When I got hit on the head." He looked down at the coverlet where their hands were nearly touching. How he craved the brush of her smooth skin, the connection to keep him grounded through the awful reliving of his worst moment. "It brought me back to when I was caring for Ena."

She reached up and put her palm to his cheek. This time he did give in to the temptation to lean into her. He put his hand over hers and cradled her against him. He allowed himself one perfectly wondrous moment to savor it before lowering her hand and easing back.

He was being weak, he knew. The pressure of the past fortnight had built around him: Ena's marriage to the Englishman when the rule preventing English and Scottish from marrying was always broken before without consequence. The Middle March Warden using it to his advantage and stringing up a rope to kill her. The bloody bargain Bran had been forced to accept so that she might live. The warden had been looking for an excuse for years to get Bran to work for him. Ena had provided him with the perfect opportunity. And now here Bran was, pouring out his soul to the woman whose castle he'd taken.

He scrubbed a hand over the thickness of his untrimmed beard, as if he could clear the sensation of her caress. And how much he wanted more. "I shouldna have told ye any of this."

A sad smile flickered at the corners of her mouth. "Everyone needs someone to need, even the strongest of us."

"I dinna need anyone." He said it gruffly, as though it might mask the exposed underbelly of his buried hurt, as if a brawny display could overwhelm his vulnerability.

"Why did you tell me?" she asked.

He shrugged, but deep down he realized he knew the answer he would never say. The considerate sweetness of her care had aided in the healing of his physical wounds. Foolish though it may be, he'd hoped she might likewise do the same for his soul.

TRUST WAS A PRECARIOUS THING, AND SOMEHOW IT HAD BEGUN to spin between Marin and Bran like a delicate web with thin, fragile threads.

Mayhap she ought to rein in her curiosity, but she could not. This intimidating man with his wild ruggedness had been a wounded boy forced to witness the violence and brutality at an even younger age than she. She didn't need to ask to know it was not a story he'd shared often. The way it had rasped from his throat, as though wrenched from a buried darkness. Mayhap he had never shared it at all.

"Why did you share with me?" She wanted to reach for him again, to cup the rasp of his beard against her palm. But the way he turned from her told her he did not wish her comfort.

"Ye're to be my wife," he answered, and shrugged as if what he'd done were no large matter. "Ye should know."

Aye, he would be her husband. This man who had stolen her castle and then helped her save her sisters. This man whose family was destroyed by reivers before becoming one himself. This man who had been a broken boy.

And she would be his wife. After years of being allowed to cast aside suitors, to focus her efforts on her sisters and weapons mastery and the upkeep of the manor, finally she would succumb to marriage—the one thing she never wanted.

Already her roles stretched her in so many directions between her father's people, the castle itself and her sisters. How could she possibly make time to be a wife?

There would never be enough light in a day to see to everything and everyone reliant on her.

The idea of a child slipped into her mind and glowed within her chest. A child of her own cradled to her breast... An ache blossomed where she'd imagined the babe, a desperate, deep pang she had told no one of. After all, how foolish to not wish to marry and yet crave a child so.

Bran's dark gaze searched her eyes. He reached up slowly, as if he feared startling her. His fingertips gently stroked over her cheek and down her jaw, the touch light and tender. "I'll be the most envied man in all the land."

Marin did not move from the caress. "Because you'll have Werrick Castle?"

"Because I'll have ye." He let his hand drop, but the intimacy of his gaze did not diminish. As if he still touched her through the intensity of his stare.

Her cheeks went hot.

"Ye're lovely, Marin," he said simply. "I'm sure ye know as much."

She glanced away. She had never paid any mind to her appearance. Not like Anice, who spent hours using creams and powders and the most foul-smelling concoctions Isla could dream up.

Marin had a care for her looks to the point of ensuring she made her father proud to call her his daughter with her fine clothes and cleanliness. There had been interest from others, but she was the eldest daughter of a powerful earl. Such attentions were to be expected.

Never had she cared if she was considered beautiful. Yet his compliment caused a pleasant twist low in her belly.

"Ye're compassionate and gentle and I like that verra much," he said.

"I assure you that I am not always so gentle." She returned her gaze to him and smirked. "And my compassion is what makes me weak, does it not?"

He tilted his head in silent question.

"It is what caused me to open the portcullis," she reminded him gently.

"Aye, it was." The corner of his mouth lifted in a half-smile that made his face look almost boyish. "But with such attributes to recommend ye, ye're a fine balance for an arse of a man like me."

He grinned at his own statement. He was handsome when he looked at her like that, eyes crinkled, full lips parted to reveal his strong, healthy teeth starkly white against the darkness of his beard. She found her eyes drawn to his mouth, remembering the heat, the sensuality, the way his kisses made her insides melt.

He reached up once more and gently caressed her cheek. The

touch of his skin to hers was barely a brush it was so light. She looked at him, marveling how so powerful a man could have had such a harrowing past. Mayhap almost losing everything was what rendered him so fearless.

She found herself drawing closer to him, pulled by some unseen force. Her mouth connected with his. His lips were as warm as she remembered and far softer. A little sound emerged from the back of her throat at the realization. His hand eased up the nape of her neck and cradled her head. The fierce warrior turned lover.

She parted her mouth and let the tip of her tongue dance against his lips. His tongue grazed hers in reply, salty from the broth and spicy with his own natural flavor. She moaned on an exhale and her body sank against him. He pulled her closer to him with his good arm so the shape of her fitted snugly against him. A hungry heat pulsed between her legs, ignited by the kisses and the solid strength of his body.

"Marin," he said her name on a groan. "I want ye."

A knock sounded at the door and Marin leapt back like a naughty girl caught sneaking a pastry. Indeed, she had been nearly caught and her cheeks singed with the knowledge.

She swept a hand over her skirts where they might have rumpled when her body pressed so flush against his. "I, um, you may enter." Was that a crease? She frowned and bent over the blue silk, her fingers working at the delicate fabric.

Isla entered and looked between Marin and Bran. "Did ye need a few more moments?" A knowing smile lit her face.

"Nay," Marin said far too quickly.

The healer didn't bother to hide her grin. "'Tis time he was fully bathed." She lifted a linen-wrapped parcel from her bag and the yeasty scent of freshly baked bread filled the room. "I brought some bread with me from the kitchens when I heard he was sitting on his own."

Bran sat forward, eyeing the bundle. "I'll take the bread now and can verra well bathe myself, though I prefer to do so in the morning."

"Ye may lose yer balance and injure yerself," Isla said with obvious skepticism.

"I'll be fine." His gaze remained locked on the bread as Isla came closer. "Have a bath sent up tomorrow."

The old healer sighed. "Verra well. If ye think ye're healed enough..."

Bran smiled over at Marin in a way that was far more charming than she cared to admit. "I believe I'm well enough to make good on my promise to make Marin my wife."

"I should go...to check on Leila." Marin stammered through the excuse. "And we truly ought to ensure you are entirely recovered." She edged toward the door to make her escape. From this conversation that felt like it was happening too soon, and from the overwhelming presence of him, of the memory of that kiss.

"'Tis been nearly a week, lass," Bran replied. "I assure ye I'm recovered enough." There was a deepness to his tone, which reverberated through her and made her slow her pace, even as her mind screamed at her feet to move faster.

Isla gave a wheezing laugh. "Ach, ye have a lusty man here, my lady." She winked. "If ye dinna mind my saying so."

"On the morrow," Bran said.

Marin stopped short and turned to him. Her heated blood tangled up her emotions and left the desire in her body warring with the stubbornness of her mind. So, this was why he'd wanted his bath in the morning.

"On the morrow?" She could not keep the nervous pitch from her tone.

"Aye." Bran settled back against the bed with a grin and winked.

Marin stood with her leather soles rooted firmly to the cold stone beneath. It was so soon. Too soon. Her heart pattered into a frenzy and her breath came faster.

"Ach, I've got something to help ye with the pain, my lady."
The healer, obviously mistaking Marin's fears, patted her arm with
good natured reassurance. "It's much better after the first time, I
promise ye."

"Perhaps you ought to help bathe him after all," Marin offered.
"To ensure he is fully clean before our wedding night."

Isla beamed wide enough to show all of her perfectly white
teeth. "With pleasure."

Bran sat a little straighter and threw an incredulous look at
Marin, his face mockingly aghast at her betrayal. She offered him
a playful smirk and slipped from the room. She almost laughed
aloud at the expression he'd cast her way. Almost.

Her mirth faded in the crush of reality.

Her marriage. The very next day. Too soon. Far, far too soon.
Heat blazed in her chest.

She pressed herself to the wall and lay her burning cheek
against the cool stones. It soothed the steady ache in her head
somewhat but did not quell the rapid pounding of her heart. She
wanted to curl up on the floor and let the frustration roiling
inside her break free in an angry howl.

Footsteps rang out just down the hall, men's heavy, bulky
steps. Marin pulled herself from the stonework and rested her
now-cooled hands to her hot brow. She would not be seen by
Bran's men weeping and piteous. Nay, she would rise to this challenge the way she had every other one placed in her path—with
resiliency and strength.

She would fulfill her obligation and marry Bran the following
morning. But first she'd have to tell her sisters.

❧ 16 ❧

First, Marin informed Nan of the impending wedding. While the older woman agreed to her mistress' orders, it was obvious the cook remained skeptical. As were the servants and the guards who had survived their attempt to flee to Mabrick, and everyone else she encountered and told. Putting on a convincing show of her affection for Bran was a difficult task when her own spirit flinched from being forced into marriage.

And yet she could not banish from her mind the image of Bran as a boy, curled into a frightened ball within the cabinet while his family was slaughtered, and then forced to care for his elder sister as they lay for days among their lifeless bodies. The idea of a child enduring such trauma opened a chasm in Marin's chest.

Yet to look at Bran, it was impossible to see him as that boy when the man who intended to marry her was as battle-hardened externally as he was within.

And this man was to be her husband.

The resignation lodged in a stubborn lump in her throat and left her thoughts racing for any possibilities that might bring her freedom. But what could be done before the following day? No matter how many times she cycled through that question, she came up with no viable solutions.

After all, she had given her word.

She stopped in front of her sisters' door after she'd dealt with the staff, knowing if she'd told the girls first, they would try to convince her to recant her vow. And such an idea was far too tempting.

Anice came around the corner urgently with Piquette trailing behind her, his tail nervously tucked low. Her eyes were wide and glossy, as though she was on the verge of tears.

Marin's knees went weak with fear. "Is it Leila?"

Anice shook her head. "She's fine. It's Papa."

Their father had gone to King Edward knowing he might have to go to war. She hadn't told her sisters in the hopes it would not come to him having to fight. Her stomach twisted. "What is it, Anice?"

"He is at Berwick now with the king, and the Scots are threatening to march to Bamburgh to capture the queen." Anice's voice trembled and she pushed a crumpled missive into Marin's hand. "He and Timothy are to fight. Even Geordie if needed."

Marin unfolded the parchment with trembling hands. Her father's squire, Geordie, was only slightly older than Catriona. Certainly not of an age to fight. "We cannot tell our sisters," Marin said. "Especially not Cat."

Anice nodded in agreement and absently reached for Piquette.

Cat had been beside herself at Geordie's departure. Though she kept up her usual cheerfulness, it was easy to see his absence had left its mark on her. The boy acted with the brave determination of a man. Such conviction might be the death of one so young in battle.

The thought ripped into Marin.

She pushed the rumpled parchment to her chest, though it did nothing to still the wild beating of her heart. Her father had seen enough war in his time. But he was the West March Warden for

England, and he was an earl. So, it was his duty, even though there were younger men who could have gone in his place.

She could not help but recall Anice's betrothed. Dear Timothy, who was always chivalrous to a fault. His heart was good, and she hoped it would keep him safe rather than put him to harm.

"Marin, they can't go to war." Anice's lower lip trembled, and suddenly she was not the confident, beautiful sister Marin knew, but the frightened young girl she had once been after their mother's death.

"Father has gone to war before." Marin pulled her sister into her arms. "He will come home to us as he always does. And Timothy is young and strong. He will come out of this a hero, no doubt. In the meantime, we will keep this between us."

Piquette's heavy body pushed against Marin's legs as he tried to join their embrace. Anice allowed herself to be held for a long moment before pushing back. "And when they return home? Will they be able to save us?"

Marin shook her head, uncertain. "I do not know Bran's intentions for the castle, nor do I know if he will allow father and his men in."

Anice took Marin's arm and led her to an alcove. "Will you still marry him?"

Marin glanced to where Piquette sat obediently several feet away. "Aye."

"We need to fight harder to stay together in such terrible times." Anice took her hand. "Tell me what I can do to help."

"I need to make the most of this situation." Marin drew from a well of strength within her, one on the verge of running dry. "Help me convince our people to accept Bran."

"It isn't fair you must marry him. You never wanted to marry-"

"None of this is fair." Marin tried to maintain her own composure. For Anice was correct, it was not fair. Thinking on the awfulness of it all would only serve to crumble Marin's strength, and God knew she needed all she could muster.

Anice nodded with a patience Marin knew to be forced. "When do you wed him?"

Marin sighed, already knowing her sister's reaction before she even answered. "On the morrow."

But Anice did not protest as Marin had expected. Instead she gazed reverently at Marin, her eyes still glossy with tears. "My poor sister." Anice's lips pursed with determination. "We must let Nan know to prepare a feast. Perhaps we ought to have the pickled eel cooked."

Marin held up a hand to stop her sister. "We will save the eel for Father's return, no matter how tumultuous a homecoming it may be." Even if they had to roll the barrel out past the portcullis for him, it would at least be waiting for him when he returned. "The household has been told to make preparations."

The skin around Anice's almond-shaped eyes tensed. "Then we, your sisters, are the last to know of your wedding day?"

"I was afraid if I told you first..."

Anice nodded. "I understand. You are always brave and fearless..." She embraced Marin in a fierce hug. "I have the perfect gown to lend you, and we will rouge your lips and cheeks. You will be the most beautiful bride ever forced to marry in all of Christendom."

Marin smiled against her sister's perfumed hair. Only Anice would think feeling beautiful might somehow set all things to rights. And yet Marin knew it was Anice's way of helping. "Come in with me, for I must inform the others as well."

Anice straightened and offered Marin her hand to hold before the two summoned Piquette and walked into the girls' chambers together. For any challenge was easier to take head-on with her sisters at her side.

BRAN WASN'T SURE HOW A MAN WAS SUPPOSED TO SLEEP THE night before his wedding, but he hadn't slept well. The irony had occurred to him that Ena had been arrested for having married an Englishman, and his marrying an Englishwoman would put them in a better position of power to save her.

True to the old healer's word, a bath was readied for him that morning, and thankfully, Isla had not arrived to assist him. The warm water eased away the remaining stiffness of battle and the deeper ache in his back from laying abed so long. His wounds were doing well and gave him few issues.

He stayed in the water until it began to cool. Bathing like a rich man was yet another luxury he found he could get used to. He stepped from the wooden tub and was just draping a linen around his naked waist when a knock came from the door.

Mayhap it was Marin, come to see him before they were officially wed. Having her find him with only the thin linen about him held great appeal. He could envision her pretty blush even as her eyes dipped low with innocent curiosity. "Enter," he called in an easy voice.

Unfortunately, it was not Marin who stepped through, but Drake. The young reiver pushed the door closed behind him and held out a bundle of cloth. "They want ye to wear this."

Bran lifted a brow. "They?"

"The ladies of the castle."

Bran gave a hum of acknowledgment and came closer, leaving a path of wet footprints.

"Lady Anice mentioned they were the fashion to wear now." Drake draped the items over the back of a chair.

"Ah, Lady Anice." Bran shifted his attention from the clothing to the younger warrior.

Color rose in Drake's cheeks and he assumed a militaristic stance with his hands behind his back, his expression blank.

Bran sifted through the clothing. "I have it on good authority Lady Anice is betrothed."

"Aye, she is." Still Drake's face betrayed nothing.

Bran lifted a pair of dark woolen hose. The fabric was fine, not rough, scratchy wool he was used to, but a tighter, more precise weave that left it soft to the touch. "There willna be much hope with her for ye, lad."

This time Drake fixed his gaze on Bran. "I would never presume, nor attempt to take advantage." He spoke with finality before returning his gaze forward, the soldier once more.

Bran hid his smile at the lad's reaction and fingered a doublet of deep blue. The sisters intended to dress him now, as though he could not be trusted to ready himself for the upcoming ceremony. Apparently, his peasant clothes would not do for a man marrying an earl's daughter.

It was on the edge of his mind to refuse, to show up in his stained gambeson and leather trews. But this was, after all, his wedding. And his first day as a wealthy man. He ran his hand over the woolen hose once more.

"Ye've become quite friendly with the lasses, it would seem," Bran commented.

Drake's mouth twitched at the corners and the determined set of his face relaxed slightly. "The younger ones remind me of my own sisters."

"And if I dinna wear the clothes?" Bran asked not because he intended to refuse the request; he was merely interested in seeing how far the younger man would go to ensure his compliance for the young women.

Drake snapped his head toward Bran. "I was instructed to remind ye that it is yer wedding and fine clothes are expected. And I promise ye, ye willna want to go against their wishes."

"Is that experience talking?"

Drake gave a half-shrug, sufficing as all the answer Bran needed. Never once did Drake have a bad thing to say about his mother or sisters. His father had been an English knight who fell in love with Drake's Scottish mother. When Drake's father died at an early age, the burden of his mother and sister fell on his shoulders, strapped to him by love and obligation, and yet he only spoke of the good in them. In fact, when he did speak of them, his eyes would brighten, as though he appreciated bearing the weight.

"Should I even ask what the ladies are about this morn?" Bran lifted the doublet and found clean linen underclothes.

"They are..." Drake squinted into the distance, as if he might find the words he sought hovering there. "Preparing."

"Preparing." Bran dropped his towel and pulled the linen braies on, securing the belt about his waist. The fabric was of exceptional quality, like the bed sheets, and sat cool and luxurious against his still-damp skin. Likewise, the shirt was of the same fine cloth, and caressed over his flesh as he put it on. Perhaps he did not mind so much having the sisters of Werrick dress him. "Do I wager to guess what their preparations entail?"

Drake's mouth twisted. "Flowers."

Bran paused before sliding the wool hose over his braies. "Flowers."

"Aye." Drake lifted a shoulder in helpless question. "Bits of blue and white." He nodded formally to the doublet on the bed. "To match, so I was told."

Bran tied the hose to the belt. "I trust the ladies of the castle dinna go gather the flowers themselves."

"I would never let them do so." Drake's chest swelled and his expression grew grave with his earnestness.

Bran approached the reiver and eyed him suspiciously. "Have they got ye wrapped about those dainty fingers of theirs?"

Drake's gaze slid right. "Nay."

"Mmm..." Bran turned from his most trusted soldier and picked up the doublet. It was thick wool, yet unlined, as it was not necessary in the summer months. Something at the base of the hem where the fabric would be folded against itself caught his eye. He lifted it closer to examine it and found neat stitching noting M and B entwined together.

It was a simple gesture, but a kind one. While he hadn't anticipated himself being the marrying sort, and he'd never seen himself as a rich man, he found he was anticipating life as Marin's husband. Certainly, he anticipated their wedding night. The thought heated his blood.

"There's something ye should know," Drake said. "While I was gathering the flowers—"

"Ach, ye picked them then?" Bran shot a glance at Drake.

"Some of Graham's men were lingering nearby the castle."

The playfulness fell from Bran's countenance. "How many?"

"We saw four. There were more of us than them, enough to send them back on their way."

Bran slipped his arms into the doublet and fastened it at the waist with a leather belt. "For now."

Drake nodded.

It wasn't good to have the Grahams sniffing about the castle. No doubt they were noting the defenses, planning ways around them, counting the men on guard. The same as Bran had done.

Damn. He knew interfering with the Grahams would make them a bitter enemy, especially when the bastards still spoke of their victory at Werrick Castle many years prior.

"How many of our men remain with us after the battle?" Bran asked.

"Sixty-four of ours and twenty-two of the original castle guards remain."

Bran swallowed down his incredulity to keep Drake from seeing how disconcerting he found the dismal numbers. Between death and desertion, their army was reduced to less than half of their forces. A great number had apparently left upon seeing Bran so gravely wounded, assuming him dead and their plunder lost. A reiver's loyalty only ran as deep as the pockets paying them.

Mayhap Bran ought to send another missive to Kerr. He had

not yet gotten a reply from his first one about the capture of Werrick Castle. Surely the Scottish Warden would understand the importance of a quick exchange.

"Is that all?" Bran asked.

Drake shook his head. There was a grim set to his mouth.

Dread wound an uncomfortable knot in Bran's stomach. "What is it?"

"It would appear the war brewing between England and Scotland may finally be coming to a head. They will fight at Berwick."

Bran cursed. "Kerr willna be coming any time soon." He scrubbed a hand over his wet hair, reminding him he still needed to comb it. At least now he would be able to keep the castle despite Kerr's delay. Marin's offer to marry him was more convenient than she realized.

"Send scouts to Mabrick Castle to see what the Grahams may be planning," Bran said after a long moment. "In the meantime, we shall hope the men assemble quickly for Berwick and the battle is quickly won."

Drake glanced at him, opened his mouth to speak, and then closed it. He said nothing as he fixed his gaze forward once more.

"What is it?" Bran dragged the comb through his wet hair.

"What will ye do when the earl comes back?" Drake asked. "And if Kerr comes first, will ye give him Werrick?"

"I'm a rich man with bargaining power after today." Bran gave Drake a confident grin. But in truth, he wasn't confident at all.

He had set down this path to simply take the castle and save Ena. It was a situation that he would need to work through as events came up. There was no better plan, and Bran had always been good at split-second decisions.

"Are ye ready to be my second?" He turned and lifted his brows.

Drake bowed. "It's an honor."

Bran adjusted his doublet. "Then let's get me married."

17

Marin should have been frightened. Mayhap even anxious. At the very least, she'd expected her stomach to be a chaotic swirl of emotion and fear. But instead, she felt absolutely nothing, as though she were simply empty within, like a doll. Certainly, she looked like one with her hair brushed to shining, and the smudges of rouge at her cheeks and lips. Her gown sparkled with small gems, made to look like a thousand stars winking in a midnight blue sky.

Her sisters sat back on their heels to admire their handiwork, all with triumphant grins. They supported her, for they knew it was what she must do. Marin, however, questioned every moment of it, from when she'd told Isla to stay the poison to now, standing to the left of the alter.

The priest's head gleamed, having been freshly shaved, and he spoke the words of matrimony in Latin without once stumbling. As awkward a man as Bernard could often be, he had truly found his calling as a member of the clergy. His bright blue eyes glanced up from time to time to regard both her and Bran during the endless stream of words that closed her fate around her like a noose.

Bran, for his part, appeared elegant in the woolen hose and doublet of the same deep blue as her gown. His dark hair was clean, and his beard freshly trimmed. He'd lost a bit of weight during his convalescence, but he was still an imposing figure of stature and virile strength.

She did not let her attention linger upon him, though, for the grip on her control was tenuous. It was better to feel nothing than to fall prey to the crash of emotion.

The flower crown Catriona had ceremoniously draped over Marin's head that morning tickled her brow. The daisies had grown limp from the heat of her skin and cast about her a cloying, damp perfume.

Outwardly, she was aware of the wet heat of her palms, despite the chilled room, and how her feet ached from standing on cold stone for so long in delicate slippers. The priest's words rattled through her mind like dice being rolled in a cup, clunky and heavy with risk.

She exchanged her vows with Bran. Her mouth moved, her voice spoke, and still she did not feel.

A band of cool metal slipped over the third finger on her left hand, directly over her *vena amoris*, not that the vein running to her heart would make her love this man she married. The fat sapphire of the ring winked up at her in the multi-colored light of the stained-glass windows. It had been her mother's and was the nearest thing possible to having her there.

Marin took a flat gold ring, procured from the smith just that morning, and nudged it onto Bran's finger. His skin was warm and dry.

"Marin." He said her name so gently that it pulled her regard up to his brown gaze watching her with lingering concern.

Suddenly, the emotion hit her with the force of a tidal wave and threatened to drag her below its torrent depths. Each one powerful as it tore into her, the sadness, the anger, the excitement, the lust.

She blinked at the surprising prickle of tears in her eyes and flicked her focus to the floor before she succumbed. Who would possibly be convinced of her love if she began to weep? Bran gently touched her chin with his fingertips and directed her face upward. She looked up at him once more.

"My beautiful wife," he murmured.

Her breath sucked in. "My husband."

The entire room watched them with the weight of the world. They observed her stand uncomfortably in front of her new husband as he drew closer and closed his mouth over hers.

The kiss was chaste, as was expected within the confines of the church, but the connection of their mouths, and the familiarity of his spicy, clean scent, left the heat of desire winding through her body. She closed her eyes and gave in to the pull of lust. If nothing else, it would serve to see the people of Werrick Castle better convinced.

Bran pulled away and ran his thumb over her cheek. Her mouth hummed from his kiss and she bit her lower lip gently, enjoying the sensation, prolonging it on purpose. She opened her eyes and turned to the waiting congregation behind them. Despite her resolve, her cheeks grew hot with reticence at having been caught publicly enjoying a kiss.

They strode from the church together, as husband and wife. Though they did not make it far before her sisters surrounded them in a flurry of excitement.

Ella threw her arms around Marin. "You played the act well," Ella whispered. "It all looked so romantic."

"I hope it continues," Marin said through a smile. In truth, her sister's complimentary words bolstered Marin's confidence and gave her the fortitude to withstand the feast. She took the arm of her new husband with a believably feigned joy and allowed him to lead her to the celebration.

Bran did not protest at her sisters accompanying them into

the great hall. It was there that Marin stopped and gasped at their efforts.

Her sisters had outdone themselves with the decor in the great hall. Thick bands of blue cloth ran down the lengths of the trestles, and clusters of white and blue flowers dotted the walls, sconces, and tables of the massive room. The fine silver had been polished and set in a sparkling array along all tables, not just the dais. A true testament to the immense wealth of the Earl of Werrick.

Marin's smile had not been forced to see such lavishness at her wedding feast, for she knew all had been orchestrated by her sisters and all had been done with kind intent and love.

Even Piquette wore a crown of daisies as Marin did, though it kept falling every time he moved.

Bran led her to the dais, where flowers had been linked together and draped over the carved wood backs of the chairs. She sat first at his behest, but he did not join her. Instead, he took a long moment to stare out at the great hall from his elevated seat of honor. He raised his chin in a display of masculine pride. A man marveling at what he had conquered. And though she sat to his right, it was she who suffered loss at her own mighty capitulation.

"My fellow reivers." He lifted his goblet, already brimming with the fine Noirien wine from Burgundy. "And the men and women of Werrick Castle."

The excited chatter of conversation fell into complete silence as he spoke. Marin's insides clenched with anticipation. He had not told her he would make a speech, that he would address her people as though they were his. Aye, he would get great wealth from her dowry, but he was in no way a lord.

He casually held his goblet by the rim with his fingertips. "We come together today to unite our lives, and our people, together as one. For peace and for prosperity."

The reivers all shouted and banged their fists on the trestles with enough force to set the platters of food chattering atop the linen-covered wood. The men and women of the castle, however, looked to Marin with uncertain faces. She was, after all, their lady, and they still looked to her for answers and safety. Their trust twisted a chord in her chest and spurred her to action.

To show discontent now would not only violate the truce she'd enacted with Bran, but it would also cast an ominous shadow of doubt. To do so was far too dangerous.

She rose from her chair and held up her goblet. "We thank you for joining us to celebrate this most joyous occasion." She rose on her tiptoes and pressed a kiss to Bran's cheek.

The hair of his beard had been trimmed back and tamed with a spiced oil. The prickly whiskers were soft against her lips and left the pleasant scent clinging to her even as she pulled away.

Several cheers rose up and Werrick's inhabitants offered genuine nods of approval as many toasted the union. The revelers drank deep from their cups in appreciation for the peace, as much as for the limitless quantities of good spirits. For their parts, Bran and Marin drank to their own toast.

The wine was rich and robust as it hit her tongue, fortifying her in a way she so desperately needed. Conversations rippled to life once more and people began reaching for the trays laden with food.

Marin sank to her seat and dipped her fingers in the rose water at her side. The cool, scented water was refreshing against her uncomfortably hot skin, and provided her some much-needed energy to get through the interminable feast. She wished she could pat a bit of it on her cheeks.

It was only just beginning. Though there had been scant time to prepare, her sisters had managed the impossible in what they'd assembled for entertainment. There was a troubadour brought in by Ella's recommendation and a new dance taught by Cat, along with bountiful food and drink and good cheer. And following everything would be the wedding night.

Nervous excitement swam low in her belly, mixing like honey and vinegar. For as much as she dreaded knowing the permanence of a consummated marriage, so too did she anticipate what her husband would bring to the marriage bed. The passion they'd only sampled before would now be feasted on together.

Heaven help her for her wanton thoughts, but she could not help the eagerness singing in her veins and the heat growing in her cheeks. As much as she did not want a husband, she found Bran immensely desirable.

BRAN HAD SPENT THE BETTER PART OF THE FEAST NOT touching his wife. The people were used to an earl, to nobility and chivalry. Bran was the son of a widowed villager from a place so small its name had been forgotten after it was destroyed.

For certes, he was no earl.

While he did not understand the delicate rules of the titled and wealthy, he knew above all else he would do nothing to bring his Marin to shame, regardless of his station or hers. It had been difficult to sit beside her and not caress the length of her arm encased in sumptuous silk or touch her skin that looked like rose petals and cream. He couldn't draw the veil of hair from her face to better see her loveliness. Not when one touch would lead to more, and the rush of his driving need to have her would leave him overwhelmed.

He had contented himself to sit and watch Marin dance with her sisters, their hair fanning about them in gold and onyx, their matching blue eyes bright with joy.

The people of Werrick castle danced as well as the reivers, the two oftentimes coming together. Even Drake had appeared tempted when Lady Anice had tried to draw him into a dance. In the end, he'd resolutely shook his head and refrained.

The evening had been enjoyable, but it had been long, and Bran's patience was drawing to a close. He could no longer be on display on the dais as he fumbled through dainty eating and frivolous customs. Ones that were apparently created to establish a distinct line between men of his station and the otherwise wealthy and overly educated. The time to claim his bride without restraint was nigh.

He got to his feet and the room hushed. "The hour grows late."

"That isna all that's growing," a voice jeered from the back. Laughter followed as well as several more ribald jests.

Bran turned to where Marin had just taken a seat once more after dancing with her sisters, her cheeks flushed from her exertions.

He held out his hand to her. "My lady, shall we retire?"

She smiled up at him with the reserved affection she'd afforded him since they'd spoken their vows. Another few bawdy calls rose above the din, and she placed her hand in his. It did not escape his notice how her fingers trembled.

"Ye dinna need to walk us to the bed chamber," he called to the waiting crowd as he aided Marin to her feet. "I'm sure enough in my abilities to see the task done without the lot of ye."

The people laughed at that and settled back to their drinking and dancing. Better to appeal to their tawdry humor than to subject Marin to the humiliation of the barbaric old custom.

His wife moved without thought, the way a warrior does in battle when their body reacts independently from their mind. Her fragile smile continued to hover on her lips as they made their way across the hall. It stayed through the long walk up the stone stairs and into Marin's room.

It had been Bran's idea to occupy the earl's former rooms, but

Marin had asked that they share hers instead. A consideration Bran had agreed to.

Once the door was completely closed, her pleasant expression wilted. The performance was over.

Whatever was left was what lay between them, cold and foreign, a yawning gap of discomforting silence. Not what Bran had been anticipating.

An unexpected awkwardness seized Bran.

He'd had plenty of women in his life, but never had he needed to work to woo them. None of those women had been ones of noble birth. And certainly, never had they been his wife, nor a maiden for that matter.

The women who had lain with him were lusty, experienced, and eager to sate his passions.

He made his way to the wine flagon and poured a cup. The liquid splashed into the chalice like a wave of blood and obliterated the quiet.

He turned to her. "Ye look lovely." And she did, like a pagan goddess with her loose flowing hair gleaming like spun gold and her eyes sparkling with the excitement of the feast.

"Thank you," she said quietly. The intensity of her shrewd stare darted briefly to the bed before returning to him.

He followed her gaze with a forced languid ease, pausing to take in the fresh linens and creamy white bed clothes as well as the pink rose petals scattered over its surface. A bed made for consummation.

He lifted the goblet and approached her. His footsteps were thunderous on the hard floor and he swore he could hear the tapping of her rapid heartbeat.

"I told ye before, ye dinna have to be afraid of me." He dipped his finger into the wine. "I willna force ye. I told ye as much in the beginning."

She nodded.

"I want to give ye pleasure, lass." He stepped closer to her and welcomed the sweet tease of her lavender scent. "I want ye to want this as I do."

He drew his finger from the cup and slowly brought it close to her mouth. When she did not move away, he traced his digit over her lower lip, painting her rouged flesh with rich wine. Her breath drew in and she watched him with wide eyes as she tucked her lower lip into her mouth to suck it clean.

Heat fired through him, singeing away the foreign awkwardness.

"Do ye know I willna hurt ye?" He dipped his finger into the wine again and drew it over both lips this time. The lower first, then the sensual shape of her upper lip. A dark red droplet beaded and threatened to run down her chin. He caught it with his thumb before it could drip and licked it from his skin.

Marin ran the tip of her tongue over her lips, so they glistened with temptation. "I know." She said it with such conviction, it cleared the lingering vestiges of his discomfort.

"I've thought about ye, Marin." He touched his forefinger to the wine and brought it to her once more. "More than I ought to have."

Her lips parted and she drew his finger into the moist heat of her mouth with a little suck.

His cock tensed with eagerness. "Have ye thought of me?" He set the wine aside. "How I kissed ye, how I touched ye?"

Her gaze darted away, and her cheeks flushed darker than the rouge.

He leaned to whisper in her ear, his voice intentionally sensual. "Be honest."

Her breathing hitched, and her eyes brightened. "Aye." She closed her eyes as she whispered the solitary word, as if she were confessing a sin.

God's teeth, he could not stay himself any longer. He held her face in one of his hands, while curling the other around to the back of her head, threading his fingers through the glossy wealth of her hair, and pressed his mouth to hers.

She parted her lips and the tip of her tongue grazed his with an innocent's eagerness. She tasted richly of wine and sexual hunger. He groaned and deepened their kiss, eager to experience her once more, eager to claim the woman who had become his wife.

❧ 18 ❧

Marin didn't want to think on what her marriage to Bran meant for her family. She didn't want to consider her father's reaction when he came home to Werrick Castle and found it overtaken, or what dangers lay in wait for him at the battle in Berwick. Nor did she want to ruminate on how egregiously she had failed to protect Werrick Castle.

With such unwanted thoughts pulling at her, it was easy to give in to the heady rush of lust stoking fire in her blood. She let her world center on pleasure, on the skilled caress of Bran's mouth, the power of his body beneath the fine doublet, the silkiness of his hair despite his powerful and undeniable masculinity.

His arousal pressed into her stomach and piqued her curiosity, as well as several other emotions she was all too eager to embrace. She put her hands to his chest without trepidation, empowered by a wife's permission. He pushed against her palms, welcoming her touch.

Her fingers moved down the fine wool of the blue doublet, one of her father's that Anice had insisted on having altered to fit Bran for the wedding. Bran groaned against her mouth and swept his tongue deeper, his kisses hungrier, more insistent. The smooth leather of the belt at his doublet met her fingertips. She moved blindly to pull the leather free of itself. It fell to the floor with a slap.

He broke free from the kiss, his gaze fixed intently on her as he shrugged off the doublet. It joined the belt on the floor.

The memory of him without his shirt sizzled in her mind. She had been too timid then to touch his firm flesh, to see if it was as solid as it had appeared.

"The leine too," Marin said boldly. "I want to see you."

His mouth lifted in a cocky half-smile. While the arrogance might have ordinarily rankled her, there was a confidence behind it that heightened his allure.

"I like a woman who knows what she wants." He lifted the hem of his shirt and lifted it over his head, revealing the rippled muscles of his stomach and the swell of his chest, all shadows of raw, masculine strength in the firelight.

Marin's mouth went dry. The tips of her nipples tingled. She'd practiced with soldiers long enough to know a physique such as Bran's was hard-won and not common. A man who fought with diligence. With passion.

The scent of sandalwood rose from his skin, enticing and sensual—his scent. She breathed him in and let her gaze stroke over him.

"Ye can touch me, wife." His words startled her, and she pushed her hand to his naked chest to mask the sudden foolishness washing over her. After all, she had asked him to remove his shirt and then merely stared.

His skin was warm and soft, the slight furring of dark hair prickled against her palm, while his heartbeat beneath was steady. And faster than normal. The same as her own frenzied pulse.

His deep brown eyes watched her intently from underneath hooded lids. Marin let her hand drift over his chest, letting her fingers dip and glide over his beautiful, war-honed flesh. First his chest, then the bulk of his chiseled arms, carved no doubt from the swing of his battle axe.

She hadn't yet had a chance to skim her fingertips over his abdomen when his hand cupped her chin and he forced her gaze upward.

"I want to see ye too." He stroked his thumb over her lower lip and she instinctively touched the tip of her tongue to the pad of his finger. He gave a short groan on the exhale of his breath, as though her action pained him.

She knew better now. There was no pain, save from the force of desire.

She turned her back to him and swept aside her hair, revealing the laces of her gown. Cool air graced the back of her neck and sent a ripple through her that was equal parts pleasure, excitement and anxiousness.

He was careful as he worked the laces of her gown, not with the lust-blind enthusiasm she'd expected from a lifelong warrior, but with the care one would expect of a troubadour. The surcoat loosened around her and his fingers lightly stroked over the exposed skin. First against the exposed top of her back, just over her girdle, a whisper of a touch that drew a gasp from her lips.

Then his caress teased higher, over the sensitive skin of her neck. Marin tilted her head to the side to give him better access. His hands slid over her shoulders, pushing aside the heavy dress and girdle as he did so. His breath fanned over the dip where her neck connected with her shoulder and the place between her legs went hot with longing.

"Ye're so verra lovely." His whispered words swept over the delicate line of her neck. She shivered.

He pressed his mouth to her there, once, twice, three times. Dear God, four and five times. Her skin burned with his touch, eager for so much more. His hand shifted to her chest where it slipped beneath the gown and cupped a breast with his palm. His fingers played over her sensitive nipple until a needling pleasure left her crying out.

He nibbled the area just below her ear and a moan made its way from her throat. The more he kissed and licked, nipped and sucked, the more she wanted. His hands moved over her as he sampled her, carefully peeling the gown from her body, unveiling her, one lover's kiss at a time. He pulled the ribbon on her chemise, and she did not move to stop him.

She wanted to be naked against him, to feel the heat of him against her, the strength of his body. The hardness of his phallus.

She drew a shaky breath at the thought of where that would go—an idea that had repelled her when first she'd heard of it years ago. An idea that now left her aching with curiosity.

The chemise fell away. Bran's chest pressed to her back and the hard column of male flesh she'd been considering fit snugly against her rump. She arched her back against him in hungry instinct rather than thought.

His hands were around her, fondling, touching...everywhere. Skimming the sides of her breasts, holding them, over the length of her upper thighs, across her flat stomach. Everywhere except the place burning for his attention.

He caught her earlobe gently between his teeth as his fingers crept toward the most private place between her legs. Before she could even register through the lust-hazed fog of her mind what he might do, one finger delivered a long, stroking sweep, and elicited a pleasure so white hot and brilliant, she couldn't help but cry out.

"Ye're so damn wet," he growled against her neck.

No thoughts of embarrassment reached her with his assessment. Not when her dampness brought forth such hunger, and not when he was touching her so intimately.

His fingertip glided over her sex once more, firmer this time, more possessive. Marin opened for him as his solid body braced her back, keeping her upright when she might have otherwise fallen. Her hips lifted to greet his touch in desperate anticipation.

He probed gently inside of her. Marin leaned her head back against his shoulder and panted at the welcome exploration. His hand cupped her, his fingers slipping through the slickness of her sex, the desire in her pounding to a point she feared she might somehow erupt into flames. One of his fingers eased up the line of her slit and settled over the concentrated center of her lust. It was a simple graze of a touch, but it left her crying out again, her voice husky.

He groaned in her ear, his breath coming faster now. She arched back against the hardness of him, rubbing her bottom up and down.

"My God, ye're going to undo me, woman." He spun her about and lowered his head to hers. Their mouths met with hungry, slanting kisses, their tongues stroking and teeth bumping with desperation.

He eased her backward, walking her slowly while his hands roved over her body until she met the bed with the backs of her calves. He guided her to the mattress and her heart slammed in her chest. This was it.

His gaze fixed on her, watching her watching him. He put his hands to the belt of his hose and unfastened it from his waist, letting it fall to the floor with his braies and hose. He was fully naked, with his powerful thighs and the thick column of flesh jutting from a nest of dark hair at the apex of his legs.

Her heart caught and beat wildly in her chest. He came to the bed, leaned over her, pressing flush against her. Hot skin and prickling dark hair and the thickness of his phallus brushed against her thigh. He caught her face in his free hand and kissed her with the passion of a man about to lay claim to his woman.

THE UNCERTAINTY NIPPED AT BRAN'S MIND ONCE MORE, A clear line of unease in the haze of passion. Marin's body was a beautiful blend of feminine curves paired with the surprisingly sensual lines of strength. She arched her pelvis toward him in a hungry rhythm, evidence she wanted him with equal lust as he wanted her.

Except she was a virgin.

He longed to draw out their pleasure despite the insistent throbbing in his cock. He wanted to take his time exploring her, his lips and tongue teasing over her petal-soft skin until he got to her center, where he would lap until she reached her crisis against his mouth.

But she was noble born, a woman who had never even been kissed before meeting him. And she was his wife, worthy of the greatest respect.

He moved his hand between them to slide against her slick opening once more. She drew a sharp breath and her hips flinched toward him. Aye, she was ready. So damn ready, it made him groan in anticipation. He curled a finger inside of her and rubbed at the source of her pleasure above it with his thumb.

He didn't know these noble's rules. He didn't know if the kind of passion he enjoyed was something she might find offensive, especially on their wedding night.

Her sheath was tight around his finger, gripping with enough pressure that he knew he would not last long within her. He slowly inserted a second finger, stretching her. She paused only briefly before moving with him again.

His cock was nearly bursting. Her sighs, the flush of her cheeks, the way her eyes sparkled beneath half-hooded eyes, he could scarcely take it. He withdrew his fingers from her, practically driven wild by her natural musk, the perfume of her arousal. Without thought, he licked his fingers and relished the taste of her.

Marin sucked in a breath of surprise at the action.

He wouldn't apologize, not when he intended to do so much more at a later date.

He held his cock in his hand, his fingers still glistening from her center, and guided himself to the triangle of downy blonde hair, stopping just at her entrance. She spread her legs wider, the delicate muscles of her inner thighs straining with her need.

He gritted his teeth and silently cursed the need for women to be virgins for their husbands. He gently eased his hips forward when he wanted to thrust, settling a scant inch within her when he wanted to sheath the full length in one hearty thrust.

She was so wet that he could easily do so.

He pushed another inch inward and she gasped. The pressure gripping him tingled from his bollocks and spiraled through him. Again, he pushed deeper, though now the grip of her turned to a blend of pleasure and discomfort. She was too tight. He strained forward to push deeper inside of her.

Her brows flinched and her starry-eyed gaze of passion firmed into one of determination.

"Am I hurting ye?" he panted.

She shook her head stiffly.

His entire body ached from holding it with such rigidity. He'd never been one for bedding virgins, and now he knew why. He started to press in deeper when she wrapped her legs around his waist and squeezed with incredible strength, impaling him the rest of the way into her.

The pressure around his cock made stars wink and dance in front of his eyes. Too tight, aye, but still hot and wet. A low groan rumbled in his chest and he gripped the coverlet beneath her.

He stared down at her, at the set of her mouth. "Are ye—"

"Stop treating me like I'm delicate." Her tense expression eased. "Please."

"It will feel better soon," he said, hoping he was right. He didn't know much about virgins, or how long it would take one to start enjoying the act. He only knew he liked women who were lusty, who enjoyed hours of pleasure and teasing.

And he knew it was awkward as hell having a conversation with his cock lodged inside her, tense with the need to release. His heartbeat pounded through his whole body, demanding he take his pleasure. The need was so bloody intense, it left his brain foggy. The obvious discomfort written on her face, however, told him he had a lot to make up for with this inferior performance.

Rather than move in her again, he bent over her, body shaking with restraint and painful need, and delicately licked the narrow line of skin between her breasts.

"What are you doing?" she breathed.

He brushed his lips over her nipple before opening his mouth and drawing in the pert bud. He arched his back, beginning to withdraw from her slowly while he did this and nearly shuddered at the bliss tingling through his body to move within her again.

Marin shifted underneath him. Resolute, he braced his weight on one hand and slipped his other between them where they were joined. He found the swollen nub of her pleasure and carefully rolled his thumb over it while switching his mouth to the other breast, to love the other nipple with his mouth and tongue.

Carefully, he pushed into her once more and found that the tension squeezing him in a merciless grip relaxed somewhat. The pleasure without the pain nearly undid him.

He played his thumb over her sex and moved his mouth from her nipple to her sensual lips. She wrapped her arms around him and met his kiss with the same ready delight as earlier. He thrust faster now, sliding in and pulling out, only to plunge in once more while their tongues mated together, and his thumb rolled and rolled and rolled over her.

Her breath became lusty pants between their kisses and her obvious enjoyment of his loving heightened his pleasure. His cockstand wasn't painful anymore; it was hot and throbbing with an overwhelming pleasure that left his bollocks drawing tight with the need to release.

Marin's body tensed beneath him and he sensed her nearing her crisis.

He drove in harder and increased the stroke of his thumb. She shuddered and threw her head back, crying out, her face a complete story of every indulgent emotion exploding through her.

Bran's own climax overtook him as he witnessed such pleasure, and his hips jerked against her with primitive action rather than thought. His seed poured into her and stars flashed once more like winking fireflies in his vision.

They remained joined together while their breathing calmed, and their lust cooled. Once his heart had ceased the frenzied racing, he rose and drew a cloth from the ewer, returning to the bed to tend to her.

He gently ran the cool, wet linen over her. He'd expected blood and saw none, which piqued his curiosity.

"Isla left ye a balm." He reached for the small jar on the bedside table and set aside the cloth.

"That isn't necessary." Marin had already begun to pull her long legs together, closing herself off from him.

But Bran's fingers were already glossy with the sweet-smelling ointment. "It will help with any discomfort." He frowned. "I dinna like having hurt ye."

"Not all of it hurt," she said in a low voice.

His cock gave a little start at the insinuation in her tone, at the obvious lust. "Enough flattering. Part yer legs for me, wife."

Marin watched him carefully and widened her knees, revealing her sex to him once more, still pink and swollen with the aftereffects of their loving. He swept his fingers over her opening, spreading the balm over her.

She closed her eyes. "That does feel nice."

The pebble at the top of her slit became engorged beneath his ministrations. He knew if he rubbed at it again, he might have her coming once more.

But she was no seasoned woman, eager for multiple love sessions in one night. He began to withdraw his hand when she reached down and settled hers over his, fastening his touch between her legs.

Her hips rolled in sensual undulations. "Don't stop."

He continued to spread the balm, keeping from her entrance and focusing mainly on the bud as it swelled and swelled and swelled. Her breath came in little pants and her cheeks went red with pleasure as they had when he'd been inside her. Dear God, she was going to climax once more.

He gritted his teeth and moved his thumb faster over her sex until she turned her face into the pillow and muted those beautiful cries of pleasure. He pulled his hand away as her body relaxed. She rolled her face from the pillow and gave him a sheepish smile.

"Forgive me." She sank her teeth onto her bottom lip. "It felt so good…"

"Dinna ever apologize for enjoying what we do." He set aside the jar of ointment and willed his cock to calm before he settled in beside her. Climaxing twice was one thing but having him inside her when she was likely still sore was another. He relaxed behind her and cradled close the body he'd only just begun to learn.

He had much more exploring to do with her. Not only physically, but also learning more of who this unique woman was. For though he'd been trying not to think on it, and despite what Marin had claimed, he knew by the absence of a barrier when they'd mated, and a lack of blood—she had not been a virgin.

❧ 19 ❧

Bran woke the following morning to an empty bed. The place beside him was cool under his palm. Some time had evidently passed since Marin had risen and departed.

Daylight streamed in through the windows. He had slept far later than intended.

He dragged himself from bed, refreshed himself with the remaining water in the ewer and pulled on a pair of gray hose and a dark doublet. He'd been about to stride from the room when he caught sight of the rumpled bed and the brilliant white of their sheets.

Her missing maidenhead niggled at the back of his mind again. He growled in frustration and pulled the sleeve of his doublet and shirt upward. With his forearm over the bed, he dug the tip of his blade into the inside of his elbow and squeezed out a couple drops of blood. The deep red droplets hit the sheets exactly where he'd aimed. He patted the mess about with his fingertips, smearing it in a way he assumed would happen naturally through the act of intercourse.

When he finished, he took care to use the crumpled linen he'd cleaned her with to remove the blood from his hands, further securing his intentional proof. It would not do to have anyone question her maidenhead.

He glanced once more at his handiwork, pulled the sleeve of his shirt and doublet down and quit the room to find his wife. Bixby sat in the hallway and leapt at Bran's arrival.

"Have ye seen yer mistress?" Bran asked the cat.

Bixby blinked up at him. The little blighter probably wouldn't tell Bran even if he did know. Bran gave him a pat on the head anyway and proceeded to the places he was most likely to find her. In the kitchen, he discovered Nan setting about the first meal of the day with clear instructions already delivered by Marin. Next, he went on the battlements where Sir Richard had the castle soldiers already scurrying about to fulfill her orders. Finally, he made his way to the solar and found her discussing the schedule with a thin, brown-haired woman.

He nodded to them both upon entering, walking closer when Marin waved him over. "Bran, this is our chatelaine, Rohesia."

The woman had a long, narrow mouth that stretched longer still with her smile. She bobbed a quick curtsey. "Will that be all, my lady?" she asked of Marin.

Marin smiled. "Aye, thank you, Rohesia."

Ah, yes, the woman who refused to even discuss cleaning and laundry with him when he first took Werrick Castle. Still, he nodded in greeting as she departed and closed the door behind her.

Marin's hair had been plaited into long braids and wound atop her head where a glittering gold caul secured them into place. Having her hair up exposed her long, graceful neck and he found himself aching to press his mouth to her perfumed skin. To hear her cry out once more at his touch.

"Marin." Her name came out in something of a groan.

She swallowed and turned her gaze to him. "Good morrow, Bran."

"Ye were up early." He closed the distance between them and

ran a hand lightly down the side of her pale blue cotehardie. The silk was cool and slick, and his hand glided over her waist and the swell of her hips, easily skimming over her curves. He deemed she ought to wear silk every day for the sheer purpose of him running his hands over her.

She stepped back slightly. Away from his caress. "There is always much to do."

He didn't reach for her again, but he couldn't tamp down the frustration at her obvious rejection of his advances. He thought the night before had burned away her hesitation.

"I believe much of the responsibility of the household ought to be mine, aye?" He gave her the half-grin most ladies went silly over.

Marin frowned. "Do you seek to take my position as well as my castle?"

"I seek to be yer husband, woman." He said it firmly, in a tone he hoped brokered no argument. "Ye canna take all this on yer own."

"I have for years. I do not intend to stop now." She spoke lightly, but he knew there was a greater depth to her words.

"Marin," he said her name again, this time more gently. "I dinna seek to take anything from ye—"

"But you have." She shook her head as tears burned in her eyes. "You took my castle and my people and my father's fortune."

"Did ye no' enjoy last night?" He braced himself for her answer and combed through his memory of the night before. He only remembered their pleasure.

Marin's cheeks went pink. "Aye, but it doesn't change what I must now face. I have given you everything, even my maidenhead. Please do not also take my tasks from me. I beg of you."

"Ye dinna have a maidenhead," he said slowly.

She stared at him and her mouth fell open before closing and falling open soundlessly once more. "Of course, I had my maidenhead."

"There was no blood."

Her brow furrowed and she glanced around the room as if she might find an explanation floating in the air. "I don't...understand..."

"Mayhap when ye were taken?"

Her gaze flicked to him. "What?"

"When ye were taken, mayhap ye dinna understand what happened..." he trailed off at the incredulous expression on her face.

"I think I would know." Splotches of pink showed on her neck and the bit of her chest that was visible.

"But if ye dinna, if ye were too young. How old were ye when it happened? Was it the Grahams?"

"I wasn't taken," she shot at him.

"Yer sisters said—"

"I know what they said." Marin drew in a deep breath and slowly let it out. "They're only repeating what I told them, as well as my father, and anyone else who needed answers."

He shook his head. "If ye werena taken, what happened?"

The confident squaring of her shoulders wilted, and she turned her face away, a clear indication she did not want to look at him. Or did not want him looking at her. "I wasn't taken. I ran away."

MARIN HAD NEVER SPOKEN THE TRUTH ALOUD. HER NEW husband was the last person she would have expected to tell. Shame burned her face and kept her eyes averted.

"Ye ran away?" His tone was slow with disbelief. "Ye, who do everything for yer sisters, yer people, yer home."

She folded her arms over her chest, a flimsy shield to staunch the agony thrumming in her heart. Her gaze slipped up to his face and she found him watching her with guarded curiosity. He stood too close to her, and his very presence seemed as if he were trying to press for the truth.

She looked away again, not only to keep her embarrassment from being so painfully transparent, but also to avoid remembering the lurid details of the night before. In truth, leaving that morning had only partly been due to the tasks needing to be seen to. The castle knew well enough its own functions and each person responsible was aware of their routine. Most had not been expecting to see her about that morning.

The larger part of her leaving had been sheer cowardice, to avoid facing the awkward discomfort of waking up curled in his naked arms, her body so intimately pressed to his own, their deeds laid bare in the light of a new day.

There had been wonder between them the night before, a heart-pounding magic that robbed her of thought and modesty. But now, with their clothes on, going about their daily lives, when only hours before a part of his body had been buried within her most intimate place. Only hours before he had licked his fingers after...he had...

He leveled his gaze with hers. Sunlight streamed in through the thick glass window and made the dark irises of his eyes glow a warm brown with small flecks of black in them. She hadn't noticed those before.

"Will ye tell me why ye ran away?" he asked earnestly.

She folded her arms over her chest. "Do you believe me that I was truly a maiden when you had me last night?"

He studied her for long enough for her to assume the answer might be no. "In truth, I dinna care if ye were a maiden or no'. But I want to know if someone hurt ye. And I want to know why ye felt ye needed to run from yer own home."

With the crook of his finger, he lifted her face higher and he gazed down at her with such consideration, she thought he meant to kiss her. Her traitorous body hummed to life with anticipation and sent whorls of hot, sensual memories flitting about in her mind.

"You want the truth," she surmised. He nodded.

She hesitated and his hand gently swept down her neck, making her skin tingle.

"I'm yer husband, Marin," he said in a seductive tone. "Ye know my past. Isna it fair for me to know yers?"

"I ran because..." She winced. Thinking the words was hard enough; speaking them was like tearing her heart from her chest and baring for him to see. "I ran because it was too much."

His callused palm cradled her jaw and the gentle sweep of his thumb whispered over her skin, too near her mouth. "What was?" he said encouragingly.

"My mother died when Leila was born." It was too easy to remember the weight of mourning as it settled over Werrick Castle and shrouded all their hearts. The laughter and joy had ceased, though in truth it had already been much muted through the months that her mother's stomach swelled with life. "There had been an attack on the castle before we had a curtain wall. They broke through our defenses. No one was safe."

Bran lowered his hand from her face. "The Grahams."

"Aye," she replied. No doubt everyone on both sides of the border remembered the Grahams and how they had wreaked such havoc and horrors on Werrick Castle. "My father tried to protect us, but he was knocked aside. We thought he was dead." She shook her head at the memory, wishing to clear the image of her father laying still and bleeding. "My mother charged at the man who meant to kill us all. She did save us, but at a terrible cost to herself."

Bran's jaw tensed and he flicked his gaze away in angry understanding. Marin shuddered at the memory of finding her mother on the floor, her gown ripped, sobbing, not wanting to live. It had been Marin who helped her to her feet, who got her to Isla for healing.

"We discovered she was with child." Marin glanced to the closed door of the solar. This was nothing she wanted Leila to hear, especially not when the girl was so loved and cared for now. For surely that was what truly mattered, was it not?

"Mother was despondent. She didn't eat enough or sleep enough." Marin spoke gently despite the closed door, ensuring their conversation remained fully private. "She was a ghost of her former self. Despite my efforts, I knew she would not be strong enough to survive the birth. And she did not."

Bran put his hands on Marin's shoulders in an oddly comforting act, as if he sought to help her continue standing upright. "That was Leila."

Marin nodded.

"Her father...?"

Marin cringed at the question he didn't need to complete. "She is our sister and that's the only thing we've ever cared about."

"Yer da?"

The image of her father's weathered face with his gray-white hair and summer-sky-blue eyes welled in her heart. "He loves her perhaps more than any of us, and we've never faulted him for it," she answered. "She's the center of our world, our mother's last gift to us. Any doubt we might have harbored has only produced a fiercer affection for her."

"Then why did ye run?" He asked the question gently, as though he worried that he might frighten her.

"Everyone needed me." The memory squeezed around her chest like a vice. "When my mother died, everyone looked to me. I cared for Leila and for my sisters, trying as best I could to aid them through their bitter loss and heartache. Mother's loss was difficult on my father as well. It was as though the Northern Star had burnt out and he did not know which direction to walk without it. Without her."

"Then there was ye."

"Then there was me." She drew in a deep breath, but the pressure around her chest seemed to grow tighter. The way it had that day. "I was too busy to accept my own grief." She gave a mirthless chuckle. "I didn't know the battlements or strategy or how to handle the soldiers. Without my father, we would not have protection, nor would we have the funds necessary to stay fed and safe. I tried to rouse him, but he would not rally. And I felt so...so helpless." Her voice caught and she drew a deep breath to calm herself. "Everyone needed me all the time and I had nothing left to give."

She had to stop for a moment to keep from letting the dismal emotion swelling inside her consume her.

Bran leaned over her and pressed a kiss to her brow. It was so surprising a gesture, so loving, it took her aback. No one had given her their undivided attention like this. Aye, the servants did for their tasks, the men for their orders, even her sisters for advice. But no one had listened to her heart. Not like this. With his focus and his concern, he sprinkled seeds of trust into her heart.

And she knew then, she could tell him the truth.

20

Marin spoke freely under Bran's encouragement, without the emotion pinching painfully at her throat. "Leila had been up through most of the night, and the other girls were abed with illness. I tried to appeal to my father to rise once more and he...he began to sob." She fisted her hand at the memory. "To see so great a man crumble beneath his heartache, to know I was doing all in my power, and for it to still not be enough..."

Her eyes went warm and she knew she was losing the fight against her tears. "It was more than I could bear. My heart was shattered, and I had nothing left to give." She sniffled and fixed her gaze on the floor. "After I left my father's room, I went outside where it was cool and quiet. I meant only to go for a walk, but as soon as I left the castle grounds, I started to run." She closed her eyes and could feel the cold air on her hot cheeks again, the incredible liberation. "It felt so exhilarating, like my body was finally alive. By the time I stopped, it was dark."

She blinked her eyes open and kept her gaze averted, too ashamed of her next words to look at him. "I didn't care. I didn't want to go back. Everyone would need me, pull at me, drain me of what precious little I had left."

It had been on that lone winter night, with fat snowflakes drifting around her like the fluff of wool bits on sheering day, that she had finally given in to the pain of her mother's loss. Her heart had cracked open and she had curled herself around its intensity, letting it suck the sobs from her throat and spill them out into the frosted air. She did not say as much to Bran. Such a private moment need not be shared, especially when she had confessed so much already.

"They found me later, laying in the snow." Marin relaxed her clenched hand and looked down at the creased lines of her palm. "They said I was near death. I didn't notice, not when my entire being had become so hollow and numb." She shrugged as if it were nothing. But it wasn't nothing. It'd been the single darkest day of her entire existence. When she'd failed.

Worse.

When she'd given up.

"Ye told everyone ye'd been taken," Bran said.

She nodded. "The truth was far too painful to say aloud. I couldn't tell everyone I had been..." Her voice caught. "That I'd been such a coward."

"Marin." His voice was a soothing purr and he finally released her shoulders, cupping her face now instead. "Ye werena a coward. Ye were a lass who was given the weight of the world. Ye took on more than any lass should have to, and the proof of yer efforts is apparent today in everything ye do. I noticed it even the first day."

She looked up and found him staring at her with heartbreaking sincerity.

"Everyone needs someone to need," he said, using her own words. "And ye dinna have anyone."

A hot tear spilled down her cheek. His thumb followed its path and wiped it away.

At that moment, her husband understood her perhaps far better than anyone else in the whole of her life ever had. It crashed down on her and left her eyes welling. Not trusting herself to speak, she pursed her lips to staunch the ache in her throat and nodded.

He pulled her to him, those strong arms of his securing her in an embrace of compassion and protection that left her heart nearly crying out in gratitude.

He pressed a kiss to her brow. "Let me be the one ye can need, aye?" he murmured against her hair.

She scrunched her eyes tightly against the scratchy fabric of his reiver's doublet to keep the tears at bay, and instead breathed in the spicy, sandalwood scent of him, of her husband. A man who not only understood her but gave her something she had been too long missing in her life. Comfort. Strength.

She wanted to stay there for a lifetime, cradled in his arms, secured to the reassuring solidity of his body. Not alone, but with a true partner who would guard her back the way he had during the battle when they'd reclaimed her sisters.

Marin pushed her face into Bran's doublet, wanting to be closer still. Her breath exhaled against the wool and spread heat against her cheeks and nose. His hand ran in slow circles over her back. Though the caress was meant to be one of soothing, she could not help the languid pulse beginning to thrum between her thighs any more than she could still her memories from the night before.

The powerful stroke of his body into hers, the straining groans as he reined in his lust to be gentle for her benefit. The way he'd licked his fingers...

She tilted her face upward, eager to be claimed by him once more, so the hurt of her past might burn away in the flames of passion. Bran's palm slid up to cup the base of her neck as his mouth lowered to hers. Her need had been unspoken, but he had answered the call. He'd been there for her as she'd known he would be.

Her sorrow was the tinder to their lust, and it ignited them both with a white-hot intensity neither could deny. Their hands moved over one another's bodies, their mouths panting and breathlessly kissing.

Bran's deft fingers found the peak of her breast, which he teased as his lips moved down her throat. He tugged at the top of her gown.

She wanted this, and yet a voice of piety nipped through the pleasure.

Marin gasped and folded her arms over her chest to stop him. "The sun is up."

He gathered up her long skirt in eager handfuls. "Aye, and I'll be better able to see all of yer beauty."

His fingertips skimmed over the backs of her thighs and up to the base of her bottom. Her body hummed in response and her sex grew damp with need. He kissed her and drew his tongue over her lower lip.

"It's a sin to do this with the sun up," she protested between kisses. "And on a Friday for that matter."

He pulled back and stared at her, his brown eyes dark and shining with want of her. "If we go by the church's rules, it willna be until Monday evening when we might have one another again." His fingertips curled around her bottom, so his fingertips were wonderfully close to her sex. He lifted a brow and swept a single finger between her legs.

Marin's knees went weak and threatened to drop out from beneath her. Bran pulled his hand away, evidence of her need glistening on his fingertips. She swallowed.

"Can ye wait that long, wife?" He pulled her closer to him and her heart pounded erratically. "I intend to show ye many ways of pleasure and can assure ye, no' any of them are sanctioned by the church."

Her nipples prickled into hard points and a breathy moan was all she could produce by way of a reply. A knock sounded at the door, startling her nerves and making her jump.

Bran released her gown and the silk fell heavily into place. He put his finger into his mouth, the one he'd touched her with, and gave her a look that shot straight to her core. Marin's knees buckled this time, but she managed to set her hand to the solid desk and brace herself. Bran's mouth curled in an arrogant smile. One she wanted to kiss off his face.

He backed to a respectful distance and bade their intruder to enter.

Drake strode into the room and nodded courteously to Marin. "Good morrow, my lady. Pardon the intrusion." His gaze met Bran's. "'Tis the Grahams."

Marin stepped forward, shedding aside the desire of moments before as the soldier in her came to attention. "Are they rallying?" she asked.

Drake cast her a regretful look. "They are here."

⚜

BRAN STOOD AT THE BATTLEMENTS AND REGARDED THE LARGE group of reivers dotting the grounds below, like vultures waiting for death. Their ponies moved on anxious legs beneath them, anticipating a battle. Not that attacking the castle would win them any victory. It would be difficult for the men on horseback to overtake the castle.

But not impossible.

Bran had proven as much himself when he took the castle by threatening Cat. It simply depended on how determined the Grahams were willing to be, how vicious.

"There's more than two score of them." Marin rested her hand atop the depressed crenellation of the wall and tapped her forefinger against the stone in thought. "Why do they stay when they know they cannot defeat us? Do they mean to intimidate?"

Bran narrowed his eyes against the cutting wind and leveled

his stare at a single man on a dark hobbler. "That is exactly why they stay."

"They are assessing us," she stated.

He grunted in agreement.

"What can we assess of them?" she queried. "Aside from evidence of their brashness, of course."

Bran had not wanted Marin to join him on the battlements, especially without her chainmail. He'd almost put his concerns to voice when the ferocity lit her eyes as Drake gave them information on the Grahams. She knew Werrick Castle better than perhaps anyone else, certainly better than him. Mayhap even more than the earl himself. Bran would do well to remember what a valuable treasure she truly was.

And yet seeing her facing the armed men below in naught but a silk gown, with her hair secured beneath a delicate gilded caul, left him with the driving need to stand in front of her. For all he knew, their wedding night had resulted in a babe.

The possibility jolted through him like lightning.

His child could be seeded in her flat belly at that very moment.

Marin frowned at him. "Why do you stare at me so?"

"What if ye are with child?"

She laughed. "I'm sure you haven't cause for concern."

He could not pull his gaze from her stomach. "Ye could be. It can take only one time."

Marin smirked. "Fire arrows upon them." She turned from the reivers with bored disinterest. "Have them scatter like vermin when met with a light."

"My exact thoughts, Wife." He caught her wrist and kept her from leaving.

She turned back to face him. Before she could protest at his behavior, he eased a hand around her narrow waist and pulled her toward him. His mouth came down on hers, his tongue grazing playfully against her own.

She drew in a sharp breath and her knees gave gently.

Bran broke off the kiss as abruptly as he'd started it and gazed down at his wife. Her mouth was soft, her eyes bright with desire already. "I dinna care the time of day or the day of the week, Marin. No' even God himself could stop me from having ye now that ye're my wife."

"Bran..." She caught his face between her hands and pressed a kiss to his mouth with equal passion.

He wanted nothing more at that moment than to sweep her into his arms and carry her to their bed chamber. But the bloody Grahams still needed to be tended to.

He broke off the kiss again, this time with greater regret. Manning a castle was apparently not all pleasantries, but a lot of responsibility. "We have to handle this first. And then..."

Marin's mouth was red from the force of their kisses and now curled into a knowing smile. "And then..."

Shouting came from the archway of the main door leading to the battlements from the castle, where Marin's three younger blonde sisters all emerged. They were clad in chainmail, their hair flying like wild gold banners behind them, their weapons drawn and ready.

"Archers," Marin called out.

Bran smirked down at her. "I believe that's my job."

"Mayhap you should have called it faster." She gave him a coy look and pulled away from him.

His blood burned hotter in his veins. God's teeth, but he had a feisty wife.

"Ye heard yer lady," he called out, still not taking his eyes from Marin. "Fire upon them and get these bastards from our walls."

Cat took the lead in front of the archers, her young voice calling out with confident authority. The men obeyed her orders, taking their aim and releasing when she gave the call. A volley of arrows sailed over the side of the castle, and the men who had been immobile now darted in various directions to avoid the attack.

Vermin scattering, indeed.

Drake appeared beside Bran and regarded Marin as she met with her sisters several paces away. "Forgive me," Drake said privately to Bran. "But I dinna like the young ladies being on the battlements."

"I confess I dinna like it myself," Bran answered, chagrined. "But nor do I think we can easily make them leave."

Drake's mouth twitched in a failed attempt to suppress a smile. "Do I have yer permission then to see to their safety?"

Bran nodded and glanced over the wall as a third shower of arrows rained down on the reivers below. Few remained, most likely ones who were injured.

"Enough," he called.

The archers lowered their bows and Cat surveyed the grounds below with a satisfied grin.

"Keep an eye on the wall," Bran instructed Drake. "Double the guards. Make it look as though we have more men than we do in case they send another party like this one. And, aye, see to the lasses to ensure they are no' injured."

Drake gave a single nod, ever the ready soldier. Ever the obedient one. Aye, the lad was a good man to have at Bran's side.

"And once it appears the Grahams have cleared the area, have a second runner sent to Kerr and inform him of the Graham attack." Bran scanned the empty horizon. "I dinna know how this will end, but I want it over with. And I want to know that Ena is safe."

Drake nodded again. "I willna let ye down."

And he wouldn't, Bran had no doubt of that. What he did question, however, was how quickly Kerr would heed his call and come to take the bloody castle. Werrick Castle was defensible, but the Grahams were a determined lot, and soon Bran might need all the help he could muster.

21

The Grahams had left not long after the archers, thank goodness. Marin did not see them the following day either.

She swept into her sisters' rooms to find Leila sitting up in bed, her face chagrined.

Isla had informed Marin the youngest sister had developed a slight fever, though one would never suspect as much now. Leila fidgeted with the irritation of a healthy girl trapped in her room.

"I don't understand why I wasn't allowed to at least go out and look down at the Grahams." There was an uncharacteristic petulant whine to her tone. "They couldn't hurt me from where they were."

The fragrant smell of steeping herbs filled the room. Isla worked soundlessly near a table, carefully adding a small portion of honey to the tea.

"You know it's only because we love you, Leila." Marin swept the hair from her sister's face. The chubbiness of youth had left her cheeks. New slender lines of strong cheekbones were showing and hinted at the beautiful woman this sweet girl would become. Marin's heart swelled with maternal pride, the way it always did when she regarded Leila.

"If they come back, may I go outside to see them?" Leila asked.

Marin put a hand over her sister's. The temperature of her skin was wonderfully normal. "They won't come back-"

"They will." Leila's mouth pursed. "There is great sadness on the horizon."

A ribbon of fear curled in Marin. She knew well enough to not dismiss lightly Leila's words, especially when spoken with such seriousness.

"You mustn't say such things," Marin chided.

"She has a gift." Isla turned toward them with the steaming mug of tea cupped in her palms. "Ye shouldna silence the child when she speaks with the wisdom given to her by the gods of old."

"A gift that can get her killed if overheard by the wrong people." Marin gave the healer a hard look.

Isla rolled her eyes. "Fools, the lot of them." She pushed the mug toward Leila.

"Dangerous fools." Marin moved back from the bed to allow the healer to approach Leila with the tea.

Leila did not accept the tea.

"This will be yer last, then ye're free to go about," Isla promised.

Leila obediently drank, her eyes large and haunted by whatever they'd seen, eyes that were far too old to be that of a ten-year-old child. If only Marin could simply wrap her sister in her arms and blot out everything awful and terrible.

Life on the border was hard enough without the threat of Leila being denounced as a witch. Isla had managed to avoid accusation thus far as her healing skills were invaluable. But would Leila's own dabbling in herbs and healing be enough to keep her safe in the future?

"This will make ye sleep a bit more." Isla took the empty mug and settled a withered hand over Leila's head. "And then ye may rise from yer bed for as long as ye have the energy to do so, aye?"

Leila's mouth lifted at the corners in a wan smile, as though she were trying to rally her own flagging spirits. Marin caught her sister in a hug.

"You don't understand," Leila whispered in a choked voice. "Our poor Anice. She will be so sad."

"You needn't worry on such things." Marin gave her one last squeeze and released her. "She is stronger than you think."

Leila's mouth twisted to the side and she looked away, giving her head a slight shake. Marin swept a hand lovingly down her silky cheek and stood by the bed waiting for the girl's narrow chest to rise and fall with deep and even breathing. Isla remained as well, which was exactly what Marin had hoped.

"You cannot encourage her visions," Marin said in a low tone. "Look at what it does to her. If accusations will not kill her, she may well be undone by the pain."

Isla frowned and shook her head. "Ye canna stop the sight, so ye might as well benefit."

"Do not encourage her further," Marin said resolutely.

The old woman nodded, and her tawny eyes sparkled. "Did yer wedding night go well enough, lass?"

Marin's cheeks went immediately hot and she stared at the healer for a long moment, unsure of how to respond. The woman seemed to revel in discussions that ought not be spoken aloud.

Isla gave a wheezing laugh and clasped her hands to her chest. "As I figured. The lad is a strapping one. Good strong muscles, no' too hairy. When they're lean like that, their bodies are—"

"I didn't bleed." The words slipped from her mouth and once they'd been loosed, there was no drawing them back. Her whole body blazed with mortification.

Isla's good humor did not abate her features. "I'm assuming ye were a maid still, aye?"

"For certes," Marin said quickly, as though doing so might assuage any doubt. For surely, she had been a virgin.

Isla shrugged. "It isna a wonder ye dinna have that wee barrier between yer legs with all ye do. It's a delicate web, ye see, easily broken. Riding horses astride and training with the tenacity of a warrior can easily see it undone. Has yer new husband questioned ye? Men have a way of needing proof they've been the first." The raise of her eyes to the heavens told Marin what Isla thought of such men.

Marin shook her head. "He did not seem overly concerned."

"Are ye sure ye dinna bleed?" Isla asked, peering more closely at her.

Marin forced herself to remain still, to not give in to the twisting discomfort knotting through her. Heavens, how she dearly regretted having broached the topic. "I confess I didn't notice if there was blood, but it was mentioned..."

A secret glint of amusement danced in Isla's eyes. She nodded her head and pushed out her thin lips. "Interesting."

"What is?"

Isla smirked. "When yer wedding sheets were brought from yer room, they would suggest otherwise."

Marin regarded Isla with momentary confusion. "Do you mean...?"

"Aye. The sheets were stained with the blood of a maiden."

BRAN HAD ONLY SEEN MARIN IN PASSING THROUGH THE ENTIRE day. Her secretive smiles in his direction had been enough to keep him hunting for her everywhere he went. He had nearly given up on getting to spend time with his new bride when Drake caught up with him on the battlements, informing him Marin requested he join her for supper in their chambers.

Apparently, dining in one's chambers was what nobles did

when they did not wish to be on display atop the highly-visible dais at the center of the great hall. They also sent servants to schedule times to see their husbands.

There certainly was a lot to learn about the complicated life of a wealthy noble. He still did not know that he enjoyed the lifestyle, but the food was significantly better. And then there was Marin and their lusty nights between costly sheets.

Bran opened the door to their rooms and gently closed the door before Bixby could follow. Marin sat at a small table, set with a fine meal. She got to her feet and met him halfway. Green silk whispered about her as she moved and caught the light of the hearth against the glossy fabric.

A pitiful meow sounded indignantly from the other side of the door.

Bran ignored it and pulled Marin into his arms.

She gazed up at him. "I've been desperate to see you all day."

Bran ran a hand down her lovely unbound hair, the way he liked it best. He tilted her face toward him and did exactly what he'd been desperate to do all day. His mouth came down on hers, light at first, then hungrily slanting, tongues tangling with eager breaths.

A knock came at the door and they broke apart. Marin's face went a becoming shade of red.

"Aye?" Bran called by way of answering.

A gentle scratching came from the other side of the door, followed by a low meow of protest.

"I came to see if you required anything further," said a voice.

"We're fine, thank you," Marin replied loudly. "Please take Bixby to Nan when you go." She looked up at Bran with a grin. "We ought to eat so they can remove our food."

"And leave us in peace?"

She cast him a grin that shot straight to his cock. "Aye."

At that exact moment, his stomach rumbled in anticipation. Apparently sating his lust wasn't all his body required. Marin took him by the hand and led him to the table set beside the hearth, where a small pie lay on each plate.

"I hope you enjoy pigeon." Marin sliced into her pie and a spiral of steam trailed upward, bringing with it a decadent scent of sage and pepper.

In fact, Bran had never had pigeon. When one was lucky enough to have any form of meat once a week, one seldom could guess its source. "I imagine I will if it tastes as good as it smells."

He cut open his own pie and nudged aside the huff paste with his knife, casting aside the inedible shell to get to the tender meat and vegetables within.

Marin lifted her goblet of wine and regarded him over the rim. "Where did you cut yourself?"

He speared a bit of slender white meat with his knife tip and paused. "Cut myself?"

"Mmmhmm," she hummed. "Where did you do it?"

He put the poultry into his mouth and almost closed his eyes to relish the flavor-rich meat. As it turned out, he loved pigeon.

"Isla said there was blood on the sheets." Marin took a dainty bite of her own food.

The piece of meat Bran had swallowed lodged in his throat and required a hearty swig of his wine before he could answer. He cleared his throat. "Ah, that cut."

"So, you did do it then?" Her tone carried enough displeasure to make him hesitate.

He stared down at his food. "Ye dinna poison this, did ye?"

Marin smirked. "If I killed you, I couldn't get answers, could I?" She set her knife down on her plate. "Besides, I did promise not to kill you."

"But ye're upset." He selected another morsel of pigeon to eat. Hell, if it was poison, it made for a fine last meal.

"I was a virgin." She lifted her eating dagger and nudged at the contents of her pie. "Isla says it is not uncommon for a woman so active on the battlefield to not maintain her maidenhead."

Her words were defensive, and she kept her eyes trained on the pie she appeared to have no interest in eating.

Bran considered offering to eat it for her, but then thought better of the idea. "Ye told me ye were a maiden. I'm no' concerned about it."

"You didn't tell me you cut yourself to smear blood on our sheets." Her mouth drew tight. "Were you so ashamed for the world to think I was not a maiden?"

He frowned. "Nay. Marin, I did it for ye."

"For me?" she repeated dubiously.

"I dinna know much about this world of wealthy men, but I know it to be a cruel place for women. I'm aware what a maidenhead is to a woman and her reputation." He reached out and settled a hand over hers. "Ye've worked to maintain yer reputation. I'd no' let ye be besmirched among the lot of pompous arses who might otherwise judge ye."

She blinked. "You did do it for me."

He shrugged and released her hand to take up his eating dagger once more. "Ye're my wife, lass. I'll protect ye to my dying breath."

"I hope that won't be too soon." She smiled shyly at him.

"Does that mean ye've abandoned yer intention to kill me?" He lifted his brows at her.

"I have other plans for you." She rose from her chair.

A knock sounded at the door.

"Get the plates on the morrow," Marin said aloud.

"Aye, my lady." The voice on the other side of the door said no more.

Marin drew Bran from his seat and pulled him back toward the bed. "You should show me where you cut yourself."

He drew up his sleeve to demonstrate the thin cut. She bent over his arm and gently pressed her lips to the slim, red line. She continued kissing, over the rolled sleeve of his doublet to the bare skin of his neck, and finally upon his lips.

"Love me, Bran," she whispered against his mouth. "I've been aching for you all day."

She needn't say more, for Bran was only too happy to oblige. And yet, even as he kissed her, as he explored her body and they sated their lusts throughout the night, he could not help the pressing thought rising in his mind. For what would become of this affection and happiness when Kerr finally arrived at Werrick Castle?

❧ 22 ❧

The following sennight flew by in a whirl of busy activity and steamy nights.

True to her word, Marin had begun to include Bran in her meetings with the pertinent members of the household to ensure they cooperated with him in helping her run the keep. Not only was he eager to be part of the castle's daily life, she found he excelled at the duties.

Each day they worked more closely together, and each day, Marin found herself all the more endeared to the man she'd been forced to wed.

Outside, the Grahams still hovered on the grounds. Their presence was disconcerting when the food stores had not been sufficiently restocked since Bran's arrival. His forces had depleted their supply when he first assumed control of the castle. Though the number of men had been greatly reduced due to abandonment and death, the perpetual presence of the aggressive Grahams had kept anyone from going out of, or into, the castle.

Leila had not developed another fever and had followed all the strict rules given to her by Isla as her wounds healed. After many,

many requests to do so, Leila was finally allowed out on the battlements.

Marin hovered over her youngest sister and tried not to let her worry and fear show.

"I'll be fine." Leila caught Marin's hand the way she had done when she was a small child.

In truth, Marin had hoped Leila might be able to offer some insight on the great sadness she'd spoken of, the one on the horizon. The one that had not yet come to pass. But seeing Leila looking out over the Graham forces, Marin didn't want the information, not when the cost was so high. Leila was too young, too delicate.

She never should have allowed Leila out there.

Bran curled an arm around Marin, protective and loving. "I promise nothing will happen to her."

Marin leaned into Bran's strength, grateful for his confident assurance. She needed it to put her mind at ease.

"If it gets dangerous, Leila, you will have to return to the keep." Marin's concern put an edge to her tone she had not intended.

Leila did not reply but stared out in the distance and tilted her face to the wind, as though doing so might enable her to read something unseen to all others.

Marin cast an anxious glance at Bran. While she trusted her husband, she did not like Leila displaying her abilities so blatantly.

She knelt beside her sister. "Leila, I—"

A tear slid down Leila's face while her eyes watched something in the distance.

Fear dragged an icy chill down Marin's spine. "What is it?"

"Do you not see it?"

Marin looked to the horizon, empty save for a few Graham soldiers. "What do you see?"

"It is coming." Leila blinked but still the tears fell down her cheeks.

Marin pulled her small sister into her arms. "We must get you inside."

"Rider," Bran said above them.

Marin jerked her attention to the distance once more and spied a man on horseback, his body slumped over his horse. Graham reivers rode on either side of him, whooping and shouting. Something was amiss.

"Summon Cat immediately." Marin stood and nudged her youngest sister toward the castle. "Leila, get inside. Now. Send for Isla in case we have need of her."

Whoever the man on the horse was, he did not appear well.

Leila ran, filling the battlements with the slap, slap, slap of her leather shoes over the stonework.

"Archers," Marin bellowed. "Ready your bows."

The creak of over a dozen bowstrings being pulled back answered her call.

"Something isna right," Bran said. "I'll be at the gate in case we need to open the portcullis. If those bastards get through, my reivers will be waiting for them."

Marin tore her gaze from the rider to that of her husband. "Bran, nay."

His mouth lifted in a lazy half smile that made her stomach twirl. "Dinna worry about me, lass. I can handle myself." He caught her around the waist, gave her one final, searing kiss and was gone.

She spun back to the rider and found two Grahams closing in on him from either side.

Footsteps thundered up the stairs. "I'm here," Cat shouted breathlessly.

"Stop them." Marin indicated the Grahams.

"Aye." Cat drew back the string of her newly fashioned bow, slightly larger than the others, and loosed her first arrow. It soared beyond the stopping point of the other arrows and continued onward, straight into the chest of the Graham on the right.

He fell from his horse and the rider lost one pursuer. Cat gave a hiss of victory and pulled another arrow from her quiver. Marin squinted in the distance. The rider did not appear in a hurry to escape them and seemed stiff, unmoving. "Wait." Marin held up her hand.

Cat sucked in a breath. "Marin, I do not think that man is alive."

The horse carrying the stiff rider trotted closer and the odor of rot rolled in on a breeze. Disgust knotted in Marin's stomach and something gripped her heart. Fear.

Her father had not come home. Timothy. Geordie. So many who had not yet come home. Could it be one of them? A taunt of the worst kind?

"Arrows," Marin said weakly. "We cannot kill the dead, but we can kill the Grahams."

Cat gave the call and volleys of arrows sailed over the battlements, peppering the field surrounding the castle. The Grahams shoved the corpse from its horse before the castle and rode away with the empty mount.

Werrick arrows flew in earnest, no longer mindful of sparing any lives. The Grahams immediately fled and not one fell before they reached a distance out of the archer's range.

Marin sent a message for Bran to claim the body. Mayhap there was something on this man's person to indicate his being there. Her chest tightened. Or perhaps he was someone they might recognize.

Not Father. Not Timothy. Not Geordie. The words came in a form of a chant in her mind. Repeated over and over again until they scored her heart.

The low, scraping groan of the portcullis sounded and Bran's men ran out under the cover of watchful archers to grab the body and draw him inside.

Marin remained with the archers until all of Bran's men were off the grass and the portcullis had dropped closed once more.

Secure in the knowledge all was safe, she locked her heart in her throat and ran down the stone stairs to discover who the dead man was, and what secrets he held.

THE MAN'S FACE HAD BEEN BEATEN AND HIS BODY MANGLED. His death had occurred some time ago given the gray pallor of his skin and the purplish hue of his lips. And the smell. God's toes, the smell. Bran pushed the sleeve of his forearm to his nose and stared down at the man. Sir Richard and several of Bran's men had dragged the poor bastard into the bailey.

The body was one of his reivers. The one sent to bring the missive to Kerr. The Grahams had caught him and had their fun with him first before finally killing him. The bailey was quiet, save for the violent buzz of a cloud of black flies feasting on the rotting flesh.

Isla regarded the man. "I dinna think ye need a healer."

"The priest has been summoned," Drake said.

"Then I'm no' leaving until I see the look on his face," Isla muttered.

A choked cry sounded from behind Bran. He spun around, but it was too late. Marin stood there with her hand pressed to her mouth, her eyes wide with terror.

"Marin, dinna look." Bran tried to stand in front of the body, to keep the worst of it from her eyes.

"My father?" She paled and reached for Bran with trembling hands.

"Nay," he answered quickly. "One of my men."

"It was the Grahams." Drake braced his feet wide, as if he required extra stability in light of the horror of this death. "This was done with intent, this torture." His lips curled and he gave a thick swallow.

Bernard appeared, his panting suggesting his haste. "I came when..." His voice trailed off and his eyes went wide.

"Are ye well?" Bran asked.

Bernard blushed and nodded. His shaved pate glistened with a sheen of sweat. "Aye, of course. We are all God's creatures. That is, it matters not how we arrive to greet him. Which isn't to say this man's body is appalling, though it is a mighty shock but—"

Isla scoffed.

Bernard's pale blue eyes shot up and found Isla. Immediately, he crossed himself.

Isla chortled at his reaction to her, as gleeful at his fear as ever. "In my younger years, he wouldna have been making that sign." She rolled her hand in the air. "Get on with it, ye spineless sap."

Bernard wiped his palm down the hip of his robe and began droning the last rites in Latin, his demeanor calming immediately with the application of his faith.

While the hum of his voice cast reverent stillness over the gathered men. Bran looked to Marin and nodded toward the castle, indicating she go inside.

She shook her head and stepped forward with her chin notched upward in that stubborn way of hers. Bran reached out and took her hand in his. Her palm was warm and damp, an indication she was not as calm as her demeanor would otherwise suggest.

But as the last rites were given over the body, Bran could not help the flurry of questions racing through his mind. How long had the Grahams had the man? Had the message to Kerr been delivered? Was there a reply?

Bernard made the sign of the cross over the body and it was done.

Bran regarded Marin. "See to your sisters. Ensure they are not too distraught over what has happened. I'll handle the burial."

Marin glanced to the body and then raised her eyes to meet Bran's. "Are you certain? I can assist you if—"

"Nay, lass." Bran shook his head. "Go to yer sisters."

Bran pressed a kiss to her brow before turning to Drake. "Take her inside, aye?"

Drake gave a firm nod.

Marin squeezed Bran's hand and released her hold on him. "Thank you."

Her look of gratitude dug into his chest and squeezed at his guilt. He needed her gone so he could check over the body, to find any missive that remained to see how much the Grahams might have found, or not found. To verify for himself how far the man had made it.

Damn.

Things could not possibly be any worse.

ᐰᐰ

With a heart fuller than it'd been in some time, Marin ran to her sisters. For years, there had been so many moments of having to choose between comforting her sisters or overseeing difficult tasks. But not this day.

In the face of horror and fear, Bran bore the brunt of the awfulness of the poor reiver's mangled body and tasked her with caring for what he knew mattered most to her.

The sisters had gathered in the sunlit solar. Anice hovered over Cat, gently resting a hand on her shoulder. Ella and Leila sat on a window seat with Piquette, their heads bent over a book. All looked up when Marin and Drake entered.

Marin immediately set to work caring for her sisters. Ella had lost herself in a book and pulled Leila with her. Cat had been distraught but had calmed down after drinking tea drizzled generously with honey from Isla. Poor Drake had hovered over them, his helplessness apparent in the way he shifted his weight from one foot to the other. Clearly wanting to offer his assistance, but unsure how. Anice had tried to set him at ease by constantly reassuring him they were all fine until he finally left to return to Bran's side.

In the distance, beyond the glass window, the sun sank into the landscape like a glowing ember and cast the sky in violent sprays of red and orange. Like watered down blood.

There is great sadness on the horizon.

A chill settled along the back of Marin's neck and slid down her spine like an icy finger. She suppressed her shudder.

"My lady." Sir Richard's voice tugged Marin from her thoughts of Leila's warning.

Marin glanced at her sisters, and after confirming they had all calmed, she excused herself and met with Sir Richard in the hallway.

His mouth set in a grim line. "I brought the man's body in."

Marin inclined her head graciously. "You have my thank—"

"I'm not telling you for gratitude." Richard kept his voice to a low whisper. "This was on the man. I brought it to you as soon as it appeared to be safe." He lifted his gloved hand where he pinched a folded square of parchment smeared with blood.

"Did you read it?" she asked even as she accepted the missive. She squared her shoulders, making herself a shield against prying eyes.

"Aye, in case it was about your father."

She cast him a grateful look, knowing his intent to be good-hearted. However, any gratitude in her chest froze solid at the words written on the parchment. It was a call to the Scottish Middle Warden to send reinforcements to help secure the castle before the Earl of Werrick could arrive.

The name signed at the bottom in a slash of black ink over the gory parchment—Bran.

Marin gasped and tightened her fist on the parchment to keep it from slipping from her fingers. So, this was why Bran had wanted the castle. For Scotland. No doubt Kerr would see them all killed, including her father. Her sisters.

She shuddered at the thought. Never once had Bran indicated his intent for the castle was so dangerous, could cost so many lives.

She had been betrayed.

❧ 23 ❧

Marin let the remainder of the day slip by without giving any indication of what she knew. Though she'd tried to avoid Bran, she had encountered him several times. She'd suffered through it with congenial smiles and let him kiss her with his lying lips.

Initially she'd assumed he'd wanted Werrick Castle for himself, and that the worst of the ordeal had passed. But apparently it was only the beginning. Didn't Bran realize what he'd done? Didn't he care?

Kerr was a rapacious Warden, one determined to claim what he could for himself above all obligations of upholding the law. Marin had heard his name mentioned often by her father in association with lying. With murder.

Once Kerr had the castle, all her people would be slaughtered, her family ripped apart, her sisters no doubt sold into marriages with the enemy—if they were lucky. And when her father returned from Berwick, he would without a doubt be the first one to die.

Her heart pounded in her chest as though it meant to burst and her hand trembled where she clutched the hilt of the knife.

She would do it this time. She would kill Bran before he could destroy her and everything she loved.

An angry scream welled in her throat, but she swallowed it down. She couldn't get emotional. She couldn't do anything to jeopardize her revenge.

The door to their shared chamber opened soundlessly and his attending servant slipped out with a solemn expression. It was time.

Marin swept past the servant and into the massive chamber before locking herself in just as noiselessly as the servant had departed.

Sandalwood filled the warm air made humid by the wooden tub placed in front of the glowing hearth. The back of Bran's head faced her, an intentional placement by the servant. Marin's head spun with a dizzying anxiety.

This way would be quiet, easy. Even the mess would be contained. She crept closer, until she discerned the swell of his powerful shoulders rising above the water.

Only the night before, she'd clutched those shoulders in passion. The memory left her stomach churning with disgust.

Bran shifted in the water and the glassy surface rippled, leaving his reflection distorted and shattered.

"Have ye ever met someone who made ye question who ye are?" he asked suddenly.

Marin stopped, but her heart raced on and on. She couldn't answer for the servant, not when it was impossible to mask her voice to sound like that of a man. Instead she remained wordless, frozen in place, hoping he would leave off the question.

"Ach, 'tis an odd question." Bran sighed. "I'm contemplative of late and I've got that wife of mine to blame for it."

Marin's eyes narrowed with her ire. What did he possibly mean by such a statement?

"Water on my head, if you please." He settled deeper into the tub. "I'd like my hair to be scrubbed."

Marin closed the distance with a final step and put the knife to his throat. She had been prepared to dig it deep, to cut through the hardy fibers of the neck to ensure his life ended.

Except his strong hand captured hers and held her in place.

"Do ye think I wouldna detect my wife's own scent?" Bran didn't twist to look at her though his hand continued to restrain her. "Do ye think I dinna notice how ye averted yer gaze from mine throughout the day, or how my tub had been positioned?"

Marin yanked her captive hand with all her strength in an attempt to draw the blade back and into the vulnerable skin of his neck. He growled and tightened his grip on her, thwarting her efforts. In one fluid movement, he rose and turned toward her with water sluicing from his powerful body. He twisted her wrist as he stood, and a sharp pain lanced up Marin's arm. The knife dropped from her hand and splashed into the water, lost.

The agony in her wrist immediately abated. Water shone over Bran's unabashed nudity and dripped into the tub. The firelight was at his back and cast his face in an unreadable shadow.

"Ye said ye wouldna try to kill me again." His voice was low, dangerous. "Marin, I trusted ye."

"I trusted you too," she spat out. She yanked the missive from her pocket and threw it at his chest.

He snatched it from the air as it fluttered downward. His body remained still. She strained her eyes into the shadows over his face but couldn't make out his expression. She hated that. The uncertainty of how he might answer the accusation.

Would he try to defend himself?

She stared into the wavering reflection of the fire atop the water. The knife was in there still, somewhere lying at the bottom. She couldn't read his face, but perhaps the missive was enough of a distraction to afford her the necessary time she needed.

Without hesitation, she plunged her hands into the water and skimmed the flat bottom with her fingertips in a frantic, blind search to reclaim the dagger.

Bran said her name, but she ignored him. The water was too dark, and her heart was pounding too hard.

She had to find it. She had to kill him.

All of this had to stop.

Strong hands closed around her arms, restraining her. The man who had lied to her, the man who would see them all condemned, the man she had found herself beginning to love.

The pain of his betrayal slashed through her. She jerked her hands free with incredible strength. He reached for her once more and she lashed out with her fist.

He avoided her blow. "Listen to me, woman."

Her chest and arms were nearly submerged in her desperation. Water splashed on her face and the sandalwood scent she once found so pleasing sputtered from her lips and clung in her throat.

Where was the blade?

Bran caught her arm once more, his grip gentle despite the firmness. "Damn it, woman. Listen to me."

"You would have us all killed."

"Ye dinna see the first page."

Marin stopped floundering against his grasp.

His shoulders relaxed, but his hold on her remained strong. "There was a first page to the missive. The only one ye saw was the second page, the one I assumed was missing."

"You're lying," Marin said flatly.

She could make out his face at such close proximity and the flex of his jaw.

"I'll show it to ye, but I'm sure ye dinna trust me."

Marin kept her face expressionless, masking the hurt and betrayal. For if he was lying, she would not let him live to witness the pain he'd caused her. He would not be worth such emotions. She shook her head slowly.

"It's in my gambeson on the chair." His grip loosened. "I'd get it, but I'm sure ye'd think I'd spring out of here bare-arsed and attempt to ride to warn Kerr of yer knowledge."

He released her, but she did not move. *Was this a trap?* It could be an opportunity to get the advantage and attack her.

"How could you do this to us, Bran?" Marin asked, her voice clogging with the emotion she had been trying to stifle.

He gestured to a nearby chair by the fire. "I'll no' say words ye willna believe. Go to my gambeson and get the missive."

She backed away from him, leaving a dripping trail in her wake. With her gaze fixed on him, she carefully searched through his pockets until she found one with a bit of parchment lodged within. Her heart slammed as hard in her chest now as it had when she had been only moments from killing him.

With trembling fingers, she unfolded the blood-spattered note, following the same creases as its twin, the sheet she'd intercepted earlier that day. There, in the same scrolling handwriting, was a plea from Bran to Kerr to see the Werrick household, the earl and his daughters all safe. But that was not all, it was a demand for the safe release of Ena.

Marin lifted her head and stared at Bran. "They have Ena?"

Bran's jaw flexed and he looked away, the way hardened men did when in pain. "Kerr tried to enlist my aid for the last several months, but I dinna work with rich men. They dinna care about people other than themselves." Bitterness laced his tone. "And so, when Ena married an Englishman from the English Middle March side, he arrested her for breaking the law."

Marin sucked in a breath. "It's punishable by death."

Bran nodded.

"But no one enforces such a law," Marin protested. "English and Scottish marry all the time."

"True, except for the Wardens of the Marches who find a way to get what they want." Bran shifted and the water in the tub spiraled out around him. "I deliver him Werrick Castle and he releases Ena."

Marin's thoughts whirled with this new development. Ena was all Bran had left of his family. "Why didn't you tell me?"

"Because ye're protecting yer own sisters, Marin." He shook his head. "Would ye willingly sacrifice them to save mine? Would I be willing to sacrifice mine to save yers?" He ran a hand through his hair, the power of his arm flexing with the simple movement. "It all would have been done if the battle at Berwick wouldna have happened. Now there's no' anything to do but wait."

Marin looked at the missive once more. "Ena." The name slipped from her lips before she realized she was saying it. "Is she safe still?"

A hard look passed over Bran's features. "She had better be."

Marin set the missive onto the chair and tried to breathe around the heaviness in her chest. All this time, Bran had been trying to protect Ena. He had even tried to use his holding of Werrick Castle to offer protection to Marin and her family, even if it meant possibly angering the man who held Ena.

Bran had been trying to save his sister, trying to save everyone at the castle, and Marin had been ready to kill him.

⚜

BRAN REMAINED IN THE TUB AND LET THE UNDERSTANDING sink into Marin. Her eyes sparkled with unshed tears.

"I almost killed you," she whispered.

"I would have stopped ye."

"Bran–I..." She slowly approached him. "You risked angering Kerr by asking him to keep us safe."

"Aye, because I wanted to ensure yer safety and those ye care about," he answered honestly. "I never want ye to know the loss I have suffered."

She gave a small whimper. "I tried to kill you. I don't deserve—"

"Ye do." He stepped out of the tub and drew her into his arms.

The ground was cool underfoot, a comfortable respite from the heat of the tub.

Her hands slipped around his back and she clung to him. The wet fabric of her gown was cold against his skin and helped keep his head focused.

Because as much as he hated to admit it to himself, her accusations and lack of trust had wounded him. True, he had taken the castle under malicious circumstances, but in the time following, he'd aided her, he'd supported her.

She was not like the ladies he had met, the privileged women of considerable wealth who looked down upon his lot. Nay, she was kind and determined and had enough room in her heart for an entire castle full of people.

Mayhap even for him.

Her mouth pressed to his chest in a kiss. Several kisses turned into a string of them up his chest and to his neck. His body responded immediately, lighting with heat and hardness, sparked by having lost her trust and regaining it once more.

Marin rested her palm on his cheek and lifted her face to his. Bran kissed her, sweetly, chastely, until she rose on her toes and swept her tongue into his mouth. He gave her what she needed then. He slanted his mouth over hers and lost himself in the shared passion between them, the spiked fear of loss, the strength of mutual want.

"Forgive me, Bran." She spoke between kisses, frantic with need, made clear by the way her hands grazed over his body.

Her fingers trickled down his stomach to where his cock had already risen hard between them. He growled against her lips and drew the lacing from the back of her gown, blindly plucking at the ties. Her touch curled around his shaft and his bollocks drew tight with anticipation.

She stroked him the way he'd shown her, starting at the base and working up to the sensitive head. His thoughts went hazy. It turned all his racing musings from before into ash and they simply blew away. From bottom to top, her small palm squeezed and worked his lust to fervent intensity. His concentration on the lacings became difficult and his movements were clumsy. Too damn slow.

He grunted with frustration.

"You said once you would feed me your cock," she whispered in his ear.

He went still, or at least all of him but his prick, which lurched to attention at such words.

"The way you slipped your thumb in my mouth." She drew her hand over him, up and down, like slow, sensual fire. "Is that how it's done?"

His mouth was too dry to answer, and his fingers stopped working at her lacing. She gave him a coquettish gaze and lowered herself to her knees in front of him.

"Should I be like this?" Warm, sweet breath bathed over the blazing heat of his skin.

He swallowed.

Her kirtle hung open at the back and drooped from one shoulder, exposing only part of her to him. The curve of a breast was tantalizingly creamy white in the shadows of the gapping fabric. Her state of partial undress in contrast to the blatantly erotic act she intended to perform on him only served to send his senses soaring higher. He wanted to shove down the limp sleeve, to kiss her shoulder and expose both perfect breasts.

She gazed up at him expectantly. *God's teeth.* Bran took his cock in his hand and guided the tip to her mouth, rubbing it teasingly against her full lips. Tingles of pleasure rippled through him. His breath hissed through his teeth.

"Open yer mouth, wife." His voice was deep with lust.

She obediently opened her mouth, her gaze fixed on him.

He shifted his hips forward and pushed his cock into her mouth. She closed around him as she'd done with his finger before, and she gave a little suck. Bran's toes curled at the overwhelming sensation.

"Aye, like that," he murmured. "Now take it deeper, aye?"

She drew him further into her mouth, suckling with sweet, torturous innocence. Pleasure raked through him, sizzling and greedy. He gave a choked cry and reached for Marin's head to bury his hands in the mass of her silky hair. To guide her over him.

She suckled the incredibly sensitive tip, nudging him into her mouth ever so slightly. A low humming moan in her throat reverberated down his shaft as she pleasured him. He wouldn't be able to take much more of this.

She teased his hard flesh for an indeterminate amount of time, until he was nearly mad with the need for her to take the whole of him. She'd wanted him to feed her his cock—by God he would do so.

He released one hand from her hair and put it over her grip on him. "Open yer mouth wider." He spoke in a low growl, his throat tight with his restraint to not plunge his cock forward. No, she needed to go at her own pace. "Take me deeper."

She obediently opened her mouth, and did exactly as he asked, letting him push his cock so it disappeared further.

It was a good thing they'd had one another so often of late, or this simple act alone would have undone him. As it was, he knew he should stop, but dear God, he could not bring himself to do so.

❧ 24 ❧

Desire built between Marin's legs in a low, hungry pulse while she took Bran's phallus into her mouth. He watched her with an almost unwavering intensity, his jaw tight, the bands of his stomach taut as iron in the firelight. His entire being was centered on her. She was powerful in her sexuality and the knowledge of it gave her a lusty high.

The thickness of his manhood pushed slowly deeper, hard and hot against her tongue, until it touched the back of her throat. His fingers at his base told her there was still more of him, but she hadn't the room. Instead, she secured her lips around him, and sucked.

His body jerked and he uttered a curse. She didn't have to look up to know he was enjoying the sensation. His hand tensed in her hair and she slowly pulled her mouth off him. His cock popped free. He still held at the base with his other hand, positioned toward her mouth, ready to push himself into her lips once more.

Desire thrummed wickedly between her legs. She licked the swollen head, enjoying the spongy heat of it against her tongue before she sucked him into her mouth once more, firmly and with more confidence. He gave a long, desperate groan and her sex clenched in response to his obvious pleasure. She cast her attention upward and found him watching her with a deep, intense ferocity.

"Keep looking at me," he said in a husky voice.

She did as she was bade, keeping her eyes fixed on him as he guided her ministrations. Giving him such bliss made her want to give even more—not because she'd almost killed him—because he had given her such evocative sensations. She wanted to give him what he'd given her, to make him feel alive in the way he'd done for her. Every grunt, every cry of delight he'd issued forth served to heighten her own enjoyment of the act, driving her forward and making her bold.

She sucked and licked, moaning her pleasure as she did so. She let him love her mouth the way he'd loved her body and allowed him to see how much she enjoyed it.

His hardness against her tongue tensed and seemed to grow larger.

"Stop," he ground out.

Marin immediately released him. His cock stood thick and hard in front of her face. He'd released it and the engorged tip pulsed in time with his racing heartbeat. Her mouth ached for the swollen heat of him against her lips once more.

"I want to be in ye when I come." Bran brought her to her feet and caught her in his arms.

The movement was quick and strong and nearly took Marin's breath away with how badly she needed exactly this. Longing burned like stars in his eyes, bright and hot. His jaw flexed and he pushed aside the loosened sleeve of her gown. He bent over her and ran his tongue over the top of her shoulder to the crook of her neck. Waves of delicious tingles spread through Marin's body; her skin incredibly sensitive with the brilliance of her yearning.

With one hand, Bran slipped the laces of her gown free. With the other, he reached into the open bodice and cupped her breast.

She had been chilled by the sodden gown and his palm was like fire against her icy skin. His fingers found her hard nipple, which he rolled with wondrous skill.

He peeled the gown from her torso and let the fabric crumple to the ground in a sad, wet pile. Bran trailed his fingers down her flat stomach and did not hesitate to slip one between her thighs where her lust burned without control, without limit. Marin's hips bucked toward him and she gave a long moan.

He grunted with pleasure, his merciless finger stroking over her again and again, gliding against her sex until the poor swollen bud made her want to rage in frustration. His lips came down on hers and his tongue swept into her mouth. He claimed her mouth as he made promises to her body. Heat prickled through her palms and she began to tighten toward the nearness of a climax. So close. So very close.

Bran removed his hand and aided her in sitting on the wooden shelf at the rear of the tub where a lord's drink and food might be placed. It rocked under her but held her weight.

Before she could ask what he was about, Bran knelt on the wet ground and gently parted her legs. Marin might have been embarrassed at being so exposed, were she not so mindless with need. As it was, she offered no protest when he gazed between her thighs, nor when his fingers spread her sex.

She writhed with his touch, desperate for her crisis. Everything pulsed with a hot, heavy need, her senses so alight, she feared she might burn from the inside out. She opened her mouth to beg for release when he leaned forward and dragged his tongue over her aching center.

It was wicked and sinful and wrong and wholly incredible. She cried out and gripped the edge of the shelf. Her senses were intensely alive, sharp with the power of her desire. The wet heat of his mouth, the tease of sandalwood floating around her in the steamy air, as though all of him were completely consuming her.

He traced up and down with his tongue as his finger had done, and finally came to rest on the swollen bud. Marin's cries were hoarse, and her knees trembled. He groaned into her while he circled and flicked and sucked.

Her gasps hitched. She was helpless to restrain herself, even if she wanted to. And she did not. She was so nearly there, teetering on the edge of losing control, ready to fall and shatter into a million euphoric fragments.

He drew away from her with a devilish grin. "In the water."

Her mind spun, trying to understand. He was killing her with this rise and fall of nearly climaxing. If she did not release soon, she might well explode.

Bran stepped into the tub and sank down into it. He paused with a jerk, then lifted the lost dagger and errantly flipped it onto the floor where it clattered. "I canna believe ye tried to kill me again."

"I cannot believe I failed again." Marin got into the bath with him. "Though if you keep teasing me thus..."

He beckoned her to join him. "Teasing ye?"

Marin sank into the water beside him, her skin tingling from having been so cold in her dress to being fully submerged in such glorious warmth. Bran caught her before she could fully sit on the bottom of the tub and guided her to him. No, not to him, over him.

"There will be no more teasing." His hands slid up her hips and he gently pulled her down. "I want ye to ride me."

"Here?" Marin asked in shock. This was where bodies were cleaned, not where--the blunt edge of Bran's hardness bumped her inner thigh. She bit her lip and gave an uncontrolled moan of need.

He gave her a lazy smile. "I think ye'll find the water enjoyable." He guided her hips toward his. The water lapped at her breasts and nipples, stimulating and enticing.

She sank onto him and the entire length of him slid deep inside her. Bran groaned with the same appreciation for the bliss of their joining. His hands cupped her bottom and he drew her snuggly against him. She put her hands to the dampness of his powerful chest to better keep her balance. "Show me what to do."

He nudged her hips back and then rocked her forward again. "Like that, aye?"

The movement rubbed at her swollen bud. She gasped and nodded, understanding immediately what he wanted in this new position.

BRAN CRADLED MARIN TO HIM, THEIR PELVISES FITTING perfectly together. She was tight where she sheathed him, exquisite. Her wet skin was slippery against his hands and glossy in the firelight.

He guided her hips backward and the water swirled around them. A gasp escaped Marin's parted lips. She watched him with half-lidded eyes, her cheeks flushed from their intimate games.

Marin shifted her hips forward on her own.

"Aye, like that," Bran said raggedly.

The next couple rocks of her hips were hesitant while she learned the motion. Bran clenched his teeth to stave off the rising swell of climax. Sweat prickled at his brow. Marin arched herself forward and braced her hands on his shoulders, her moves growing more confident. Her lashes fluttered and he knew she'd not only found the rhythm, but the exact spot she'd needed.

She had the power and she knew what to do with it. Exactly as he'd anticipated she would.

He growled in approval and slid his hand up her narrow waist to where her breasts bounced near his mouth. Too tempting to ignore.

Water churned around them beneath the surface where they were joined together, heightening the pleasure of it all. They were light in the water, buoyant. Bran pushed against the rising tide of release threatening to overwhelm him. By God, he would not come yet.

Her hands gripped his shoulders harder and her breath came faster. He cupped her bottom once more and pumped into her as she rubbed over him again and again. Bran's breath hissed from between the clench of his teeth. Water splashed over the sides of the tub. Her pace increased.

She slammed down hard on top of him and her sheath clenched him in so powerful a grip, his own crises tore from him. She tossed her head back and cried out with abandon while he roared at the ferocity of his own release.

Flashes of white danced in front of his vision as his entire body succumbed to pleasure.

When at last the waves of euphoria finally ebbed and trickled away, he opened his eyes to find Marin watching him with a wicked smile curving her lips. His cock twitched within her, eliciting a flinch of oversensitive pleasure from her. Her hair fell around her face, the golden cloud of it floating around them in the water. With her naked torso and perfect breasts rising from the choppy surface, she looked like a water nymph who slipped from the sea to slake her pleasure. The image was erotic, intoxicating. This would not be the last time they used the tub thus.

Marin blinked, slow and languid and gave a shaky exhale. "I didn't know it could be like that."

He chuckled at that. "There are even more ways we havena tried."

Her eyes widened and brightened; her eagerness apparent. She drew her hands from his shoulders, down to his chest and swept one finger against his tight nipple.

His release had left him highly sensitive and he sucked in his breath at the simple action.

"Will you show them to me?" Marin asked with the husky voice of a wanton. "All of them."

"There's no' anything I'd rather do." He glided his hands up her body to tenderly cup her face. "I was worried doing such things as this might scare ye."

She blinked. "Scare me?"

"Ye're a nobleman's daughter." He tilted his head. "It is Saturday. No' a sanction day by the church." He ran his hands down her body again, grasped her fine, round bottom and pushed her against his cock. "And this isna a sanctioned position."

Marin arched with a sigh and her breasts lifted high enough for him to flick his tongue over. She shivered. "I believe I've become relaxed in my views."

"I see that." He drew her toward him and kissed her gently before unseating her from him. He rose from the tub and brought her the linen meant for him.

In truth, he'd been fearful of showing her such pleasures for fear she would find them to be perverse. But his Marin was a noble unlike any other. The lot of Werrick Castle seemed different than those of wealth and title Bran had associated with in his past.

He had found a lusty wife, one eager to fully enjoy the intimacies of marriage. And he was a damn lucky man for it.

He held the linen for her. She opened her mouth to protest, but he shook his head.

"I'll use it after ye," he said. She was so much more petite compared to him, if he'd used it prior to her, there wouldn't have been a spot left dry.

Marin rose from the water, stepped out of the tub and into his waiting arms. He wrapped the linen around her and breathed in the sweet lavender of her hair, now mingled with the spice of his bath. He ran his hands over her body, ensuring she was thoroughly dry. A task he found immensely enjoyable.

He paused in his ministrations and gazed down at her. This incredibly sensual woman was his wife. *His.* A woman of beauty, confidence, authority and caring affection. Her damp hair fell in messy waves around her face.

"You're staring." She spoke playfully, and he knew his attention flattered her. "Dare I ask what you're thinking?"

"I'm thinking what a lucky man I am." He ran his hand down her arm and took her hand in his. Some baser part of him needed to touch her, to confirm she was real. After a lifetime fighting for everything he owned from the clothes on his back to the crust of bread in his belly—after all of it, this incredible woman was his wife. "Ye make me want things I dinna imagine I ever might have."

She lowered her head and aimed a coquettish look in the direction of the tub. "I feel the same."

He grinned. "More than that though." He ran his thumb over the back of her hand where the sapphire ring glinted on her finger. "I never wanted children. A family of my own. No' after what happened to me as a lad, or how vulnerable that love makes ye." He shook his head. He'd never uttered such fears aloud before. But the idea of a family had always frightened him. It kept his intimacies with women casual, safe. "I worry about ye and I havena worried after anyone in a verra long time. I should be driven mad by it, but I...but I care for ye more than I am vexed at fearing for ye."

"And I tried to kill you." She winced. "Several times."

"Ye were protecting yer home." He released her hand. "And I should have told ye about Ena."

The caring glow in her eyes faded to concern. "Bran, what are we going to do?" She lifted the linen from her shoulders and passed the length of damp cloth to him.

He accepted it and draped it over his shoulders as he went to his chest to pull out two leines. One for him and one for her.

What were they going to do? It was a concern that grew ever more pressing, and one he had pushed aside for too long, especially as the threat of war grew between England and Scotland.

No doubt the Earl of Werrick would have other properties where his family and people could go, assuming he had survived.

And assuming the English king would not strip away his land and titles for the loss of the castle.

And Marin, she would go with Bran. But where? To a life as a reiver, one of many in the drafty peel towers set at the border? Could he subject her to a life so dangerous that they had to draw up the ladders at night for fear of being murdered in their sleep?

"We will ensure Ena is safe, and yer family as well." He handed her the long leine. "We can discuss how in the morning, after we've both had a good amount of sleep."

He wished it was possible to put even more time between now and the discussion they needed to have, once more variables came into play. Had Kerr gotten his first letter? Would he come? Was the Earl of Werrick alive?

So much rode on the answers to those questions. Unfortunately, there was no choice but to wait and hope Ena did not pay the price.

🌟 25 🌟

The following day, Bran paced the battlements, staring out
past the cluster of Graham soldiers to where the brilliant
green grass stretched on for miles.

The enclosure of the keep's walls was taking its toll.

The reiver's horrible death the prior day had cast a somber
shadow over the mood within the castle. The threat of the
Grahams just over the walls rattled like a stone in everyone's
mind, a constant irritating reminder of imminent danger.

The soldiers were less anxious, confident in their knowledge
of the safety within the structure, but the reivers, who had grown
used to open freedom, were agitated and edgy. Bran understood
their restlessness. Reivers were nomads, belonging to no one,
reliant on themselves for care and food and lodging, takers of
their necessities.

He did not give in to the pressure, although it didn't mean he
was free of its effects. He stared down at the mass of Grahams
outside the castle walls and a tight itch prickled at the back of his
neck.

Marin stood with the stillness of a statue at his side, her

narrowed gaze focused on the cluster of several dozen men. "What will we do about them?"

Bran rubbed at the spot on his neck, though it did little to alleviate the discomfort. "There's no' anything we can do, save pick them off with our archers when they come too close."

The wind tore at their clothing and left Marin's veil snapping. Her attention was fixated on the Graham reivers, her dissatisfaction evident in the clench of her jaw. She settled her hands on her hips and tapped her finger lightly on the hilt of the sword strapped to her belt. "If your reinforcements do come in, would they help us put the Grahams off?"

Bran glanced down at his wife. He hadn't expected her to mention the possibility of Kerr sending troops, though he could tell from the stern expression on her face that it weighed on her thoughts heavily. "Aye," he answered warily.

She nodded. "If he received the missive." Her neck tensed. "I think he did not. Regardless, the strife at Berwick would detain him."

Her worried expression did not lift. He hated that he couldn't offer her any reassurances. He hated even more that he was the cause.

A Graham warrior edged closer and an arrow shot out from the castle in his direction. He managed to scramble to a safe position before it sank harmlessly into the earth. A cheer rose up from the Grahams. One of them tugged his doublet up and pulled his hose aside to reveal a bared white arse pointed in their direction.

Bran almost chuckled at the antics, for even if the situation was not funny, these men were his kind. Marin, however, was not so amused. Her fists tightened and a flush crept up her neck.

"My father would never have allowed any of this to happen." She muttered the words, but Bran heard them before they were snatched away by the wind. Her brow furrowed, and he knew she was piling the blame upon herself.

"Yer da isna here." He reached out to her. "But we are."

The Grahams hopped on their horses and rallied in a group. Bran strained his gaze. What the hell were they doing?

The lot of them rode off in the direction of a nearby hill. Marin turned and gave a sharp gasp. "There's someone coming." She spun to the archers on the other side of the battlement. "Ready your bows. Summon Cat this instant."

She leaned forward, peering into the distance and gave a sharp gasp. "They are flying our banner. The Werrick coat of arms."

Bran stared at the lone rider and caught the familiar green crest with the yellow stripe running down its center. Marin darted toward the stairs.

Bran caught her arm. "What are ye doing?"

She shrugged him off and raced down the stairs before disappearing into the stables. Whatever she was planning was not an idea Bran liked. If Marin was in the stables, she was intending to acquire a horse—and she wouldn't need a horse if she wasn't planning on riding out.

She burst from the stables atop her horse and nearly ran him down.

"Marin," he bellowed. "Ye canna—"

She twisted in her saddle to face her sister. "Cat, get to the archers."

The slap of feet on the cobblestones behind him told him Cat ran to obey her orders.

He reached for Marin. "Dinna go out there." His heart scrambled in his chest. She couldn't go out there, not when the Grahams were thirsty for her blood.

"That could be my father." She cried out and her horse bolted forward. "The gates!"

Damn it.

"Dinna ye dare open those gates," Bran called out.

The castle soldiers did not bother to give him a second glance before following their mistress's orders. The portcullis groaned open.

God's teeth.

Bran spun angrily toward the stable. "My horse, Peter," he growled at the Master of the Horse. Peter leapt to obey his order and within moments, Bran was at Marin's heels.

But it truly wasn't anger spurring him onward–it was fear. They could capture her. If so, they would certainly torture her, as they'd done with his messenger. An image flashed in his mind of her in front of the castle, dumped as the last body had been, bloody and twisted.

He urged his horse faster as he went through the gates. She was in front of him, her back straight in the saddle, the thunder of her horse's hooves lost beneath the sound of his own. The Grahams divided suddenly. Half of them going toward the man riding to the castle, half of them turning toward Marin.

Bran's heart lodged in his throat.

An arrow zipped from the battlements and caught one man in the throat. He fell from his horse, his cry inaudible. Another arrow came, and another, and another, every one finding its mark. Marin reached the lone rider and Bran was finally able to catch up to her. Finally, able to help her.

He drew his blade from its sheath and together he and Marin fought the dozens of Grahams while they turned and darted back to the castle together. The rain of arrows had dwindled to a trickle. One lone archer still taking carefully aimed shots while the others ceased to fire.

Cat, no doubt.

It seemed like a lifetime had stretched on before they finally reached the gate. Several archers had been relocated to the entry-way, their bows readied with nocked arrows. Drake stood at the lead, shouting orders.

Marin and Bran guided the man in, and the arrows began

firing until the portcullis closed once more and the gates securely drawn.

Once they were inside, Bran and Marin dropped from their horses while the visitor was aided from his.

Bran caught Marin's hand. "Ye scared me."

She looked unrepentant. "I had to go."

He edged closer to her. "They could have taken ye, tortured ye."

She lowered her head and looked at their joined hands. "I thought he might be my father." Her gaze found his. "What would you have done if you'd thought it was Ena?"

With that, she slipped her hand from his and went to the rider. A man who, based on the civil greeting and invitation to join them inside, was not the Earl of Werrick.

৩৯৫৯

THE MAN FOLLOWED MARIN INTO THE CASTLE WITH A DISTINCT limp. He was one of her father's soldiers, she knew this for certain, having recognized him from weapons practice. His skill had always been exceptional.

He did not look like that powerful warrior now. Dirt and blood caked his once-glittering chainmail and lines of defeat creased his bruised face.

Marin strode alongside the man, her feet nearly tripping over themselves in her haste, while she attempted to read his face. His expression was grim and hard, his stare vacant, and it caught her heart in a vice of fear.

"My father," she whispered. "Is he safe?" As soon as the words had fled her lips, she regretted them. She ought to wait until they were alone, when they had privacy.

His gaze slid toward her and everything in the vast nothingness within turned her soul to ice. Her step faltered.

Hands clasped her arms, and held her upright despite the pull of the floor below her. The comforting scent of sandalwood filled her nostrils.

Bran.

He was there for her. As he said he would be.

She drew from his strength and waited to hear the words every daughter dreaded. Bran guided them not to the great hall, but up to the solar, where they could be alone. It was uncustomary, but it was perhaps the most private place for Marin to receive her father's soldier, and the news that had made him appear so mournful.

"My father?" Marin asked.

The man swayed on his feet a moment. He ducked his head and clasped his hands in front of his body. "Forgive me, my lady."

The breath choked from her chest. The man did not go on. Did he mean to torment her thusly?

Drake pulled a chair forward and the man sank gratefully into it. When had Drake arrived? Had he always been there?

Marin's head spun; her whole world held in a state of purgatory.

"Go on," Bran said from beside her.

The man lowered his gaze. "The Earl of Werrick is dead."

Marin staggered. The news slammed into her heart with the force of a war hammer and purged her of all thought and breath. Only pain remained. An ache that cut so deeply, it bore into her soul. Strong arms caught her shoulders and curled her in a protective embrace she scarcely registered.

Not her father. Mother had already left them in a horrific death, and now her father... Her father...

Her mind flinched from the words she could not say even in her head.

How could this be? He was a powerful man, not only in ranking, but also in stature. After he'd recovered from Mother's death, his bravery and strength had returned. How could a man such as he be cut down in battle as though he were a simple soldier?

Her heart crumpled under a clench of hurt.

Her father's face filled her mind, the crinkled corners of his eyes when he smiled at her, all the love shining there when he told her how proud she made him. She would never see that expression on his face again, never hear the rich timber of his voice, never feel the comfort of his hand upon her shoulder.

The door flew open and her three blonde sisters fell into the room along with a large dog.

Cat opened her mouth as though she meant to offer a witty remark. Her eyes sparkled with unshed tears and she merely shook her head.

"Papa." Ella's gaze cast to the ground in solemnity. "Just like Mother."

"What news of the other soldiers?" Anice asked in a trembling voice. "Have you heard news of Lord Clarion?"

The man grimaced at the name. "Forgive me, my lady. I fear I bring grave news of him as well."

Anice curled her fingers around the base of her throat, as if she could no longer draw breath. The small ruby ring on her finger caught the light. "You do not mean..."

The man lowered his head with sorrow. "Aye, my lady. He is dead."

"Geordie." Cat fell to her knees in front of the messenger's chair, peering up at him. "Did he fall in battle?"

The man regarded her and shook his head. "Nay, young Geordie has survived."

Anice staggered back on legs that did not appear to hold her. "My father...and my betrothed..." Piquette whimpered and edged nervously around her.

"Forgive me, my lady." The man's voice had gone gravelly. "There were so many dead." His eyes went distant, haunted. "So very many."

Anice sagged against the doorway and the color drained from

her face. Drake was there in a moment, sweeping her into his arms as if she weighed nothing.

Anice turned her face to Drake's chest and sobbed, deep, wracking tears that tore at Marin's heart. Piquette watched his mistress anxiously.

"Was Berwick such a loss?" Marin asked, incredulous.

"Nay, we won Berwick with nearly no casualties on our side." The messenger scrubbed a hand over his weary face. "It was reivers. They attacked us as we headed home. We overpowered them, but not without our own losses."

Tears burned hot in Marin's eyes, tears she could not stop even if she tried. "Drake, please take Anice to the girls' chambers. We must tell Leila."

She cleared the grief from her throat, for the moment at least. "Thank you for bringing this news to us," she said to the soldier. "You did so at great danger to yourself and we appreciate your risk. Please go to the kitchen for food. I will have Isla see to you and ensure you have a bath and bed waiting for you when you have finished."

He lowered his head, more in a hang of defeat than a nod of compliance. "Aye, my lady. Thank you."

No sooner had she finished speaking, the tightness in her throat welled once more with the threat of tears. But she was not a girl. She was the lady of Werrick Castle. She was her father's daughter. Determined and strong.

She would not let others see her tears as she straightened and led the way to the room all the sisters shared. She would be their support now as she'd been when their mother had died. Drake lay Anice into the bed, concern etched deep on his face. Piquette leapt up onto the mattress by Anice's side and Drake departed with apparent hesitation. Ella and Cat cuddled beside her, their own sorrow leaving their eyes and noses red.

Leila sat in the chair by the fire, her legs tucked up on the seat, hugged against her chest. Her eyes were large in her small face as she regarded Anice's heartbreak.

Sweet Leila, who they all cherished in their own precious way. In the depths of their minds, buried so deep none would ever admit it, they realized Leila had been the byproduct of their mother's brutal rape. The knowledge lodged like a stone within them all. Affection masked guilt, and their father had been the most affectionate of all to this final gift from the woman he had loved with all his heart.

Leila had been his favorite daughter.

Marin blinked against the unforgiving grip of grief around her heart and went to her youngest sister. "Leila."

She shook her dark head and turned toward the fire.

"I must speak with you." Marin knelt beside the chair and peered up at the girl, hoping to catch a glimpse of her face beyond the curtain of dark hair.

There is great sadness on the horizon.

"You already know though, don't you?" she asked.

Leila nodded and slowly lifted her head. Her hair parted to reveal her face as she did so. Her eyes, while large with emotion, were dry.

Marin reached out and stroked her youngest sister's cheek.

Leila looked away and pursed her small lips.

"What is it?" Marin asked.

Leila did not answer.

"Leila."

The large blue eyes shifted back to Marin once more. "I...do not believe all is as it appears."

Marin's heart lurched in her chest. "What do you mean? Is it Father? Is it Timothy? The reivers who attacked them?"

Leila's hands fisted and she kept her mouth closed, obviously not intending to say more.

Desperation raked over Marin's raw nerves. Was this hope? Was this another warning? A pent-up sob ached in her throat.

But then Leila was hurting too. They all were.

"I am here if you need to talk," Marin offered patiently. She leaned over her sister and pressed a kiss to her brow. Leila slid from her seat and joined her sisters on the bed where they all held one another in their grief.

Marin ought to join them, to comfort them. Except that it was too similar to when their mother had died. The pain in Marin's chest was exquisite. It choked her and made the room spin. In the end, she knew she could not stay. She pushed from the room and out into the hallway.

Bran was leaning against the wall but straightened as soon as he saw her.

Torrents of emotion whipped at her, lashing in deep, gouging bites. Part of her wanted to run into his strong arms and let him comfort her, to take advantage of his offer to be the man she could need to need. And yet another part of her was appalled at the life he had led, at the simple fact he had been a reiver. In her life, reivers had destroyed the safety of her home, raped her mother, killed her people, waged a siege against the castle and now they had murdered her father.

How could she love a man who had led a life which had brought her such sorrow?

❧ 26 ❧

Bran was helpless as he watched the emotions playing over Marin's face. Her wide-eyed surprise at seeing him, the softening of her features that left him thinking she might possibly run to him, and then the pucker of pained confusion on her brow.

"Marin," he opened his arms to her.

She looked at him like someone she wanted to trust, but someone she was suddenly frightened of. "Reivers killed him. Just like it was reivers who attacked our castle and hurt my mother. And still more reivers are waiting outside the curtain wall to kill us all. How could you live such a life, Bran?"

The question punched into his chest like a knife, especially when said with such bewildered hurt.

"Let us go to our chamber to discuss this." He did not step toward her despite the ache in his soul begging him to do so. In part, he wanted to allow her the space she so obviously needed, but also because a fat, lazy cat had taken advantage of the opportunity and lay sprawled across his feet.

Marin nodded and cast a sad look down at Bixby before making her way to their chamber.

Bran shifted his foot slightly. Bixby didn't move. He squinted one eye open to convey his irritation before resuming his nap. "Ach, off with ye." He bent and gently slid the bulk of the wee beast from holding him captive and followed Marin to their chamber.

He found her leaning against the bed with her arms tightly crossed over her chest, her gaze fixed unseeing on the floor. His chest ached at the depth of her agony. While it wasn't his reivers who had killed her father, they had been men who led similar lives as his own.

He stood there helplessly grasping at what to say and remaining foolishly mute. While she waited, her eyes were glossy with tears and her throat flexed violently at the force of keeping her sobs contained.

Bran cast aside any attempt at discussion and went to her, his arms outstretched to the woman who had been so strong. Not only for her sisters, but for her people. The woman who sometimes needed someone to need and had never had it until now.

This time, she did not fight him. She collapsed into his arms, clenched her fists into his clothing where she clung to him, and cried.

Her back jerked and shuddered against his hands with the force of her weeping and the steady flow of her tears left his chest sodden with her sorrow. He held her tightly to him, being the strength he knew she needed. His hand moved over her in the same soothing circles he'd seen her do with her sisters and he pressed kisses to the top of her head.

He would do anything in his power to draw away the hurt of her loss. For he knew how poignant it could be. It had shattered his heart irrevocably. It made all of him ache to think it might do the same to her, especially when she had so much love and goodness in her.

After some time, her sobs tapered off to deep, sucking gasps and her hands pressed feebly to his chest.

Bran released her with great hesitation. She had asked him a question before he found her like this, and he would answer it. "I dinna like what I've done, Marin. I dinna like the life I've had to lead, and I force myself to no' think of the consequences."

She shook her head. "You do not have to do this."

"Aye, I do." He smoothed a lock of damp hair from her forehead. "I'll no' have ye locking these questions inside and letting them fester without answer. Ye need to understand what happened after my mother and Gregor were slain."

Marin bowed her head and took his hand in her cold one.

"We wandered for a bit of time, but we were beggars in a world filled with too little food." He ran his thumb over her knuckle. "By the time the first winter came, Ena was healed well enough, but we were near starving. No nobles took us in, no priests offered shelter for more than one night, no villagers filled our bellies with the good-smelling food roasting in their pots. No one was there for us. But the reivers, they took us in. They showed us mercy when the rest of the world put their backs to us."

A tear fell from Marin's eye and spattered on the back of her hand.

"I became a reiver because I dinna have a choice." He lifted her tear-stained face with the forefinger of his free hand. "I thought I hated nobility until I met ye."

"Because they made you a pawn," she whispered.

"Because they dinna understand." He cradled her lovely face in his palm. "They always had coin enough for food. Their homes were safe with feather beds and clean clothes. I had only what I could steal, and many times went days without eating. Reiving was survival. No' just for me, but for Ena."

Marin nodded then, a slow resigned acknowledgment to what he'd said, and he knew then that she truly did understand.

Marin had never fully appreciated how fortunate she'd been to have the life she'd led. In fact, she'd oftentimes found herself overwhelmed, snared within the triviality of her sisters and their squabbles, or letting an incorrect order for their larder ruin her day. She had become lost in the ignorance of her own naivety.

Never had she experienced what Bran had described—the starvation and lack of security. What type of person might she have been had she endured such daily uncertainty?

To think he'd done it all in the beginning merely to have what she'd taken for granted through her whole entire life. The ache in the back of her mind became a dull thrum, its beat echoing in her temples.

"I imagine I might have made the same decision you did," she said at last.

The tension in his face did not drain away.

A quiet scratching sounded at the door. Bran cast an irritated glance over his shoulder. "That damn cat willna leave me alone."

A bubble of laughter burst from Marin. She immediately bit back the giggle.

What right did she have to laugh when her father was no longer alive? The memory struck her deep in the chest and threatened to consume her in a cyclone of grief. Her people were relying on her for their safety. With the Grahams on the outside of the castle walls, circumstances were becoming dire.

She shoved at her loss, gently tucking it to a silent corner of her mind. Too many others relied on her.

"Do you think something might be done about the Grahams?" she asked Bran.

He lifted a brow at her.

"If we perhaps gave them food in good faith, provided them with coin to see to their basic needs..." Her words trailed off at the ridiculousness of what she suggested. She put a hand to her brow where her head throbbed. Her fingers were cold and offered a semblance of relief against the heat of her skin.

She gave an exasperated sigh. "Bringing them Nan's meat pies and giving them coin is foolish and would only serve to encourage them to attack."

Bran smiled sadly. "If only it could be so easily done as Nan's meat pies. Though I must say, I've no' ever tasted anything savorier or tenderer in a crust in all my life." He pressed his lips together, as though he could taste the rich gravy as he spoke. "Nay, I've committed a great offense against them, and the Grahams do not forgive easily."

"Can they be bargained with perhaps?" she offered.

He shook his head. "The few bargains I've seen them propose have been exorbitant."

"We have coin enough." Marin couldn't keep the hope from her tone.

"Their prices are no' with coin generally, but with what they know ye'd least be willing to sacrifice."

"You know them well," Marin surmised. "You knew they would retaliate against you."

He nodded and her heart sank.

He had incurred Graham wrath for having come to her aid at her behest. He'd done it for her. Even after he already had the castle and needed to save his own sister, he still sacrificed everything for Marin.

"You knew and you still helped us," she murmured. Until that moment, she had not understood exactly what he'd done for her. Aye, she was grateful for her sisters' lives, but she had never fully understood what he had given up for her.

He nodded again and she found herself aching to be in the comfort of his arms once more.

"Bran, I—"

He held up his hand. "I got a bonny wife out of it." He gave her a boyish grin that made her heart tilt.

The castle lay in the back of her mind like a stone, weighing at her thoughts. "What can we do to get the Grahams to leave?" She asked. "They've been at the castle for almost a fortnight and with the increased need for food for your troops, our stores are dwindling. I do not wish to wait and be starved out."

Bran rubbed the back of his neck. "We canna wait for Kerr, no' when we dinna know if the first letter was delivered. And if the Scottish were soundly beaten at Berwick, he may no' be coming at all."

"Waiting for the Grahams to come within close range for our arrows has provided little success," Marin mused. "When my father's men come home, they will be exhausted from battle. We cannot rely on them to help."

"What of the passage?" he asked. "The one ye used to get yer sisters out of Werrick the first time."

"It would be fine for sneaking out a small group, but without horses and with the constant patrols of reivers, we would surely be found. Unable to flee with haste and prime for slaughter."

Bran's stare intensified. "Ye know what we must do."

Steely determination flared through her. This was her chance to exact revenge for the soldiers they lost in the battle to save her sisters, an opportunity to allow the helpless rage coiling inside her to blaze out in savage glory.

"Aye," she said vehemently. "We fight."

❧ 27 ❧

The day of battle had come. Bran's pulse pounded through his veins as it often did before a fight. Mayhap even harder than usual, for there was so much more at stake than a bit of coin or food.

Though their army was small, the battle took a solid three days to plan between himself, Marin, Drake and Sir Richard. Judging from their collective estimation, there were usually six dozen Graham reivers loitering outside their walls. As they had not seen within the walls of Mabrick Castle, they were unsure how many of their numbers remained, or if they had sent for reinforcements. Or if they even held the castle still at all.

Mabrick could well have been reclaimed by the English after their victory.

Marin was at his side, prepared for battle with her full body chainmail clinking. While she had tried valiantly to hide her sorrow, its proof smudged under her eyes and drew tight at her normally lush mouth.

With her now at his side, he knew she did not suspect anything. Her blind faith twisted at the honest part of his soul. She would possibly never forgive him. And yet, he had lied when he'd said she could join him on the battlefield. If he'd tried to keep her back, she would have fought and railed against him until he finally agreed. But he knew the truth of it. How could he fight with her at his side when his worry for her was so great?

It was about more than a babe possibly being in her belly, or the comfortable life her dowry would afford him. It was *her*. The way she had become a part of his heart.

It was because he loved her.

Wind swept through the bailey and set the banners rippling in their full glory. The men—reivers and castle soldiers alike—wore the Werrick coat of arms emblazoned across their chests. The fierce black hawk stood out against the green tincture of its field with a bold stripe of yellow running down its center. A way to identify one another in the chaotic confusion of battle.

Restless energy charged the air. Men hopped from foot to foot, shifted and twisted their sword arms, readjusted their armor, all the anxious prep work men did to ensure the odds of victory tilted in their favor.

Marin's sisters waited near the soldiers, clad in chainmail and set with grim faces. They would not be fighting.

Both he and Marin had agreed to leave them behind, partly to ensure their safety, especially in light of the cruelty their mother had endured at the hands of the Grahams. But also, to ensure the safety of those remaining within the keep should they lose. If the tides of battle turned against them, the sisters were to lead the women and children through the secret passage.

While the Grahams were occupied with the spoils of war and a renewed attempt to enter the castle, the lot of them would slip through the passage and find help. Hopefully.

If help could be found.

The girls ran to Marin like daughters to their mother. Bran stood back and allowed them to offer their well-wishes and love. Anice slid him a knowing look and nodded in his direction. The knot of tension in his chest eased.

She had remembered their conversation and would comply. And she would see to Ena's safety if he did not survive battle.

Bran allowed himself the luxury of watching Marin as she spoke with her sisters, the way her graceful hand stroked their cheeks, how she wore the chainmail as regally as if it were a gown of the finest satin. She was beautiful. Perfect.

Aye, she would be livid. Mayhap even try to kill him again. But for the same reason they had agreed to not allow her sisters on the battlefield, Bran knew he could not have Marin beside him. He could not clear from his mind the horrible offense done to her mother. The very idea of being helpless as men violently harmed her made him burn with enough rage to split a man in two with his axe. Nay, he would rather face her wrath if they won than witness such horrors if they lost.

Marin turned from her sisters and met his eyes.

It was time.

"I would speak to ye first," Bran said when she approached him.

She smiled up at him, her full pink lips parting over her straight white teeth. Her blue eyes sparkled at him in the flirtatious way he enjoyed. He drank in every detail of her loveliness, as though he might fill up on it and make it last forever.

For this might be his last opportunity to see her. Such a realization jolted through him and left his heart slamming in his chest. Fear. Ugly and metallic and foreign.

He nodded, not trusting himself to speak, not with the way his throat had suddenly gone tight. He indicated the stables behind them. She caught his hand and drew him with her.

Sunlight slanted in through a narrow window and motes of dust drifted lazily in the brilliant shafts of light. All around them was the sweet, musty scent of hay. God in Heaven, she would be furious with him.

"Marin, I—"

She threw her arms around his shoulder and kissed him,

hungry and hard. "We will win. Together. We will save Werrick Castle."

His gut twisted, and a thread of doubt wound its way into his mind. He had only to consider what they would do to her if she was captured and his resolve steeled once more.

"Marin." He cradled her face in his hands and stared at her until every lovely detail of her face had carved itself into his mind. "I love ye." He pressed a tender kiss to her mouth, savoring the familiar taste of her.

"Forgive me," he said.

Her eyes widened, but he was too quick, and she too surprised, for her to stop him. He fled the room, slammed the door shut and clapped the beam over it, locking it into place. She screamed on the other side, begging him to let her out.

"Forgive me, Marin." His throat hurt to speak, but he pushed past it. "I canna lose ye."

She pounded at the door in response, but he'd already turned his back and was heading in the direction of the readied troops. Anice held the sisters in place, her head bowed as she spoke in low tones to them. It was odd to see the second eldest sister without her large beast who had been left within the keep to ensure his safety in the upcoming battle.

Bran pulled his focus from the sisters and steeled himself for the battle ahead. He had the portcullis raised, and together with Sir Richard and Drake at his sides, he led the men out on to the open field to fight.

In the distance, the Grahams leapt to their horses, ready to fight at the moment's notice. One broke off at a full gallop in the opposite direction. Most likely to get reinforcements.

Damn.

"Sir Richard," Bran bellowed.

The soldier nodded and veered his horse out of the group to follow the lone reiver. Though older, Richard was the fastest rider they had, and Bran knew he'd rather die than see the castle fall. He would not fail.

He could not. For if Graham reinforcements arrived, they were all dead.

☙❧

MARIN POUNDED ON THE DOOR UNTIL HER ARMS ACHED, AND still she continued to slam her fists against the solid wood. Had the window not been so narrow, she would have climbed through it. She'd actually tried but had found it impossible to even wriggle her torso through.

Her cries were left unanswered: first when Bran walked away, then as the thunder of footsteps passed as the men marched to their waiting horses. The groan of the portcullis opened, and all those heavy feet and hooves painstakingly made their way out beyond the castle walls.

Marin had switched to kicking the door then, slamming her foot against the solid frame repeatedly until her thighs burned. Each solid hit let in a seam of light, but never resulted in the door swinging open.

The groan of the portcullis sounded again, followed by the hearty thunk of the gate closing. Only then, in the absence of sound and soldiers was there a clatter of wood at the door before it creaked open.

Anice stood in the open doorway, her face pinched with anxious uncertainty. "Forgive me, Sister."

"How could you?" The cut of betrayal gave her words volume enough to echo out over the empty cobblestones.

Anice flinched. But Marin pushed past her to the gates, which were fully closed.

Marin knew well enough they wouldn't be opening again. Not until after the battle. If they won.

She stalked toward the stairs leading up to the battlements

where the archers stood at the ready. If she could not be part of the battle, she would at least watch it play out.

"I couldn't lose you too," Anice called out to her.

Marin stopped.

"We lost Papa," Anice said. "I lost Timothy. I couldn't..." her voice cracked and tugged at a wounded place in Marin's soul.

"I couldn't lose you too," Anice repeated softly.

"And so, you have not." Marin said it gently but resumed her trek to the battlements. Such offenses were not easily forgiven. Not when one skilled soldier could turn the favor of the battle.

Cat stood at the head of the archers; her slender figure so small beside them that she appeared far younger than her sixteen years. She cast a glance back at Marin, her eyes wide with anxiety. "They're coming."

Marin rushed to the crenulations in time to see the two forces charging at one another, horses at the front and men on foot running at a wild pace in the back. Leading the band of men was Bran. He rode on his horse with easy confidence, his face fixed toward his enemy.

The summer breeze blew against the grass, sending waves rippling over the long blades. Overhead the sky was a perfect blue with clouds like stretched wool. It was a day for a banquet beneath a copse of trees, not for a battle and death.

Shouts rose up from either side, carried to her on the wind. It sparked her warrior's blood and sent her pulse racing. Her muscles ached with the need to be there with her men, racing toward the enemy. She clenched her hands into fists and pressed them hard into the stonework of the wall, as if that might somehow ease her angst.

The men increased their pace as they got closer. Marin tensed.

"Ready your arrows." Cat lifted her hand.

A dozen bows creaked. The reivers and soldiers below crashed together in a cacophony of ringing metal, clattering shields and cries of effort and pain.

"Launch!" Cat drew her hand down and nocked her own arrow. The release of her weapon was soundless beneath the terrible roar of battle.

Bran had managed to stay on his horse, his battle axe glinting in the golden light of the sun. He filled her thoughts as she recalled the way he'd looked just before locking her in the stables. His gaze had been so desperate, emotion shining in his eyes, as if it tore at his heart to leave her.

I love ye.

She had replayed those words in her head again and again, savoring them, clinging to them.

Already several bodies fell to the ground, some Grahams in their plain gambesons, some bearing the Werrick coat of arms.

Marin's heart snagged in her throat. Her men. Ones who had protected her all these years and now made the greatest sacrifice to see her and her people safe.

She put a hand to her mouth to cover her sobs. Her tears could not be so easily squelched. She watched the entirety of the battle and yet kept focused on where Bran led their army with commendable bravery.

He remained at the front line. His movements were as powerful as they were lethal. His strokes were rhythmic in a smooth repetitive motion she knew well enough from her own time in such melee. He operated on well-honed instinct, pausing only to aid a fellow soldier or reiver, the way he'd done as they were side-by-side when they'd saved her sisters.

But to observe him like this, from a spectator's place, he was magnificent.

A Graham pulled his blade free and spun to face Bran's back. Marin clutched at the stonework beneath her hands, but before she could even draw a full breath to call out his name in warning, a white fletched arrow sailed toward the man and hit him in the eye. The Graham fell to the ground, no longer a threat.

Cat did not pause to appreciate her own incredible shot, not when her fingers were flying from plucking and firing with abandon. Despite Bran being saved by her sister's extraordinary talent, the tension did not leave Marin's shoulders. Watching the fight unfold was the greatest hell she'd ever endured.

When she was among her men, she had the element of control, inasmuch as one could wield during the chaos of war. At Bran's side, she could keep his back guarded, ensuring his safety. Instead, she was confined to the battlements in the weighty trappings of useless chainmail, completely and utterly helpless.

Each man in her livery who fell dragged at her heart and left her wondering what she might have done to prevent the death, had she been among her men. Where she belonged.

Anger fired through her again. She wanted to scream out her frustration until her throat bled. When this battle was done, she would ensure Bran got a good piece of her mind.

Her heart squeezed at the thought of seeing him again. God, how she wanted to see him again. After she kissed him senseless, she decided. That was when she would give him a good piece of her mind.

Several more of the Werrick coat of arms fell to the ground, and then several more. The battle was turning in the favor of the Grahams.

She shot an anxious look to the gates. They could open them and partially raise the portcullis ever so slightly. Enough for the men to scramble underneath. Enough for Bran to be safe.

When her gaze settled back to the field, her blood ran cold. The Grahams were easily consuming the Werrick men. The battle would not last much longer.

Movement on the horizon pulled her horrified attention from the fighting. Men lined up along the crest of a hill in the distance. A good number of men.

The cool blood in her veins turned to ice. The Grahams had brought reinforcements.

"Marin, we must go." Cat pulled at her.

But Marin could not leave, not when her feet were rooted to the stone ground. "Bran," she whispered.

He continued to fight, oblivious of the men soon heading in his direction. Heedless of the impending slaughter. She had not told him she loved him when he left. She had shouted curses at him she hadn't meant, and she never, never told him she loved him.

She shook her head and the world swirled in a blur of colors.

"Forgive me, Marin," Cat said in her sweet voice. "We must. The women and children need us."

A small hand pulled at Marin's, leading her away. Before she could disappear completely, she jerked her face back toward the battlefield and took one last long look at her husband, knowing it would be her last.

❧ 28 ❧

Bran was in the full glory of combat. His movements glided in rhythm with the countless motions he'd practiced since he was a youth, and his senses were tuned in to everything around him. While his heightened awareness focused him, it was impossible to not hear the grunts and pathetic cries of the dying coming from behind and beside him.

The odor of death clung in his nostrils, tinged with the metallic note of fear. He roared with energy and swept his axe down with all his might. It sank into the skull of the man attempting to plunge a sword into his side. The man fell and another took his place, forcing Bran a step backward.

Bran gritted his teeth. It was not the first time he'd moved back. In fact, he had been steadily pushed in the direction of the castle with each man he killed or maimed. Ahead of him, the carpet of bodies grew larger, many colored with the Werrick livery.

Beside him, Drake's sword whipped and jabbed effortlessly, the weapon light in the warrior's grip. "They keep pushing us back," Drake said between attacks. "Is it so we can see how many of our men have died?"

"Aye." Bran jerked his battle axe upward to block a blow aimed at his face. "'Tis meant to fluster us." He readjusted his grip and swung his axe into the man's neck.

Drake slid him a glance and plunged with his blade once more.

The tactic wouldn't work on Bran, or Drake, or even most of the castle's soldiers. His reivers were another story altogether. Already many of them had been restless within the keep. Even as they'd run out for battle, several had slipped away. Whether they survived or not, he did not know, but he wagered he'd see some of the fine coat of arms cloth for sale in the market in the future.

And there would be a future, because he would win this battle, damn it. He would see Ena saved, and he would see his wife again.

Once she forgave him, of course.

"Let's kill these bastards and go home," Bran gritted out.

Drake bellowed out a war cry in response and speared the man in front of him. Together they fought on, empowered with the need for victory.

Movement caught in Bran's periphery. A considerable amount of movement. It pulled his attention momentarily from the fight. He was not alone. A unified respite hummed through the melee at the cluster of a few dozen soldiers rushing toward them. They did not cry out as they descended. Nay, they were silent, their faces grimacing with savagery. Their armor was tarnished and spattered, their clothing beneath unkempt.

Bran's heart fell at the state of their dress. These were not soldiers who happened upon them to help. They were more reivers. The reinforcements had come through, and they were Grahams.

ALL AROUND MARIN CAME THE CRIES OF HEARTBROKEN WOMEN and their fearful children. The few men who remained behind held somber, desolate expressions at their own sealed fates.

Bernard made his way from person to person, offering his blessing and his ear. The awkward priest had cast aside his public discomfort and prayed so fervently with each desperate soul that his bald head glistened with his efforts.

The thick stone walls of the castle left it impossible to hear the fight raging on. Part of her was grateful for the reprieve from the cries of the dying, and yet part of her wanted to cling to the battle, to the men who were still alive. Panic threatened to break her, fear for those who fought for them and for the man she loved. But she swallowed it down and remained resolute. Her people needed her. As lady of the castle, she had to remain strong.

Everyone had been accounted for and were gathered in the great hall. Everyone save Leila and Isla. Marin rushed to her sisters' shared chamber and found the girl curled up by the hearth once more, her chainmail glinting in the firelight.

"We must go," Marin said with urgency. "The reivers have brought reinforcements. Leila, the castle will fall."

Leila shook her head.

Panic jabbed hot at Marin. "There are lives depending on us."

Her youngest sister slid a gaze to the seat beside her where Isla sat. "You may leave us," Leila said, as if it were the simplest decision.

"I will not leave you." Marin came around the chair and reached for her sister.

Leila simply shook her head. "It isn't as it seems."

"It isn't as it seems?" Marin shook her head, her nerves scraped raw and her patience expired. "That makes no sense."

Isla lay a sympathetic hand on Marin's shoulder. "Yer sister knows more than any of us ever will."

But Marin had seen the battle being lost with her own eyes, as clearly as she'd seen the reiver's reinforcements arrive. It was all too certain what lay in store for Bran and the men he led. There would be no escape.

She clenched her fists. This hope her sister tried to offer was too much, especially when such loss would be Marin's destruction. She pressed her hand over her chest, but the pain burning there did not cease.

"Is Marin here?" Ella's voice cut through Marin's lamentation. "You must come. Quick!"

Marin stared in bewilderment.

"Come, child." Isla's gnarled hands grasped Marin's shoulder with surprising strength and hefted her to her feet.

Marin staggered forward on legs she did not trust. "What is it?"

Ella twirled and came to a stop with a lovely smile. "A miracle."

৩৯৯

BRAN'S BODY TENSED AT THE ONSLAUGHT OF THE NEW ARMY. Their men would be fresh and bloodthirsty, not worn down from the endless swinging and blocking of their weapons.

"Dinna stop fighting, men." Bran swung his axe down. "We do this for Werrick Castle, for the women and children, for those that we love. We do this for us."

The men at his side remained there, both soldiers and reivers alike. Together they braced as the army fell upon them. The first of the new soldiers attacked, thrusting his blade with savage strength into a Graham. The man staggered, a look of surprise on his face, and toppled to the ground.

The second new warrior attacked another Graham, while the first found yet another to kill. They were helping.

No doubt for a ridiculous fee that would be charged once the battle was won. It was common of mercenaries low on work to force their need upon hapless souls in order to earn their living.

Though at this point, Bran would pay them what they asked, no matter the price. Their safety meant that of the people within the castle walls.

Bran pulled his axe from the dead Graham in front of him and glanced at the new men fighting at their side. Their chainmail was even filthier up close, layered in mud and black slime. Beneath it all was a coat of arms. Through the muck, a green background was bisected by a yellow stripe with a black bird emblazoned on its front.

Bran's body tingled.

The Earl of Werrick's soldiers were home from Berwick. A Graham knocked into Bran, nearly sending him to the ground. Bran shoved the man to create space between them, enough for the blade of an axe, and swiftly ended his life.

If the men were alive, then perhaps... He surveyed the men fighting and found one in particular who was surrounded by soldiers. Guarded. The way one might do for an earl.

Bran's heart raced. Marin's father might truly be alive.

The battle had turned in their favor. Bran's forces were the ones pushing their enemy backward now, allowing them to see the rapidly growing number of dead Grahams. The men at the back of the battle began to break away and leave, choosing to flee and live.

Soon their enemy was no more, with most dead and many more running.

"We'll be back." An aged man with long gray and white hair glared at Bran. "Ye mark our word, we will be back."

The words of a coward to be sure. Bran hefted his axe and the man turned with haste to flee.

All around him rose the shouts of victory, cheering until voices went hoarse. Brethren greeted one another and reunions were had. The crowd of men had begun to move as a solid mass in the direction of the castle.

Bran fixed his gaze on the man he suspected might be the earl. The man removed his helm to reveal a head of silver hair. Sir Richard was at his side in an instant, saying something Bran could not make out. At least, not until the possible earl's face hardened and an icy blue gaze slid in his direction.

Shite.

Bran had never been one to back down. He shifted toward the earl, preparing to march over to him when a hand caught his chest, stopping him.

Drake caught his eye and shook his head. "Better to do it in front of yer wife," he said in a low voice.

"I'll no' hide behind my wife's skirts," Bran snarled.

"Better that than lying dead at her feet." Drake nudged him forward with his shoulder. "Ye took the castle by force and have married his eldest daughter. Many of his men are dead because of battles that wouldn't have happened were it not for ye."

Bran groaned. "When ye word it in such a manner..."

Drake did not reply, but instead urged him forward.

Bran grunted in reply and allowed himself to be nudged away from the strewn bodies remaining, out of the grass gone muddy with blood, and back to the place he realized he now thought of as home.

"Papa!" A girlish squeal sounded from the battlements and echoed over the field. A figure in front of the archers leapt up and down several times before disappearing.

So, the man was indeed the Earl of Werrick. Despite the hollowness that knowledge wrought in Bran's gut, he could not help but smile at Cat's delight to see her father alive.

The portcullis opened and the men shifted with restless eagerness to be reunited with their families, whether their time outside the castle walls had been over an hour, or over the last month.

Two women waited on the other side, so eager for it to open, they finally ducked underneath and ran to the earl. As they got closer, Bran realized they were Anice and Cat, Anice racing with the same girlish excitement as her younger sister. They flew into their father's arms and remained there a good, long time.

The earl kissed each of their heads in turn and held them as though he never intended to let them go. When his eyes opened, tears shone, making them glow like a summer sky.

The rest of the men pressed onward into the bailey, giving the earl his privacy in the reunion with his daughters. Though not all of them.

Bran scanned the courtyard as he entered the castle grounds, but he did not see the rest of Werrick's daughters. Not Ella, nor Leila. And not Marin.

The other men were greeted by the grateful women and children, kissed and held and crooned over. The earl returned to his men once more, his face beaming with pride and love. He was exactly the man Marin had described him as, the kind of father any child might want. Even a boy who had never known his own.

Before foolish thoughts of a happy outcome could take root in Bran's mind, the earl released his daughters and the expression on his face went from adoring father to fierce warrior. The summer-blue eyes frosted to a wintery gray and the lined scowl transformed his features into something menacing. His stare pierced Bran and chilled his soul.

"You forced your way into the castle by threatening my daughter." The earl's lip curled.

Cat stepped toward her father. "Papa, he—"

"You took my castle, you slept in my bed, you ate my food and sat at the head of my table." Spittle flecked out of his mouth and shone in the brilliant sunlight. He stopped just before Bran and glowered down at him with such authoritative disapproval, Bran had to force himself to remain upright. "You married my eldest daughter." He blinked slowly, as if the act pained him to do so. "You laid with her."

Bran opened his mouth, but the earl reared back his fist and pain exploded in Bran's cheekbone.

"I'll have none of your excuses, you reiving bastard," the earl hissed and strode away. "Guards, this marauder has led a life he does not deserve, his pleasures stolen for too long."

The men surrounding Bran hesitated only a moment before seizing his arms. Drake lunged toward them but was immediately restrained by three of the filthy Werrick soldiers.

Bran bit back any explanations he might offer. It didn't matter. Not with a man like the Earl of Werrick, a nobleman exactly like every other Bran had known. He only hoped Anice would remember her promise to save Ena, and that Marin would help.

Sir Richard appeared beside the earl and stared at Bran. "Shall we take him to the dungeon, my lord?"

The earl spit on the ground. "Kill him."

❧ 29 ❧

The hum of voices greeted Marin before she exited the castle, far too many to be the remaining people left behind, and far too tame to be a winning band of marauders descended upon them for rape and pillaging. Her pulse stumbled and resumed with a wild patter.

Was it true? Had they won?

Ella and Leila gripped her hand with the same level of excitement, and together they ran the length of the castle entry. Sunlight blinded them, but they did not slow, not until a familiar voice slammed into her heart.

"He has brought dishonor to us all."

She stopped, blinking against the brilliance to the mass of faces before her. Ella and Leila ripped their hands free of Marin's grasp and continued to run. "Papa!"

Marin's knees went weak and she almost pitched to the hard ground. The only thing keeping her upright was the beloved figure of her father standing tall with the light of the late afternoon sun limning his slender frame, as though he were some kind of saint. For truly, to them, he was. A man full of goodness and love, a man returned from the dead.

"Father." Her lips were numb and yet still she managed to whisper the word. She repeated it louder, in a shout of joy. Suddenly the legs nearly too weak to hold her were carrying her across the cobblestones and into his arms.

He caught her beside Ella and Leila and crushed all three of them to his chest in a great bear of a hug, the way he'd done when they were girls and they would squeal for him to stop. His whiskered chin rasped at the top of her head and the odor of peat and death clung to his filthy chainmail.

"You're filthy." She pushed back with a chuckle and reached out to gingerly touch his silver beard. A bit of dried mud dropped from the once well-trimmed hair and fell to the ground.

He grinned at her. "Is that any way to welcome home your father?"

She laughed, a giddy, happy laugh, earnest and free of all the tension built up over the last month. "I would welcome you home no matter how you looked."

Though, in truth, it pulled at her how much he had aged, the lines on his face were creased deeper beneath the spatters of muck. He was thinner, almost frail. All the men carried about them a haunted look. Their faces were streaked with peat. Even Geordie, Sir Richard's squire who had gone into battle for experience, appeared to have the worn features of a man rather than the boy he still was.

Cat stood at his side, beaming up at him as she chattered on. Despite his apparent exhaustion, the young man grinned down at her and nodded along with whatever she was saying.

"Papa, they told us you were dead." Ella hugged at his arm and pressed her face to his sleeve, heedless of how it left a streak of mud on her cheek. "Where is your armor?"

Marin had not noticed until her sister mentioned it, but the fine decorative helm with gilt whorls was now a simple, serviceable helm.

He scoffed. "Some jackanape stole my armor before we were attacked."

"They told us you were dead," Marin said weakly. Her gaze shifted to the crowd of men, seeking out her husband, and finding him almost immediately. In a wild chain reaction, she immediately experienced the rush of elation at his safety, followed by the fear and confusion of his capture.

"Aye, many died, daughters," Father said solemnly. "A great many. The battle had been a victorious one. The attack on us was meant to get us when we were away from England's forces. When we were vulnerable. The bloody Kerrs."

"Father, why is my husband restrained?" Marin asked sharply.

Her father's face darkened. "Sir Richard told me about him. You needn't worry after him any longer, Marin."

"What do you mean?"

"He forced you to marry him. No one else need know, save those of us in this castle." Father's eyes narrowed. "I'll kill the whoreson and take back my castle."

"Kill him?" Marin gaped in horror. "He's my husband. You can't—"

"He forced you into marriage, Marin."

"I offered my hand in marriage to save the lives of my sisters." She shifted to put herself between her father and her husband, to break the glare of hatred he cast Bran's way. "He made sacrifices to save them and has saved us all many times over. He is a good man."

"A good man? He raped you. Like your mother, he—"

She put a hand to her father's chest to stop his ugly words and shook her head. Her cheeks scorched with heat to be discussing her consensual fornication with a man. As a wife it was her right to do so, but as a daughter, it was humiliating. Still, it was better for him to believe the truth than the lie Sir Richard had put in his head.

Sir Richard.

She shifted a hard look at the man she had trusted so often in her father's absence. "What is the meaning of this? Is this your plan? To see him destroyed. First with the letter and now with this...this betrayal."

Sir Richard did not so much as have the decency to wince at her words. "You needed to see the letter; you needed to know what he was about. He forced his way into our lives. He brought war when there was none. He endangered the lives of every person in this castle and lost just as many. His men ate up our food stores and left us to the dire situation we're in now."

"One page," Marin growled under her breath. "You only gave me one page of it."

"The one you needed to see." Sir Richard lifted his chin.

"I don't know what bloody page you are discussing," Father said in an exasperated tone. "But I'm tired and hungry and in urgent need of a good bathing." He stepped around Marin and addressed the soldiers holding Bran. "Kill him."

"Nay." Marin threw herself in front of Bran, blocking his body with her own, and looked frantically to the soldiers. "I order you to stop."

"You no longer give the orders." Her father spoke sternly, as though she were a chastised child.

Bran's chest was warm against her back. His breath blew delicately against the nape of her neck. She shook her head with the force of her insistence. "You will not kill him."

"I will do as I damn well please with this usurper." Father nodded to the soldiers. "Marin, cease this behavior at once. Guards, kill him."

The men cast glances at one another, apparently unsure what to do.

"Lock him in one of the chambers, please, but don't kill him." Marin cast a look at the countless eyes watching in fascination while their family battle publicly ensued. "We can discuss this privately."

Father's eyes narrowed into a shrewd squint and his eyes glittered with something she could not make out but knew she did not like. "Put him in the dungeon."

"Father," she admonished.

He glared at her. "You forget yourself in this madness, Daughter." He nodded to the guards. "Take him to the dungeon."

"Nay," Marin gasped. She spun around to face Bran and clung to him. His arms were restrained, and he could not wrap them around her. The loss of his embrace was palpable, painful.

"Nay," Marin whispered against him. "I won't let them take you to the dungeon."

Bran pressed a kiss to the top of her head. "Aye, ye will, lass."

Surprised, she looked up.

He stared at her with a solemnity which cut into her heart. "'Tis better than death."

"I don't want you down there," she protested.

"Separate them," Father's voice said from behind her.

She tightened her grip. By God, she would never allow them to drag her free.

"Let go," Bran said. "I'll no' have ye getting hurt." He pressed a kiss to her mouth, greedy and desperate. "Save Ena. Please."

Strong hands grasped Marin's arms and Bran was wrenched from her grasp. Sir Richard and another soldier dragged him to the mouth of the castle.

"Nay," she cried. "Please." She tried to run after him, but the hands on her arms held her back. She was entirely helpless to do anything save watch her husband be forcefully taken to the dungeon.

BRAN PACED THE NARROW FLOOR OF HIS CELL. ALL AROUND HIM was darkness, so heavy it seemed to be a living thing more than nothing at all. It squeezed at him and made his eyes ache with the strain to see. Ten paces and he stopped short to avoid running into the grates. Turn. Ten paces and he stopped short to avoid running into the grates. Turn.

He had been down there a while, without even the courtesy of a torch. Though it was obvious they were not attempting to be conciliatory. His stomach had begun to growl two thousand, four hundred and twenty paces ago, and his throat burned with thirst. He'd given up trying to swallow, for it only made his throat stick together and caused him to cough. And that made his throat drier still.

He still wore the chainmail from battle, the blood of his enemies long since dried and stinking on his armor. All of his discomforts were minor though, at least in comparison to the torment of worrying after Ena. Would Anice be able to help her? Marin?

Marin.

Her name was a dagger in his heart.

Her shrieks had accompanied him to the dungeon, or at least into the heart of the castle where the sounds from outside were dulled by thick stone walls and countless winding corridors. And yet sometimes he swore he could still hear her cries, echoing in the darkness.

Two thousand, four hundred and fifty-five paces.

He staggered and fell to his knees as though dragged down by the weight of his suffering. *Marin.*

He dug his fingers into the hard-packed earth, ignoring how his fingernails bent backward and gritty dirt scraped at the tender skin beneath. He would sell his soul for one last moment with her, to hold her in his arms and confess the extent of his love for her. But in truth, he would doubtlessly never see her again. Something awful and wretched twisted in his chest and a gasp of pain choked from his lips.

He clenched his jaw and pulled himself to his feet while

releasing the handfuls of earth back to the ground. Two thousand, four hundred and fifty-six paces. Fifty-seven, fifty-eight...

He would need a plan and wallowing in self-pity would not get him out of the damned cell any faster. Footsteps thumped over the flagstones, distant at first before growing louder, closer. The flickering light of a torch filled the room from a low glow to brilliant light that left him blinking and squinting. The torch shoved toward the bars, as if the wielder knew the discomfort of bright firelight on a man too long in the dark.

"Your time to do as you please has come to an end, reiver." The volume of the earl's voice echoed off the walls. "You'll no longer have access to my castle, my people, or my daughters." He emphasized the last word.

Bran stood resolutely in place. "Let me speak with Marin."

"Nay." Werrick set the torch into a metal sconce jutting from the wall. With the light over his head, Bran could make out the older man, his wizened face locked in a scowl of displeasure. He'd bathed and changed into a fresh tunic and hose. Freed of the filthy garments he'd worn mere hours ago, he appeared every bit as regal as was expected of an earl. He examined Bran with a sneer. "She fancies herself in love with you, the foolish girl."

"Girl?" Bran repeated. He curled his hands around the cold metal bars and peered through them at Marin's father. "She hasn't been a girl since her mother died."

The earl's eyes narrowed. "You have no right to speak to me in such a manner."

"They're words ye should hear no matter who they come from." Bran pinned the earl with a hard gaze. "Ye know she took over the role of mother to those girls, and mistress of the castle. Then later when ye ran away from the castle to escape, she had to become the master. Ye tell me to have a care how I speak to ye when ye dinna even give her the respect she deserves?"

Bran curled his lip at his father-in-law. "I tell ye: have a care when ye call my wife a girl, as she is more woman than any other in the whole of this world."

The earl's narrowed eyes widened briefly. Finally, he scoffed. "Because you feel this way about her, you believe yourself entitled to see her?"

"Nay," Bran replied slowly. "I'm her husband, and I love her."

"Love." The older man shook his head. "What do you know of love, boy? You forced her to marry you as surely as you'd forced yourself into the keep. You've spent every moment here forcing people to do things against their will, especially my daughter. And what's more, you did it with the intent to sacrifice Werrick Castle to Kerr. To Scotland."

"I dinna have a choice."

The earl lifted a brow and his forehead crinkled. "So I heard. I also heard the missive had been stopped before it could be delivered."

Bran's shoulders sagged in defeat. "There was another missive sent to Kerr." The confession was damning, but then there had already been enough other evidence stacked against him for it to not matter now. At least he could protect Marin's people. "It was sent the day I took the castle."

"The one given to your reiver who saw the laundress before he left?" The old blue eyes sharpened. "Aye, I know."

"The laundress?"

"Aye, a lass all too eager to keep your reivers from destroying her life here." Sir Richard entered the dungeon with a flat expression. "The missive never made it to Kerr. It's been sitting in the chest in my room. Yer man thought it best to see the laundry lass the day he left, and she slipped it off him."

"So, Kerr never knew." Bran's blood ran cold.

Sir Richard shook his head. "He did not."

If Kerr never knew Bran had secured Werrick Castle, then Ena would never have been released. She would be in prison still, thinking Bran had let her down. Or, if Kerr had grown impatient...

Bran's stomach churned. "Nay," he gasped. "Please. My sister."

"Is it time?" The earl asked of his captain of the guard.

Sir Richard nodded, his mouth a hard line.

Bran's heart knocked against his ribs. "Let me see Marin. Just one last time. Please." He was begging, pleading with these men, and he didn't give a damn. He'd kiss the dirt at their feet if it would give him one more second with Marin. To beg her to save Ena, but also to be with her. To stroke Marin's lovely hair and commit every sweet curve of her face to memory. He wanted her scent on his clothes and her love in his heart when he met his death.

"You cannot see her," Werrick said with vehemence. He drew in a slow, deep breath, as if trying to reign in his control. "She does not know of this plan."

Plan?

Bran squeezed the iron bars against his palms to keep his thoughts from whirling out of control.

"If it were up to me, I'd kill you." The earl slid a regretful look in Bran's direction. "But my daughters have spoken for you, as has my captain of the guard." He nodded to Sir Richard. "I will allow you to leave and never return. I also will work with Kerr to have your sister freed. However, if you do return, I will kill you myself and put your bloody head on a pike for all to see."

Bran would be free to go. Ena would be freed. But Marin would assume he had abandoned her.

He rested his brow on the icy bars. His choices were grave indeed, with neither one letting him fully win and either consequence breaking his heart.

❧ 30 ❧

Bran couldn't imagine his life without Marin any more than he could imagine leaving without her at his side. She was his wife. He would rather go to hell and back than have her think he had left without her, abandoned her.

But he could not sacrifice Ena.

Yet again, he was a pawn in a rich man's game. Being moved around at whim. But this time he did not try to fight it. Nay, he bowed under its burden.

"Please," he said in a ragged voice. "Let me see my wife."

"Don't be preposterous." The earl cast him a look of incredulity.

Bran gripped the bars with determination and stared directly into the earl's hard blue eyes. "I love her."

"What life will you give her?" Her father asked. "You have no home. You have nothing save the clothes on your back."

Bran's stomach clenched at the statement, and its underlying truth.

"Will you have her starve as she hopes her next meal comes soon?" The earl prompted. "Will you be content as her fine clothes turn to rags on her? Would you see the powerful woman she is shrivel in a life where coin goes from hand to mouth and security is in as short supply as luxury?"

"I have been in love, Boy." Werrick's voice lowered. "I would never have wanted for my wife what you intend for Marin. If you truly do love her, leave and spare her the pain of your death. For I refuse to allow her to live such a life."

Bran would have preferred to have been beaten and kicked by these men rather than subjected to their justification. For all of it was true. Raw and abrasively true.

His thoughts went to the women who rode with the reivers. Some fought in battle alongside the men, their weapons as shoddy as their pieced together armor. Some remained at camp, exposed and vulnerable to attacks. With him, Marin would not have safety. He had nothing to offer but love, and that would not fill her belly.

The sad reality of it shuddered through his heart.

"I see you understand." The earl spoke gently. "Save Marin and we will save Ena."

Sir Richard unlocked the cell door and pulled it open, his manner solicitous. "Can we trust you?"

Bran nodded. "I willna do anything to cause Marin further harm." The words choked from the tightness of his throat, leaving them sounding foreign to him.

The day before, he had a powerful castle and scores of men who trusted him enough to follow him into battle. Most importantly, he had Marin. He had love.

He would lose her. He would never see her again.

His heart crumpled under the force of his loss, as painful as what he'd remembered with his mother and brother, when he'd been so helpless in his meager care for Ena. And yet despite the bitter, soul-sucking agony of it, he could still not bring himself to regret his time with Marin. Not when it had been so precious.

He would never see her again, never hold her again, never see that playful smile or kiss her full lips. She was gone to him forever.

"What of my men?" Bran asked.

"We've had considerable losses," the earl replied. "We've offered to keep them on with the pay of our usual soldiers."

"All accepted," Sir Richard filled in. "Save one in particular who refused to leave your side. He waits for you now."

Sir Richard indicated the hallway stretching before Bran, one which was shrouded in darkness with no light to guide him toward its end. Bran shuffled forward.

The castle was soundless around him and the light beyond the animal hide coverings at the windows had gone dark. A chill of night seeped through the stonework underfoot and through his leather soles. The hour was late.

They led him from the castle and into the bailey where one man stood with his back to the castle. A horse stood on either side of him.

"The one man who refused to accept our offer to stay at the castle," Sir Richard said again.

The man turned around, his expression solemn. Drake.

Bran hesitated. "Ena will be safe?"

Sir Richard clasped Bran's forearm with his own. "You have my word as a knight that she will be safely recovered."

"Care for Marin, aye?" Bran released the man's arm and turned away to his one loyal friend. "They have a good offer here," Bran said in a tight voice to Drake. In truth, he hated to turn away the one man willing to stand at his side, but nor could he allow the youth to lose the opportunity for greater things than Bran could offer.

"Aye, but ye have my loyalty." Drake inclined his head respectfully.

Bran smirked to cover the tightness in his chest at the lad's impeccable honor. He didn't know what he'd done in his life to have earned such fealty, but he'd never been gladder for it.

Sir Richard strode ahead of them and called to the soldiers

manning the gates. They groaned open and the portcullis began to raise.

"I believe that is our nudge to remove ourselves from this place." Bran leapt onto his horse.

Drake did likewise and the two rode toward the open gates.

"Are ye sure ye want to do this?" Bran asked under his breath. "I dinna have a location in mind, I have no men but ye, and the Grahams will want my head and that of those around me."

"I go where ye do," Drake said stoically.

"Dinna say ye were no' forewarned," Bran muttered.

Together they left the safety of the castle walls. Neither of them looked back. Bran wasn't sure why Drake didn't bother, but he knew for himself if he looked backward, he might never be able to take another step forward.

Outside, the fallen Graham soldiers had not yet been handled, due to the limited resources and exhausted men. The bodies had attracted swarms of flies that the buzzing was enough to set Bran's teeth rattling. The odor of death swelled up around him, forcing him to put his sleeve to his nose to avoid breathing any more of the purification than necessary to draw air.

Beside him, Drake gave a choked cough and they both picked up their pace—away from the dead soldiers, and out into the night, into the unknown, where Bran would never see Marin again.

MARIN STARED AT YET ANOTHER LOCKED DOOR. HER HANDS ached from the repeated strikes against the solid wood to her room. Still, it remained in place, a barrier between her and the man she loved.

Bran.

Spent tears rendered her exhausted and left her eyes swollen and gritty. At one point, she'd fallen asleep curled up before the door. As uncomfortable as it had been when she'd finally awoken with a stiff neck, her own unease paled in comparison to what Bran doubtless endured.

Her eyes filled with a fresh bout of tears.

Her father had taken him away and had her locked in her room, a prisoner in her own castle, in the home she had worked so hard to run. And not one soldier had come to her aid. Not even her sisters. Already the skies had grown dark and she had heard nothing of Bran's fate.

She howled her anguish and pummeled her heel into the door with all her might, summoning the energy from the depths of her wounded soul. Her heel slammed into the door, but it did not cause so much as a shudder.

Would her father kill him?

The breath choked out of her chest and refused to be caught again. He wouldn't kill him, would he? Would he try to marry her off to some noble? Would he help rescue Ena?

Mayhap if she found out she was with child, then her father would relent. Marin put her hand to her flat stomach and scrunched her swollen eyes shut.

Her mind warred with the father she'd grown up loving and the hardened man who had returned from Berwick with only part of his troops, the man desperate for vengeance. She shuddered.

She did not know what this man was capable of.

A rattle came from the door and Marin sat upright. "Who's there?"

A shushing sounded on the opposite side followed by more muted clattering. Marin's pulse raced. Was she being let out? Was someone helping her at last?

The door creaked open and Leila's narrow face appeared.

"Leila," Marin said in a whispered rush.

Her youngest sister gave her a small smile and rushed into her arms. They stood thus for a long moment, wrapped in each other's embrace, pulling and giving comfort all at once.

"What has become of Bran?" Marin asked, desperate for news with a mix of dread and anxiety.

"He is alive," Leila whispered. "They have let him go."

He was alive. Every knot of apprehension loosened. Marin caught herself against the wall lest she fall to the ground with the force of her relief.

"They let him go?" Marin straightened. "Where? Where is he?"

Leila shrugged. "Beyond the castle gates. He has been told never to return, or he will be killed on sight."

"He's gone," Marin repeated slowly.

"Aye, over an hour ago."

Marin sank to the floor, no longer trusting her legs to hold her properly upright. Bran was gone. She would never see him again. She'd never had the opportunity to say goodbye. That last thought lodged in her mind and rattled around like a pebble until it was the only one thing she could hear.

She'd never been able to even say goodbye.

"Are you going to go after him?" Leila asked.

Marin snapped her head up.

Leila shrugged her delicate shoulders. "I didn't sneak here to open your door simply for an embrace." She smiled sheepishly. "Though it was nice."

"You did that for me?"

Leila nodded.

"Do the others know?" Marin asked of her sisters.

Leila shook her head. "You know they would not want you to leave." She twisted her lips to the side and gazed intently at the floor. Her small sniffle pinched at Marin's heart.

"You don't want me to leave either, do you?" She got to her feet and went to her smallest sister.

"Nay," Leila cried. She threw her skinny arms around Marin's waist and hugged her with the strength of a warrior. "I love you so much. It was hard to come."

Marin stroked her sister's head. "Then why did you do it?"

Leila turned her luminous blue eyes up at Marin. "Because I want you to be happy more than I want my heart to be whole."

"You are selfless and wonderful, Leila."

"As are you." Leila toyed with a loose string on the sleeve of her pale green kirtle. "It's what finally made me come to you. All our lives you've been there for us, giving so selflessly. You've never wanted anything for yourself, even though the rest of us needed you for everything. You were the mother I didn't have." Her voice caught.

"Leila." Marin knelt and looked at her sister.

"I know how much you love him. The Grahams suffered a great defeat with many of them slain. I do not think they have the forces to rally once more. But I would avoid large groups if I were you." Leila pulled a dagger from her pocket and gave it to Marin. "Nan is waiting."

"Nan?" She took the dagger and slipped the sheath onto her belt.

Leila motioned for Marin to follow her into the hall. Together they wound their way down to the kitchen. The castle was still around them, the soldiers all sleeping soundly after a hearty battle, many having just returned home for the first time in a month. The moment that they entered, Nan sprang up from a small wooden chair by the hearth.

"My lady." Nan stopped in front of her and her kind brown eyes crinkled with emotion. "Oh, my lady."

"Thank you for helping," Marin said earnestly.

Nan smiled sadly and nodded. "I'd have followed my Hewie had he gone to a place I could join him. I cannot think what life will be like without you here, but I know I want you to be happy."

"Will you be well here?" Marin surveyed the limited food stores and could not stop the nip of concern at leaving the castle thus.

"The earl is sending a large party out for food on the morrow."

Nan bent and stroked a black cat winding between her feet. "I am not sure Bixby will ever be the same. He misses Bran."

"God willing, we shall see Bixby again. We shall see all of you again." Marin's heart gave a little twist. It was probably an impossible dream, but it was one of her heart regardless.

"It's time," Leila said.

Marin nodded and made her way to where the empty wine casks sat over the trap door to the tunnel. Nan pulled it aside and opened the trap door while Leila readied a torch.

"If you don't mind my saying, my lady." Nan looked down at her hands.

"What is it, Nan?"

"You know my Hewie and I were never blessed with children of our own."

Marin nodded.

"Forgive me, but I've always thought of you and your sisters as mine, especially after your mother..." Nan's explanation faded away rather than say the words none of them wanted to hear. "I love you girls as though you were my own."

Marin hugged Nan and the cook returned the embrace with ferocity. "You be safe out there, aye?"

"I will," Marin assured her.

Leila entered with the torch, its flame making a low crackling in the large room. Nan handed Marin a bag with a shoulder strap. "Food in case you need it. It isn't much, just a bit of bread and cheese and some ale."

"Thank you." Marin embraced both Nan and her sister one last time before accepting the food which she draped over her shoulder, and took the torch in her hand. Even as she descended into the tunnel, she knew what she did was madness. Yet she had to try.

She had to find Bran.

❧ 31 ❧

The tunnels had been frightening to Marin as a girl. And now, alone in the tunnel with only its dank air pressing against her, she found her heart firing at a rapid beat, teetering on the edge of that childhood fear.

She forced her thoughts to those of Bran, of where he might go, and how best she might find him. It was far better than considering what might lay in wait for her beyond Werrick's walls. The Grahams had been run off, but it did not mean they were gone for good. Not to mention the other bands of random reivers wandering the borderlands in search of anything they might steal to survive.

Nay, she had to have faith she would find Bran, that they could be once more reunited. She clung to that idea as she wound her way through the dark tunnels with only the glow of her torchlight to combat the darkness. At long last, she found the exit to the tunnel. She pulled the precious key from her belt, unlocked the grate and eased out before locking it in place once more.

Once she was freed, she replaced the key carefully in her belt, and doused the flame. Her eyes took a moment to adjust to the absence of light, and in the moments of true darkness, the world came alive with rustling leaves. A droning hum sounded in the distance and the wind carried with it the odor of death. All evidence from the battle that day. How could it have only been that day, when it seemed so terribly long ago?

She secured the bag on her shoulder and strode in the opposite direction from the bodies. If the Grahams returned to collect their dead, she did not wish to be found.

After what seemed a lifetime, the small bit of forest came into view, lit by the glow of the moon and the sparkling stars above. She trudged onward, careful to avoid any part of the surrounding areas of the castle where a soldier might spot her from the battlements. She'd donned a kirtle after having been locked in her rooms and knew she would now stand out from a distance. Ladies did not wander about on their own in such lands.

She walked on through the night for what felt like ages, knowing Bran would eventually set up camp somewhere. It was not impossible that she might find him. There was no need to avoid any traveling parties along the way, for she saw not one soul on the path. No Grahams, and no Bran.

Exhaustion pulled at her legs and her temples still throbbed with the remnants of a headache from so many tears spilled. Her feet had grown tired and she regretted her inability to have taken a horse. She'd already eaten a bit of bread from the bag Nan gave her and happened upon a stash of coins. A considerable amount that most likely came from Nan's own pocket.

The sun had begun to rise and gild the lush green grass with its golden light when she finally saw a lone rider approaching her. He sat atop his horse in a familiar gambeson covered in filth, his dark head lowered, the way a man might if truly defeated.

Her heart skipped. Was that him?

She clapped a hand over her mouth to keep from shouting aloud. After having been raised since infancy on the borderlands, she knew better than to trust anyone, even if they looked familiar. She edged back slowly to a thatch of bushes and sank into them to observe from a safer location.

The man passed, and her heart dropped. He was not Bran.

She remained in the bushes until he had ridden by, her gaze still fixed on him, and rose from where she'd been hiding. A quick survey of her surroundings reflected not another soul. At least, not until she turned and found a group of five men riding in her direction.

It was impossible to have not been seen by them. Their pace quickened in her direction and she loosed a curse she'd heard Bran use several times. How could she have been so careless?

She'd been too mired in her disappointment, her mind too exhausted to produce sufficient logic.

Energy fired through her, spurring her feet into action as she darted from the bushes like a rabbit being chased by hounds.

While she ran, she fumbled with the dagger at her waist, pulling it free. The pounding of hoofbeats grew louder and made the earth under her feet rumble. Her heart was ready to explode from her chest and still she ran.

The scent of sweat and horseflesh prickled at her awareness and something hard slammed against the back of her head. Her feet flew out from under her and she connected with the ground in a hard *oof*.

Several rolls of bread tumbled from her bag, scattering about her. Marin yanked the bag from her shoulder as she flipped over, her dagger clutched in her fist. She was ready to fight.

The world tilted, but she ground her teeth and forced herself to focus despite the injury. She'd had worse.

There were five men. She'd fought five men before. Granted, not with a dagger, but it could be done. It had to.

A man with ruddy skin and a thick black beard stared at her with amusement. "She's got a dagger." He waggled his hands in the air in mock surrender and the other four men laughed.

They would not be laughing long.

"Hold her," the man said. "I took her down. I get her first."

Despite her confidence in her own abilities, Marin's blood turned to ice. They intended to rape her. Like Mother.

A man with red hair came forward, but she slashed at him with her knife. It nicked his forearm. He hissed and jerked his arm back.

"Get on with it," the dark-haired man said irritably.

"The bitch cut me." The redhead grimaced like a sullen child.

"You'll get your revenge." The dark-haired man gestured to her again. "Now hold her down."

This time a balding man came forward, his face screwed up in a scowl, his eyes cold and soulless. A shiver wound down Marin's spine. He pulled his foot back and kicked with incredible speed, before she had a chance to lash out.

Pain shot from her side and radiated through her body, sending stars flashing and blooming in her vision. She cried out and curled toward the injury. She blindly stabbed at the air with her dagger to prevent from being grabbed in her moment of weakness.

The blade caught and someone grunted in pain. A second kick landed in the exact same place as the first. The breath choked from Marin and did not easily return. She gasped and sputtered, made weak by her injuries.

She dragged in a hard inhale and her insides lit up as though on fire. Her arm was wrenched painfully, and the dagger fell from her grip. Strong hands shoved her wrists to the ground, grinding them painfully into the packed soil. A primitive part of Marin's mind shoved past the discomfort and her body writhed in helpless desperation to get free. One kick landed at the redhead's temple and sent him reeling back.

"Damn, but this lass is a fighter." He drew back and his fist flew toward her face.

She jerked her head to the side, but not quickly enough. His fist connected with her jaw and fresh waves of agony rocketed through her awareness. Her world was starting to dim, and a salty warmth filled her mouth. Blood?

There were too many men, their tactics too brutal. Despite her father's efforts in teaching her to be stronger, she had not been strong enough to fight off these men. Not when she started on her back, already injured. Not with simply a dagger.

She would end up just like her mother.

The bald man grimaced down at her, a large angry cut showed on his cheek and dripped blood down his chin. "Too much a fighter for her own damn good."

Marin braced herself for another hit, but it did not come. Instead, her clothing was tugged, and the rending of fabric filled her ears. She shook her head and tried to speak. A low, pitiful moan erupted from her chest. Hot tears leaked from her eyes. She wanted the darkness to take her away, to keep her from living through this hell that had destroyed her mother and would surely kill her too.

⬥⬥⬥

SLEEP HAD EVADED BRAN. AFTER EVERYTHING HE'D LOST, HOW could he possibly calm his mind?

He left the makeshift camp, letting Drake sleep as only young men could. They'd stopped as soon as they'd gone into the Scottish border to rest before deciding where to travel next. What to do next.

Movement to the right of the patch of forest called his attention. A group of men leaning over something.

No doubt a fresh kill of some sort.

Bran was just beginning to turn his attention away when he noticed one of the men get on his knees while his hands moved over the ties of his hose. A warning bell clanged in Bran's mind.

They didn't find a beast—they found a woman and were clearly going to rape her.

"Drake, get yer arse out here now," he growled. He didn't wait for the lad to rouse. Years of working together gave Bran the reassurance of knowing the young man would be moments behind him. Especially when a lass was in danger. Drake always had a special sense of awareness when it came to ladies in need.

Bran hefted his battle axe and ran toward the men. His blood fired with a rage that could not be quelled, a rage that had a purpose now to be sated.

The kneeling man didn't see him coming any more than he expected the war axe slicing through his neck. He pitched to the side with his head knocked from his body. A woman lay beneath a ruined gown, one leg naked and exposed from a massive tear in the silk. Her blonde hair spread over her face, bright and wet with fresh blood.

A bald man flew at Bran and managed to land his elbow into Bran's jaw. It was a hard hit, but not enough to break Bran's savage concentration, or deter him from his path. He roared his rage at the man and swung with his axe. Fear showed in his opponent's dark eyes.

Bran was relentless in pursuit of punishment, arcing his axe like a pendulum of death, sweeping closer with each step. The man turned and tried to run. The way that the lass on the ground no doubt had done. Bran launched his axe through the air, letting the handle leave his palm at exactly the right moment. It flew forward and sank into the back of the man's skull. He dropped like a sack of rotten grain.

Behind Bran came the ringing of swords and he knew Drake had joined him. Bran ran to reclaim his axe and turned, ready to help Drake fight the last three men. Two already lay dead and the third remained locked in combat. The red-haired man's attacks against Drake lacked confidence and finesse. The fight would be over quickly.

The woman on the ground shifted and let out a long, deep groan of agony. Bran's heart wrenched at the sound. What the bloody hell was this woman doing out alone and without a damn guard?

He knelt beside her and gently covered her leg with the tatters of her dress. She flinched, and he immediately regretted the action. Of course, she would not want him touching any part of her or her clothing after what she'd just been through, especially when she couldn't see with all her hair in her eyes.

Damn, but he was daft.

He pulled his hands back from her. "The men who hurt ye are dead. My man and I have made sure of that." He glanced over his shoulder to see Drake run the final brigand through with his blade.

"We're here to help ye," he said as gently as he could.

She whimpered.

"I want to move yer hair out of yer face, aye?" he said. "I willna hurt ye. I need to see yer injuries. To help ye, aye?"

Her right arm curled protectively against her side and the breath shuddered in and out of her as if each inhale and exhale caused fresh waves of agony.

She spoke, but it was an indistinguishable mumble.

"I'll take that as an aye from ye." He reached down to pull the hair from her face. "I'll no' hurt ye, I promise."

She whimpered again, and this time he understood the single word she spoke.

"Bran."

His heart stopped and his blood ran cold. Though he could not recognize the voice, considering how garbled it was through her agony, the connection immediately shot through him. The long blonde hair, the fine dress. *Dear God.*

One of Werrick's daughters. Bran drew the tresses back from her face with trembling hands and his heart crashed into his stomach in horror. The face he'd once stroked so affectionately was already bruising an angry purple at her jaw, and her teeth and mouth were red with blood.

A cry wrenched out of him, from the very core of his soul. This wasn't just any one of Werrick's daughters, she was Bran's wife.

She was his Marin.

❧ 32 ❧

Bran was careful to lead his horse at a steady pace, quickly enough to get Marin to Werrick Castle where she would receive the best care, but slow enough that it wouldn't jar her any more than was necessary. He cradled her gingerly against him, minding her injured side.

His throat was tight with emotion and his chest ached as surely as if he'd been stabbed. In truth, getting a dagger in the heart would be more easily endured than the pain of witnessing Marin in such a state.

She had sucked in her breath when they'd gotten her on the horse and started on their journey, her lips pressed tight to suppress her tears. Some time back, her whimpers had ceased, and she lay silent and limp against him.

At first, he'd feared the worst, but after confirming she still breathed, he pressed onward. Now, at long last, the castle rose before them.

"Give her to me," Drake said. "I will take her in."

Bran ground his teeth. "Nay." He swept his hand under her nose and gave a sigh of relief at the huff of air coming regularly from her nostrils. It was light, but it was breath. She was still alive.

His fear did not fully abate. Not when she was grievously injured, not when the reality of her survival was so perilous.

"Let me take her in," Drake said again.

"Nay," Bran snarled. He would sooner die than release his hold on Marin. It would be impossible to relinquish her to someone else and be ignorant to her fate. He had to be with her. He had to know.

"They'll kill ye, Bran." Drake's tone was somber.

Bran gazed down at his wife and everything inside of him twisted in agony for her. "I know," he said finally. "But I canna..." His words caught on the knot in his throat, croaking out before stopping short.

The odor of death came before the castle rose into view. Soldiers stood outside, gathering the bodies of the fallen and loading them onto carts. Bernard, visible in a green robe, moved his hand in the air in the sign of the cross.

They all stopped to watch Bran and Drake approach.

"Tell them," Bran ground out.

Drake nodded sharply and rode on ahead. He returned moments later. "Ye are instructed to give her to me," he said somberly.

Bran said nothing and continued to ride forward. An arrow soared toward him and sank harmlessly in the soil beside his horse. A warning shot.

Damn their warnings.

There was not another shot fired. This time, the portcullis opened to reveal Marin's sisters and her father. The earl's face went gray. "Marin." Anger flashed in his eyes. "What have you done to my daughter?"

"I dinna know it was her." The words choked out of Bran. "I saw a lass being attacked and went to aid her and it was...it was..."

He couldn't say her name, it was too agonizingly awful to relive that moment he'd realized it was her.

His Marin. His beautiful wife with all her fierceness, her passion and vitality.

The earl's eyes filled with tears. "My daughter. Is she..." He clenched his fist and did not finish the question.

"She needs Isla," Bran replied. Drake leapt from his horse and held Marin as Bran got down from his own horse.

Just in time too, for young Leila slipped to the ground like a puppet who'd lost its strings. Drake rushed forward, narrowly catching her in his arms before she could hit the cobblestones.

The earl stepped forward. "We will take my daughter. You may leave." He glared at Bran. "You've done enough."

"Like hell I will." Bran cradled Marin in his arms. "Kill me if ye like, but I refuse to leave her side. I left once before, knowing she would be safe, and then I find her like this. I refuse to leave her side again."

"Cease yer bickering." Isla approached somewhere between a run and a walk, certainly at a faster pace than she'd surely moved in some time. "Bring her inside so I can have a look at her. I'll no' have the lass die while ye stand there arguing like merchants at market day."

She leaned forward and peered at Marin. The lines on her crinkled face deepened. "Bring her." She bade Bran follow with a crook of her gnarled finger, and he obeyed with haste.

All around them, the keep had gone still, every person riveted on the battered body of their beloved mistress. Several made the sign of the cross as Bran passed by with her in his arms, pressed near his heart. Many of the women wept openly, their eyes bright with tears. Even several men averted their glossy gazes.

Isla led them to a small bedchamber with a single bed. "Set her there." She nodded toward the thin mattress.

Bran did as he was told, taking care to move Marin as little as possible. He gingerly swept the hair from her face and draped the ruined dress over her bare leg.

"Dinna bother with that." Isla appeared beside him with a pair of shears.

Bran shifted in front of Marin, ready to protect her.

"Easy, lad." Isla wriggled the shears. "Ye're covering her, but I need to see her, aye?"

A hearty knock shattered the stillness of the room. "Let me in," the earl's voice boomed.

"No' during this part, m'lord." Isla's reply came calmly, and she swept her hand to the side, indicating Bran need move.

He did not. "I'm no' leaving."

"Ye're here, are ye no'?" She lifted her brows and waved him away again.

This time he sidestepped out of her way. The older woman peered at him. "Dinna hover over me, or ye'll be joining her da outside."

He edged back even further, lest he give in to the temptation to do exactly as she asked him not to. Isla took the tattered edge of the once-fine gown in her withered fingers, put the shears to it and sliced into the fabric. Watching Marin be bared in such a way held him riveted with fear, worry and the overwhelming need to hide her naked body from observation.

The healer pulled the fabric away from Marin's ribs and gave a low curse in Gaelic. Bran could stand the distance no more. He stepped forward and choked on a cry.

The entire left side of her ribs was a mass of violent, angry purples and wicked reds against her fair skin. Isla ran her fingers along the swollen, bruised flesh and sighed. "She has a few broken ribs for certes, and she's had quite a blow to the face. I'll know more when I've looked her over more thoroughly. I must move fast to ensure she does not wake. 'Tis a blessing for the pain to have taken her to slumber."

And move quickly she did. Her fingers shifted in a nimble

exploration, skimming over Marin's naked skin, combing lightly over her scalp, assessing every intimate part of his wife. Bran's cheeks burned by the time Isla had finished and his hands ached from clenching them.

"She's got a knock at the back of her head as well." She slid a glance in his direction. "She was not used."

"I would love her even if she had been," he stated.

"Aye, but at least now ye know any bairns ye may have are yers." She shrugged. "It matters to most men. Be glad for her sake then. 'Tis a harrowing thing for a woman to live through."

Bran nodded with as much understanding as he could. A woman's body was precious, sacred. He could only imagine the horror of such desecration to their intimate parts. His gut twisted, and he found he could not think further on it. Not now with such pain already on display.

"Can ye heal her?" he asked.

"I can heal anyone but the dead." She considered Marin for a long moment. "She will need to be kept still lest her broken ribs pierce her lungs."

"If that happens?" Bran pressed.

Isla frowned. "She dies."

"She willna move," Bran vowed.

The aging healer patted his back. "This is why ye were allowed in." She glanced to the door. "Her da will no' be so easy to tell."

"I would do anything to save her," Bran swore. "Even lay down my life if need be."

Isla smiled sadly up at him. "Ye may have already done exactly that."

"I NEVER SAW IT. I NEVER SAW IT. I NEVER SAW IT."

The fragile feminine voice chanted the words, each phrase ticking through Marin's conscious like drips of water from a leaking roof. "*I never saw.* Forgive me, Marin. Forgive me, forgive me, forgive me."

A harsh sob came from beside Marin.

Pain effused her body. Pain everywhere. It was agony to even breathe.

She opened her eyes. That didn't hurt. Good. She slid her gaze toward the ragged weeping. A glossy dark head lay against the mattress of the bed.

"Forgive me," Leila said in a choked voice. "I never saw the attack, or I wouldn't...I couldn't..."

Marin drew a breath to speak. Fire lashed through her lungs and the air she meant to draw broke off in a cough. Her chest wheezed at the intensity of the pain and she tried desperately to inhale as minimally as was possible.

"Marin." Leila stared at her in bewilderment. The tip of her nose was red and shiny, and her eyes swollen and red-rimmed. A tear trailed down her cheek. "I never saw the attack." She shook her head. "I never saw it. If I had, I never would have freed you."

Her hand grasped Marin's, ice cold and clammy. "I almost killed you by doing so. Please, please forgive me."

Marin shook her head, confused. "What attack?"

Her blood chilled as a memory came to surface. The men. Too many of them. They overwhelmed her after the strike to her head. Then Bran was there, his voice soothing and his touch gentle. Her heart ached with more intensity than even her lungs. "Bran. Where is he?"

"Ye're da will bring him to ye. Leila, get the earl." Isla approached the bed. "We've been keeping ye resting so ye'll heal."

"I must see Bran." Marin tried to sit up and a lightning bolt of pain streaked through her, freezing her in place.

"Ye're no' well enough to move around, lass." Isla put a comforting hand on her shoulder. "It hurts like fire to breathe, aye?"

Marin nodded, grateful that the healer understood her discomfort. Understanding meant there might be relief.

Isla smiled with sympathy and her kind eyes crinkled beneath folds of wrinkles. "Ye've had some ribs broken. We've kept ye asleep on and off for six days with some of my teas, only giving ye time to eat. But I think ye've healed enough now to remain awake safely. Calm yerself, take smaller breaths and it will feel better."

Marin obeyed, drawing in smaller breaths. She could not calm herself so easily though, not when Bran was not there. Not when she was not getting answers. Where was he?

The smaller breaths did help, at least.

Her door opened and her father walked in. He looked stronger than when last she'd seen him, the way she remembered. His beard was closely cropped and his silver-gray hair neatly combed. He stood for a moment staring at her, his eyes glittering with unshed tears.

"Dinna ye go upsetting the lass," Isla warned.

Father put up a hand and nodded. "Marin," he whispered.

"Bran. Where is he?" She couldn't stop the rapidity of her breath. It made her head spin and her ribs ache.

He sank into the chair beside the bed, the one Leila had been sitting in, and took her hand. The action made her feel like a little girl again with how his palm engulfed hers with his love and strength. "You love him, don't you?"

Marin tried to force herself to calm, as Isla had instructed, but it was impossible to do so. "Aye."

"He risked his life to bring you home." Her father's jaw flexed, the way it did when he was agitated. "You shouldn't have gone out there. You put yourself in considerable danger. Leila—"

"It wasn't her fault," Marin said firmly. She regretted now having been so confused when she woke and unable to accept her youngest sister's apology. It was a wrong she would ensure was righted later that day.

"I would do it again," she said. "I would leave again if it meant finding him and being with him."

Her father winced as though she'd hit him.

"Father, I have spent my entire life giving to my family, doing everything—being everything—for everyone. I've done it gladly and with the whole of my heart." Her words came out breathy and jagged with her shallow breathing. "But leaving to be with my husband was the only thing I've ever done for myself."

Her father rose to his feet. Marin watched him with trepidation, fearful of what his next words might be.

"Bran made me realize something the day I released him and cast him out of the castle." He tucked his hands behind his back and paced about the narrow room. "You are no longer a girl, but a woman. You've been a woman since before you should have been. Because I failed you."

He stopped and lowered his head. She could not make out his expression, but it took a long moment before he spoke again. "I lost myself to my grief, first when your mother died and even in these past years when I haven't been here. You've taken on the responsibilities she left behind, and those I'd inadvertently pushed upon your shoulders. Bran was right. You are no girl to be ordered about by her well-intentioned, yet wayward father. You are a woman, powerful in her own right and capable of making her own decisions."

He turned to her and swallowed. "I will not fail you again, Daughter."

"Bran?" she whispered.

He nodded. "He is being summoned from the practice yard. This time while you've been resting, he has been treated not as a prisoner, but as a guest."

Marin gave a shuddering exhale and scarcely acknowledged the streak of agony it produced in her lungs.

"Ena?" she gasped out.

"She is on her way as we speak." Marin's father smirked. "With

Kerr's gross misuse of his power, I was able to quickly summon all the wardens together. He was all too easy to deal with when confronted about his plans to take my castle. The other wardens sided with me. Kerr will be punished appropriately, and Sir Richard was sent to where Ena was being held captive to bring her here. I came home as quickly as I could, out of my concern for you."

Marin closed her eyes in relief. "Thank you. You have saved her life."

"She is an innocent in all of this. As was Bran." The earl stared down at Marin and his face softened. "I have a wedding present for you." He smiled now, the loving grin she knew so very well. "The castle and lands in Kendal, the one we visited when you were a child, if you remember."

She did remember. The sun's heat on her face, the sweet perfume of roses around her in the sculpted garden, the ornate beauty. There had been happy times at Kendal Castle.

"They are yours," her father said. "For you to go to with your husband. For his sister and her new husband to be safe. I have already made arrangements to hire more servants there and have accommodations made ready for your new life."

Marin blinked, unsure what she could possibly say in gratitude for such generosity and understanding. "Father, it is so much."

His brow furrowed with concern. "Are you unhappy?"

A choked cry emerged from her heart. "I could not be happier with your generosity, Father. You have given me everything."

"As you have for me." He approached her bed and gingerly embraced her. "I love you, Marin."

"And I love you too, Papa." She had not used the girlish endearment in more than a decade. It filled her heart to do so now and brought tears to her father's eyes.

"Marin." The deep, familiar voice of her husband interrupted the embrace.

Her father cleared his throat and eased back. For the first

time since she thought her husband lost to her, Marin laid eyes on Bran.

BRAN RAN TO HIS WIFE'S BED AS THE EARL DREW AWAY WITH A smile. The older man nodded at him and left the room with Isla, leaving Bran and Marin alone.

"Marin," Bran said again. He wanted to say her name over and over again, to reassure himself she was here. With him. Alive.

"My father told me the most joyous news." She beamed up at him in the beatific way he remembered.

"Ena is safe." Though he said the words, he still did not believe them. He could not until he saw her standing in front of him.

"Aye." Marin held out her hand and he took it. "She will be safe with us as well, for father is giving us a castle near the sea that once belonged to my mother."

He gently drew his arms around her, fearful of causing her pain. She was sweet and precious in his hold, the way he remembered. Her head came to rest on his chest, and he found himself stroking the silky length of her hair before he realized what he was doing. He wanted to touch all of her, to ensure himself this moment was real and not yet another dream.

He'd had too damn many of those. They'd been so vivid, each time he'd rushed from his chamber, sure he would find her sitting up and fully recovered. Once he'd found she had developed a fever instead, and he sat with her the two days it took to finally loosen its grip on her hot, reddened cheeks.

"I thought I'd lost ye, Marin." His voice clogged with emotion. "When I realized that battered lass on the ground was ye." He gritted his teeth to fight for control. "There were so many times after. When ye became so still on the way here, when I saw the extent of yer injuries, when ye developed a fever. And all the while, even as I feared losing ye, I could never regret having let myself love ye."

"I love you with all my heart, Bran."

"Ach, I know it." He closed his eyes and reveled in the feel of her in his arms. "A wee bit too much, judging by yer attempt to try to find me. It was reckless and impulsive and—"

"You would have done the same for me," she said against his chest.

"Aye." The love he had for her was so great, it welled in his throat and made his voice tight. "I would do anything for ye."

"With good fortune, neither of us should face such circumstances to save the other again."

He stared down at her and imagined her in their new life. In a castle where the land was safe, and the border territory was only a distant memory.

"What are you thinking?" she pulled her head from his chest and glanced up at him.

"I'm wondering what our life will be like together in our castle." He ran his thumb over her cheek where the discolored bruise was fading to a deep yellow. "And I wonder what ye want out of our life."

"What do you mean?"

"Ye've never thought about what *ye* want, Marin. Ye've always done for others." He let his thumb brush over her lower lip. "This is our life and I want ye to think of yerself for once."

She smiled. "I have what I want."

"But there is more. Ye could take up gardening." He kissed her gently. "Ye could swim out in the sea like a selkie." He kissed her now-smiling mouth. "We could have children."

"Aye," she breathed. "Children." The simple word made her smile with wonder at the idea of having her own, ones who looked like a perfect mix between her and Bran. A sweet babe to cradle in her arms, as she had with Leila all those years ago.

"We should try for them soon." She slid a coy look up at him.

"When ye're healed," he replied gruffly.

Her fingers ran down his chest to his abdomen. "We can stay in our chambers late every morning and retire early every night. Mayhap even in the afternoon."

"The afternoon?" He dropped his jaw with exaggerated shock. "Ach, next thing ye'll be suggesting is Friday, or some other day not sanctioned for copulation."

Her brow quirked upward like a shameless flirt. "Every last day of the week."

He held her face in his hands and kissed her, so glad to have her safe and in his arms, and so eager to see what their new life would bring them. If nothing else, he knew there would be passion and love and happiness.

"Bran." A familiar voice called his name from the doorway.

He froze. *Ena.* He released Marin and spun around to find his sister rushing toward him. Her long dark hair was bound back, and her slender face was clean. She did not appear to have any bruises indicating beating, or other signs of misuse.

He took his sister in his arms. She squeezed him with impossible strength. "Ye saved me." She released him and blinked back tears. "My Renault will be joining us soon."

She glanced around Bran. "Is this Marin?"

Marin smiled. "Aye. It is good to meet you after all this time, Ena."

"Thank ye, my lady." Ena bobbed an uncomfortable curtsy.

"Marin," Marin corrected. "Please. We are sisters and there is no greater joy in all the world than a sister."

"Mayhap a brother." Ena grinned at Bran, then back at Marin. "Or mayhap even love."

"Or mayhap children." Bran reached for Marin's hand while he held his sister's shoulders secure in his right arm.

Regardless of where the love came from, or whether the person was noble or poor, they all found wealth in joy. And Bran knew himself to be the richest man in all the world.

EPILOGUE

March 1336
Kendal Castle

Marin closed her eyes and tilted her face to the heat of the sun. The air was cold with the last of the winter chill, but it was a lovely contrast.

"Ye look bonny." Bran's voice sounded beside her.

She opened her eyes to find him smiling down at her. A breeze blew in through the open window and ruffled his dark hair.

"This castle suits ye, as does the land here." He drew her into his arms where his skin was warm despite the coolness in the air.

"This was my mother's favorite castle. We have many fond memories of visiting here." Marin glanced to the dormant gardens below and could almost see her mother's golden head bent over a bush filled with massive roses. Leila had inherited her way with plants, a skill Marin had always envied.

"Why dinna yer da bring ye here instead?"

She tore her gaze from the garden and let her stare fix out on the glittering sea in the distance instead. "Werrick Castle was too important. With Father being Warden, he had to remain there, and Mother could not stand for us to be separated. Their love was greater than any ever known." She smiled at Bran. "At least for their time."

He gave a deep chuckle against her ear and snuggled her closer.

A baby squalled in the distance. Ena's new son, who was ready to eat nearly every hour. The poor woman had finally conceded to hire a wet nurse just to get a moment's rest.

The boy brought great joy to the castle, as well as renewed hope for Marin that she and Bran might soon have their own child.

"It would be a wonderful place to raise children." She ran her palm over her flat stomach. "Someday."

He swept her hair away from her shoulder and kissed her exposed neck. "Someday if God wills it. Until then, we will continue to pursue our efforts in conceiving." There was a playful, sensual undertone to his voice.

Mayhap with another man, Marin might have been more discouraged by her inability to bear a child in three years' time. But with Bran, with his unwavering love and the beautiful, peaceful life they lived together, the issue had not been one of great import. How could it be, when her life was so perfectly happy?

A sharp knock came from the door. "Stay here," Bran said in her ear. "I'll send them away."

And send them away he did, but when he returned to her, he held a missive in his hand. Anice's neat writing spelled out Marin's name.

He held the note aloft with a wicked grin. "A kiss for a letter, my love."

Marin laughed and gave him a kiss as she pulled the folded

parchment from his fingers. She unfolded the note to find Anice's neat writing had gone sloppy.

"She says she does not know if we will receive this," Marin said as she read the note. "She wants me to know they have been under siege from the Grahams, but that all will be well, for she has a plan."

Bran leaned closer, the playfulness gone from his expression. "Does she say what she intends to do?"

Marin read on and shook her head. "Only that this is to warn us not to come until she tells us it is safe to do so."

Bran ran his hands down Marin's arms. "I fear for the Grahams being at the mercy of yer sisters."

"This is serious," Marin chided.

"Aye." Bran held her face in his hands and met her gaze. "The curtain wall is strong, and yer family is resourceful. Dinna forget Drake is there and still has connections on the Scottish side, aye?"

It was true: Drake had remained at Werrick Castle. Sir Richard had deemed himself too old to ride into battle and Drake had been eager to fill the role when Marin's father had offered him the position of Captain of the Guard. The Earl of Werrick had always been one to recognize skilled warriors.

"We will find out more details," Bran said. "All will be well, my love. I'll send a runner today."

Marin nodded.

"All will be well," Bran said once more. This time the reassurance sank into Marin's heart.

She nodded again with more conviction.

"And if ye need someone to need, I'm here for ye, lass." He winked at her.

She couldn't help but smile at such an offer. Because he had always been there for her, his strong arms open to ease away her fears, his smile there to lift her spirits.

Everything would be well with Bran at her side. Even this.

He was her husband, her love and the best promise she ever kept.

Thank you for reading MARIN'S PROMISE! I read all of my reviews and would love to know how you enjoyed MARIN'S PROMISE, so please do leave a review.

All the sisters have their own story:

- Anice in *Anice's Bargain*
- Ella in *Ella's Desire*
- Catriona in *Catriona's Secret*
- Leila in *Leila's Legacy*
- Drake's sister, Ena, even has her own story in *Ena's Surrender*
- Drake and his sisters will be getting their own stories as well, starting with *Faye's Sacrifice*

Check out Anice's story next in ANICE'S BARGAIN where Anice realizes the only way to save her family, is to marry a Graham reiver.

***Keep reading for a first chapter preview of ANICE'S BARGAIN**

ANICE'S BARGAIN

ANICE BARRINGTON, THE MOST BEAUTIFUL OF THE EARL OF Werrick's daughters, will stop at nothing to protect her family during a siege, including offering herself as bride to her enemy.

James Graham has grown weary of a life of destruction and

longs for peace. While marriage to Anice offers a new opportunity, it comes at a high cost.

Forced together by desperation and held by passion, will love take root, or will the bitterness between enemies tear them apart?

Sign up for my exclusive newsletter to stay up to date on the latest Borderland Rebels news. Sign up today and get a FREE download THE HIGHLANDER'S CHALLENGE.

www.MadelineMartin/newsletter

ANICE'S BARGAIN
Chapter 1 Preview

March 1336
Brampton, England

It was not their first siege, but it was certainly their longest. The Grahams were determined.

Lady Anice Barrington, second daughter to the third Earl of Werrick, regarded the dismal larder with her father at her side. Their gazes were mutually fixed on the lone sack of grain.

"The last," he muttered. His brow furrowed into a complex map of creases, carved by a life of sorrow and hardship.

"Is there nothing else?" Anice asked. The large red brown dog sitting near her feet shifted and gave a low whimper as though he could understand their dismal discussion. Piquette was not allowed to receive his own ration of food and so Anice split her meager portion with her beloved pet. It was hardly enough to fill either of them. They were left persistently desperate with hunger, though neither offered up complaint.

Nan, the cook of Werrick Castle, crossed her arms over her chest in a show of authoritative knowledge. "Nothing left save any new vegetables we manage to grow in the garden, my lady. But they get eaten as soon as they're plucked from the earth."

"We'll need to reduce food distribution." The earl nodded absently to himself, content with his decision.

Nan cast Anice an anxious glance, the steel in her back melting. "We've already done that several times. The people are starving." The cook had once been round and plump, the way one in her position ought to be—or so Nan had said. The lean months, however, had left her sharp chin jutting from sagging skin and her kirtle swinging around her once generous frame. They were all too thin, too hungry.

Anice stood mutely, unable to come up with a solution. They would be out of food within days. Reducing their rations further would do nothing but anger the people of Werrick and prolong the inevitable by a day or two at best. But what would happen when it was all gone?

Anice shivered at the possibilities, all of them awful.

Lord Werrick dragged a hand down his tired face. "I wish Marin were here," he said quietly. "She would know what to do."

Anice bit the inside of her cheek and focused on the sharp pain rather than the cut of her father's words. He had not meant them, after all. Or at least, he had not meant for them to hurt. Anice's eldest sister, Marin, had been gone from Werrick for almost three years, living in their mother's favorite castle in England. Hunger made Anice's head swim. It was all too easy to remember the peaceful life there with lovely rose gardens and sunlit gardens. And food. So much food.

Sweet, fresh apples with juice that ran down one's chin when she bit into the crisp flesh. Crusty bread that broke under her fingers and revealed the soft, steaming doughy center. Slathered with butter. Greasy, salty—

Stop.

"Perhaps we can speak to the Grahams," Anice suggested

abruptly. Anything to take her mind off food. "I've heard reivers will sometimes bargain."

Her father shook his head, his stare going distant. It tugged at Anice's heart when he did that, lost to the horrors she wished she could blot from his memory.

"I cannot lose another messenger." He looked down at her with his large, solemn eyes—eyes that had shone with joy when Anice had been a girl. How she missed those long-ago days, back before her mother died.

In a brave attempt to bring a message to the king requesting his help, their messenger had rushed past the Grahams, gotten caught, and paid with his life. He'd lived only twenty summers, the same age as Anice, and had volunteered hoping to save the lot of them. Anice's father had reluctantly agreed. The young man's body had been left in front of the gates the following morning with the missive torn, the dozens of pieces fluttering in the grass about him like macabre, blood-spattered moths.

Several more men had followed that messenger, either to escape the stomach-gnawing hunger within Werrick's walls, or in an attempt to help. And while Anice did not know if any of them made it through, they remained without aid.

"We haven't tried discussing it with the Grahams ourselves," Anice protested.

"And who would go?" he asked.

Anice straightened. "Me." She ran her fingers over her dog's soft fur. "Me and Piquette."

At the mention of his name, Piquette stiffened to attention, always loyal, always brave.

He blinked and his face reddened. "Absolutely not."

"Mayhap they wouldn't kill a woman."

"Nay, you know what they would do to a woman." His jaw flexed beneath his gaunt face. Anice opened her mouth to protest, but he swept a hand in front of her. "I'll not discuss the idea of sending one of my daughters to be left at the mercy of those barbarians. "He turned on his heel and strode from the kitchen. His footsteps rang out on the flagstones until the door closed behind him, muffling his derisive departure.

A little black cat wound its warm body around Anice's feet and cast Piquette a wary glance. Poor Bixby hadn't been the same since Marin left. Though in truth, it was most likely her husband, Bran, who the cat missed the most. Bixby flopped in front of her and she gently nuzzled his chest with the toe of her shoe, much to Piquette's grumbling agitation. Anice bent and rubbed her fingers at the little white star on Bixby's chest, while scratching behind Piquette's ear. It was easier to offer affection to the animals than to regard Nan and the pity dulling the older woman's eyes.

Anice wasn't Marin. That much was obvious with each passing day. She didn't help their steward, William, with the books the same way Marin had; she didn't have the soothing patience; she wasn't as organized and couldn't keep the castle together as Marin had. As with much else in Anice's life, she was failing where others had succeeded, no matter her immense effort and good intentions.

Nan's warm brown eyes fixed on Anice. "I'm inclined to agree with your da. There now, you needn't be upset." Nan settled a hand over Anice's cheek. Though there was little food to be had, the comforting scent of baking bread still clung to Nan's sleeve.

Since Marin had left, Nan had taken on more of a maternal role with the remaining four sisters—yet another area where Anice had been found wanting.

Bixby rolled abruptly. His ears flicked and he darted into a shadow. At least one of them would eat well today. He always knew where to find the rats.

Piquette watched him with a furrowed brow, too big and clumsy for an attempt of his own.

"If I went down there, mayhap I could make them listen." Anice kept her back held straight as she spoke. She was a woman of twenty, running the Werrick Castle as lady of the keep. Had Timothy not been slain in combat she would even be a wife.

If only he hadn't been pulled to the battle of Berwick with her father. If only he'd returned home, they could have resumed their plans to wed. Memories of her time with Timothy twisted at something inside of her, the same as it always did when thoughts of him surfaced. Not with the regret of a lover, but rather, with a pang of guilt.

"How about a smile on your lovely face instead?" Nan smoothed Anice's hair from her brow. "Your beauty is enough to cheer up the whole of Werrick."

Anice swallowed the rising ire within her and complied. Not for herself, but for Nan.

She kept the smile pitched to the corners of her mouth until she was out of the kitchen where she let it fall without ceremony. Piquette nuzzled her palm with his big wet nose.

No doubt her father would have trusted Marin to go speak to the Graham reivers. He might even allow Ella, whose intelligence could unravel any stitch of trouble. Or Catriona, whose immaculate aim with an arrow could knock a feather from a bird mid-flight a hundred yards in the air. Or Leila, with her ability to foresee what was to come.

But Anice had none of those qualities. She was simply beautiful. A dull, shallow label she loathed. Regardless of how much she despised it, she clung to the praise. While paltry, the notoriety was better than being nothing.

Despite her father's refusal and Nan's warnings, Anice knew best how to aid her family. And it had everything to do with her beauty.

She waited until the castle went still that night, then crept down to the kitchen. In more ordinary times, servants would have been awake still with dishes to scour and foods to prepare for the following day. In their new life, everyone went to sleep early, even the servants, conserving their little strength remaining.

She slipped into the pathetically empty larder, where wine barrels were piled against one another. Beneath the collection lay a secret door, leading outside the castle walls. Piquette padded silently behind her.

Though she'd tried to get him to stay in her room without her, he'd refused. Forcing him would have resulted in a fuss she could ill afford, so she had finally conceded to allow him to join.

He sat and watched her with his head tilted, as she shifted about the casks, long since empty of their contents. The barrels were easily moved, the passage opened and within seconds, they were navigating the earthen tunnels beneath the castle. Anice cupped her hand over the candle flame to prevent it from snuffing out in the dank, cool air. Outside of the flickering light, darkness pressed in on them, threatening to swallow them whole.

In truth, she was grateful for Piquette's presence, for the warm comfort of his massive body hugged up against her leg. He brought what she needed most—strength.

At last, they made their way to the gate of the narrow exit. She pulled the key from her pocket, clicked the lock open and eased out into the night through the tangle of concealing vines. Above, the stars winked down at her with such brightness, they appeared to be slivers of forgotten sunlight caught in a blackened sky.

Once the gate was locked and the vines rearranged to conceal where Piquette had barreled through, Anice hid the key beneath a large boulder. In the full face of a brilliant moon, they made their way through the dewy summer grass to the scattering of firelight below.

She had spent hours preparing for this moment, ensuring she'd chosen the right gown, that her hair gleamed like spun gold; her scent was feminine, but not overpowering. Mayhap everyone was correct. Mayhap there was nothing more to her than being beautiful. After all, what she was about to do lacked skill and thought.

If indeed, she did stop to think, she would no doubt run back into the safety of Werrick's walls.

She spun the small ruby ring on her right hand, the one her mother had given to her before their world had abruptly changed. Anice did not intend to quit this mission. Not until she was at the Graham encampment and had the opportunity to speak to whoever was in charge of the marauding band of murderers.

They had to listen. And if her beauty was the only way to make that happen, so be it.

❦

JAMES GRAHAM REGRETTED HAVING COME TO WERRICK Castle. He'd been fool enough to think he might be able to sway his father from the war-torn path he had blazed for years over the border between England and Scotland.

"We're wearing them down, lad." The elder Graham grinned in the light of the campfire. Shadows danced over his aged face and gave him a ghoulish appearance. His hair, once a deep brown like James's, fell in wisps of white around his skeletal cheeks. He bobbed his head in slow consideration. "I can feel their surrender coming, deep in my bones."

Such words used to bring pride to James. Back when he had believed their way of life was the only way to live, before he acknowledged the damage left behind their success. Back when he looked up to this father and contemplated his words wise.

No doubt the laird of the Grahams was correct now, but it did not mean James found joy in such truths. They'd been camped at the base of the massive castle for nearly five months now. In the last month, their fires roasting freshly caught game had lured soldiers to the parapets. No doubt the scent of cooking meat made them wild with hunger.

The people of Werrick Castle would be on the barest bit of

grain, if they had any left. The village nearby had not suffered at the hands of the Grahams, not when they were too important for their purpose in supplying the camping force with food, ale and women.

James hoped the sparing of the village also had to do with the lessening of his father's blood lust, mayhap even a modicum of guilt. The acts of their prior years had been more than James could bear. He suppressed a shudder.

"Just think, Son. When they surrender, ye can have the land ye've been wanting." Laird Graham bumped his elbow against James's arm.

He cast a dark look at his father. "I dinna want the land like this."

"Ach, aye." Laird Graham nodded to himself. "Someone is just going to give it to ye then, provide ye with heaps of coin to start anew and we'll all sprout rainbows from our arses." He gave a wheezing laugh that bled into a wracking cough.

James looked away to afford his father privacy, while the old man gathered his breath once more. He was dying. They both knew it, but neither bothered to say it aloud.

"We have enough coin," James ground out.

"For caring for the land." His father cleared his throat in a great, rattling hum. "We dinna have enough for land *and* living. These people dinna need a farming tenant. Especially no' when its frozen or been buried under rains like in the past. Nay, lad—our people need a laird. They are used to battle, to being led into war and winning, no' tilling soil."

"Better to till soil than to murder." James met his father's gaze. "To live a life they dinna have to regret."

Laird Graham stared at James, his eyes glittering like flecks of onyx. "I liked ye better before that witless English bastard got to ye."

This argument again. The one about the man who had saved James first from death, then from a life of lies and theft. He'd showed James there were other ways to live, ways Laird Graham might never agree with.

Somewhere in the distance came the shouts of several men, followed by the clatter of weapons striking. Another fight. Sieges led to bored men and bored men seldom possessed good intentions. They wanted a fight, something solid and ripe for their blades to split. They wanted war, a break from the tedium of endless waiting.

"Ye should settle into the life ye had before." His father's tone was impatient. "Find yerself a wife, have a few bairns."

It was a tender spot and James's father knew it. There'd been no other woman since Morna. James scowled.

Laird Graham gave another winded laugh, this one shallow in his obvious attempt to prevent another coughing fit.

"Ye're always on about having me change my ways." The elder Graham smirked at his son. "Mayhap I'll consider altering my set ways when ye decide to wed."

It was no secret Laird Graham hoped to see grandsons before his death, to pass on his marauding influence, more likely. For James's part, he wanted his father's remaining time to be spent in peace, in a world built on hard work and honesty rather than theft and greed. As it was, the old man's dark heart would send him straight to the flames of hell. Before that, as death was stretching a hand toward him, there would be the reminder of all the hurt he had caused.

James knew all too well how horrific those final moments truly could be. "Dinna ye see I'm doing this for yer own good, old man?"

Laird Graham scoffed. "As do I, lad. As do I."

James pushed up from the roughhewn bench and stepped away, desperate to let the cool night air smooth the ragged edges of his irritation. His father's wheezing laugh followed him, until it became distant enough to fade into the backdrop of the camp. James drew a deep breath to calm his racing pulse and appreciated his ability to do so without the lancing pain in his chest he'd experienced so many months before.

The scar stung at times in a sharp, internal way; nothing he could soothe, but for the most part, he had recovered from the thrust of a sword into his chest. He'd used the idle time at camp to strengthen his body once more and was grateful to have recovered so fully.

He knelt at the edge of the small creek, cupped water into his palms and splashed it over his face. It was cold against his hot skin. Refreshing. He sighed and leaned his head back before opening his eyes. It was then he realized he was not alone.

He put his hand to the hilt of his dirk, his muscles tensed to spring from his crouched position as he slowly glanced to his left. He went still.

It was no warrior standing several paces away, but a woman. Nay—a goddess of the old ways—for truly no mortal woman could possess such an ethereal presence. Moonlight glowed off her in a radiant sheen, from the purity of her white gown, to the perfection of her fair skin and the brilliance of her golden hair. She was a moniker of peace, a symbol for everything beautiful and right in a world that had gone so damn wrong.

A massive dog, the size of a small pony, came from behind her and stood before her like a sentry.

The woman beheld James with long-lashed pale eyes, her gaze beseeching. When she finally spoke, her voice was soft, gentle, far too appealing. And completely English. "I need your help."

AUTHOR'S NOTE

One of the things I enjoy most about being an author of historical romance is the research involved. With every book, it seems like I discover something I hadn't expected to find. Marin's Promise was no different.

Cooks were generally men in the medieval era, but in my mind, I always saw the cook of Werrick Castle to be a woman. And not just any woman, but one who was warm and comforting, almost like a mother. So, I dug into my research and was elated to find it could still work with Nan as the cook.

Apparently with tradesmen, their wives often assisted in the running of the business. If the man died before his wife, there was no one better equipped to handle the business than the wife (except maybe a long-term apprentice). It was not uncommon, and sometimes even expected, for a wife to continue with her husband's trade after his death. Therefore, it would be perfectly fine for Nan to resume being cook at Werrick Castle after her Hewie's death.

Want to learn a little more about each of the characters and the history of the Borderland Ladies? I have a history of the Borderland Ladies, character bios and free short stories on the supporting characters on my website:

Read more about the Borderland Ladies here

ACKNOWLEDGMENTS

THANK YOU TO my amazing beta readers who helped make this story so much more with their wonderful suggestions: Kacy Stanfield, Monika Page, Janet Barrett, Tracy Emro and Lorrie Cline. You ladies are so amazing and make my books just shine!

Thank you to Janet Kazmirski for the final read-through you always do for me and for catching all the little last minute tweaks.

Thank you to John and my wonderful minions for all the support they give me.

And a huge thank you so much to my readers for always being so fantastically supportive and eager for my next book.

ABOUT THE AUTHOR

Madeline Martin is a USA TODAY Bestselling author of Scottish set historical romance novels filled with twists and turns, adventure, steamy romance, empowered heroines and the men who are strong enough to love them.

She lives a glitter-filled life in Jacksonville, Florida with her two daughters (known collectively as the minions) and a man so wonderful he's been dubbed Mr. Awesome. She loves Disney, Nutella, cat videos and goats dressed up in pajamas. She also loves to travel and attributes her love of history to having spent most of her childhood as an Army brat in Germany.

Find out more about Madeline at her website:

http://www.madelinemartin.com

- facebook.com/MadelineMartinAuthor
- twitter.com/MadelineMMartin
- instagram.com/madelinemmartin
- bookbub.com/profile/madeline-martin
- amazon.com/Madeline-Martin/e/B00R8OGFN2/ref=ntt_athr_dp_pel_1

ALSO BY MADELINE MARTIN

BORDERLAND LADIES

Ena's Surrender

Marin's Promise

Anice's Bargain

Ella's Desire

Catriona's Secret

Leila's Legacy

BORDERLAND REBELS

Faye's Sacrifice

Clara's Vow

Kinsey's Defiance

Drake's Determination

REGENCY NOVELLAS AND NOVELS

Earl of Benton

Earl of Oakhurst

Mesmerizing the Marquis

HARLEQUIN HISTORICALS

How to Tempt a Duke

How to Start a Scandal

HIGHLAND PASSIONS

A Ghostly Tale of Forbidden Love

The Madam's Highlander

The Highlander's Untamed Lady

Her Highland Destiny

Highland Passions Box Set Volume 1

HEART OF THE HIGHLANDS

Deception of a Highlander

Possession of a Highlander

Enchantment of a Highlander

THE MERCENARY MAIDENS

Highland Spy

Highland Ruse

Highland Wrath

Made in the USA
Las Vegas, NV
04 November 2021